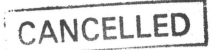

Viaréggio

Paul Kestell

authorHOUSE®

AuthorHouse™ UK Ltd.
500 Avebury Boulevard
Central Milton Keynes, MK9 2BE
www.authorhouse.co.uk
Phone: 08001974150

This book is a work of fiction. People, places, events, and situations are the product of the author's imagination. Any resemblance to actual persons, living or dead, or historical events, is purely coincidental.

First published by AuthorHouse 2/19/2010

ISBN: 978-1-4389-0191-6 (hc)
ISBN: 978-1-4389-0190-9 (sc)

This book is printed on acid-free paper.

The lyric poems are from my collection, "My very first book of poems."

Cover photographs by Thorn Island Films.

This book is dedicated to Stephen, and Carolann with all my love.

Death will come when thou art dead,
Soon, too soon--
Sleep will come when thou art fled.
Of neither would I ask the boon
I ask of thee, beloved Night--
Swift be thine approaching flight,
Come soon, soon!

Percy Bysshe Shelley

Acknowledgements

Special thanks to the people of Courtmacsherry, for their kindness. Thanks also to Sumpci and Marco, for their kind help with Italian translations. To my sister Yvonne, for helping to edit the text, when I thought all was lost.

Prologue

Viaréggio, Italy 2006

On the rooftop terrace of the Grand Palace Hotel, Viaréggio. The woman with me is Lucia, my wife; we have been married twenty-four years.

I am forty-eight years old; she is forty-nine. The man at the next table is Gardiner.

He is quiet for an American; he sits alone drinking wine. Rosa, the waitress has taken a shine to him.

She fills his glass, he drinks it, I don't think he is mad about the taste; he drinks it anyhow. Lucia looks at me oddly, I think she thinks I may have gone mad.

Maybe she is right.

Below us the crowds are thinning; the Italians like to go home early. Early on, the crowds were huge to watch Italy versus the USA in the World Cup on the big screen.

When Italy score, the crowd roars. A guy from an attic apartment runs out onto the roof.

"Fuck you, USA," he says and runs back in.

When USA score, he is nowhere to be seen. I say to Lucia he should have run back out to shout, "Fuck you, Italia." He didn't.

Gardiner tries to avoid us, he can sense us looking at him, Rosa has become his muse.

There's a guy inside playing a keyboard. He sings, "Vonderful, Vonderful." Dutch people dance to his music.

They are heroic; they dance well, the singer with the

1

permanent smile sings, "Susannah, Susannah." Dancing, they are too few to create an atmosphere.

Lucia wants to dance; she wants to dangle over the concrete surround that stops you falling a hundred feet to the pavement below.

I try to hug her as the music plays. I feel a hurricane is blowing me away.

Grip her shoulders, rigor mortis–like.

Lucia finds it funny, she's forgotten I was frozen for twelve hours? Showing her strength she faces my mortality for me. It is of no consequence.

Eventually she decides to look over the parapet down to the street below the bicycle lane still has traffic; the prom is almost empty.

The restaurants and bars are closing. Trickles of people move stealthily towards open-top cars, many escape on foot or on nifty small head-lit scooters.

Beyond, the beach is a graveyard with folded brollies and deck chairs. People don't go there at night, in the folds of darkness the sea continues imagined, overhead, stray stars touch faint ripples of whitewash, they appear only to disappear. Lucia is taking photographs.

Gardiner is watching. The music stops. Rosa checks to see if we need a last drink. We do. Gardiner has one more.

The Dutch people disappear; the musician, still smiling, is packing his gear.

Lucia calls me Stephen. The American introduces himself. He is older than me, not much, recently divorced. This is his third time in Italy, first time alone.

We tell him it's our first time in Viaréggio and our second time in Italy.

"We were here five years ago, before I got ill," I said.

Seems like a different era, a different planet a stupid thing to say to a stranger, "Before I got ill."

Follow that with the last time we flew to Bologna, we were an advertisement for coupledom, we flew, we drove, we hired a car; we like our hired car, our little deck chairs on the beach. Gardiner got stuck into his wine.

"Children?" Lucia asks him.

"No." He is blunt.

"We have two," Lucia says triumphantly. "James is twenty-one, he's doing engineering. Amanda's still at school she's seventeen."

I like Gardiner's face, it is crumpled, full of lines that trespass into dips, his hair is grey, he has a modern style,

I like the sharpness of his nose and the tough curve of his mouth. His style, wearing expensive clothes, his wrists tanned. When he looks at me he fakes sincerity, yet somehow he generates sadness. An apparition, he exposes his soul.

"My ex-wife, Susie, she loves Italy, she's gonna look for a place near Siena, it's further on, begins with R."

"Radda," Lucia says, "Chianti, Radda in Chianti."

Next I hear myself blurting, "Love a place in Italy, so cold at home in the winter."

"Home is Ireland, right?"

"You got it," Lucia answers for us.

"Ain't as cold as Brooklyn, I'd bet."

Gardiner finishes his wine, Rosa is gone.

Then he gets lucky because Rosa re-appears smiling. "Ah! Night cap?"

Even I love her. Lucia eyes her unsteadily.

"Sure, we may have one more!"

I remind her it's being charged to the room. "Smart," she says, she is reaching for a fag, eyeing my wallet sitting on the table.

Gardiner smokes too, soon they are both puffing.

The clouds of smoke are cartoon-like as they form over the tables. Rosa replenishes the wine.

"I've never been to Ireland, in my job I don't get to travel so much!" Lucia goes, "So what is it you do Mr Gardiner?"

"I write copy for magazines and TV advertisements you know, 'Welcome to Marlboro country,' that type of thing,"

"Wow," says Lucia.

"What do you do?" Gardiner asks me.

"I work in pensions, investments."

"Finance." Lucia said.

"Sure," says Gardiner, adoring his new tall glass. "Did I hear you say you were ill?" He asks almost with mischief. "Yeah," says Lucia. "He's had a double bypass." She says it like it's a matter of fact as in, "we drive a BMW." Gardiner goes, "I had a bypass myself just after our divorce." "Two?" Lucia asks. "Three," says Gardiner. "Cheers." He downs half his wine. "Stephen hates the medications, he has type 2 diabetes as well." "So have I," Gardiner says. He is only short of adding, 'it's a small world isn't it?'

We get one life, and I was going to live it. How many times had I wanted to write that novel? How many times did I start and give up? Not this time. The hurricane lashed against my skin, it seeped through to whirl round in my head.

I had enough, the wine was starting to warm my stomach, the cold pain was abating, my brain starting to drain. Finance, pensions, I thought how it all contributed to my illness, how much did Lucia understand that?

Lying in my bed I searched the bedside table for my wallet, I always left it beside me even when home. Lucia was tired and cross when I woke her, "where the hell could it be?" "Was there much money in it?" she asked. "About a hundred euro," I answer. "My notes, my cards, photographs of the kids, my work ID. Shit, what a pain." "When did you have it last?" "Dunno, thought I left it on the table when we were chatting to the American guy."

At Bagni di Lucca, Italy August 1977

Cardinal Edgell took a deep breath. The scent of the garden's perfume rising through the air brought him back to his youth. He loved the sounds owned by summer.

The bees were busy; the butterflies were seeking images of similar beauty in the shade, tiny green lizards darted into the shadows of dark stones.

How the scent in the air brought him back to his childhood in Germany.

The birds flying low, skimming the ornamental pool, cooling themselves from the fearsome heat.

Don Dino was indeed an enigma. His villa was so grandiose, full of beautiful trees, water sprinklers, and exotic plants shaded by small hedgerows.

Edgell thought the Italian dislike of natural flowers replaced by dubious marble effects very odd, yet the wonderful pines and cypress trees contrasting against the backdrop of the golden hills made the whole scene.

He wondered what Damasky thought of it all. Where he came from, the landscape was barren. It only yielded coal and minerals, there was no beauty of this magnitude.

Fucilla was different of course, Joseph was from culture, his people wealthy bankers from Milan, his family of the highest order. Joseph was sitting reading on the opposite side of the ornamental pool. Every now and then he would wave away an unwanted wasp.

The dedication to detail was exquisite, he returned to his paper immediately not allowing even a puff of wind disturbing his page to distract him.

Marie Abele sat in a proper garden chair. He preferred not to read and instead gazed skyward, the pale blue was his own personal canvas.

He watched tiny birds, joined by the pastoral wood pigeons, fly through his vast blue universe.

Damasky was nervous, he traipsed up and down disturbing the gravel. Edgell was about to silence him but thought better of it.

Damasky was the wrong stock; those persecuted by the Red Army educated him.

He was tall and robust like an officer. Like so many Poles he had deep piercing eyes, he could pass for either a serf or a king.

Edgell could not fault his dedication or his appreciation,

for it was he who pulled the young Priest from anonymity.

It was he who pulled him kicking and screaming to the position of power he held today.

Damasky did owe him favours for sure, many a pretty seminarian was sent to him for advice on how to climb the ladder.

Edgell laughed to himself at the plodders, the straight men, the buffoons who thought they were at one with God and the world.

Edgell believed in the nobility of men. Fucilla for all his nobility had never quite learned the correctness of it all,

he was too infected with the richness of blood. His father had been a wealthy banker, his grandfather founder of Italy's largest bank.

Maybe he didn't need to play games, a mere monsignor?

Edgell mused, Fucilla hardly wept for the creed or any real sense of idealism, he was just expressing what was part of him; he knew of nothing else. The doctrine was unspoken, it passed through his blood through generations to reach him as a relaxed state of normality.

This particularly pleased Edgell, as a man like Fucilla needed no further enlightenment or training.

Marie Abele was older than Fucilla but was just as dedicated. He was not from the same rich bloodline, somehow his blood was tainted by the peasants of Provence.

He repeated his story of gathering sticks in the snow during the harsh winters of Cucuron and how the wisdom of self-reliance was revealed to him. His words never impressed the Cardinal.

Edgell looked at the balding Abele, whose role was as secretary. Marie Abele was on the make, his loyalty was born of necessity rather than belief.

Edgell sat back in his seat to grasp the pleasure of the garden; it shaped his thoughts. Don Dino had a lovely garden for an Italian. Damasky was concerned, and rightly so concluded the Cardinal. If the truth ever came out how Benedetto died! It was unlikely.

6

The tracks were covered; he painted the dark paint himself.

It was unfortunate that the boy's wife was in the car with him. There it goes he surmised, God's grace, a moment in time.

It was important Don Dino thought his enemies were ruthless, he should see the Cardinal and the entire Sodality movement as a source of protection. Damasky was right – Don Dino was not a stupid man.

In Rome, on many occasions Edgell was impressed, even stirred, by the Don's clarity of thought and his unrivalled bravery in the face of adversity.

Marie Abele, hosting the bereaved Don finding solace in Cucuron, perhaps he knew him best.

"How long will he leave us waiting?" Damasky kicked at the gravel, getting several small stones stuck in his shoe.

"We must be patient my dear Gregory," Edgell said.

"He may be plotting to have us shot here where we stand, out here in the open!"

"Gregory, your imagination runs riot, you people spent too much time defending yourselves. You fought heroically against us, then ran afraid of the Red Army, I'm afraid your race has not yet recovered its equilibrium." Edgell spoke softly to pacify Damasky.

Damasky stopped kicking the stones and walked over to Fucilla, sitting alongside him on his makeshift seat. The Italian sighed and moved only slightly. Edgell thought of Drozdan, he reminds me of Damasky.

The young Croatian seminarian who was his muse, such a beautiful boy. Edgell's thoughts were interrupted by the words of the chauffeur, Gregor. "Don Dino is ready now."

Don Dino was so relaxed.

She sat by the door leading to the veranda, the shutters closed over allowing only a single ray of light through.

She was blonde, her hair tied back, her dark glasses didn't allow Edgell to inspect her eyes as he liked sensing how young she was; she smelled of youth.

The way she sat, with her left leg bare to the thigh crossed over her right, unnerved him for a moment.

He wanted to walk right over and touch her to see if she was real. How could one so innocent looking come with such a fearsome reputation?

Edgell stared at her. There was something about her, she gave off a perfume.

This girl, little more than a child, unhinged his senses, she radiated power – he concluded this was her perfume – undiluted power. It was this sense that grabbed his soul and aroused him.

She flinched, as if she sensed his gaze upon her, Edgell's concentration broken he was suddenly aware that Don Dino was staring at him disapprovingly.

The Cardinal moved slowly to the soft armchair. Damasky, Fucilla, and Marie Abele took hard seats behind him.

"This is Eva Devlin," Don Dino said, as if introducing his daughter.

Edgell moved to get up, but she looked away from him to peer through the crack in the shutter, and he changed his mind.

"We will be joined by another member of the cloth, Father Burdon. I think you know of him?" Don Dino directed his words at the gathering; he was looking at Abele in particular who was busy writing notes.

"This is Archbishop Damasky," Edgell said standing up,

"Monsignor Fucilla, you must have met my secretary from Cucuron, Father Marie Abele." The don stood up from the piano stool out of courtesy. "Father Burdon will join us shortly," he said.

Edgell smiled. He chose to stand again turning to look at the expectant faces of his own disciples first.

"I wish to thank Don Dino most graciously for his hospitality; we were fatigued when we arrived. The refreshments and access to fresh air and the wonderful splendour of your gardens were enough to rekindle our spirits and empower us to continue."

The door opened behind him. Father Burdon entered and

went straight to Eva's side not bothering to recognize any of his fellowmen of the cloth.

Cardinal Edgell nodded at him aware of the antipathy the cleric held for the rest of his ecclesiastical brotherhood.

"Don Dino, I wish to be honest. We are here because of you, Miss Devlin, your reputation."

"My reputation?" The girl said.

Edgell wasn't expecting the retort; he fumbled,

"Your reputation, if I do not put too fine a word on it is the stuff of legend!" Edgell paused pleased with himself.

"I am a legend," Eva whispered to Father Burdon.

The Irish priest muttered.

Don Dino noticed him trying to bite his words as if afraid his spit might be venomous.

"What is it you men want? Just get to the point. We don't need any lessons concerning the past spit it out why are you boys here?"

Damasky rose from his hard chair as if to speak, but Edgell cut him short.

"We don't mean any insult Don Dino we would never enter your house with any malicious intention. Rather we heard you had acquired a certain reputation, Miss Devlin.

Our visit is purely to request that you assist us in our quest."

Edgell hesitated unsure as to what to say next. Fucilla taking over said,

"I don't intend to give you a lesson in history or allow myself to get overenthusiastic about our hopes for the future we in Sodality may need a person like you, Miss Devlin." "Name your price, Don Dino," the monsignor ventured.

Edgell, picking up on the words, said,

"To save time we are thinking in the region of two million US dollars."

"Two million?" Father Burdon went on.

"Judas went for forty pieces of silver."

Damasky rose.

"I am tired of this; you are no longer a priest Burdon, no

longer recognized by Rome. You want to start your own church based on the teachings of Marx not Jesus Christ."

"Father Burdon is a friend and a confidant of Don Dino. Should we show disrespect?" Cardinal Edgell said politely.

Don Dino answered, "Cardinal Edgell, I have heard what you have to say. We can consider the offer you have made."

"The don shows his true strength I only wish to test the waters, as they say."

Don Dino turned as if about to play the piano but more to avoid the gaze of his companions sitting by the window. Edgell sat in his chair with clasped hands resorting to the benign expressions of old; he knew he must act soon before Damasky ruined all.

"Can you give us any idea Miss Devlin?"

"I need time to think. I dunno what to say." She looked appealingly at Father Burdon.

Don Dino stood up indicating the meeting was over. "I have one question Cardinal, before you go."

"Yes," Edgell said, turning.

"When do we see this money?"

Edgell, warming up, took a step closer to the don. "Half up front. You'll get the rest when our first task is completed."

"I see," Don Dino said. "I hope your trip wasn't wasted Cardinal. Maybe when we are next in Rome we could meet for coffee you are going back to Rome?"

"Why, yes Don Dino all save for me." It was Father Marie Abele who answered the question. "I am returning to Cucuron just for a short while." "Yes. Cucuron is a favourite place of mine."

Don Dino bid them farewell.

The Cardinal strained his head to look back at Damasky.

He was on the verge of asking Hans to slow down so he could sit in the back.

"I don't like it, Your Grace. They were too cocky. That woman is a bitch and a whore for a priest! Those stories are cock and bull," Damasky said.

"No, I have it on authority they are all true," Fucilla said softly, his eyes scanning the countryside.

The Mercedes drove fast along the country roads. Hans was expert a trusted compatriot of the Cardinal.

"You do well, Hans. We will be in Lucca soon," the Cardinal said. The chauffeur nodded, smiling like a kid when praised by his teacher.

"They were too smug Cardinal," Damasky said. "I tell you, Don Dino is smart, it worries me he may have found out about his son. They were laughing at us, Your Grace. They were not considering our offer appropriately. What is your opinion, Fucilla?"

Edgell intervened, "Let Joseph think, it seems the Archbishop of Lublin is a conspiracy theorist."

"I agree with Gregory, Your Eminence. I got no impression of any serious analysis of our offer. We could have offered five million; it would not have ruffled a feather,"

Edgell sighed, looked at the road straight ahead firstly to relieve his aching neck and also to get thinking time. As they approached Lucca the traffic got heavier, forcing Hans to slow down. For a moment the Cardinal was sorry he excused Marie Abele, allowing him to spend the night in Bagni di Lucca. He was going to Bologna with two fellow priests the next day, returning to Cucuron to tend to some personal business.

Marie Abele had a stabilizing influence on Damasky; also the Frenchman kept the exact minutes. He had a gift for recalling all things spoken or expressed by facial movement. If anyone was qualified to comment on the merits or demerits of a meeting, Marie Abele was the one. The Cardinal sighed as the Mercedes slowed to a stop.

"This is the only road that allows us access," Hans said to all in general.

"So be it, Hans," said the Cardinal sighing, the traffic ahead was so slow.

"She is evil. I vouch for her not been of sound mind, Burdon covers for her; he is only short of holding her hand, as you would a child," Fucilla said, sounding surprisingly vicious.

11

"Burdon is mad," Damasky said.

"The British are nothing, compared to the Russians they are angels."

"Indeed," agreed Fucilla.

The Cardinal managed to turn around once again, trying to protect his neck by making only a three quarter turn. "It is shocking for a priest to loose all his moral conviction to fornicate with a minor and then present himself to the world as an advocate of leftist theology. I do agree the meeting was contrived; it was as if Don Dino was not listening in the real sense. Honestly, my two loyal friends, I found the experience to be perverse."

Damasky nodded, like he was suddenly vindicated. Fucilla muttered under his breath, but nobody could hear. The traffic moved forward but only for 10 metres before stopping. Hans made a gesture, lifting his hands to indicate his powerlessness. He didn't notice the scooter with a rider and pillion passenger weaving in and out of the cars behind him. It made good progress, coming closer.

"I think we should change our approach!" Damasky said to the Cardinal.

Edgell felt his spirits rise as the car moved forward at least 30 metres this time. Damasky went on,

"If we used our contacts in the middle east?" Edgell was unimpressed. He didn't like Turks.

"We should remove them all without delay." Damasky let his words cut through the air.

Fucilla, stared at Damasky. Edgell challenged the Pole with eye contact.

"It is drastic," Edgell blurted. "It is what I sense must be done as soon as we reach Rome!" Damasky said strongly.

Fucilla tut-tutted, "We are in danger of losing our way, to take out his son, I want no more of it, cold blooded murder," Fucilla appealed to Edgell.

"Your Eminence, you said Sodality stands for justice redressing wrongs, surely we must do everything with full moral justification."

Edgell went puce; he didn't know which one to censure

first. The scooter about to pass, but the Mercedes moved away again. "I will hear none of this, it is an outrage. We will not discuss our meeting in detail till we sit again with our people in Rome. Do you hear me, Gregory, Joseph? I forbid it. We are acting like children, we must take our time, examine their motivations. Review our position carefully, in a considered manner. I forbid anymore talk of this."

Cardinal Edgell turned to face the traffic eyeing Damasky scowl in the rear-view mirror. Fucilla, like a small child scolded by his mother, sat still, his head bowed forward. The Mercedes stopped again, this time behind a foul-smelling refuse truck. Hans wound up the windows. The stench seeping in, making them uncomfortable. The scooter about to pass, Hans watched enviously. As it passed he felt the pillion passenger beat hard against the roof of the car.

"Bloody kids, Your Grace. No respect," Hans said, Edgell was deep in thought.

The bike disappeared. Finally the traffic moved slowly before starting to speed up. After a minute the refuse truck turned right entering a municipal compound. Hans increased his speed despite seeing a red light ahead.

As the car ground to a halt one more time, Hans said, "Your Grace, I will open the windows for a few minutes whilst we're stuck in the city traffic; the air is foul from the refuse truck."

"Very good," said Edgell half turning to his companions. "The air is putrid in here."

The Mercedes was an inferno in seconds; its roof blown off, the flames fanned by a light breeze. All four bodies were burned beyond recognition.

1.

The cold is the same when you're dead, the only difference is this time I was woken from it. Lucia laughs when I say it, feeling sorry for myself. You were lucky to survive, some people just keel over. To be honest, I don't remember the cold, somebody said it to me afterwards, I suppose I just hung on to it as thinking about death is relentless.

OK, it's not that I feel special or hard done by, death has taken on a new significance, it is not in our nature to think of it, each of us knows it's coming, there can be no other outcome. I see it now, it's like after the operation, everything is clearer, all my companions are walking that same road. I go through all the processes: the rotting body, maggots, heads, skeletons, coffins, priests, selfish thought. Maybe it's just that nothing makes any sense anymore, borrowed time, loaned companions. Anything mundane is so boring, I have this sense of being treated, some great God in the universe feels sorry for me, allowing me live, mind, invalid needs his brain wheel chaired, pushed along, walk 2 kilometres each morning here in Hilton Head.

Go walk places like Plantation Drive, Greenwood Drive. I walk by a tiny cemetery adjacent to the footpath. The names on its headstones are barely visible, Sissy, Tobias.

Harbourtown itself is pretty. I sit at an outdoor bar admiring the small craft tied up for the winter.

Still the late evening sun dazzles my eyes, I think of the ferry ride through Calibogue Sound to Daufuskie Island.

This is only half a river as the Atlantic steals in its waves, crisp fresh surf to bathe deadwater,

I am on a riverboat called The Cripple Creek Ferry. I'm aware of history, of plantations, young blacks tie up the boats, they serve beer in the Golf Club bar.

In Harbourtown, the white bartender serves me Charleston brown ale, dark and bland, maybe I will acquire a taste. I don't it sours as I swallow, all the froth disappears. I drink dark water. A woman opposite is loud. She talks down to an older woman. The expensive boats are behind her. She squats, the louder she speaks the more knicker she shows. I, blinded by the sun squinting wisps of cloud cover allow me view her in spasms taking stills she becomes an amateur lap dancer, men by the stage throw dollars for her.

Gardiner didn't mind the journey. It was only an hour and twenty from Newark to Savannah. The man that picked him up was a regular guy. Gardiner could tell by the way he dressed and spoke. The man was older, retired early, holding up a card with Gardiner's name on it. Later at the checkpoint on the bridge to Hilton Head Island, the old boy was still talking he reminded Gardiner of Lou Costello the way he talked nonstop. "I mean, you take this George Bush, ask me, does he give a damn? Guys like me, they don't matter to him. If you ask me, there's none of 'em any good! All are in it for what they can take themselves. I am right, mister, I am right!"

Gardiner agreed, it was the wisest thing to do. Life was too short to engage this old guy in a debate, chances were he wouldn't change his mind in a month of Sundays anyhow.

The driver still babbling on dropped him off in Harbourtown. "Cheers man, that's terrific. See you know I been paid already!"

Gardiner gave him two hundred dollars, the old guy sped away mighty chuffed with himself.

He wondered whether he should get a beer or go straight for the ferry, carrying his holdall using his shoulder strap.

The ferry berth was empty with nobody waiting.

Walking on by the lighthouse down the Marina, he sat at an outdoor bar. He ordered a beer, it was late in the afternoon and the sun was sleeping in the western sky.

The bartender told him the ferry would be back in a half an hour. Gardiner made himself comfortable people watching mostly, taken with the array of small pleasure boats tied up for the winter. The bartender gave him Charleston Brown ale, he liked its strong taste. A young woman opposite was attracting attention to herself. She was talking loudly to some older woman. Gardiner noticed her precociously holding her legs up as she sat back on her seat. The more she caught his glances the further she revealed her thighs. Gardiner tried to look away, but was helpless, and kept sneaking glances, waiting for something to happen.

The ferry returned as darkness fell on Calibogue Sound. By the time it came to boarding at least ten other people had arrived, most of them were tourists returning to their hotel. Gardiner was glad he made a reservation. The ferry slipped out of Harbourtown. It seemed to regard the darkness nonchalantly. He stood at the rear; it gave him a view back towards Hilton Head, the coastline lit like a necklace with pieces missing. The moorings on Daufuskie were wooden; a shuttle bus came, transporting them along an uneven road shaded by large trees. The hotel was alight, an oasis. Around it small ornamental gardens were half lit.

"Mr. Gardiner." The receptionist was a middle aged male wearing thick black frames. He was sharp and to the point. "I have a message for you sir, left for you this a.m. at 11.30 to be precise." Gardiner stood silently waiting for him to finish.

"There you go, sir."

The hotel-supplied note simply said suite 207.

"OK," Gardiner said.

"I will get the porter to carry your bag," the receptionist said, condescendingly eyeing the holdall.

"No it's no trouble. I will carry it myself, thanks."

Suite 207 was a floor up from his. Gardiner took the stairs, his doctor encouraged it. He had taken his Coversyl 5 mg, reminding himself not to forget the Lipitor later. He knocked politely and the door opened almost immediately.

A young man wearing braces over his white shirt with the trousers of an ordinary suit said, "Come in, Mr Gardiner." This guy looked too young to be anything, Gardiner mused.

Another man with his jacket on sat over by the window.

The drapes half drawn, he was writing copious notes into an A4 pad.

"My name is Robert Quinn; this is Jack Kellerman," the young man said pointing at his colleague who was still writing without acknowledging Gardiner's presence. "Take a seat, please." Gardiner stared at Kellerman, wondering what was so important, why couldn't he lift his head just for a second.

Robert Quinn pulled a chair from a dining table placing it in front of Gardiner.

Finally, the man stopped writing and looked up at him. Kellerman was the older of the two, his eyes betrayed him. Gardiner put him in his early thirties; Quinn was much younger, a freshman.

"Thanks for coming down all this way. Can we fix you a drink?"

"I'm fine."

"How about a coffee?" Robert Quinn said, walking to a coffee blender sitting neatly beside a kettle on a sideboard.

"Sure, why not?" Gardiner said.

Kellerman added, "Its piss but its drinkable."

"Good."

"How is the retirement going?" Quinn asked amiably.

Gardiner was taken aback, he didn't like being studied, having only responded to the invitation out of boredom and curiosity.

"We hear the missing person's bureau is missing you!" Kellerman was embarrassed at his effort to joke.

"The NYPD file on you Mr Gardiner is impressive. Three commendations." Robert Quinn tried to rescue his partner.

"You guys know a lot about me. Hey, ok, I know by your contact method you're CIA, how's about a little, huh?" Quinn gave him his coffee.

Kellerman tried to make light of it all. "We were just impressed; it's very impressive."

"Till I have a heart attack," said Gardiner coldly.

"You can understand the department all the same, especially in your line of work. No picnic searching for abducted kids, don't know how you could stomach it."

"Kellerman was just saying," Quinn interrupted, "we don't operate the same rules as the NYPD; our work is strictly private."

Quinn looked at him, drinking a mouthful of coffee like he was slightly disgusted with himself.

"I don't look for kids anymore, all washed up." He only sipped at his coffee.

"We don't need you to find a kid, at least she isn't a kid now." Quinn handed him a photograph. It was nothing remarkable: a black-and-white shot of a girl about fourteen. She was fair and thin. Gardiner noticed her nose was long and straight; it made her look a little severe.

Kellerman, anticipating his question, said, "Her name is Eva Devlin. The photo is circa 1975; it's all we got on her. She is Irish, from the North; the photo was taken a couple of weeks before she disappeared."

Quinn took over. "The British have more on her for obvious reasons, they were very active, MI5 were unhinging whole communities there. She fucked them and they got pissed when she went missing."

Gardiner stepped forward to hand the photograph back. Quinn made no move to receive it from him, giving him a large photograph instead.

"That is Cardinal Edgell, a German who died in 1977; the other is the esteemed American Cardinal Auldridge."

"He died a few years back." Kellerman added. "This guy had his own key to the White House."

Back in his room Gardiner sat on the bed wondering should he call Susie about the kids? It had been three weeks. Maybe he should leave it till the morning. He washed down his Lipitor with spring water and poured a gin and tonic from the minibar.

So he was to find this girl and bring her in. She was under the protection of the Mafia for over thirty years. Why did they pick him? He would need to find that out. There was a reason, always was. The money was pretty good—straight up half a million dollars. It was more than he earned in five years at the very top. Where to start, what do you do with just a photograph. What was it Quinn said? She was in Italy. But where? The photographs of two dead Cardinals: one blown to pieces in a car bomb, the other dead due to natural causes. Kellerman had shown him another photograph, this guy was alive and well, Drozdan. Fuck it, thought Gardiner, these guys were a little vague. "We need to find her!"

"Why not the fuck ask her; give her a bell?" She's probably listed in the phonebook.

"She has made contact," Kellerman said. "Through a priest in Cucuron, a small town in Provence. She wanted to trade with the British and then us."

"Trade what?" Gardiner asked.

"We dunno," came the dumb reply.

"You need to track her; then we will know."

Kellerman was irked by him. Gardiner could sense the man was more comfortable writing copious notes than giving out information.

Gardiner got no sense of his own importance in the matter, he wasn't CIA; he wasn't even NYPD anymore. Shit! He lay back against his propped-up pillow, feeling tired. Sipping his average gin he found it warming, which helped him to relax.

Tell them in the morning, I will sleep on it—always a good thing, he thought, falling asleep. The niggling voice of Quinn rang in his ears, "You know, Edgell was a fascist; he wanted to prolong the Third Reich. His thesis was simple, the Western governments were mad to defeat Hitler and go kiss Stalin's ass. This guy Edgell wanted to do the lot. He started this organization called Sodality, they aimed to overthrow every single government in the world!"

"Auldridge was his American contact. He ran scared after Edgell died.

Drozdan, a clone of Edgell, now he thinks it's all gonna blow in his face, he wants the girl," Kellerman's droning voice responded. "She has a son, a kind of lay preacher who performs miracles."

Gardiner jumped up checking his watch, it was only 12.30. He tried to sleep again yet the booming voices returned doing their damnedest to interrupt. He pulled the sheets up over his head creating a vacuum, the sound of his own breathing bringing relief. Soon the heat made him strip the sheets off, damp from his sweat. He turned on the bedside light. Gardiner sat to drink water looking at the shapes carved in the wooden headboard. They were perfect, each shape matching circles save for one randomly half done at the very end. He lay on the pillow again staring at it, soon his mind was caressed, odd shapes filling his eyelids till sleep came.

2.

Gardiner took me a long time yet like everything else in life I had my good and bad days, sometimes I wouldn't think of the book at all, I might just tune out. Maybe Gardiner tired me out, put it this way it was becoming more of a hobby than anything I seriously planned. The search for the others happened by accident. Some I never met at all I just made them up. You see, when you're not regarded as a writer people don't expect you to research, so if you happen to tell them what you're up to they can get cheesed off, like you're some kind of fraud or you're not to be trusted, they clam up and look at you differently. Over time I met some of the others. To be honest, I might have chosen lots of people, in some cases I might meet someone in the morning then somebody else at night, usually whoever I met when I was pissed won out. So I found them over a period of time. Here goes my list.

Don Dino Bernado, Edward Boyce, Don Maestrino Giordano, his son Philippe, his daughter Monica. There were others!

Toby, faith healer, child of a child killer, I finally met her, Eva Devlin.

Of all of them, she was the hardest to find.

Lucia didn't even know I was looking, our days were filled with walks down the prom after breakfast, a hot shower and lunch in the café right by our beach entrance.

Each day we got the same seats on the beach, greeted by the same fat lady, showing her the same ticket.

The walk took us by a tiny bar area showing World Cup matches on a tiny TV watched by a few interested locals, a few compatriots of whatever teams were playing.

We were shown to our seats by the same boy, he was pleasant, about seventeen.

I always tried to tip, that's if I could find any change.

Invariably I would spend my time searching in my pockets, whilst Lucia produced three Euros from nowhere.

"Grazie," he would say to me smiling

Lucia liked his courteousness.

Once seated we could recognize the other hotel guests as they availed of their preferential passes.

Some of them seemed to have more upmarket status than us. This type of thing would normally bother Lucia, but somehow she didn't mind.

I was taken with an Italian woman who sat opposite. She always gave me a full rear view before turning to reveal her neat Italian breasts smiling from her bikini top.

Her daughter was very beautiful also. I presumed her to be only twenty or twenty one.

I did everything to evade her glances and even searched the masses of hairy-legged men and hawkers to avoid her. The father made only flying visits, he was a big fat man.

He wasn't old but his weight made him look older than he actually was.

We sat patiently under the shelter of our brollies, the sun making the sand almost impossible to walk on barefoot.

The hawkers were continuous, trying to sell cheap jewellery or beach towels.

One guy was selling something resembling doughnuts.

Two oriental girls were offering a massage right where you sat, legs, back and body. Young kids raced up then down the boardwalk, they sprinted along, their young feet oblivious to the heat.

After an age of people watching, feigning sleep, even I had to resort to the sea to cool off.

Lucia was a strong swimmer, she had the strength to swim way out of her depth. I was scared of the water, didn't like my feet not to touch the sand.

She would be gone for a half an hour or so at a time.

I might be in and out in ten minutes, embarrassed by the scars on my chest as I passed the woman and her daughter opposite.

In the evenings, the same ritual. A heavy-chested Italian man walking the boardwalk, smiling as he went.

This evening he was followed by three children. An overweight teen with a thin younger boy. They in turn were followed by a young girl of about ten.

The overweight teen shouts to the man, "Dove sono i nostri soldi?"

The man turns to all three children and says,

"Non ne ho, andate via,"

He makes to hit out but smiles at anyone watching.

The weighty teen goes running back up the boardwalk towards the pool area and bar, followed by his conspirators.

He shouts to the fat lady, who arrives to greet him,

"Mamma, non ci vuole dare i soldi."

The mother laughs and turns away much to the children's disgust they fail to receive the payment due. The heavy-chested man laughs to the remains of the crowd, walking through the lines of huge umbrellas, ducking like a circus performer as he releases each catch, his timing is perfect, he then proceeds to tidy each table, fold each chair.

Gardiner's apartment partially looked over the East River. He saw it cold and dark. At night the moon made shadows forming fake murals on the walls opposite. Some mornings he walked down to Prospect Park, it helped him relax. He watched young mothers tend to their children. Sometimes he might sit for an hour on a park bench. Nearing home he saw the air was full of hidden spray, his face dampened by fraudulent rain.

Trying Bateman in his office. As usual Bateman was full of crap.

"What you're saying Gardiner is the guy they locked up for trying to kill the Pope wasn't the first, at least maybe somebody else planned to have a go. Who cares? I'm no Catholic. Don't even think they give a shit, Gardiner, you sure are a strange one! Even after you're heart attack you still think people give a shit if you're dead, tell you pal nobody gives a rat's shit. My two uncles passed away, wives remarried in a year, kids counting the dough. Maybe you're different eh Gardiner? I know how

you love your kids, when you're 6 foot under it's fuckin' no good cause they can't squeeze yeh!" "Yeah, Joe, just check it out for me, will you?"

"Sure, buddy, I don't hold with all that stuff, you know me, Gardiner. I'm a man of the people, I for one was sure glad you didn't die from that heart attack, not many guys get through that!" "Let me know as soon as you can," Gardiner said exasperated.

"Sure thing; hang loose..." the line went dead.

Gardiner was wondering whether he should contact Quinn or Kellerman, tell them the whole thing was a waste of time. They were in touch only twice since Daufuskie—Quinn the first time, and Kellerman, his voice showing more gravitas, the second.

"She's not ready to come out yet, there is no point in you going till May." "Where is she?"

"The British seem to know and they won't share this one." He spoke like a child in the schoolyard sulking over not getting a sweet.

Kellerman commanded, "Sit tight, Gardiner. It will be worth it."

Susie and the kids were staying with her father down in Coney Island. That's where he should go, the old man was still on good terms. Susie would never agree. Gardiner could never figure her out. It wasn't like he was away all the time having affairs, his job took him nationwide. He was a searcher, the guy who searched for little kids as far away as Washington State, the Heidi Heisler case was the worst ever.

Every lead he followed meticulously. She had gone missing from outside her home off the Eastern Parkway. She was eight years old at the time.

Within two years Gardiner searched all over the United States. He and his team followed every lead, every scrap of information, anybody with even a hint of a history was interviewed. They took thousands of statements.

So Susie divorced him citing irreconcilable differences, like he was never home and he didn't know his own children. Truth was she met somebody at work who paid her more attention. It didn't last, she was single again as soon as the new guy found she was available full-time and didn't have a heap of cash. Susie still wanted to go it alone. She cited stuff about his drinking, his mood swings, his depression. She sure was his light of spring Gardiner thought bitterly, remembering those nights spent coaxing Susie. She would take comfort in his arms as she relived the trauma of growing up with an alcoholic mother.

"All is sweet with you, my darling," he said out loud.

The phone rang. Bateman's number came up. "Gardiner, how's your's hangin', hey? I didn't mean nothin' on account of the drugs you take."

Gardiner interrupted, "Joe, what you got?"

"I'm gonna bike this over to you You're right about her being in with the Mafia, especially this guy Bernado, Don Dino. He was chief suspect in the murder of this dude Edgell all those years back, see he got this idea they done away with his son so he blew three high-ranking clerics into thin air, as for the girl, we dunno, her story is different; whatever it is, the British have it. She got some reputation back then for a kid; she wasn't fourteen? Hey, I will send it to you, ok? Got stuff on this guy, Drozden; this other dude Auldridge, you know he's dead. So nobody gives a shit!"

"Send it over, Joe."

"Sure, just you call me—anything you want."

All went silent. Gardiner lay out on the sofa. He was going to watch a ball game yet he felt sleepy. When he woke an hour later the apartment was cold. He turned on the gas heating and the electric fire. His dreams disturbed him. He put on the kettle to make a pot of coffee.

The lights of the East River flashed like beacons through

the spaces in between the buildings opposite, the noise of the traffic heading down Atlantic Avenue soothed yet somehow irritated him simultaneously. His house phone rang; instinctively Gardiner looked at his watch. It was 11.15.

"Hello," Gardiner said. There was a pause and the line wasn't good.

"Messaggio dall'Angelo della Morte."

"Who is this?" Gardiner tried to think on his feet.

"Ci vediamo."

"Hey buddy, I don't talk to strangers this hour. Come on, who's playin' games, eh?"

"Vaffanculo, ti vedo mentre dormi, ti vedo mentre sogni."

3.

I thought St Tropez would be this big fast town, affluent, where the beautiful people live.

Film stars lived there. Diana and Dodi romanced in his fathers mansion the year they died.

Lucia thought it was splendid, she liked the South of France. One day we took the ferry from St Maxime.

The usual mix of tourists, the stereotypical Japanese with their cameras, some token Germans, the mannerly English. The Americans were either old or fat or both. Aboard the ferry we got a tour of the bay.

Anchoring off shore, the guide pointing out the houses of the super-rich. I wasn't impressed with the list of movie stars, rock singers, and supermodels but when we got close to the harbour I changed my mind. The yachts were absolutely huge as we sailed in, the guide was going on about Elton John, Princess Grace, Diana, and Dodi.

Never had I seen anything to rival these vessels. Two Texan-type oil billionaires, like two Larry Hagmans, stood eyeing us as we passed. They weren't exactly dressed for the sun with their Stetson hats and blazers. Once ashore the place disappointed a little.

It had lots of beach-front café bars, frilly discount clothes shops. I suppose I just expected it to be bigger, more grandiose.

We strolled around. Lucia was hungry so we bought two baguettes from a sandwich bar. She was content to sit on a small wall by the harbour. Errant ripples, the mullet darting to the surface, silver against the rainbow of leaking fuel. Lucia watched them struggle to catch the light of the sun.

A local gathered an audience. He was pulling them in by the dozen with a simple rod baited with bread.

The man would unhook them and cast them lazily on the stone slabs of the harbour promenade. His black Labrador sat faithfully by his side, the fish flapping its way back towards the safety of the water, the Labrador tracking its every move.

The fisherman either pretended or was oblivious to the entertainment.

As soon as the fish neared the water, one more flip flop then safety, the dog would pounce, picking it up carefully like a retriever, returning the poor creature to its original start point beside his master.

The whole operation became more complicated as the fisherman reeled in more and his faithful dog had to follow and retrieve not one but three, then four.

Lucia was fascinated by the dog and his master's apparent indifference.

We walked on towards the pier itself. This part of St Tropez was more like I had imagined. The pier was on two levels with a stone archway. People walked from one side to another, some walked on the upper level to try and catch the cooling breeze. The buildings were coloured exotic yellows, creams, some even orange. I thought I had landed on the set of some pirate movie, I half-expected to see Maureen O' Hara as we turned the corner beyond the pier itself.

There were people swimming, diving from specially constructed platforms into the cold sea. This is where I first saw Boyce. He was sitting out on a single protruding rock.

I knew it was him straight away. He sat lazily, his swimsuit too small, showing an unreasonable amount of buttock. I watched him as Lucia changed into her swimwear.

Boyce was staring at the array of boys who dived athletically into deep water. People were removing their sandals as they crossed tiny coves leading to the swimming areas. This whole place was lined with quaint buildings, they looked condemned from the outside but were probably masterfully modern inside.

I looked away as I sensed Boyce catch me staring at him. He moved, self-consciously looking out to sea.

Lucia found the water cold, her feet were burned by hard stones.

You would think St Tropez might have a sandy beach? Lucia swam out too far. I kept an eye on her wondering what the hell I would do if she ever got into trouble.

Drown with her, I suppose.

Why would I bother to save her? She played tricks on my mind.

For as long as I have known her, there has been this ambiguity between us.

We had our moments, deep loving ones, then she would make a comment or act in a certain way.

Made me wonder what it was I ever saw in her. Maybe she felt the same way about me, that's why she swam out so far, I became just a tiny small dot sitting uncomfortably on a rock. She smiled as she braved the tiny sharp stones. I could tell by the way she walked they were cutting at the soles of her feet. I could imagine the underwater gravel give way making her lose her balance and laugh as she slipped over. It was a desperate move, her left arm reaching into the mire to save herself.

Boyce hated driving. The roads were decent; though once you got into the country they got narrow. He put his displeasure down to his mood, he didn't want to concentrate.

Staying alert, following the road signs, he soon got lost in the country along winding roads, stopping occasionally to read the signs. The further he travelled the more rural the landscape till he found his mood lighten as the neat haystacks dotted the bare fields around him.

By the time he returned to the coast he was exhausted. The idea of a swim seemed the only way to cool his body. His stomach playing havoc all the way. He put it down to the previous night's malt.

Just a dip to cool off, nothing flashy, cold water to numb his body. Later he planned more malt and maybe a treat, he hadn't quite made up his mind. Was he gone too far, the drinking, the cigars, maybe he had but he didn't care. The waves crashed against the slippy rock where he rested, the spray imitating ferocious storms, to a tiny creature this was a hurricane. Back in Oxford he will see his doctor, the man always reads the riot act. What of it, if he was to tell him the truth!

Coughing up blood was now habitual each morning, the constant pain he had down his right side was a worry. He was too old for all this.

The lure of one final payoff was enough to coax him out of retirement.

Would he recognize her after all of this time? He doubted it. His new employers were not in any hurry, they needed time to set up their own structures; his job was to assist in a practical fashion to finish things off in the end. The lack of real urgency made him sigh, it was not bad all the same to see out retirement in a place like this and get paid a half million dollars for the trouble. He felt it was getting cool and thought he might walk back to the steps to retrieve his robe. The enjoyment he got from admiring the young boys was beginning to wane. The boys were very nice. Boyce loved their angular bodies and the strength of their arm muscles yet when they turned away from him he saw they had buttocks like women. He had not ventured close enough to judge their eyes or more importantly their lips. As he walked, dodging the jutting stones and grimacing at the pain the tiny pebbles could inflict, he wondered about himself. Soon he would be seventy years old, having spent thirty seven years in MI5. What was it that made him tick?

He retired to Oxford ten years previously, the idea to live out his life in comfort, his own special comforts, the ones only he knew. He never took a wife for women did nothing for him. If there was a part of them that excited him, it was too little to be of consequence. Glancing around for his robe, slipping on his pool sandals. The tourists were so nosey, they expected everyone to be grandiose, French, and have the smell of affluence. Boyce knew his own smells; he smiled, they were never affluent.

Boyce, in truth, was never really a patriot nor did he ever feel motivated by any sense of patriotism. The word seemed rather pointless to him. Perhaps this explained his total disregard for those who were swallowed by the notion. He may have been as happy making cuckoo clocks in Switzerland as long as the money was right. Of course Edward Boyce would have been a master clockmaker, his motivation was clear: to be the very best no matter what! He hurried back towards the promenade, up the narrow street to his accommodation. He didn't like to think back to how he dealt with so called patriots, it was simple: if a part of the clock was faulty it needed mending. If he could not mend it, break it up, throw it away.

His disturbed sleep did concern him though, always the same bloody thing, the bloody boy Rock. Why did he invade his brain so regularly? Was it the malt or was he getting old and tired?

"Rock." He was the only ghost his mind ever entertained, he lost no sleep about the girl.

Passing the obese Madame on the way up the stairs, she gave him a nasty look of disgust. Yet when she addressed him, she addressed him politely.

"What time do you eat breakfast, Mr Boyce?"

Boyce glanced back at her with disdain.

"Madame, I shall have it at the usual time," he said.

Madame Fusco cursed under her breath and went back to her kitchen, where a television played loudly. Boyce filled his glass with malt. Think of the girl he told himself with purpose. In no way did he hold himself responsible for her, she was created by them; they allowed her. His instructions didn't involve her, never. Boyce drank half the glass; it steamed down his chest, he gasped to take in air before refilling.

Wondering whether he should dress up for the evening and go to the nice restaurant by the harbour, deserving a treat after all the driving and the meeting in Cucuron. The thoughts of muscular youths still appealed to his brain. Maybe, he mused, I will call Maurice in St Raphael.

Boyce helped himself to more malt to ease his mind, to help chew things over he showered washing away the smell of the sea.

Deciding not to put on a suit as the evening was too warm, he chose his old naval-type blazer instead.

Boyce smiled to himself, he still had that quirky Methodist control over finance, inherited through countless squires and scoundrels.

Really, he could have done lots of things: rented a house out on the coast or stayed in one of those fancy hotels. It wasn't a question of money or indeed any inclination towards tightfistedness. Training is the very essence of survival. All those years of experience, lie low, be a sheep not a wolf, lie low woolly back. Besides, Drozdan was really impressed with him.

The Croat thought everything Boyce did was masterful. Boyce felt the man may have remarked on the complete ingeniousness of how his bleeding hemorrhoid allowed him to pass off as a human being.

Boyce laughed as he looked at himself in the mirror still looking the part when dressed up—not the man of yesteryear but more complete now in his maturity.

Brushing along the edges of his sideburns, wondering whether he should have shaved for a second time. "Damn it!" he concluded. "Will I do for the boy that wants me?"

Madame Fusco watched him as he passed by.

"You see key?" Boyce looked back at her waving his key ring.

"No need to stay up if I'm a little late Madame, I may bring a guest later, and I may not, you understand?"

The stout French woman twisted her mouth like she was being force fed castor oil.

"Madame Fusco, you may misunderstand me," Boyce waved a crisp note before her eyes just as a snake charmer charms a snake.

"Mr. Boyce, you have your key to come and go as you please, but only you yeah?"

Boyce gave her a practiced impatient nod.

Leaving without saying goodbye he headed down the street to the harbour.

The young people flying by on scooters made him nervous, driving the machines dreadfully fast without due care or caution. Boyce avoided them for weeks, weaving in and out of the traffic, showing no respect.

He checked at least three times before crossing the road to sit at his favourite spot overlooking the yachts. The harbour looked beautiful in the late evening, the water a dark green. The evening clouds smothered its reflection, a faint breeze cool against his skin. Walking on, he got a table at his regular restaurant which was getting busy yet some people didn't eat till after 9pm.

He ordered his meal, a chicken dish to negate his combustibility. An order of single malt, made him relax and feel good.

The waiter, a tall African, was cheerful making jokes in English as he eyed the fine women taking their seats. Boyce felt almost relieved to find the guy was straight, there was no time anymore for flirting or titillation, life was closing the door gently, whatever he needed he could buy; money was power, unaffected by his quirky Methodist upbringing, nothing diluted his fantasies. The restaurant started to get full. Evening light was fading, soon darkness arrived, the sky turning dark blue for a moment. The waiter lit candles on the tables and groups of people like moths were attracted to them. Soon the whole place was full with small groups of tourists.

Boyce didn't feel odd to be sitting alone. His malt was good. He ordered more. His waiter made a fuss about pouring it, more so to impress his clientele.

Two American couples close by were entertained by the waiter's antics as he pretended to empty the whole bottle into the glass. However their entertainment turned to disgust as Boyce lit a cigar. Though he tried blowing the smoke seaward, the offending cloud returned to form a film above their table. Complaining to the waiter; he just offered to move them to the far side of the restaurant where it was smoke-free. Choosing not to move and lose their view of the harbour or the magnificent yachts.

He puffed, admiring the lighted elegance of the yachts before him. He preferred to look at them in the dark, somehow they were more decadent in the night-light. The Americans, particularly the women, gave false coughs with dubious splutters, the smoke was killing them. Boyce continued to ignore them.

He didn't like Americans, having worked with them hand in hand over the years. He always felt it was un-English to like them. He always found them diligent if not a little predictable yet his dislike for them was based on something else altogether, feeling their reluctance to accept the superiority of a race who basically conquered the world centuries before they were even a country. Holding only contempt for the British and all those wonderful things achieved through colonization. Again he reminded himself his views were not based in anyway on patriotism or jingoism.

It was a fact the Yanks were jealous, they had only a short history. All their colonization a work in progress. They were like the spoiled boy allowed to do magic tricks at his birthday party only to find all the other kids dying of boredom.

Boyce blew his smoke into the air nonchalantly. His Americans were scheming to see whether they should elect a spokesperson to complain to him directly. One rather stout middle-aged woman got to her feet and took a few strides towards him. He promptly doused the butt. She stopped dead in her tracks, stunned, making a hasty retreat, expecting something like a victory salute from her companions. Boyce chuckled. "Bloody Yanks," he thought. "Spoiled kids."

4.

Lucia took her turn driving to give me a break, she liked scouring the map that led us everywhere,

I was content to let her organize, she probably thought she was doing me a favour, taking the pressure off, letting my brain rest.

Lucia was a very good driver, safe, very thorough.

I spent the time looking at the landscape, searching for the lavender fields, I read so much about them. Before me were farms set among low-lying fields. Sheep with strong-looking cattle grazed on grass which struggled for the greenery of Ireland. I was used to deep greens, Ireland is a dark land.

However, this was a pretty country, dominated by haystacks and fields painted with sunflower. We stopped to take photographs, me laughing at Lucia squatting midst the giant flowers. She looked like she was taking a wee, standing up embarrassed fixing the soft hat I bought her in St Maxime. I was sorry I had said anything; men find things funny that women just don't.

She took some photographs. I dreaded to see myself, my inner vision always had me in my mid-twenties, early thirties.

The photographs totally disproved my theory. I gazed at the image in complete shock. Is that me? After my operation I must have dropped nearly two stone.

I was thin, balding, so old-looking, my hair grey, it was like Mother Nature crawled out of those sunflowers just to kick me in the ass.

It was nature's way of reminding me that I was past it as any sort of serious proposition for the female sex unless I handed over a wad of notes. Maybe if I found some older female who was in worse straits than me!

Lucia laughed when I said it to her. I looked in the vanity mirror of our hired Citroen.

"Yes," she agreed playfully, "you are an old man. Aren't you lucky I still talk to you?"

I looked at her side-on under her soft day tripper's hat. Her skin was still taut and her hair retained its natural blonde. Catching me looking, she smiled, "What are you looking at?"

I could only chance it, saying how much more photogenic she was compared to me. "Yeah," she said turning a sharp corner, her eyes hidden behind her shades. I knew her whole countenance screwed up when she concentrated.

"Don't worry I will find you lavender fields," she always thought my mind was living in the present. We passed some fine horses, beautiful brown foals, a large white horse that reminded me of Desert Orchid, I know he was a grey.

The fields started to shape upwards. In the distance I could see the snowy tips of enormous mountains. This was France, this was Provence. We rounded another bend.

"See?" Lucia said.

There were fields after fields of lavender.

We stopped the car to take more photographs, Lucia smiled as she posed.

"Look serious," I asked her. "You look better when you're serious."

She sighed, not understanding me. Really though, when posing, she overposed, she always looked like she was photographed after somebody told her the best joke in the world.

She compromised, smiling in a few, serious for me in a few.

Drozdan didn't like coffee yet he didn't want to insult Marie Abele. The Parish Priest of Cucuron had gone to great trouble, with plates of sandwiches and also a plate of wafer biscuits.

Drozdan looked mournfully at Argüelles, who said politely, "Father Marie Abele, there was no need to go to so much trouble. The Cardinal is forever in your debt."

"I consider it an honour and a privilege for a student of Cardinal Edgell to grace our parish."

Marie Abele was pouring the coffee; he was at home in his darkened study.

"The Parish Priest of Cucuron is more a student of Cardinal Edgell than myself, Monsignor Argüelles."

"Indeed I hear that is true," said the Monsignor.

"Gentlemen, you flatter me really, after all of this time." Father Marie Abele took a seat pulling it in to the table. He sipped his coffee, careful not to spill it on the saucer; he was silent, knowing he should listen.

"Tell me, Father, has there been more word of our miracle worker or his mother?" Argüelles looked at Marie Abele curiously.

"I have heard not a thing for at least a year," replied the priest, risking more coffee.

"No? We have heard nothing either. A little odd isn't it? Monsignor Argüelles and I think it was odd she should meet you, then nothing. Obviously she still enjoys the protection of the Mafiosi. Is that your understanding Father?"

Argüelles was all eyes and ears to Drozdan, watching Marie Abele for any hint of insincerity, any clue the Parish Priest might be holding back. Marie Abele was near retirement, serving the church for over forty years. Argüelles could tell the strain was beginning to show; he had shadows under his sunken eyes, his knuckles were sharp—almost worn skin powdered and scratched, the Parish Priest looked like his body was attacking from within.

"The young man stays in Italy; it seems certain Don Dino Bernado is keeping him close," Father Marie Abele said finally.

"I see," the Cardinal said.

Argüelles intervened. "How is your English curate?"

37

Marie Abele seemed uncomfortable, drinking his coffee too hastily.

"Father Cryan has improved, Your Grace." The Parish Priest directed his reply at the Cardinal.

Argüelles was unperturbed; the Spaniard asked, "Really? After throat cancer? What do the medics say?"

Once again, Marie Abele hesitated before saying, "They say he is in remission Monsignor."

"Remission?" Argüelles said, dismissing the idea as a hoax.

"It concerns me," the Cardinal said quietly.

"If we are to re-establish Sodality the last thing we need Father is for some nut running around Italy doing miracles."

"Is it your view Father she was worried for him?" Argüelles asked almost accusingly.

The Parish Priest frowned, there was no coffee left to wet his throat. Reaching to take the jug of water, he said, "I only think it was because I recognized her she knew me at once, it would be accurate to assume she wants to protect him. Yes, I believe she wants to call a halt and clean the slate."

"Did she say that, Father?" Argüelles was tapping his fingers on the hard table to show his patience was being tested.

"Monsignor, she said she holds the truth all recorded. If anything happens to her son she will go public, let the whole world know. It is all she said, no other words passed between us."

"So you contacted British Intelligence before us," The Cardinal said coldly.

"The Americans are pouring over Auldridge's archives; we cannot rekindle Sodality under such scrutiny Father," Argüelles said, sliding his chair back, making a scraping noise, walking to the window pulling back the drape to allow light.

"It's very dark in here Father. My eyes are straining to see you. Why did you go to Boyce and not us?" Marie Abele slid his chair back in turn; he went to the rear window, pulling the drape right back, the lower end of the room flooding with brilliant light.

"Because I was afraid Monsignor, after what happened to us all those years ago, the imprint is left on my heart; Cardinal Edgell, Archbishop Damasky, Monsignor Fucilla— all murdered. I had no idea you were planning to start all over again. I was never told or given that impression when I was in Rome." Marie Abele spoke with a passion, it was impressive. Argüelles grunted, pretending to look out over the gardens.

The Cardinal offered, "Father Marie Abele, you understand our need to be careful, we must proceed with the utmost care."

"We cannot allow Boyce to know too much about our aspirations. They tell the Americans everything, you see they have common interests. We trust you, yet we have to be careful!" The Spaniard said dryly, returning to his seat.

"Father, we have to make sure all present at our meetings in Rome are vetted; history has taught us caution. You are right, after what happened all those years ago - you were scared, hah?" Marie Abele smiled at the Cardinal.

"Your Grace, you know I offer my service to you without precondition!"

Drozdan laughed, as he always did, and Argüelles laughed with him. "We never doubted your loyalty, Father,
    you have been a servant to our cause for so long."

"What did Boyce say when he came to visit?" Argüelles interrupted the gaiety sharply.

Marie Abele looked at him; he was too intimidating for such a small man. He didn't like the Monsignor's tone, the Spaniard was arrogant; his manners rude. It was on the tip of his tongue to say something to voice his true opinion, it was a great pity these people inherited the cause Edgell gave his life for.

"Mr Boyce came to see me his curiosity aroused by my initial contact with him almost a year ago. I could tell him nothing, not a thing. As far as I know they are still in Italy. He wished to know more about what this woman has on record. I, Your Grace, could not enlighten him on that count. Mr Boyce was very pleasant; he was happy I told him the truth!"

Drozdan eyed Argüelles for a reaction. The little Spaniard thrust his head forward as if thinking. "Yes it makes sense, Father, he never asked about us? I mean he never mentioned Sodality or the events of the past?"

"No, Your Grace, he never asked."

Argüelles stood. "When are you next due to visit us in Rome, Father?"

"I am not sure. My diary is in my desk." Marie Abele pointed to his writing desk at the other end of the room, almost invisible in the shadow.

"No, Father, please don't go to any trouble, no need." Argüelles stopped Abele from leaving his chair. "I will fix a date for you, say in a month. We can relive your experiences and talk in more detail about this great Mafiosi Don Dino Bernado. You can remind us of your lucky escape, after all, you know more about this woman than we do.

Perhaps you are the only member of our movement who has ever laid eyes on her. Come help us understand what we need to do, the action we need to take."

Father Marie Abele felt his stomach tighten as the Spaniard spoke. His tone had a ring of sarcasm, he was patronizing, yet chastising in unison.

5.

In Cucuron we ate lunch at a little café bar adjacent to the only decent place we could find to park the car.

The flies were swarming, so Lucia used her hat plus an insect spray she carried in the bag that carried the world.

It made not a heap of difference to the flies but at least it made us feel better. The food was good if the service was a little slow. Taking a seat outside the waiter came out speaking to us like we were the first visitors he ever met in his life.

I will tell you the guy was middle-aged, however, as previously explained, he was probably younger than me. He took our sandwich-and-baguette orders without fuss. We ordered a litre of spring water with gas.

The place-mats had photos of scenes from old French movies. The stills were of high quality; the characters looked like the Marx brothers, others were very beautiful females, or self-satisfied men in dinner jackets smoking fags.

Lucia went "yeah?"

She was busy swatting flies. I wondered what French movie the photographs came from.

She didn't hear me. The waiter returned.

"Ah," he said. "I buy in Paris."

He went on to say something about Marseille.

I hadn't a clue what he was on about. Lucia seemed to understand every word he said. When I asked her to explain she admitted she hadn't a notion what he was on about.

Later I waited nearly twenty minutes to pay the guy, who somehow had changed into his twin brother. He didn't know

41

who I was, or why I was in his café bar. Eventually his twin returned, greeting me like a long lost friend before taking my money.

Our walk up the town led us along narrow streets, up steep hills, passing a shop selling postcards which Lucia examined. They were mostly scenes of lavender fields, others with adoring sunflowers in the shade of dark mountains. Further on, the street opened up, the buildings became more defined. A man with a beard, sporting a stereotypical French beret, invited us into a local museum. It was free, so Lucia walked straight in, me behind her. The exhibits were mostly photographs of the locality from times past, various types of farm machinery, photos of labourers digging a trench. One large photograph of people walking through fields of snow, on the day that was in it with the sweltering heat it was hard to imagine the environs of Cucuron ever seeing a flake of snow.

Lucia goes, "Snow? My goodness."

The museum turned out to be a little disappointing, more like roaming through somebody's house and examining the relics of their ancestors. We didn't leave anything in the voluntary contributions box as Lucia was too wise, I was too lazy.

Further up the street, on the brow of the hill where the town ends, the church of St Michael stood high and mighty.

I almost fell and broke my neck going in as the place was so dark and there was a drop of at least a foot from stone step to stone step.

Boyce almost lost his life when he stepped into St Michael's; he missed the step completely, only because he retained some of his old agility he ended up sitting on his bottom on the cold floor. "Fuck it," he cursed, automatically scanning around him to see if anyone had heard him fall. The church was dark, it took him a minute or so to adjust his eyes to the blackness. However, he could see nobody. What he thought to be a person was indeed a statue of St Michael, obviously it was due to be discarded or refurbished. Boyce knew this by where it stood over by the big heavy door with a ring handle which he presumed led to the presbytery. Following Father Marie Abele's instructions he entered the first confessional to his right. Boyce was a big man; he barely squeezed in. Once inside there was no room to sit, so he had to kneel. The hard wood was cutting through his knees, he felt a cramp eat up his leg from his toes. First his right leg, then both legs started to give trouble. Knowing he would never last this, he was about to move outside when the grill slid open.

Father Marie Abele said, "Hello, Boyce. I can barely see you in this light. Your shape is as I remember; maybe you have put on a little weight?"

"I can't see you at all Abele, maybe just as well, time is not a favoured thing'!"

"True," the priest said sadly.

"We meet again after all this time Father because she wants to speak?"

"No, my friend, we meet because she threatens to speak if anything happens to her son. She will... what is it you secret service say? Come out; that's it. We French say she will spill the beans."

Abele, his breathing heavy, waited for Boyce to comment. Boyce was distracted by the pain in his calves, knowing if he didn't restore the circulation from his knees down he would probably lose one leg or both!

"She can, as you say Abele, spill the beans. For a start nobody gives a damn about Northern Ireland anymore or particularly what happened there in the seventies. She is barking up the wrong tree. Who cares if she knows there was a plot to kill the Pope?"

Boyce hesitated, he tried in vain to move his legs. "Father, we left no prints on this; she is a fake, her priest Burdon and his kind are no longer of any use."

"You know Burdon is dead five years. A long illness."

"So much for their miracle child; the son couldn't save him, eh?" Boyce said, trying to move his left leg out the door so he could keep talking.

"The boy didn't know he was sick. Farther Burdon came back here; the boy only came here after he died." Abele hesitated; it was his turn. He didn't want to give the Englishman too much information. "So where are they all now, Abele?"

"I don't know Boyce, perhaps they still live with Don Dino Bernado at Bagni di Lucca. I dunno."

Boyce, knowing he had very little time with his knees, said, "Where was it you met her, Father?"

"Only by accident. I went to the spa. My sinuses needed treatment. I met her there."

"I see." Boyce was on his feet outside, bouncing his left foot off the stone floor.

"You have my number Abele, let me know if you hear anything or if she tries to make contact again."

"Sure, I will let you know if I hear anything,"

Father Abele slid the grill closed. Afterwards Abele sat alone in his study. Drozdan and Argüelles were to visit the next day. It made him nervous, drinking his coffee, thinking if only Edgell had survived where would he be now. Edgell had plans for him, he said it more than once.

I would have made Cardinal, long since gone from here, perhaps Paris, or Rome itself. Maybe I might have made the States?

The world a better place, with more order, less of this racial mix that causes such discord. Cardinal Edgell was a man of great vision, such a pity he died when he did. It happened just as they were beginning to take shape and possibly change the world forever.

Remembering the first time he met Boyce, he was totally different now.

I suppose we all change given time. Boyce was very handsome, very impressive. Now his frame betrays his years. Abele could see he was slow on his feet as he struggled up the church steps. What the passing years can do to a man!

Father Abele didn't know if he either liked or trusted Boyce, he wasn't his type of man. Boyce made contact after Edgell died.

He wanted the girl and offered Abele huge sums of money for information.

Abele told him all he knew. Boyce paid him on that basis; however, the information led to nothing. It pained Boyce, who compared it to allowing a prize fish jump from the net. Yet it was more cash than Abele had ever seen or would ever hope to see.

She was under the protection of Don Dino, that was it, Boyce couldn't get close.

With time it all went quiet, the main people in Sodality all dead, besides Auldridge, it was the end of the road. Abele never told Boyce she spent time in Cucuron, no point in complicating the issue. It was in his parish Father Burdon hid her for over six months. Boyce didn't need to know; he was only interested after Edgell died.

He drank more coffee, remembering sitting at the same table discussing his dilemma, if one can call speaking to himself a discussion.

He relied on his own wit to seek grace, for who was there to seek advice from. Nothing much had changed for Abele, he was too keen to sit back, watch. It was an old thing he had learned growing up in the seminary in Paris - wait, watch, listen, learn; never rush in, Father Abele. He watched helplessly as Cryan re-enforced Burdon's already dangerous philosophy. She was young with child. Burdon claimed the girl was abused by her father. Abele had great sympathy for her on hearing this; yet he knew she could not stay long, not in Cucuron.

Edgell advised him to receive the broken-hearted Don; it was his way.

The idea the Don would retreat to Cucuron, repent his sins.

The man was close to mental breakdown after the death of his only son. The Don did not speak for a month. One day Burdon overheard what was a private conversation. Father Abele banged his fist on the table in frustration, if he had been more discreet Edgell might still be alive.

To compound matters he made contact outside of instruction.

The contact was totally out of concern for Don Dino's health. Abele knew Sodality needed the power the Don wielded. The Don told his sins to Burdon, his Confessor. Burdon must also have confessed to the Don, telling him about the girl and their history in Ireland. He told him about the conversation he overheard. Abele remembered thinking the Don had lost his mind, it was his duty to plead with the Edgell.

The coffee was cold as Father Abele placed his head in his hands.

He was safe, he comforted, nobody ever knew besides Burdon, he felt a sharp pain across his chest.

6.

Lucia led the way along the narrow isle. The church was deserted, both sides adorned by minor altars. It reminded me of my childhood.

Our local parish church, it always fascinated me how three masses could be said simultaneously. One on the main altar, then one to each of the side altars.

How did each priest keep his concentration? Sometimes there were only one or two people at the side altars. They got mass all to themselves. The confessionals in the church of St Michael were so small, narrow, it was a wonder a body could fit into them at all. They were carved from the wall with wood so old I expected it to crumble. Lucia was away to my right trying to decipher the various notices on a tiny notice board.

I could sense the cold, turbulent air pockets filled with dust rising to the ceiling. Lucia had enough, walking back out she warned a Canadian tourist to watch his step. The light outside was blinding. We looked over the old boundary wall, it lent a view of the vast countryside.

"Different, isn't it?" Lucia said as she scanned the hills and the lush valleys below. I was still inside the church wondering at the richness of its golden tabernacle, the gold-plated rail serving to divide its three altars, the statues that adorned the side aisle, the crude beautifully hand-carved stations of the cross, I felt a great peace in this dark lonely place.

I remembered marching banners, the Men's Sodality, unquestioning parishioners.

My father at the end of the pew with his sash, the Men's

Sodality. I hated thinking this way, boys march home from war, catholic banners, bloody victory.

I feel I touch the skin of men, so safe years ago. Lucia watches me, she is afraid.

"What is it?" she said.

I didn't answer.

Putting on a false smile, "Didn't you like the church?"

"Yeah, it was beautiful." I said.

She stared at me; still not satisfied I was telling the truth.

Collection plates passed by serious men, Irish Mafiosi suits for Sunday, passing wooden plates, damp coats, dubious hair oil, whispered prayer.

Safe generals carry banners, the marching boys follow blindly.

Gardiner prepared himself for Bateman. He was becoming increasingly frustrated, the phantom chest pains, fatigue swallowing his spirit.

"You're right on with your translation. Gee Steve, this thing is spooky. Got one of those interpreters on to it, no shit she was spooked; hey I mean she was wacko, nice ass though..."

Gardiner thanked him, trying to remain patient, he must stay on good terms, it wasn't like the files held anything new. It was late afternoon he decided to call Susie. She was shopping, she had a weeks vacation from her secretarial job.

"Yeah," She adopted this distant approach since their split. Gardiner didn't pretend to know she was in Coney Island.

"Hi Sue, just calling to see how you all are?"

"I'm out shopping, got to get my dad's stuff too, you know his knee is gone again the Doc thinks he'll need surgery!"

"Geez. How's he taken' that?" Gardiner seized the opportunity to make the conversation normal.

"He doesn't like it, it reminds him of Mom, can't say I blame him, there aint many people going in for a routine procedure end up dead!"

"He will be fine; your Dad's as strong as an ox. How're Shaun and Marsha?"

"Fine," Susie said defensively.

"Shaun is good; he's playing a little hockey. The study is hard, you know him when he gets the bit between his teeth. Wish she could buy a little of his diligence, Christ she is so difficult you know. Life is a drama, one big drama."

"I was thinking maybe I could drop by and see them. Dunno, maybe do some shopping? Shaun might want to take in a hockey game or something?"

"I thought you were going to Europe?"

"Not yet."

"Shaun said you were going to Italy, your daughter says she never hears from you!" Susie gave a kind of false chuckle as if to imply that Marsha was unreasonable.

"I call her every chance I get. She is always powered off, she never calls back, the only time she calls me is if she needs stuff and you said no already!"

"I got to go Steve, it's mad in here. Will you call me later? I dunno, the kids are kind of busy and with Dad's knee let me think hey?"

"Sure ok." Gardiner wanted to sound meek. "See yaw." Susie ended the call.

An hour later Gardiner crossed the Brooklyn Bridge. The East River was reflecting the dark cloud, flowing slow it begged for light. The sight of the river depressed him, it always did, even as a kid. Kellerman called out of the blue. He wanted a meet in the Chelsea Sheraton, the CIA liked to do it posh. Quinn let him in. This time he wore the jacket, Kellerman was in braces.

"It's a funny day Gardiner. I don't know, with this place you look out the window, hard to know if it's winter or summer. All these cities look the same." Quinn pointed to the coffee brewing. Gardiner shook his head.

He wanted to get out, get home as soon as possible; coffee meant he was happy to be there.

"These country boys hey Gardiner, Washington State, you know Quinn here started the fire on Mount St Helens."

The two men lamented their demise into small talk, Kellerman in particular at his really bad jokes.

49

Gardiner took a seat by the window. The air was heavy; the arrival of summer to New York meant sweltering heat.

"We went through the archives, everything we have on this old boy Auldridge." Quinn sounded like he was Indiana Jones giving a lecture. Kellerman as usual interrupted, "The old boy had powerful friends. We had to go to a lot trouble to get what we wanted; we went as far as the director's office to get these."

Gardiner was handed a file with a dozen or so photographs, mainly of Cardinal Auldridge, one or two were just straight portraits. There was one with Jimmy Carter, George Bush senior, a couple with Ronald Reagan. The last few were older, Gardiner recognized the subjects. Their names were printed boldly below: "Edgell, Damasky, Fucilla, Rome, 1976." Gardiner looked at the two men blankly.

Quinn responded, "We are worried, this guy Auldridge was slightly right of Adolf Hitler. If this woman's got something we have got to know what it is."

Kellerman looking serious added, "We think it's time for you to track her down find out what she's got?"

"How do you know she wants anything?" Gardiner was sorry he said it the way he did, it sounded smart. He chose to look out over the Manhattan skyline. In the distance the cloud had grown mushroom like away in Newark.

7.

Lucia looked different at night, she was taller, more womanly.

She wore dresses, put on eye shadow. We walked down the promenade, Lucia keeping an eye on the designer shops. She might stop suddenly out of the blue, wander into an empty shop, me spending five or ten minutes walking behind her as she picked up items then putting them down after an age. She liked to joke with the shop assistants, she liked to appear eccentric showing she possessed a wonderful innocence.

I started off in positive fashion offering her advice and encouragement on the goods enticing her. The more time she spent, the more my assistance receded. Soon I either ended up dumb, what do you think of that, dumb? She pondering on some very expensive article.

Or, I ended up standing outside pacing, awaiting her arrival, it was a dangerous game I was playing, one she would only tolerate to a degree.

If I got sullen or smart it could have led to total disaster. Most times I would make light of it, throw in a ruse by saying, "My God! I had to walk out, did you ever see such an expensive place?"

She would agree immediately stating, "You would want to be out of your head to buy anything in there." However, I knew if I sneaked back and bought any of the offending items I'd be hailed the best in the world.

It was on one such stroll down the prom in Viaréggio that I met Raymond. Later on the very same night I met Philippe and Monica. The head waiter at breakfast in the Grand Palace Hotel, was already Don Maestrino Giordano.

I needed to find his son and daughter and his key henchman. Lucia had no idea how lucrative her shopping could be. We passed a very modern high-fashion store, the owner standing in his doorway. He was a striking man in his early fifties with a tailored suit. He was unusual in that he had long grey hair falling onto his shoulders, a little like Chief Dan George in Little Big Man if you ever saw the movie.

The man was born to be Mafiosi. Whilst he was odd-looking, he was just perfect for Raymond. His elegance and sincere countenance, if ever anyone possessed that intellectual-henchman look it was he. When Lucia and I passed by he was on the phone doing business. Later we saw him take a table in the indoor section of the restaurant we had chosen. He was a big shot buying wine for his table of guests. Master of ceremonies. Perhaps somebody was leaving his employ or it was a birthday.

We ended up in the New York Bar. Lucia liked it as it had an outdoor covered area for snacks and cocktails. Inside you could have a beer or a gin and listen to a guy play what looked like a white grand piano. This indeed turned out just to be a hidden synthesizer.

The pianist was able to play violin, piano, drums, electric guitar—all on the same instrument. We had a gin plus a beer in the extension, which was done a little like a sheiks harem with net curtains and a canvas roof.

When we sat the waiter brought us sliced fruit and peanuts. A guy sat beside us watching a movie on satellite television. This was Philippe. He sat grim-faced, all his concentration on the screen. He peeled his fruit into a bowl without moving his eyes from the television. All I could imagine was somebody planting dialogue into his mouth, stereotypical mafia speak,

"You let me down Georgi, you show no respect." Philippe would keep peeling his fruit oblivious to the anguish of his victim. Lucia laughed when I whispered Mafiosi into her ear. Philippe turned the sound down on the TV, paying no notice to any movement around him. The karaoke guy playing the synthesizer is joined by this beauty.

She is dark, tall; she sings sweetly in Italian. The crowd outside are quiet for a change. I have found her, Philippe's sister, this is Monica. I study her as Lucia helps herself to peanuts. I try the freshly cut kiwi fruit. They sing "Time to Say Goodbye." The pianist is smiling, enjoying himself.

Boyce made the call, Maurice answered straight away. Boyce was speaking slowly, his accent more pronounced when he had a drink. "How long can you wait?" Maurice asked.

"An hour, no longer. It gets cold here after eleven." Boyce said, already feeling the cool night air.

"I will drive Eric, we are near St Tropez," Maurice was gone.

Boyce sat back in his chair, lighting another cigar. His American friends had left making a lot of clatter. So loud he thought, of course they never inherited the English reserve or culture. The restaurant was fairly full. As the night went on its clientele got younger. A few people arrived by launch from the yachts.

Boyce enjoyed looking at their finery, the women were elegant, the men dashing. Taking more of his malt, wondering whether he should order more, worried save it make him too drunk or too tired. After all Maurice was bringing Eric to entertain him.

He drank more malt, it was good, cold down his throat yet hot when it passed into his chest and tummy. Maybe, he mused, tomorrow I will not have gas and pain. The waiter cleaned his ashtray looking at his empty glass, affirming a re-fill was in order. Moving on, admiring the elderly gentleman's capacity for drink.

Boyce wiped his lips, then closed his eyes to hear the water gently fall against the harbour walls. It was like someone opened then closed the drain of a wash hand basin.

So long since he was satisfied, Maurice knew what he

wanted, the way he liked it to be. Feeling the little heat of excitement as it warmed in his genitals, then his brain as if they were married. How he discovered where his tastes lay. As a young man he had dated women and scorned men adoring the naked poses of trashy porn magazines, often relieving himself wildly wherever he found privacy yet somehow over the years dissatisfaction grew. Boyce smiled at a passing beauty, taking a large drink of malt, his drink relaxing him, allowing his mind to wander. Where did he first discover his penchant for boys dressed as women? Why thick lips, feminine eyes soft searching, skin smooth contrasting with their rude maleness, this excited him. Crossing his legs in an effort to control his body responses, hot fires invading his mind, he dominant, abusing. From where did this need arise? He saw Rock's face, he saw the look of fear, the horror, his boyish skin soft! Why is it the boy haunts him so?

Boyce could not snap out of it. Each time trying to slip back into relax mode, seeing the same thing. Young Rock in terror, crying, asking to be allowed go home.

He could hear his own voice, threatening, vile. The boy shrinking, the horror was too great. It wasn't my fault, Boyce tried to counteract his own conscience, it wasn't my fault. Rock was a Roman Catholic; he paid him well for the information.

So what if he wanted to have a bit of fun?

Buying the wig and lipstick whilst back home in Oxford.

This turned him on, turning Rock from boy to girl, he was a beautiful girl, in the end the cold look of resignation, frozen Rock all manly, the frost lending him dignity. Boyce knew the kinks in his armour; he wasn't the monster they all said he was.

He just knew the rules of the game, knew how to play. The Swiss clockmaker makes his clocks. Wars and skirmishes are there to be won. It was Mick Devlin who allowed things get out of control, Burdon the skinny priest, whining, maybe they might have made a deal? Boyce saw the mist hang on the fields, he saw half trees stand naked, weak light facing the prospect of a slow thaw.

8.

Don Maestrino Giordano supervised breakfast. He was robust, small. It was as if he wanted to smile and be friendly, only his face wouldn't allow it.

He gave his orders in a peaceful fashion, his underlings happy to do his bidding.

Not that there was all that much to do. Once they set up the buffet the same confused faces arrived. This was Italy. The only hangovers in view were Lucia's and mine. The woman from the beach was there with her pretty daughter. They sat alone at a table opposite, the Don overseeing their every move. The fat father made a guest appearance. He gestured, sat, said a little, then moved on. They had a weird arrangement. I figured he must run a business somewhere locally, or else he was stock broking from his room.

How such an ungainly creature could have secured such a beautiful wife. Of course Lucia hit it on the nail when she put him down for being loaded.

"Yeah," I said jealously, "he must be rotten with money." This was something that fascinated me about the female kept with riches, rewards, material goods.

The only demand to lie on your back every now and then, take your due, one more satisfied customer. These women could have children, maybe even stay loyal all their lives.

These slobs, the neglectful successful businessmen, the ones who have it all, wealth, beautiful women. Lucia deplored my views, a woman needs to be secure. "What happens if the old man ups and kicks the bucket?"

In these types of scenarios Lucia defended all women as a group. It was something I have rarely seen a man do, if ever. The woman helped herself from the buffet, which in fairness the Don made sure had everything. Fresh crusty rolls and bowls of fruit salad were complemented by every breakfast cereal ever made.

There were boiled eggs, brown bread, oranges, grapefruit juice. On a table removed a selection of cold Parma ham and salami. She was elegant, followed by her daughter who was radiant. The Don looked on, his hotel uniform a tiny bit too tight, maybe he was just that little too robust. I wanted to use the woman. I thought of Eva; she didn't fit. I may use her as Monica, to replace the singer of the previous night. She was very beautiful, if a little too perfect. I decided to stick to my original decision. It was with sadness I watched her leave with her daughter. They were met at the doorway by her husband, his shorts too big for him. He mumbled something to her; she mumbled something in return.

Boyce knew Maurice was discreet. He saw the Mercedes coupe pull up opposite. He watched as the occupants studied their geography. His cigar was just a butt; he sucked the last of it. The waiter offered more malt, he nodded, this would be the night cap.

"Give me a Martini or a cocktail of some sort," Boyce instructed. The waiter answered "Martini sir." To anyone looking on an attractive North African woman got out of the car. The dress, figure hugging gold, offered a clear view of both thighs. Boyce sat back whilst the chair opposite was occupied.

"Hello," Eric said.

"Maurice, ever reliable, I ordered you a Martini."

"Good,"

Boyce looked at Eric's thick lips. His eyes were glittered, the lids painted with a mixture of blue and green. Looking at Boyce he painted his lips wet using a kind of lipstick. Brushing his long dark hair from his smooth skin, he said, "I like Martini Mr. Boyce." The waiter returning was taken with the attractive specimen before him. Boyce was pleased when he said, "The lady and you sir." Eric sipped his drink.

The interrogations had no set time. It frustrated Boyce, he wanted them all fast, concise. All it took was some stubborn little shit with the Republican ethos stuck to his soul; they could be at it all night. Boyce didn't like hurting his hands; he left the beating to his subordinates. Anyway it wasn't the part he enjoyed, Swiss clock makers make clocks, working on mechanisms. He enjoyed the fine work, when the suspect was close to passing out, most of them gave up in the end. Blood pumping from the nose, all bashed and bruised till it resembled no more than a hole within the mass of facial skin. The ears were usually bent backwards, dark purple; often blood would ooze from them as well. He was always careful to warn his interrogators not to blunt the power of speech.

Despite the small streams of red trickling from broken teeth, bitten gums, purple tongues, his suspects were useless if they were rendered speechless he mused, that was always a concern. One suspect had initially led him to Mick Devlin. "You see if you can let me have a little I can tell these bastards to stop, they are not like me, just want an excuse to use extreme violence, help me stop them," Boyce would always pat his victim on the head, rubbing the boy's hair with his right hand.

"You want to go home don't you, to your family, I understand that."

One of the interrogators, shouts,

"Let me at the Fenian bastard Captain, he'll fuckin' squeal. I'll tear his fuckin' balls off." The boy squirming; Boyce enjoyed examining the terror in his eyes.

"Tell me what it is I need to know?" The boy finally broken, tears flooding his wounds, his mouth shivering like a fish pulled from a frozen stream. He sobbed, whispering names, places, things he heard. The experience was relentless, Boyce pacifying him with a kind stroke of his head every time he gave a snippet of information. "Very good, very good." Boyce said softly.

Madame Fusco was in bed yet Boyce could still smell her presence. She used perfume tainted with garlic. He led Eric upstairs to his room. The African was quiet, a little nervous, so Boyce offered him a drink. Eric refused, "I cannot have more."

"Fine." Boyce said, pouring malt from the bottle by the dresser. He moved to the window, surveying the harbour one more time before drawing the drapes. Boyce lit the side lamp that illuminated the small writing bureau standing idle in the corner. Eric sat on the small armchair which rested by the stained coffee table.

He eyed Boyce, nervously shifting backwards in his seat. Boyce sensing his discomfort saw the dress go back further revealing more of his dark thigh. This pleased him as the more uncomfortable the young African became, the more it excited him.

Rock was a quiet fair-haired boy from a farm beyond the village. Boyce met him first when the squaddies searched their barn. His parents were old, he an only child. Boyce could see it in him, Rock didn't have the hatred in his eyes that consumed the others. The boy was used to working the fields, driving the tractor. His parents, the father older than the mother, were nervous. Boyce knew they were quiet people, intent on making a living from the few acres they farmed. The boy their lifeline, at eighteen he was their strength. His life was dedicated to those who gave him life. Rock had a full interest in the world around him.

Boyce could see he was at ease with nature, the animals in the fields were comfortable when he passed through to open outhouses, the soldiers at ease in their search.

His blue eyes were attractive. Boyce saw girl's eyes, soft, yet his bone structure was manly, his ancestors were good stock.

He spoke in a series of statement like monologues, saying things in a hurry, his face pale and sincere, looking the captain straight in the eye.

"It's in there we keep the hay, Captain," He would answer Boyce's questions with, "Aye I see," "Never a bit of trouble, all is quiet here."

Boyce asked him did he ever go to the village for a drink or a chat, to see his mates. Rock hesitated, looking at him fair and square said, "Only on a Saturday night, if there is something on in the parish hall!"

The Captain looked at him disdainfully, "So you know this Father Burdon then?"

"I do, everyone round here does, a brilliant priest, great for the old people,"

Boyce noticed the sincerity in his eyes. Here before him was the epitome of maleness, a big broad athletic youth, but Boyce could smell the femininity sap from him till it crawled under his skin. "Do you play this game, you know?" Boyce said frustratingly, "Gaelic football, or Hurling?"

"I'm not good at the Hurling Captain, it's mostly football round here."

Eric was ready for him; he painted his lips wet as Boyce requested. A true professional, he performed his duty expertly. Boyce found it difficult to relax, his mind wandering to the darkness of his private quarters. The bubble bath, him lying back talking, Rock vomiting in the cold white sink. Eric was too practiced, Boyce was disappointed it was over so fast, an uneasy silence followed. Soon the African was gone, Maurice waited. Boyce slid into bed after his exertions, exhausted from the malt. Rock left when it was dark, how many nights watching from the window, the boy walking away, the sentry on the side gate allowing him leave, one last glance before he vanished into the night.

9.

Viaréggio at night stimulated my imagination almost beyond my control. Lucia said it was the slow evacuation of the anesthetic drugs. Her theory was based upon my continued silence, which to her mind was down to complete ignorance, maybe she was right, I was still half-conked from whatever they gave me in the private clinic.

Still I will always love Viaréggio for allowing me to go crazy.

A real artist might say it allowed me the freedom to think, imagine.

Where was I when I first realised I was crazy?

On the beach, the Orientals offering their massaggio, when I was eyeing the fat guy's wife, she was bronzed, she glistened in the light. I just happened to glance at Lucia wondering how she retained her attraction within the remit of her paleness but she did. With Lucia, her eyes light blue allowed ripples of intelligence, washing the spirit .The beach sprayed with colour, the heat steaming to the sea. Waves crashed to the shore false as children appeared from the foam, yachts sailed by in deep water, the sunlight creating stepping stones, fallen stars cooling down. I saw Shelley, his body floating face down, falling to the sand, the sea eventually regurgitating him, loose skin effervescent, his clothes ripped by predators. People bathed avoiding his remains. Children ran screaming with delight carrying small buckets, standing by the shore their tiny feet swallowed by quicksand. Byron leaving through the crowds, Edward Trelawny watches as Shelley's body burns. 'Heart of

Hearts.' Trelawny reaches into the pyre, he removes Shelley's heart from the ashes. I watch as Lucia looks on, she wants to swim, cool down. This woman, my wife, what hold has she, I am infected by her, addicted to her conversation, our shared memory. She steals away, bathed by cold surf, my woman who shares my skin, she is stolen by the current. I am reminded Mary Shelley kept her husbands heart it was interred beside her when she was laid to rest.

Drozdan watched Argüelles the Spaniard was reading the documents intently.

Finally, after what seemed a lifetime, he lifted his head and said flatly, "I was right. Edgell says it all, doesn't he, Your Eminence?"

Drozdan waited to reply. Looking at the ceiling he was repulsed by its plainness, hardly good enough for a man of his standing. The Vatican was full of offices with stained glass windows and decorated ceilings. They thought they could belittle him.

"It is clear Marie Abele betrayed them." Drozdan was matter of fact.

Arguelles said, "The French are like that, passive, weak. He told this Father Burdon, cracked under pressure. Edgell guessed, had no proof yet he was sure in his own mind?"

"Yes, if he had not needed the woman?" Drozdan replied firmly.

Argüelles looking at him blankly said, "She is not speaking; she has nothing on us!"

"Maybe enough if it gets out, embarrassing at least. We need to take them out, all of them."

Argüelles nodded "As soon as possible," Drozdan took the file from Argüelles; he half opened it, then closed it tight.

"Edgell never got a chance; we must not make the same mistake Monsignor!"

Argüelles smiled, "Don't worry, Your Grace. We are ready I have only to press the button." When he smiled Drozdan saw his teeth were perfect, saintly white.

Monica stared at her brother in disbelief, then turned to Don Maestrino shouting, "You don't honestly believe him, Father?"

Don Maestrino, turning his back in disgust, went to open the window shutters.

"Philippe, you always have this place like a morgue. No wonder my temper frays. In Volterra, we keep shutters open to allow light, allow the presence of God in."

"Father, I tell you the truth, she is sleeping with a miracle man. What is worse, he is tied to the protection of your mortal enemy, Don Dino Bernado."

Monica gave Philippe a foul look. He smiled at her contemptuously. She ignored him, beseeching her father as he turned from the window.

"Toby is not tied to Don Dino; he has no interest in the past. He cares not for anything to do with business, neither is he a miracle man. He has cures, but since when is that a crime?"

"Quiet, both of you!" Don Maestrino commanded. The room was different with the light. Don Maestrino felt he could sit and maybe have a coffee to relax his brain, make him trust his judgement. Monica was looking at the ground. Her brother had taken to the window as if he had just discovered the view.

"Hey, Raymond, how about a coffee? I want a cappuccino," Raymond moved from his seat with no obvious degree of urgency.

"No, no." Philippe said. "Not for me." Monica was still looking at the ground.

"OK, Philippe, what is it has you bothered? You are my son. Monica, my daughter, what are you asking from me, to choose between you?"

Don Maestrino looked pained as if all his dreams just suddenly ended in tears. "I buy you this bar Philippe! I buy Monica a car. I still get trouble, hey? I don't ask for much, maybe a little peace. You present me with this fix, what am I to do? I know you, Philippe, you have a motive. I fail to remember you doing anything for free since you were this high," Don Maestrino gestured the height of a small boy.

"I think you watch too many movies in your head, you live in New York. You are a hood. I think you are Al Pacino in the Godfather, hey?" Don Maestrino said, half smiling.

Philippe, his face purple, moved from the window to retake his seat.

"Monica you are my beautiful daughter, you remind me of poor Stella. Everyday I see you, I see your poor mother. You sing like an angel, yet your head is full of romantic nonsense. I don't care if this man has connections with Don Dino; it is of no interest to me. My interest is in your heart, you are sure to have it broken, now tell me tell everything," The Don looked at Philippe.

Raymond returned with the Cappuccino, "Grazie," Don Maestrino said as Raymond returned to his seat. Philippe hesitated, "I was asked by some very important people in Rome to help them Father. Have you ever heard of Sodality?" Don Maestrino moved in his chair, otherwise he showed no emotion.

"Sodality is dead, Don Dino killed them, all of them," Don Maestrino sat more upright to listen to his son.

"Father, Sodality has been reborn, led by Cardinal Drozdan. They need our assistance. They have offered us more money than we have ever laid eyes on," Philippe was pleased with himself. His sister covered her face with her hands.

"Philippe, you say they want our assistance. How do they need our assistance son, be more specific, you're talking in riddles,"

Raymond eyed Don Maestrino more closely as the Don went to stand. This he always did when thinking or excited.

"They want Don Dino, they want this woman he shelters, the mother of this fake miracle priest my sister is whoring with."

Monica got to her feet "Father."

"Sit," Don Maestrino commanded. She obeyed.

"Philippe you never use the word whore when referring to

your sister again. You will promise me this or our meeting ends." The Don walked over, placing his hand on the crying Monica's shoulder. Philippe glanced at Raymond sitting passively in the corner.

"I apologize Father and Monica; it was a slip of the tongue. I will never comment like that again."

"What was their request Philippe, how much have they offered?" Don Maestrino was seated again, enjoying the light that warmed his face.

"Two million euro Father. We must take out Don Dino, and this woman."

"Philippe," The Don stood suddenly. His movement even caught Raymond by surprise; he went to rise also but changed his mind. Monica looked at her brother coldly.

"I tell you, I can't get to your brain," the Don said, frustrated.

"You love movies with gangsters; all those bullets," He mimicked firing a machine gun. "Those days are over, we are no longer powerful; all the families have gone legitimate. The days of 'sleeping with the fishes' and horses' heads, are gone. Don Dino would laugh if he heard our discussion. This Cardinal in Rome wants to restart World War II. He wants to bring the families back to life and go to war again!" Don Maestrino walked to the window and inhaled the fresh air. "Why do they seek to harm this woman? I can understand the motive for Don Dino, but the woman, she is harmless, no?" Don Maestrino kept his eyes on the landscape. He could see over the row of villas opposite stacked along the winding foothills of the Apennines.

"I dunno Father. I beg you to understand this is not some plot from a movie. My heart is here in Viaréggio. My head wants you to live out your life in comfort in Volterra, you can live out your days in peace. These people are serious; they have a vision of the future. They will stop all the decay we see in our streets every day. There is a need to change things Father, to return to the social order of times past. I have seen the money Father, it is good money. We barely make anything from my bar. All our business has suffered. We need to reorganize, make our family strong again." Philippe looked hard to Raymond for some sign of approval. Raymond was still, passively staring straight ahead.

Don Maestrino turned from the window, his face slightly red.

"I need time to think. I won't be rushed into a decision. I have harboured a great hatred for Don Dino since I can remember. I have memories Philippe, of when we got sucked in by these religious fanatics before. We did their ugly deeds and it sapped all our energy, our freedom. I need to think. I will go away to think,"

The Don left the room with Raymond. Monica rushed down the stairs behind them.

"Father, I beg you, this is not our fight, this is asking for ruin, I can sense it. Philippe, he has changed Father, he is mad, I think he is mad." Don Maestrino turned to his daughter,

"Quiet it is not good, your father needs time."

10.

The drive to Bagni di Lucca brought us out of Viaréggio I taking a wrong turn ending up in an industrial estate. Lucia laughed as I cursed under my breath, reminding her to make sure I stayed on the right hand side of the road.

We went via the Marco Polo exit; we didn't have to go far before the slip road, the exit for Lucca. Countless bridges hung, some still in construction. It was like the beautiful countryside had been rained on by hailstones of concrete.

Below, small cars whizzed by. The dual carriageways were narrow, functional, with a kind of corrugated divide. We drove round Lucca, its ancient city walls still intact, the old stone had a dark yellow feel to it. I was driving, Lucia was reading the map. She enjoyed her role, making funny comments as we left the outskirts of the city. We climbed, the roads winding with endless hairpin bends. I thought of cyclists racing over these roads, up these mountains. The Apennines were spotted with deep wood; through gaps cold streams made crystal-clear waterfalls, they sprang from hidden high rocks.

Lucia laughed as we dodged our way through the streets of tiny villages. On further the ravaged landscape, mountains with large chunks missing, their marble gleaming, man rupturing the earth in search of wealth.

Lucia was reading from the Lonely Planet. When she read, she reminded me of my father; don't ask why, she just did. The same deadpan delivery, the same emphasis on words. She was practiced at reading out loud. "Many of Italy's finest buildings and palaces are adorned with marble mined in this area."

"Really?" My insulting reply, my mind miles away.

We went through Bagni di Lucca almost accidentally, the road was steep beyond it; I asked Lucia where it was we were actually going. She re-checked her map, she wasn't quite sure.

"I think we should have stopped back in that town. It says here they have wonderful spa waters."

"Maybe we should stop so you can read it properly," I said pointing to the map.

We pulled over into a lay by. I could hear the torrent of a river below getting out of the car to stretch my legs.

The forest hugged the riverbank, the water flowing fast through large chunks of rock. The landscape so different from Volterra, from San Gimignano.

"Maybe we should turn back? What do you think?"

Lucia looked at me comically, her sunglasses masking a sunburnt nose. I worried that I looked the same to her, all white with red blotches.

"I think we should. We might meet the lads from Deliverance if we go any higher." Lucia didn't get it. Smiling, she pretended to.

I turned the car. We headed back towards Bagni.

"What is that place there?" Lucia asked as a small turn right was signalled ahead.

"Don't know but we will soon find out," I said trying to be manly.

We turned up a steep hill bordered on one side by a railed field with meadow grass. As we neared the summit the road veered hard left. A young man sat on the rail, his mobile phone to his ear.

"Look at him," Lucia said as she made a good attempt to wave. The youth never lifted his head.

"Friendly," I said, not really meaning to be funny.

There was a tiny car park against the outer wall of what was just a mountain village. We parked beside a small Fiat. Another car sped past, it was going further up the hill. Lucia had no time to inspect the occupants, which displeased her slightly.

"You're day tripping," I said laughing at the straw hat and the shades.

Her broad shoulders looked larger in the light; her pink skin was burning. She laughed back.

"Let's explore," she said peeking around a corner.

When Boyce woke the room was dark, he hated to wake so early. Looking at his watch he saw it was only five twenty. His stomach ached. The malt was trapped in his gut along with food. Rubbing his navel with his right hand he exhaled loud gas. He pulled his pillow over his face, feeling secure as it suppressed the odour. His mind racing the dark green barren land full of dead trees, secret ditches, cattle half starved watching him with dead eyes. His body interrupted this time, the pain in his side was worse.

Soon he knew he would have to visit the toilet. He was out of Rennie, the empty box on the dressing table. Can't drink malt anymore, getting too old? Making it to the toilet just in time, gasping with relief as the burning pain receded and an air of normality returned to his being. He sat there, as was his habit, for twenty minutes, until he was certain he had completely emptied his bowels. Often he would wait for ten minutes between evacuations. The relief was rapid once he had expelled the offending food particles or the remnants of liquid effluent.

When he first met her it was a cold day in early November. She was shy, cowering from him. Her father was a heavy man yet weak-looking. His cheeks were rosy red like he always suffered from high blood pressure. Eva was standing behind him. Her mother was picking at straw and putting it into her fat mouth. She looked like a half-wit. She was double the size of her husband. Boyce could feel the frost in his boots. The squaddies had completed the search of the barn but found nothing.

Mick Devlin was trying to be brave. "We have no dealin's with the likes of 'em, Captain. I only graze a few cattle and grow enough to feed ourselves."

Eva had crawled from behind him, her curiosity getting the better of her. Boyce smiled at Eva, as her mother chewed on straw. The mother watching Boyce intently, spat contemptuously. Eva stepped back, her turn to stare at the Captain.

"You get a lot of visitors for a small farming chap, Mick. We had you under surveillance for three months. This place attracts a lot of funny people. They come at all sorts of times—sometimes day, sometimes night. You, Miss," Boyce pointed at Eva. "tumbling down the hill like you're in a playground." Eva cowered behind her father again.

"Who are these people?" Mick Devlin said his voice trembling.

"Mr Devlin, I was hoping you could tell me. I am most interested. The priest Burdon, does he pay you rent?" Boyce moved to where the door was half open.

"My wife has been sick, Captain, very sick." The woman ate more straw as if in support of her husband.

"We know McCabe comes here with the mechanic from the village, Dwyer. They have been here so many times, Mick. I can give you days, dates, times, whatever you want. Come to play poker, do they?" He pretended to examine the door hinges.

Boyce wiped his bottom wondering why it was so sore. Banging his foot against the base of the sink, it was asleep. Suddenly he felt pins and needles in both legs, below the knee. Making his way back to the bedroom, he considered pulling the drapes.

He felt cold, slipping back into bed to enjoy the dim light. He wanted to sleep, not to think, and most of all not to remember.

Mick Devlin didn't fully understand. Boyce could see that immediately. "I will make myself clear. You won't have a fucking farm; there will be nobody to look after these two," he said.

"I don't want no hand or part of it. Those men you refer

ta... they come here to meet up with each other. I don't know what they talk about. I just bring them tea in the parlour."

Boyce knew that the man was telling the truth mostly. He was too scared to lie, however, things needed controlling. Things had gone wrong mostly through a lack of control. "I don't think you understand, Mr Devlin. I could have you locked up in less than an hour. I have enough to take you away. What I ask is fairly simple, not a huge task. The boys we send you will talk, all you do is tell me what they say." Boyce made his voice loud, laced with anger.

Mick Devlin winced; Eva moved to stand between her father and mother.

"We let em go when they tell us? These people, I don't know, who will they be, Captain?" said Mick Devlin.

Boyce stepped back into the barn properly, the door swinging on the rusting hinges behind him.

"Don't get it? You let two well-known activists use this house. You will be given a list, Mr Devlin. I will send you anyone I suspect with links to the Provos. You convince your men McCabe and Dwyer. These boys are squealing to me. Let them go? Are you mad? Let the IRA deal with them by your own rules." Boyce went to place his hand on Eva's right shoulder. She shivered, taking a step backwards. He didn't attempt to touch her a second time.

Finally he mustered the strength to go to the window. St Tropez was still asleep. The yachts looked less imposing in the early light.

Boyce could see the sun climbing in the sky, only warming to its task. Next stop Italy he mused, he didn't fancy moving. Feeling tired. Still it was their demand, they were paying the bills, calling the shots. He wondered whether he might skip breakfast altogether. Certainly right now food had no appeal to him. Madame Fusco was a dragon, though she cooked a nice breakfast, plenty of croissants with scrambled egg. Yuk! The thought of it made him run back to the bathroom.

Feeling helpless. Argüelles organized everything even to giving Madame Fusco notice. Anyway he concluded, maybe a change of scenery may do him good. Maybe in Italy he would forgo the malt and stick to wine or try a local beer. Boyce laughed, knowing he could never keep any promise made to himself.

Madame Fusco was quiet serving breakfast. She normally chattered endlessly; today she was quiet.

Boyce struggled to eat, preferring to read the letter from Argüelles again for the third time. If he read it again he would find new things, words he had missed, hidden meanings. He drank copious amounts of coffee, sitting much longer than normal. Soon it was time for Madame Fusco to clear away the plates. She too had received a letter from Argüelles containing a generous cheque. However, it didn't help her mood.

"Monsieur Boyce, you go soon to another place with your girlfriend; she beautiful, yeah?" Madame Fusco startled him with her words and the way she eyed him sadly.

"I must move on. It's a business matter," Boyce said, with trepidation.

"I saw her. She is a young dark woman, very young, naughty man."

As she went to bring the dishes through the streamers to the scullery, she turned and said, "I don't think St Tropez is good for you, make you ill, too much drink, easy women here, good you go on eh?"

"Never good to stay still," Boyce said calmly pretending to read his letter again.

11.

The houses were separated by old walls. The pathways were cobbled, with manholes looking like they were from the last century.

A slug lay dead, out of place. Lucia was fascinated with it, just falling short of picking it up. I was admiring the mountain view and the vast forests below.

We decided to stroll down a little cobbled lane, it ran as we thought to the rear of the houses. Half way down we were struck by the silence. Was the village deserted? Yet the houses were in good repair. Lucia wondered were they holiday homes, as most had their shutters closed.

The tiny laneway was leading nowhere. From a nearby house came the happy sound of children at play. Instantaneously Lucia smiled, she found the sound relaxing. Almost as quickly silence returned, all went eerily quiet again.

Lucia was uncomfortable. She thought maybe we were trespassing in some private hamlet. We walked by the car, by the small road leading up the hill where earlier the passing car disappeared. The small Fiat was gone, just our hired Lancia remained parked.

I walked ahead lazily up the hill, concentrating on my breathing, watchful for the wind pains I always felt in my chest.

Lucia followed at a more leisurely pace, the cigarettes evident as she politely coughed.

I was walking on, minding my own business, turning the odd time to admire the valley below.

"Stephen," Lucia called. I was watching a small herd of goats tied inside a pen which was shaded by a tall tree. She too was looking into the meadow.

"Let's get out of here," she said, using a voice I knew meant business.

I walked back to her side quickly.

"What's up?"

"There's a huge dog in there minding the goats, he's more like a wolf," she said. "He's giving me nasty looks."

Lucia was an animal lover, so if she was afraid I took her at her word. We walked quietly back down the hill towards the car.

Occasionally I turned to look over my shoulder. I never caught sight of the wolf myself.

Back at the car Lucia sat in gratefully, lighting a fag to comfort herself.

I looked back one more time up the narrow road. An old lady crossed over to empty the contents of a basin into the ditch.

I waved and smiled a sort of salute. She ignored me, glancing down, pretending not to see me. As I drove out I noticed the youth was gone from the rail.

Lucia smoked with the window full open, the breeze ventilating the car. We reached the bottom of the hill before turning right to the main road. I checked my rear-view mirror. To my astonishment the youth was back on the rail, his mobile phone pressed to his ear. I said nothing to Lucia. We drove back in silence towards Bagni di Lucca.

Gardiner found the heat different, not like New York; there was more air. They don't get it quite so hot, he surmised. The Grand Palace Hotel was ok; it could do with a facelift. It was one of those old hotels. Once it was stately and grandiose. The changes in culture of society led to its standards becoming outdated, even unwanted. The result was a certain fall into the realms of shoddiness. Sipping his drink on the rooftop terrace.

The waitress was pretty. She had a small tattoo tastefully just above her right buttock. Gardiner noticed it as she bent over to replenish the shelf stock. He liked her smile and the freshness about her. She must have been just as beautiful as a child.

Still, life could be worse than to be supping wine in the heat of the afternoon.

His conversation with Marsha earlier was still on his mind. His mobile rang out of the blue as he rested on his bed after a shower.

"Hi Dad, where you at?" Marsha asked casually.

Gardiner laughed as all good parents do. "You won't believe this, hon. I'm in Europe in Italy,"

"Gee."

"How are you?"

"I'm ok but I can't stay long cause I'm using Breezier's house phone. His dad will flip."

"Sure, sure," Gardiner said, wanting to ask who the hell Breezier was when he was at home. Heck, he would check it with Susie.

"Dad, I wanna go see Green Day. Mom says I'm grounded 'cause I stayed out past curfew Saturday. You know me, I never miss curfew. The cab didn't come for me and Ellie, so we got late."

Gardiner could sense the tears coming, so he interjected, "Hey, hon, no point in being upset. How's about I talk to your mom, eh?"

"She won't listen, she's lost it ever since her and Jonathan messed up. She's takin' it out on us. I can't do nothin.' She screams. Honest, Dad, I was one hour late, like it was a big deal! The city's gonna fall down! Makes me feel like I'm a loser, Dad. You gotta talk to her 'cause I need to go see Green Day. Ellie's boyfriend, Tim, he got the tickets!"

"Hon, your mom's just worried for you. It's not..."

"OK, gotta go. No really. Love you. Gotta go talk to Mom."

Gardiner heard the click. Pulling the towels up over his chest, he said, "Shit." He wondered where he left the container of Coversyl 5mg. He was a little worried about the left side of his chest. It was sore, as was the deepest base in his throat dry, like pulled taut with string. He drifted into a half sleep. Once more the voices of Quinn and Kellerman came to haunt him.

They were not making sense. They were speaking in unison, contradicting each other. Gardiner bolted awake, feeling his chest heave as if his heart had missed a beat. He closed his eyes, feeling his lids heavy. Trying to remember when he last checked his blood sugar. It was three in the afternoon; he never checked before lunch.

He would check later. No big deal. He started to fall asleep again, his head planted firmly in the pillow. He heard the ambulance siren. It was one of those Italian minibus types. It was travelling very fast, the bell was ringing with a screaming sound. Gardiner found himself running up a steep hill, the perspiration pouring from his face, his head full of steam. The stills of Heidi Heisler, as he stared at them a million times, came before him. He saw the newspaper headlines: "Child still missing." As he ran the hill got steeper. There in front, a boy sat on a rail, a mobile stuck to his ear. The ambulance got louder. Gardiner shot up in bed, his body caught in spasms. It took him some time to realize where he was.

"I am not listening to it because this is nonsense," Toby said.

Eva went to where Monica sat with her hands resting on the small kitchen table.

"Sssh now. No need to cry," Eva said. Turning to face her son, "What is it with you, Toby?" Monica raised her head as if surprised by Eva's outburst. "Do you have a death wish? I have enemies. I have told you all these years since you were a boy we have to take care, didn't I son? What did I tell you?"

Monica dropped her chin again, almost out of respect for Eva's agitation. Toby was pacing the tiny kitchen in an effort to secure his concentration. "Mother, it is no use. I promised Father Cryan I would assist him. The baptism goes ahead in a week. The man is travelling to Volterra from Cucuron. What should I say to him? Mother, Monica, do you want me to say I cannot assist you to baptize this dying child?"

"Toby, you don't know what Philippe is like. He is capable of anything. He has befriended powerful people in Rome who want to get rid of you both," Monica said, looking at Eva tearfully.

Eva walked to where the kettle was boiling on the stove; she remained silent pouring the boiling water into the pot, her hand shaking slightly. "I will make us tea Monica, a drop of tea is much better in times of crises than coffee. Toby, you should have tea as well," she said.

Toby nodded. Finally, drawing a chair he clasped Monica's outstretched hand.

Monica watched Eva's hand shake as she spilled tea onto the cooker. Eva dried it nervously with a dirty tea towel.

"Does your father have anything to say, Monica? You tell me he is a fair-minded man," Toby implored.

"Philippe has confused him. He paints the picture, putting you as part of Don Dino's entourage. I keep telling him you know nothing of the Don's business. Philippe is trying to persuade him, Father is getting old, he is not able to resist such coercion."

"I will consult Don Dino," Eva said. "I will drive over to see him this evening. We can't have this situation and allow it to fester. We will all be like the birds in the garden, afraid of the cat." She poured the tea into mugs; it was piping hot.

Monica seemed appeased, Eva had lightened her anxiety. Eva handing the mugs by the handles said, "The Don will know if it's wise for you to go to the church in Volterra. He may forbid it Toby, we have always accepted his word, he is the arbiter."

"Then, Mother, I must go with you to explain about Father Cryan," Toby said earnestly, lifting the hot tea to sip and then putting it down again, it was too hot. "I will drive you." He saw his mother glance at him nervously.

Eva gave him a cold look. She sipped her tea. "OK then, Toby. We agree that whatever the Don decides, we do eh?"

Monica nodded for him. Toby stared at the table in silence.

Don Maestrino Giordano was feeling tired, much too tired to assist Raymond who was giving instructions to the housekeeper. He preferred to sit on the terrace overlooking the fields below. At last the sun had come out, he wondered for how long it might stay. Where was summer? If the vines were not nourished it would go down as a bad year. The mere thought depressed him. Yet the smell of wild flowers and the distant neighing of horses helped his mind relax. He was busy, his age was beginning to take its toll. No longer were the problems he confronted tiny obstacles which made his day more interesting, now they became bothersome to the point of leading him down the narrow path to fatigue with a blinding headache.

During one such event he chose to take his seat on the terrace to smoke a cigarette. The sounds of the country played a bigger part in his recovery than the Aspirin Raymond supplied. The water was possibly of even more assistance. He was still mulling over his troubles when Raymond interrupted,

"We are wasting our time with that woman, Don Maestrino. She is impossible. I ask her to clean the kitchen, she cleans the study. I ask her to make your room nice and airy, she closes the shutters. What am I to do? She says she has a bad back, I say bring your daughter to help; we will pay her. She then cries, says she is a lonely widow, I have designs on her daughter, I want to be alone in the Don's bedroom with her daughter! My God." Raymond sat on the iron garden chair opposite the Don, who was slightly taken aback by his outburst. Raymond pulled his long grey hair away from his left cheek where it had strayed; it now rested normally over his shoulder. "I could have every prostitute in Pisa or Firenze. She thinks I want to fuck her daughter who is ugly and fat. What am I to do, Don Maestrino? Clean the house myself?"

Raymond had a look of resignation the Don didn't like. He was not used to it.

"I don't know. It is not significant, Raymond. I came out here to solve the problems facing my family. What do you do? Unload your problems on me, make my brain weaker than it already is. It is not a good thing. You are my mentor, my trusted advisor. You bring me domestic problems. Go pour us some wine, will you? Water also. I am too hot here, maybe I will go inside shortly."

The Don gave Raymond a most dissatisfied look. Raymond hopped to his feet to serve the Don's request, filling the glasses promptly. He kept one eye open for the housekeeper, listening for any hint of hysterics coming from upstairs. Don Maestrino sipped his water first, only taking a sip of Chianti before placing the glass on the garden table. "It is this problem with Philippe," he said staring at Raymond, sensing he was still thinking of the housekeeper.

"Yes, yes, Don Maestrino," Raymond said urgently, to deny there was even a hint of idling in his head.

"The boy is not right, Raymond. Let's be honest, I admit it's a desperate thing for a man to concede about his son. We know he is not right. No sign of him settling down with a woman and starting a family. He is keeping whores from God knows where. His passions are all from Hollywood—fast cars, the quick buck, what do you think, eh?" The Don asked sadly.

"I don't think he is well since Stella died. Your wife doted on him too much in the old days."

"Sure, you're right. It is my daughter I feel sorry for. What is it, Raymond, that makes women dote over their sons, to neglect their daughters? You would think the opposite to be true."

"I have no answer, save Stella was the finest, Don Maestrino. We know she was!"

"She was. Stella was the best." the Don said ruefully. "What do you make of Philippe with these people from Rome? I can't figure it out in my mind."

Don Maestrino lit another cigarette. Raymond watched him take a puff. The smoke gathered around his mouth like candyfloss. "It could mean great danger. I don't trust those religious fanatics any more than you. Like you I get older, I look forward to a comfortable retirement, not a return to the days of old when we both lost many friends. What purpose does Philippe want to serve? Does he want to serve us as a family, or himself?"

"Fine words, you see into my brain Raymond. You are right. Philippe is self serving. I personally can see no gain from mixing with these fanatics. He has, as the cliché goes, got his money counted."

Raymond leaning forward interjected, "What is it you intend to do? I think we commit suicide to enter a war against Don Dino. He still possesses great power."

"True, Raymond. Philippe is still my son. It is my duty to protect him, even if it is from himself, no matter how it goes against my instinct."

Don Maestrino drank more wine; he looked again out over the fields, once more hoping for a rich harvest.

Boyce hated airports, always had. To him they were stifling places. He detested the way they made even the most menial workers look important, from the broom operator to the idiots driving the trolley collecting minitrain. Then you had all these uniformed men and women trying to look cool. It was a fashion statement, all of this metal flying through the air business. These glorified waitresses and hip young pilots! He hated the clientele even more. Lots of lazy-looking women returning from sunny holidays with their rolls of film. He played a game to see if he could find the most obnoxious happy holidaymaker in Nice.

Boyce had a beer in a small bar just inside the main door of departures. He was an hour too early for check in. Sitting at the tiny bar wondering if he should buy lunch. There was no guarantee of food on the plane. There were all sorts of people wandering around, lots of black boys, an army patrol complete with submachine guns. The world post Sept 11th. He ordered a pre-made ham and cheese sandwich from the little Algerianlooking bartender.

When Rock told him, it made him angry. The boy cowered down in the small toilet off his quarters. Boyce remembered hitting him hard twice across the face. It was impossible the boy was lying, his nerves shattered after they found the third body lying face down on the road. The priest confronted him at the scene. Burdon was one of those long-haired Jesus-type priests who got up Boyce's nose; they were so full of shit.

"It's the truth. I swear it." Rock cried, his hands up to his face. Trickles of blood seeped through the holes in between his fingers. Boyce kicked him this time on the side, causing the boy to wince, his arms wrapping round him.

"Don't bullshit me, you little Fenian toe rag," screamed Boyce.

"You think you're fuckin' smart?" Burdon said as they both gazed at the body face down against the hard tarmacadam.

Boyce looked at him contemptuously. "Is your duty not to say a few prayers in his ear? Do it then and get the fuck out of here before I have you fucking shot."

The priest didn't flinch. "You're breaking the rules, Captain. I will not rest till this is brought out into the open, do you hear me? I won't rest. I have contacts. You have to stop this."

"Go fuck yourself," Boyce said with spite.

"Who are you listening to, the faggot priest? Or are you trying to give me a bum steer, hey? For your mates in the Provos? Is that it, Rock? Answer me." Boyce kicked him in the side again.

How many times he studied the surveillance tapes? The

80

farm was on the side of a hill; the house above a triangular field. Three telegraph poles linked to the road below.

The house itself was yellow; someone added a clumsy extension on the side. On the left the large green barn, to the sides the old whitewashed walls. Watching McCabe and Dwyer coming and going, mostly at night. Boyce watched the priest visit every other day. The girl played in the front field, rolling down the hill, tumbling through the dried hay. The camera picking up her smiling face as she played with the straw. Weak sunlight made her features soft.

12.

We had lunch in a quiet place by the street. Bagni di Lucca is a small place with a one- way system that would tax a rocket scientist.

Lucia needed the loo. The young girl serving spoke good English, her mother spoke kindly to us in Italian. She understood English better than she could speak it.

"Wonder where the spa is?" Lucia said.

She was consulting a brochure she had picked up in the hotel lobby, still sounding unnerved. I ordered her a glass of white wine to calm her.

The place was a bar in the main, the food was pre-cooked for heating in the microwave. The toasted "Prosciutto e formaggio." was welcome. I washed mine down with some bubbly water.

Weird, wasn't it? Lucia was taking a bite of her "Formaggio Caprino.". "Was weird." I agreed, "That kid on the railing freaked me."

"The children playing, they stopped so abruptly." Lucia looked at me intently, as she did when she meant business.

"It was like somebody played, then stopped a tape," she said.

"What about the dog?"

"The bloody dog was more like a wolf, I tell you, Steve, the eyes on that thing!"

"Freaky," I said, sounding like somebody from Scooby Doo.

Soon we were back in the car, which I had politely parked against a bush in the private car park of the local post office.

Trying to obey the signs and watching out for the one-way system, we went in search of the thermal waters.

After much deliberation, wrong turns, steep hills and cul de sacs, we eventually found it, nestled on the side of a mountain only a few hundred metres from the main road.

Lucia was back to her cheerful self; she wanted more photos. I must admit my mood was lightening and the peaceful location made it possible to relax.

The spa itself was a mixture of the old and the modern. The old spa, which had been visited by Byron and Shelley, was crumbling with parts of it already lost. The new building was flashy, like a modern leisure centre. We walked in to a large reception area where we were greeted by three women in white coats. They could have been dentists or junior registrars.

A list of treatments plus prices was displayed on the wall beside a coke machine, which looked alarmingly out of place.

Lucia hid her embarrassment by trying to be funny and sound eccentric. It didn't work so well.

Only one of the three white-coated females appeared to have a grasp of English.

It was a toss-up between a dip in the thermal spa and a complete sinus irrigation, or, for the really warped, a complete vaginal irrigation.

The other stuff they offered didn't appeal to us, so we opted for the thermal dip.

I clutched my swimsuit and towel and wondered would it be deep. Lucia went puce, as she always did, as we climbed the cold stone steps following the signs for the spa. Up one floor and we were confronted by our second fright of the day.

This Italian lady, who had certainly been attractive when young, came from the shadows of a doorway. She wore too much make-up for her age. Perhaps what was most frightening about the poor lady was that her hair was dyed completely blonde, which neither suited her face or the light.

We made our excuses, testifying for each other's sinuses. The long corridor we took worked on a sensor system. The lights extinguished as we moved on. We went about 10 feet and another light came on. Ahead was semi-dark. Lucia laughed nervously till at last we came out of the shadows into another reception area. This time a young man sat at the desk wanting to see our ticket.

Through a glass door I could see people wading in the water. It looked green and pretty deep. Oh shit! I thought, I can barely swim out of my depth.

My mind raced. I must have been killed in a road accident on the way here. This was always how I imagined heaven's reception to be, a counter with a particularly dour young man, the small mini-bar stocked with gin and whiskey, a thermal spa through a glass door—all green and very deep-looking.

Lucia stepped in bravely. The water was just up to her waist.

"Reckon it's the same depth all over?" I asked, pretending to be only half interested in the answer and yet hanging on to her reply, "I don't know what you're worried about." Still the water was different, it looked and smelled of sulphur. When it touched the skin, a faint tingle, it was tonic. I splashed letting the water touch my face. I was John the Baptist immersing my head.

A group of young nun-like girls got in, a smile painted on their faces. It was unreal, like either they were all related or were blighted at birth by some sinister curse, or they were morons.

I thought I was imagining it, until Lucia came to my side as I sprayed my head with the healing water gushing from a chute overhead.

"They don't look the brightest, do they?"

"This place is as bad as the village."

"I know. It's like the house of horrors."

I started to wonder had we eaten something we shouldn't? Did Don Maestrino Giordano give us magic mushrooms for breakfast?

It was then I saw her, just a glimpse of her, she was middle-aged, looking through the viewing window into the pool. She was, as I imagined, stern, her nose prominent to guard eyes of steel, in many ways she was very beautiful.

She wore white dresses, grass stained at the end of her play. Eva did handstands revealing her tiny white thighs. She sat knees up allowing her skin fall on meadow grass. Watching the visiting birds as they ran hen like round the hard cowpats.

Rock was lying; Boyce was sure of it. "No, Rock. What sort of fucker do you think I am?" he said.

Rock sat on the floor; his legs half in the en suite. "OK, Captain. I made it all up don't hit me no more,"

Boyce had kicked him in the side again, the hardest yet. He retreated to sit by his dresser, the wig and lipstick both touching the mirror. Boyce could hear Rock still sobbing as he admired himself. "Rock, you have to learn, I can smell lies at 50 feet. Lies are my job, like you feed cattle bales of hay. I listen to little Provo murderers like you and I can tell you're lying. It's instinctive, you know. You probably don't know, believe me. Can't remember ever being wrong. Take your priest friend, that Mullah Burdon. He's lying. He wouldn't be here in the asshole of South Armagh if he had contacts high up. No, Rock, he'd be in Dublin or London, wherever, but not here, don't you agree?"

Boyce continued to look in the mirror lifting his head to see if his nose hair needed trimming.

Rock said, still sobbing, "Yeah, I agree, Captain. It's the truth."

"Now, now, Rock, you are very sensitive today. My God, when I think of how my father disciplined me when I was young." Boyce, satisfied with his nose hair, looked at the figure still squatting half in the en suite. "Really, Rock, get up, wipe the blood from your nose and clean up the whole mess. Use the basin, there's hot water." The boy struggled to his feet dipping his head forward to clean the blood off his face. "I don't think any of you people realize what is going on here. I mean, I watch the news most nights. How do I describe it to you, Rock? Clean the floor with the rag, that's the idea. As I was saying," Boyce was on his feet again.

He walked over to where Rock was cleaning the blood off the lino. He continued talking to the top of Rock's curly hair. "It's like throwing a stone into a pond, and expecting no ripples."

Rock tried to look up at the Captain to gauge his mood. His neck and head were sore, as was his side, which throbbed like the bones inside it were broken. "You people have no respect for the rule of law. You are, in essence, every one of you, traitors to the state that feeds and houses you. What are we to do? Sit back and allow you to destabilize our country? What would you suggest we do, Rock?"

Rock could see Boyce's shadow as he cleaned, knowing from the tone he used he was getting angry again. "I know it is true what you say, Captain."

To Rock's relief, the Captain withdrew again, this time to sit on the corner of his bed. "Who told you to tell me lies?" Boyce said calmly, as Rock continued to clean the floor.

Rock looked at the Captain, then away, accidentally catching the wig sitting on the dresser. "Just made it up, Captain. I'm sorry I had no news for you so I made it up." Rock said convincingly.

"I see," Boyce said. "Tell me it again."

The Captain smiled at him, his lips curved like he had hurt them. "But it isn't true."

"I know, Rock, but tell me again. I will let you go home early."

The sandwich didn't sit well. It was too cold, like the setting in the display cooler was too high. Boyce hated airport food. It was always shit, miles too dear. The place was even busier now with people milling around. The "no smoking" announcement was getting on his nerves. Not only was the recording repetitive, it repeated in three languages. As if anyone cared! However, it gave him the idea to go to the car park for a cigar; then he planned to find a Pharmacy and buy some Rennie. He could check in for his flight, find a toilet as well. He felt better making his way out to the fresh air. The hunger abated, even if the food sat cold.

"I heard they went chicken like they couldn't do it to the first boy."

Boyce was on his feet once more. Rock winced as Boyce brushed by him. The Captain went to the washbasin to wash his hands.

"The first time round, they were all ready, Captain. Mick Devlin, Dwyer, McCabe. They had the boy, from Monaghan, Jimmy Curran." Rock said looking at Boyce. He was busy scrubbing, but sensed that Rock was hesitating. He shouted above the flow of the water, "Go on, Rock, go on."

"Like I said earlier, Captain Boyce, they beat him to pulp till the lad couldn't speak no more. He couldn't say a single word. Dwyer did the hittin', McCabe, he sort of hit him, but not so much.

Mick Devlin was askin' this boy lots of questions like things about you. When it got to the end, Mick Devlin took out the gun. They left the boy tied to the chair under the only light in the barn. So the three of them walked away to discuss among themselves.

When they came back the boy was half dead from swallowin' his own blood.

Mick Devlin handed the gun to Dwyer. He couldn't do it, hadn't got it in him." Rock was almost out of breath as he recanted his story. Boyce finished cleaning at the washbasin and was back sitting on the bed. He had a spare drying towel which he wrapped round his hands, making sure to clean the soap from the creases between his fingers. "So Mick Devlin put the gun down on a barrel of diesel he used for his tractor. They started a sort of argument. McCabe said he couldn't do it either.

The boy passed out see, it looked like they tied him too tight.

So anyways they argue on about it. Mick Devlin is pleading with both of them to do it.

The next thing is they hear a shot, one single shot. When they look, Eva Devlin, the child, is standing there with the gun in her hand. The boy, his head slumped forward, is dead. She shot him right through the back of his head.

She puts the gun back where her father left it. Then walks out the side door of the barn."

Boyce clapped his hands, "Bravo, Rock, it is a very good and plausible way to tell a lie."

13.

I will always remember the drive from San Gimignano, the road has outstanding views, busy, winding, hand-carved through hills.

Twisting round a particularly sharp bend, a strange building stands alone to our right. It is totally out of place midst the beauty of the landscape. We videotaped the large penitentiary-type structure, resting to sip spring water, washing down our rolls, 'Crudo e formaggio', which I bought in San Gimignano.

Lucia, hydrating herself with the cool water. She was sad looking at the line of coloured towels hanging from the cell windows. We continued on, twisting around tight bends through small villages, lost in the hills.

In Volterra, Lucia found a good shop selling products made from alabaster which is mined locally. The shop was interesting with products ranging from cheap to the very expensive. I was taken by the beautiful chess sets displayed in various forms from the very small to full coffee-table size. Lucia bought some reasonably priced souvenirs.

We walked around by the old town walls; searching the view below. We didn't realize how high we climbed, the view stretched forever over the burnt landscape. Miles of green mixed with browns and yellows, hills rising from the earth with such ease.

Lucia led the way as we walked uphill into an open square. A small outdoor café called Bar Priori lent us rest and also much-needed refreshment. We ordered two glasses of Rose. Lucia relaxing, people watching.

I decided to have a quick look in the old town hall opposite.

Up the stone steps inside I was surprised to see the building still operated municipal offices on the upper floors. On the ground floor, through a medieval set of heavy doors, was an old well. I was surprised to find it dry, fouled with plastic bottles. It was most un-Italian.

I rejoined Lucia who was taking photographs. We visited another alabaster shop which was smaller but more upmarket than the one before.

On one street, the narrowness of the medieval set opened up and we found ourselves suddenly in touch with the modern.

A church, small and sacred, with its doors open, the dark interior battled the bright heat of the sun, paintings adorned the walls on both sides.

You got the sense you were looking into some peaceful untouched world, far removed from reality and the hustle and bustle of today's manic world.

On the way out of Volterra, I met Don Dino with Toby. They were father and son, their shop sold replica swords and daggers.

Don Dino was a small man around mid-sixties. He was balding, his large dark eyebrows hid his dark brown eyes. His chin was strong and noble. When he spoke he pushed it out making him look younger. I knew in my head I must have him age. Toby was just right, around thirty-two. He was young-looking for his age with splendid blue eyes set in blonde.

He was thin and when he smiled at us it was genuine and true. Toby had this form of banter with his father, it was like the older man was mocking him. His father laughed at the end of each sentence, making a grating noise with his throat.

Toby ignored him, smiling to himself and discussing the pros and cons of the items on sale in perfect English, whilst Don Dino ranted on in a punctuated Italian cackle.

On our way back we passed the prison again. Lucia, tired as she was, did the driving. I fell asleep, head forward, not waking till I opened my eyes, groggy, in the environs of San Gimignano.

Eva tried several different tops; none fitted her, they were all too big.

She was losing weight again, her red top she had a good three years.

Sitting in her room, thinking of the kitchen table with empty bottles packed into four shopping bags.

She would get rid of them before Toby called. Who was she fooling. He knew right well. The shake in her right hand was worse. She slept much too late each morning. Now that she had left the spa, what else was there to do? Toby was no fool. He had found her often enough lying on the kitchen floor. She had locked herself into the room where she sat so many times. Don Dino would send Gregor and a couple of henchmen to kick it in.

Five times in ten years the Don had paid for the best treatment. Don Dino used his influence to get her the job managing the spa. The last time she thought she was going to make it. Two dry years. Then she met Marie Abele and everything changed. She knew he recognized her at once, her old life continued to haunt her! Later Don Dino gave her the files, he was really serious about it. One last time; she could not fail him. The files were sick. She felt it her duty, naturally. Yet there was Toby to consider.

If only James Burdon were here, he would know what to do. She needed a drink.

A full bottle of gin was stashed at the back of the wardrobe so as Toby wouldn't find it. She took a glass from the small scullery. The taste bitter; it hurt the back of her throat. After a few gulps she began to feel its effects. Her brain thawed, the cold replaced by warmth. The alcohol brought its own clarity. Replacing all those dark voices with amiable ones.

Her justifications, her hurt made sense; when sober they didn't.

Eva drank half a glass down. She was preparing to plead with the Don. She couldn't face him with the jitters. Half the bottle was gone. Eva, staggering, went back to the scullery for water. Maybe she should have no more; she wouldn't be able to talk to Toby when he arrived.

Eva shuddered with the cold. She wondered why she never opened the shutters, why fate left her alone in the dark without even the memory of happiness to sustain her?

When Eva went to bed at night she dreamed before she fell asleep. Even at the age of thirteen she knew what it was she wanted from life.

She saw her mother to bed, she doting and reciting nursery rhymes like she was only four years old. Her mother settled early; for Eva it was a role reversal.

Eva kissed her softly on the forehead pulling the blankets up tight to be sure she was warm. She would close her mother's eyelids with the soft tips of her fingers whispering, "Night night. Sleep tight," as she turned out the lamp and left the room.

Bringing her father tea at the kitchen table as he did his accounts and filled out forms for his cattle. Her father accepted his tea. Leaving it untouched for a minute he said,

"Your mother asleep?"

"Just gone off." Eva said, tidying the sink.

"That dog needs his bed."

"Alright, Daddy. Sure I will call him in."

"Good girl," he said and followed it with, "To bed then, you."

"Aye," Eva called back from the door, whistling for her dog.

When tucked up, she dreamed of the future.

She wanted to be married, have two maybe three children, a boy, two girls.

She pulled the covers in around her, to hide from the world. Who should she marry? All the boys she knew fell into the no category.

They were, she surmised, too giddy, silly for her. She needed a man who would treat a girl properly. Father Burdon would be ideal with his long dark hair brushing the shoulder and hiding the collar.

Now, he would be such a nice man. He called regularly to see Mother and to say prayers for her. Eva always sat in, not ever understanding a thing the man was talking about. Father Burdon. Priests can't get married. Pretend Eva, she spoke to herself, he will leave the priesthood for you.

They would cause scandal. There would be talk of this great love all over the parish.

This excited her until sleep came. Her dreams were tranquil.

Eva fell asleep with the bottle overturned on the floor, only a tiny dribble left.

Toby stared at her in the half light. Checking his watch, he went to wake her, then hesitated. The smell of alcohol was all over the house. It hit him hard, like the darkness. In the scullery, the many empty bottles she had spirited away. He could not bring her to see the Don like this.

He sat alone thinking how useless his gift, when he could not cure the only person in the world he truly loved.

The soldiers arrival changed everything for Eva, her father was terse and nervous; he spoke to Father Burdon about placing her mother in a home. At one point she had heard her father say that he would be selling up, the Captain had made it impossible for him to stay. Mick Devlin, his voice chilling, told the priest his life was stolen, his wife may die in an institution; his daughter will be forced to run away. Eva listened at the parlour door as the priest comforted her father, promising he would go all the way to Rome to stop this injustice. They were mighty fine words, said with a lot of venom. The words of a chivalrous knight. Mick Devlin continued to tend his farm, Eva still dreamed, sitting on the brow of the hill with Rusty never too far away. She rolled down the grass banks, sometimes doing handstands, then idling; she sat in awe of the world.

She saw the men arrive in their van, chat for a good while

with her father in the yard without ever turning off the engine.

Her mother was getting steadily worse, wandering around the back fields pretending she was a cow. When Eva found her, she had soiled herself, making animal noises, one minute like a cow, then a pig. Father Burdon came over that evening to discuss the situation. Eva listened again at the parlour door.

The priest had found a place for Mother; it was in Belfast, an hour away. Her father cried, his tears loud and pathetic. The priest tried to comfort him, but his words were wasted. All her father could say was, she wasn't always like this; she was normal when they married. It was as if she'd been bitten by the devil.

The next day her mother was taken away by a man and a woman in an ambulance.

Her father saw to his duty. Once the ambulance left the yard, he went to his tractor and drove round to the back field where he was mending fences.

Eva watched as the ambulance meandered down the twisting drive, appearing then disappearing, part hidden by trees. She watched till it reached the white walls at the main gate and turned left towards the main road. The ambulance gained speed. It was the last time she ever saw her mother.

The following day the soldiers came again. The Captain spoke for an hour with her father. Rusty nearly lost it with his barking.

A few nights later Eva was woken by sounds coming from the barn. Its barrel-shaped roof was directly below her bedroom window. The noise was like nothing she had ever heard before.

At first she thought it was a stray cat or a trapped animal. As she came to her senses she realized it was the screams of a man. He cried, "Stop it, please stop. I dunno know. I swear to ya."

Eva threw on a few clothes, making her way from the house to the side door of the barn which was unlocked.

She stepped in to see the man tied to a chair under the naked light bulb, blood dripping from his head, pools of blood congealed on the floor beneath him.

She saw her father away in the corner in the semi-dark, he was talking to McCabe and Dwyer.

Moving a little closer, each one looking at the man bound to the chair.

They discussed him like he was a pig to be slaughtered.

McCabe said to her father, "'Tis you... You brought him here. You do it!" he was scared, his voice uneven.

Dwyer added, "We are only actin' on the information you gave us. So Jackie here is right. You can do it."

Both men retreated a few feet.

Her father, never taking his eyes from the man helpless, tied so tightly, walked closer. "I think we may have killed him already, Jackie," her father said.

"How can you be sure?" Jackie replied.

It was then that Eva noticed the handgun, her father gripped it like his own life depended on it. After a minute passed, her father put the gun down on the barrel of diesel that stopped him from seeing her. He walked slowly back to the others who were lighting cigarettes, the glow out of proportion in the dim light.

Eva looked at the gun sitting there glistening under the glow of the swinging light bulb.

"I can ee do it, I can ee do it," she heard her father say.

Eva picked up the gun, releasing the safety catch, as she had watched a soldier do only a week before.

She went to the rear of the man. The blood on the ground soiled her shoes. Holding the gun, pressing tight into the groove above his neck, she squeezed the trigger. The blood spurted out over her white top.

The man fell forward. Her father walked closer, as if to actually verify what he had witnessed. Jackie, with Dwyer following, walked slowly forward.

Eva placed the gun back on the barrel of diesel. She walked back out the way she came in.

Toby lifted her onto the bed, smelling her foul breath. She moaned in her stupor. He spoke gently to her so she would know it was him, propping her head up with pillows so as she wouldn't vomit. If she did he knew it was important she was on her side.

"Toby, Toby," she whispered. He could still get the foul scent of half-digested alcohol, it came in waves of warm air.

"I want you to tell Don Dino I am finished. Will you tell him that for me, my son?"

"It's time to rest, Mother." He patted her forehead, the way she did to him when he was a child.

"I am serious. You go tell him that Eva Devlin is all done. She says he is to take care of you for me."

Toby half smiled. "Mother, you forget I am a grown man."

Eva opened her eyes. Her lips curled as if she wanted to smile yet found it impossible.

"Toby, you must stay safe. Tell the Don I fear for you, the same fear he had for Benedetto all those years ago."

"Sssh, Mother, you must rest now."

"Sit with me for just a wee time," Eva said, closing her eyes in surrender.

14.

There were times I was sure I loved Lucia. These moments always brought me back to when we first met.

I would try to re-invent the sense of excitement when our eyes met and I was so sure. Perhaps this sense of excitement represents youth, hope, or maybe it is an admission of my own failure to capture self.

Did I always have such a low sense of self-esteem to imagine only the love and support of a woman could comfort me and make my life complete?

I am sure it is one of the fallouts of bypass surgery, the daily realization that life is fickle; it can end at any moment. I have gone through the complete rationale.

If I had died, what would Lucia have done? Sold our home? Moved back to the country? Met another man, maybe in a year or two? She is still a young woman. Could I expect her to live the next thirty years, or more, waking alone with no warmth? The children will eventually grow and move on.

It was a particularly hot day, we were exhausted by the sun. On the beach

the dark North African women carrying their wares on their heads, like you see in documentaries. I watched dark women dazzled by the sun, lost in the remote desert, the sea made of sand. Lucia decided it was time to go.

We reached the comfort of the hotel room, the air conditioning cooling. Removing our clothes, lying on the double bed, I staring at the ceiling.

"Where will we eat tonight?"

Lucia always wanted to know way in advance. She covered herself with a hotel towel.

"I dunno. Maybe we will walk on down a little further, we might find somewhere nice."

"Yeah," she said, "we can have some cool Rose, hey? I think I might go for a real Italian Pizza."

"I might go steak," I said turning to her.

She turned to face the wall on the far side. I left the wardrobe door open, looking at my shirts hanging neatly.

"Do you remember when we first met each other?"

"I do," she answered as if the very idea calmed her.

"Funny, isn't it, how people meet? Do you ever think if you hadn't met me at Veronica's party, more than likely you would have married someone else?"

Lucia was quiet when I said this, like she was hurt by my comment.

"Yeah, but I did meet you, not somebody else."

"I know," I said softly, sensing I was treading in shark-infested waters.

"You could say that about anything," she said suddenly, turning to me till I felt her breath skim across my skin. "It means that James or Amanda could be Betsy and Bill, what the fuck is that?"

She laughed, turning away again to reach for her cigarettes innocently lying on the bedside table.

"What I mean is that if I hadn't met you, we may have met other people and got married to them," I said, all with an air of childish triumph.

Lucia was sitting up straight, her towel now purposefully keeping her covered. "What does all that shit mean?" She looked at me incredulously.

"It means, there is nothing to stop you meeting people all through your life who are suited to marry you. Is it why loads of marriages fail? People have affairs? Nobody will admit we are not designed to have partners for life."

"Horseshit, Steve, you're forgetting about love and commitment. Of course, you will meet people who you find attractive. That's only natural. Is your loyalty not to the first partner, your life partner, the mother or father of your children?"

Lucia took a deep drag on her cigarette suddenly enjoying herself.

I sensed she was on the verge of victory, so I went on, "So if I died in hospital, you would never fall for anyone else? Your devotion to my memory would be sacrosanct?"

Lucia finished her fag, stubbing it vigorously, singeing the tiny tip of her finger,

"That would be different," she said. "You would be dead, I widowed, totally different. Maybe I could stay alone, that's the difference between men and women."

"What's the difference?" I asked, turning away embarrassed.

"Women can live without a man. We can go without sex for a long time. We don't see relationships purely in sexual terms."

"That's 'cause you don't have a cock!"

"What?" Lucia laughed.

"You don't have a penis," I said, laughing.

"What has that got to do with it?"

"Everything. If you had a cock you wouldn't go years without sex, your whole system would be different. You the hunter, not the hunted."

"I'm going for a shower," Lucia said, checking her figure in the full-length mirror.

"Anyhow ,I can hear you say to some posh businessman the fuckin' eejit just upped and died. Laugh about it, women the great survivors, eh?"

"We have to be with men ruling the world the way they do. Take it like this, a woman has to work twice as hard, twice as long, to prove herself in a man's world."

Lucia was now removing small black dots from her eyelids. She sat on the hard chair in front of the vanity mirror of her travel bag.

"It's inherent in women to survive if their men-folk die. They will live on, despite all the wailing and outpourings of grief."

I knew I was on dangerous ground, so I physically tried to keep my tone light.

"Then they will look for another strong member of the tribe to look after them, comfort them. You take it how the church survives!" I was on my feet, pretending to be interested in peeking through the window at the empty street below. "Women propagate: the church without women, it would die. Kids go to Mass, make First Communions, Confirmations, all this nonsense! Who makes them go? Women. Where are all the women priests, hey? None, Lucia, because women don't want to be in charge, it's part of the deal. Men are seen to be in charge; women, really, are in charge by stealth. It's preordained, excuse the pun."

"What are you on?"

She turned, laughing, looking different without whatever the black dots were stuck in her eyelids.

She rolled onto my side of the bed, her face smiling honestly.

"Come here, you idiot."

I did and I loved her for listening. She stroked my forehead till my mind drifted into a peace.

Boyce puffed on his cigar. Argüelles coughed, so Boyce took another puff blowing the smoke across the table. It magnetized the air around the Spaniard's sharp nose; he looked at Drozdan for help. Drozdan was preoccupied with matters in hand. He was studying the photographs in his manila folder.

"Where is the air conditioning?" Boyce said mischievously.

"Mr Boyce, we are guests here," the Monsignor tried to chide him, yet he couldn't muster enough menace in his voice. Boyce was a different proposition to Marie Abele. Drozdan intervened, not interested in the exchanges around him. He handed the manila folder to Boyce, saying, "Here's all you need. I have checked it myself, it has everything."

Boyce took it slowly, like the old pro he was. He stubbed his cigar butt into the dirty ashtray. He smiled at his companions before slowly opening the folder, examining its contents. He separated the photographs from the pages of text. Each individual had been clearly assessed, their details put on paper in scholarly fashion. Argüelles, as if reading Boyce's mind, smiled. Boyce knew he could not digest all the information at one sitting. Summarizing as best he could there was

Eva Devlin, Don Dino Bernado, Toby, strangely, Marie Abele also Philippe Giordano. This time Drozdan was reading his mind. "Hush now, Mr Boyce, you must put those items away now before our host arrives." Drozdan's voice was just above a whisper.

"You surprise me, Cardinal," Boyce said, looking at Argüelles.

"You are shocked, Mr Boyce?" Argüelles asked in his practiced sarcastic tones.

Boyce smiled at him, glancing at the door to make sure nobody was coming.

He leaned forward, gently eyeing the owl-like Monsignor, "I have worked for some of the biggest lying ruthless scum ever to walk this planet. I must say, Monsignor, you rival them." Boyce laughed heartily, giving the impression he was pleased with the Monsignor. What he just read through empowered Argüelles with a great deal of respect.

Boyce was surprised by Philippe Giordano, he imagined a stocky small Italian who had eaten too many pies.

Philippe was in his early thirties, but he looked younger. His sallow skin, a gift from nature. Boyce thought him handsome. When he spoke he was business-like yet held back on occasions, like he went to negotiation night school.

"I understood we were to act independently," Philippe said.

He chose not to eyeball Boyce, but rather to fix his gaze on the Cardinal.

"My dear Philippe, whilst we know of your family's reputation, we feel Mr Boyce here can act as consultant advisor on the matters discussed.

You may not understand, but we must learn the lessons

of the past, harsh lessons. Mr Boyce is experienced in these matters. You understand, Philippe?"

Philippe looked at the smug Argüelles playing with his pen, tapping it faintly on the table coaster. "If the Cardinal pays the bills, we will accept his condition. However, I insist Mr Boyce and I work on equal terms," he said and sat back as if expecting an argument that never came.

"Sure. We never saw it any other way," Argüelles said, ceasing to tap his pen.

"Good," Philippe said with a faint grin.

"We will take our leave now," the Cardinal said standing up. Argüelles stood as if to mimic.

"I will leave you with Mr Boyce to discuss your plan of action. You will report directly to Monsignor Argüelles. That is understood?"

The Cardinal offered his hand to Philippe, then to Boyce. Argüelles shook hands like he was afraid of picking up some deadly germ. Boyce watched them leave the room.

"Now Philippe, we can discuss what it is we have to do. I did notice that you run a bar downstairs. So may I implore you for a glass of malt whiskey?" Boyce said.

Philippe smiled; he seemed relieved Boyce requested something so innocuous.

15.

Lucia called it paradise, our own outdoor pool. Standing by its edge the view of the valley, empty fields, out buildings of soft stone, rooftops orange and red. Beyond small hills caressed my eye. The sound of a cockerel singing in the mornings, Lucia smiled each time he let go. The pool wasn't big, more or less the same depth most of the way along.

I liked it because I could stand in any part.

The usual pool furniture adorned its sides. The sound of sprinklers in the nearby garden was ever-present.

Lucia spent her time rescuing ill-fated ladybirds, drowning, deposited by the breeze. She took time, concentrating fully, washing them to the side, brushing away monster ants that attempted to devour them. I lay back, swallowed by the blue sky above. I was thinking of the children at home.

Wondering did they miss me like I missed them, or was that just a parental thing?

Here the birds skimmed down to the water to cool off, like warplanes, swift dive bombers in unison taking trickles of water before gaining speed, accelerating into the sky. Once airborne, they flew at amazing speed in big wide circles.

Lucia eventually gave up on her 'save the cute insect.' campaign to return to her poolside bed. She adjusted the deck chair and brolly with great skill.

"Better to keep in the shade," she said. "One doesn't want tears later."

She laughed at me when I chided her for fussing.

"Well we don't want to be burnt alive, do we?" She said.

The tiny lizards appearing stealthily from the undergrowth fascinated her, turning to the flat of her tummy to watch them.

"Isn't this just fabulous? A small twelve-room hotel all to ourselves?" We were literally a five-minute walk from the medieval city of San Gimignano. I remembered our first visit to this place, remembering her walking up the steep hill by the small row of café bars. Living within the old facades were utterly modern houses. Old men drooling over their window boxes as Lucia strode up the hill with her figure-hugging red dress. I was so proud of her, so happy she was my wife. Walking through the pedestrian tunnel, up steep steps by the old city gates, stopping for a quick drink and a fag. She pointing to a small on-street café to our right. I'd smoke a Major, she a Silk Cut Purple, I'd have a beer, she'd have wine. People watching. Every now and then Lucia might stop people watching, saying "Wonderful isn't it?" I agreed, walking on up the hill by the tall towers so unique to the city. Each one represented the wealth of a particular nobleman, the smallest to the biggest. Further up the hill it opened into a square with cobbles and a quaint fountain, punctuated with bars, good cafes, hotels, and banks; it never did lose its charm. Lucia was taken with the gelateria. She drooled over the heavenly selection of ice creams. That was the last time I remember Lucia happy, the last of our carefree days. When I came out of hospital all innocence left us. I went through the motions, I suppose in her own way, so did she. My thinking pattern changed. To sit among birds, listen to the sounds of the garden, to watch the sunlight lost in the clear water of the pool, yet to think back on pain, the cold white of the hospital ward, the fellow patients all scared, all vulnerable.

In Ireland, going from public to private medicine is like staying in a boarding house one night, only to wake up in the Four Seasons the next morning. The only good things that can be said for the system is that it spares nobody. If you're admitted through accident and emergency this is where you end up. It's also where you are most likely to stay if you have heart disease, at least till they are ready to intervene. When they brought me in it was on account of my falling from my perch one Christmas night whilst Lucia and I watched television. The off-spring were upstairs, entertaining friends. To this day the doctors are baffled as to the reasons I fell off my perch. My heart was like a dodgy starting motor, it hit the wrong cog. Otherwise my blood sugars went sky high due to the undiagnosed type 2 diabetes. Anyway, I ended up on the flat of my back, surrounded by another five unfortunates. They ranged from a farm labourer, who lived in a converted outhouse, to the retired CEO of one of Ireland's semi-state jewels. This poor man was well into his eighties and would openly admit to the onset of dementia. Another man opposite me didn't know who the hell he was and why he was in hospital. It was doubtful if he was 100 per cent certain this was a hospital. Lucia was very kind; she came to see me every day religiously. The dutiful nurses more than made up for the arrogance of the junior doctors, although I found the registrars and the consultants brilliant, one and all. I had an infection so after a week's stay eventually I was allowed an angiogram. It was strange, I knew Lucia was waiting in the ward below. I wasn't frightened, well, not really. They had done heart ultrasound echoes, as I came to know them. My heart wasn't operating to its full capacity, it was operating at something like thirty percent output. I think the consultants knew I had heart disease, they couldn't really call it as to the extent of the damage. It was either that or I had a massive infection which had slowed everything down. I somehow believed my own infection version of events. When the consultant told me it would be inaccurate to say I was shocked, I was in truth almost relieved. It was like the finality of the diagnosis was better than the maybes or if's which haunted much of the previous week.

Toby watched as Monica brushed back her hair, its length sheltered her hand it fell on the ravine protected by her shoulder blades. Monica lay flat on her tummy, she lifted the small of her back. Toby studied her skin, she was sallow all over. She helped him, soon they were one, he whispered to her. Monica, lost in a world of her own, barely heard his words. Soon Toby lay back, breathing deeply. Monica sighed, she looked towards the shutters, cracks of light sneaking through. Toby let his right arm dangle over her thigh she turned to look at him, her face soft. Toby stared deep into her dark eyes; in a trance, endless eyes. She placed her hand round his shoulder, rubbing the corner of his neck gently.

"How is Eva?" she asked.

Toby looked at her intensely.

"She is very ill; Don Dino wants her to go away for a while." He spoke lyrically. In this case, it was to sad music.

"Where on earth can she go, if not back to the sanatorium?" Monica spoke with fear.

"I dunno," Toby said.

"She is lucid, not like before. I think the Don wants her to go away and rest someplace, not too far away. He is concerned for her. He thinks she is getting things out of proportion, imagining danger." Toby moved to rest his back, his head buried in the soft pillow.

"I don't think she is exaggerating. I told you, Toby, Philippe is mad. Father has lost control; he is too old. I know the Don is old also. He has grown old with more grace, more refinement," Monica said. She went to stroke Toby's forehead; he moved away without meaning to. Walking slowly to stand naked by the window, opening the green shutters.

"Toby, what did the Don say about Volterra, hey?"

He could sense the fear in her voice, yet for her sake he turned calmly to face her,

"We are criminals to be here in the dark, Monica; the sun is splitting the stones." She watched him silently as he started to dress.

"I told Don Dino Father Cryan asked me to assist as a special favour. I told him about the dying child. I said to him you were concerned about Philippe, the fascists from Rome." Toby was walking to the mirror to comb his hair. Keeping his gaze on her reflection Toby continued,

"Se fosse cosi, mi prenderei delle guardie del corpo per proteggermi."

Monica waited for him to turn around; she had half covered herself with sheets.

"Ti amo," she said.

Toby smiling walked over to her sitting on the bed. He kissed her gently on the forehead speaking softly,

"Monica, so quello che provo."

16.

I saw it in the faces of the nurses. They were sad for me. Looking back I suppose they had a much better idea than I what lay ahead.

Still, I was coping well trying to convince myself anything was better than falling from my perch, never getting up.

It could be worse. They can fix hearts. I'm lucky they found me.

All of these were mind weapons I used to get over the next couple of days before being transferred to the private hospital for my bypass.

This pretty rehab nurse came to see me to advise me on the practicalities of heart surgery. She described to me the process, more importantly the process of recovery. I fell in love with her, well, infatuated with her. She gave the impression that she would have the operation for me if she was allowed.

My diabetic nurses were a rave as well. They advised on the glucometer, how to use it to record my blood sugar levels four times a day. They sent in a nutritionist who gave me work sheets with low-sugar diets. She advised on what I could and could not eat.

The best of all though was my surgeon. He appeared one evening unexpectedly. He was a young guy, didn't look anything like a surgeon. I thought somebody was having me on. The guy was dressed in dark colours not unlike he was in mourning.

He was smart though, I figured that. It was like somebody saying I will meet you at eight-thirty for a pint.

He looked me straight in the eye.

"I will do you on Friday," he said.

"You will be up and about by Monday."

He was gone and I took a long deep breath. The guy meant what he said.

It's hard to know or care how Lucia took all this. I chide myself for being selfish. It's the truth that when you go through this bypass surgery you don't think of or care for others.

Maybe it's part of the survival process, both before and after.

She tried her best to be upbeat and cheerful.

Doing her best to change the subject, give me useless details about the neighbours, bland things about the kids. In her own way she was trying to protect me from all thoughts and worries associated with the real world outside. I, unknown to her, had already started the process by not buying newspapers or reading about the awful slaughter of the Tsunami.

On that point my hatred of the media was formed, the day when the newspapers showed us the rows of bodies lying on the fly-infested streets.

They greet such events with an air of voyeuristic glee, till along comes the next tragedy. Large or small is of little relevance to these people whose favourite buzz word is "Breaking news." God save us!

"Your blood pressure is too high!"

"Yes, Don Dino, I work here seven days a week. I drive, I cook.

I serve you like a wife."

"Gregor my wife!"

Don Dino didn't like the look of Gregor.

"Your face is too red. It doesn't come from the sun. You should see a doctor.

Anyhow, my wife ran away years ago," he said.

"I hope they made it to Switzerland or someplace," Gregor growled.

Don Dino chuckled as Gregor handed him his orange juice.

"What I love about you Gregor is you always manage to see the best in your employer. Sure, I did many bad things in my youth. I regret and confess to my priest, but I could never touch a hair on Bendetto's mother's head. As for Claude, miserable Swiss son of a bitch—"

"I don't want to know. I am too old, no good at anything now. I'm not even a good driver. You should let me retire."

The Don laughed louder this time, enjoying the banter, the evening sun on his face.

"Retire? What would you do, Gregor?

Go back to the miserable house your ex-wife has in Volterra? She would nag you to death in six months. Sit down there, share my juice. I have a jug full. I will sit in the toilet all night long if I drink it. Besides I want to discuss Eva with you. I need your advice."

Gregor sat reluctantly. He poured the smallest drop of juice into a glass and sipped a tiny amount.

"When the Don wants my advice he always pulls the same trick. Lets me talk for ten minutes, then tells me to 'Shut up, what do you know, Gregor?' till I wonder why he has asked me in the first place."

Don Dino, ignoring him, said,

"Gregor, Eva is bad again. She is drinking herself to death. Toby found her on the floor, it is a bad case yet again. Her nerves are shattered. She suspects these Sodality people are reactivated. She fears Don Maestrino may be involved, his son Philippe is a hothead.

They want revenge for Edgell, they are afraid of Toby. Perhaps he could embarrass them."

"Could be true, Don Dino."

"It is true, yet Eva forgets we can protect ourselves. She goes hides inside the bottle like alcohol has the answer, huh?" The Don downed his orange juice.

"Eva has always had a love affair with the bottle Don Dino, ever since her priest died."

"We must find out Gregor, find out their plans. I need you to contact our people. I want Eva and Toby protected. Will you do that for me?"

Gardiner lay awake, the room was too warm.

The steep hill…the rail…the meadow,

did Kellerman and Quinn feed him with drugs, some mind-expanding concoction?

He felt his head go weak and his fingers tremble. The boy was taking position on the railing. Gardiner could feel tightness in the back of his throat; he wondered was he having another heart attack?

The woman appeared, she was tall and slim. She wore a pretty white dress that fell just below the knee. She walked down the hill purposefully.

Beyond her the boy was speaking into a mobile phone. It was like he had it buried in his ear, was it him that phoned him in New York?

'Messaggio dall'Angelo della Morte.' Eva stepped into the car.

She looked at him as if he were a long lost friend. "Un uomo dovrebbe fare attenzione mentre dorme."

Gardiner glanced up the hill; the boy was still talking into the phone.

"I know what the words mean. I don't know why you use them." Gardiner called on all his experience. He had been in tight scrapes before.

"I knew you would come," Eva said.

Gardiner turned to her, about to speak. He caught her eyes which were dark yet gave life to her pale skin.

"What is it you want to tell us?" He tried to sound hard and businesslike, like he gave a shit for Kellerman or Quinn.

"I have everything you need. I will contact you when the time is right." she said softly, looking up the hill to where the boy was.

"What have you got on us?" Gardiner sounded foolish. "I mean, is it this stuff on Auldridge or the Pope?"

She smiled at him, she was about to leave. "Who is he?" He pointed to the boy still talking on his mobile phone. "Who is he?" Gardiner asked once more.

"He is strange looking even from here," he said.

"The boy is Agnolino," Eva said softly.

Getting out of the car she turned and said, "Does he appear in your dreams?"

"You will meet with me?" she said holding the door.

Gardiner glanced up the hill. The boy was gone.

"Remember," she said again, "He knows where Heidi Heisler is." She shut the door like a girlfriend after an argument.

"Hey, Steve, I mean I love you and all, sure was glad they didn't haul your ass with the heart thing. The fuck, do you know what time we are here? We're in the middle of the goddamn night, right? What the fuck?"

Bateman would have kept going on but Gardiner interjected,

"Joe, shut the fuck up, will you? Listen to me now. Calm, ok? I can't do this till you're calm." Gardiner waited till the line was quiet. "Agnolino, he lives here in Bagni di Lucca, it's a little place up here in the Apennines. That's all I got. You get me something, any goddamn thing, ok?"

"Steve," Bateman sounded calm and reasonable. Gardiner started to relax. "You know, when you nearly died, they rushed you to hospital."

"Yeah, I know," Gardiner said impatiently.

"Well, fuck you, Gardiner. It's a good thing you didn't fuckin' die 'cause nobody gives two fucks about you when you're dead.

I feel like going over to fuckin' Italy, ripping your heart out myself, you mother fucker. Waking me in the middle of the fuckin' night with shit! A fuckin' name, how the fuck many people in Italy with that name hey?"

Gardiner waited till he heard Bateman run out of steam at the other end.

"Bateman, Gardiner here. Remember me? Your ex-boss,

112

who used to fix you three days extra vacation every goddamn year, just get the information,"

Gardiner hung up smiling.

17.

Lucia was out of sorts. We tried this off-licence, it was down an old passageway, something from the middle ages. The shop itself was modern and the young assistant spoke excellent English.

His hair was neat with a twist of curls that covered his ears, tantalizing against the soft brown of his skin. This was Agnolino. His eyes falling to dark, like the night sky minus stars.

When he smiled he showed perfect teeth. He smiled only when prompted. His face was in general serious, which made his top lip pout over the bottom one.

He was elegant, smart, a salesman but more of a friend. His knowledge of wine was extensive, yet he imparted this knowledge as somebody would share their last morsel of food.

Lucia was preoccupied with her tummy. She had a cramp; she was quiet.

I hated to see her sick, it made me feel vulnerable. She became a little sad, like she had suddenly discovered a part of life she never knew existed.

I followed her in and out of quirky little souvenir shops.

When Lucia wandered, she was either bored, sick, or both.

Finally, after grudgingly looking at more porcelain ashtrays and scarves, I made us sit and have lunch.

We found a little outdoor place, they did a decent "Pane Tostato."

Lucia also drank some refreshing Acqua Imbottigliata.

When you think too much it's not a good thing. Most people just get on with life, get up early in the morning, go to work, come home in the evenings, play with the kids, watch television. Most men enjoy meeting a buddy or two in the pub, having a pint and a laugh watching their sports.

Me? Whatever happened to me? I sat in our little outdoor café eating my pane tostato. What happens that my head goes in a spin?

I think its fatigue. I usually start the day fine, yet sometime around lunch or just before, it starts.

I even mentioned this to Lucia, but she just laughed when I told her about my brain flu. When I was about eighteen I got this head cold. I was laid low, taking to the bed for three days.

My mind started to race. Now every time my mind races I get the same feeling, even if it lasts for only ten minutes or so. My brain virus; it lives in there. I don't know if I keep some little viral-type bugs. I feel a sensation resembling a cold breeze.

Perhaps I have a huge ugly worm. It sleeps when I am fine, wakes and starts moving around when I have my brain flu.

I eyed the waitress's bum. It was fat, so rounded she was luscious. I marveled at the old lady opposite with her middle-aged fat son. She had a full moustache like a man. I wondered how some poor bastard slept with her.

I marveled at a lot of things. People put up with imperfections, grief —in these moments I decided I wasn't a very nice person, which visual people really aren't. Here's to us visualizers, we are never satisfied, and how can we be? The world is too imperfect for us to inhabit safely.

I also reckon most men are lying all of the time.

My thoughts deserve jail, at least for intent, if not incitement. I think nearly all men are potential paedophiles.

Horror, horror, I also think all men are part homosexual. It is a certainty that violence is a manifestation of sexuality.

There now, you try telling Lucia that, and I haven't started on women.

We had a grand lunch before setting back towards Poggibonsi. We stopped at the Castellare Vineyard where Lucia made a video portrait like a demented female Richard Attenborough.

I digress. Lucia was feeling better. The sight of the golden sun baking the tracks of brown that ran mid rows and rows of sacred vines settled her.

We bought some wine from the shop, really splashing out; we loved our wine.

Funny, there was something about the time we visited the Castellare that brought us close.

As we walked back to the car I studied her from behind.

The sense of autistic distance I felt was melting in the heat. I was somehow stumbling back into reality, like the man who longed to find the sea but found a great lake instead.

Where was this perfect world I sought? In what selfish sinew did it live? My fake attempts to scream at mortality, yes come soon you son of a bitch, come soon. Lucia driving, innocently smiling to herself, her eyes watching the sun shining, nourishing the wild flowers decorating the roadside.

By the pool I felt her presence, her blonde falling to the blue, splash white she swims like a swan. Lucia makes it ten lengths before stopping, holding the side. She feels the sun drift west, shadows move across her face. When her hair is wet she is dark. I know later she will dry off to become blonde again. She sees me fake reading a novel, she asks me am I ok, I, say I am. Falling backwards she does the backstroke, her hands tense as flippers. The sky is deepest blue, her hopes are lost in it. She stares into the void, the failing sun sparkles round her. This is my wife, floating model, mother earth, visitor, friend. I want to sleep but I can't, my tee shirt sticks to my back, my face is wet, groggy head immersed in cold water. Lucia comes to me, she gives me a hug. Water dripping through drains, fresh water pumps from beneath.

"Toby, it's been too long," Father Cryan said.

"Much too long. You remember Monica?"

"I do, of course I do,"

Monica smiling held out her hand.

The priest kissed her gently on the back of her fingers.

"You are still so beautiful."

"Thank you, Matthew." Monica blushed slightly at the Englishman's sincerity.

Toby rescued her, "Come, Matthew, we shall sit in the garden or by the pool. There is nobody about."

"Sure," Father Cryan said. He followed as they walked through the gravel to the garden table. It allowed glimpses of the valley below. "We are blessed with the weather at last. The sun adores us this day." He sat beside Toby.

"Can I get you lemonade or a soda?" Toby asked earnestly.

"There is nobody at reception," Monica said standing,

"I will go look and get us some soda."

"You are so lucky Toby," the priest said, calmly stretching his legs beneath the table.

Toby laughed heartily.

"Matthew, you presume the world to be as pure and ideal as you are. It is in fact the opposite. As they say, God keeps a special room for the innocent."

Toby touched his arm playfully; Matthew smiled. "True, for I am sure even Monica is not perfect."

"Where is the girl?" Monica emerged from under the trees with her tray of soda.

"Yes," said Matthew, distracted by Monica.

"She will come here soon. I have to text message her."

The priest reached for his mobile phone, holding on to it like he never saw one before.

"Thank you," they said in unison as Monica laid the tray on the uneven surface of the table.

"How old is she?" Toby asked.

"Still a child. She is just gone sixteen."

"Who is the father?" Monica asked.

Father Cryan, dropping his eyes said, "Unknown. It was a relative that wrote to me."

"What is the illness exactly, Matthew?" Toby asked.

"The baby has multiple tumours in the brain. The doctors in Firenze give her no hope. She wants the baby baptized in Volterra, hoping that perhaps your hands may repeat the wonder I myself witnessed."

Monica looked at Toby admiringly. Toby, half embarrassed, turned to the priest. "She has no expectation I hope, Matthew?"

Father Cryan met his eyes. "No Toby it would be foolish. It is a comfort for her. I explained we can only view this as comfort. As I said, it was a relative who contacted me originally. The girl herself is young. She is without a passion for religion. I found her to be smart, even if uneducated. The girl has intelligence."

When the girl arrived she sat with them embarrassed. An older woman had driven her. She waited in the parked car by the ornamental pond.

Father Cryan introduced her, "This is Marea."

Toby studied her. She was like most young women of her generation.

She was clean, her skin pale for an Italian girl. He liked her face which though full was softened by clear blue eyes. It was obvious her tight blonde hair was natural.

He noticed small holes in the sides of her nostrils, she had recently removed studs or pins. Marea spoke softly. Toby could not imagine her as wild, he could only surmise that whatever encounter she had was either a misjudgement or a violation. He noticed she was nervous; she refused his offer of a soda. "The baby is called Donata, meaning gift from God," she said.

Father Cryan moved uneasily when she said this. Toby caught her eye.

Monica wanted to comfort her; she wasn't brave enough to reach out for her hand.

Marea was holding the steel of Toby's water-coloured eyes till it became clear to the ensemble that some communication was taking place.

Monica was about to speak. Matthew raised his hand for her to stop.

Marea, who was almost ice-like, suddenly smiled. She got to her feet, walking back to the car, a spring in her step. When she reached the car she stopped. Turning round she smiled again before leaving.

"Are you ok, Toby?" Matthew asked.

"Fine, Matthew," Toby said watching the car leave through the rising gravel dust.

"Anyone for more soda?" Toby said getting to his feet.

"You know what it is about guys like you, Gardiner? You're kinda sick, like you're sick inside. The disease you have works into your brain.

You give me the name of some kid and you expect miracles. What is more, I don't give a shit 'cause you don't work here no more. All the vacation shit means nothin'. I don't need anymore vacations since my divorce.

All those extra days meant was another three days screwing my mistress, till my wife found out 'bout us. She threw me out. So that's where those three days extra vacation got me." He stopped, running out of breath but gathered himself to continue.

"So this is the shit on Agnolino from God knows where,"

"Bateman, just give me what you got, will you?" Gardiner said calmly.

"What I got? Are you for real?"

"Give it to me, Joe."

"Alright, this is all I got. This kid Agnolino, he comes home from school one day five years ago thereabouts, he was ten years old. He finds his father has shot his kid brother and his mother, then hung himself from a tree. So he gets the gun. It took the cops three days to get him out of the house. He nearly killed one of them. So he was taken into care. Then he runs away, escapes again and again, always back to the house.

Each time the cops bring him back, he escapes again.

The people of the village said they would look after him. They made submissions to the courts. So he gets an education.

He's been clean since they let him go home. That's it. All over the Italian press five years ago."

"That's it, yeah?"

"All I got, you goddamn dirt bird."

"OK, Bateman, remind me I owe you."

"Yeah, sure, Steve. You owe me a wife and a goddamn bitch of a mistress!"

Gardiner saw the hill, the boy on the rail, siren sounds. Susie, on the beach, bare feet on the boardwalk. His heart burns. Agnolino, dream visitor, walks from fire, his face lost in vegetation. Gardiner senses the cold, water lilies midst ripples, bleak bones lost in the forest.

18.

Each morning I walked as far as I could up the prom. I was heading towards Massa. In fairness to Lucia she tried to help by walking with me, well, at least some of the way. She was a better swimmer than walker. The way she moved her arms was even more ridiculous than me.

After breakfast I changed into shorts and runners, she into a tight top and shorts. We set out past Raymond's fashion shop and on past the New York Bar, dodging the cycle lane.

Lucia could keep pace. To be honest, I kept it sedate as I didn't want to show off. When we reached the end of what I called the business prom, we split. I moved ahead to walk another kilometre or so,

Lucia, dawdling behind me, walking on at a slower pace.

The shop fronts and restaurants were replaced by rows of private villas stretching to the sea. These were classy places with manicured gardens hosting table tennis and in some cases deck chairs and tables. They had pavilion-like designs with wooden walkways and changing booths. I walked right to the end where I turned at a huge building. I never quite found out its use.

Turning to retrace my steps, feeling the heat, trying to preserve my energy as the walk back to the hotel was daunting.

Spying Lucia a half kilometre ahead. She walked really fast. The first few times I made great strides to reel her in, catching up with her on the cycle path just at the pedestrian walkway beside our hotel. She glanced at me, disappointingly one day, saying, "You are moving it," then she laughed and I allowed her win the walk to the steps leading to the lobby.

We laughed more in the tiny lift we squeezed into. I commented on the sweat gathering in rounded beads around her neck and shoulders.

"The word is perspire," she said. "Horses sweat, ladies glow."

I laughed. As time went on either she got better or cheated or I got tired, less able.

Over our last few walks I didn't catch her. She was easy about it. To be honest, it wasn't a part of her I disliked. It showed she cared for herself, and in her own way she was able to compete with me. Some women spend all their lives competing openly with their husbands, with men in general. They are rarely acknowledged for their victories, even when they do win; I suspect they win more often than we men like to admit.

Don Maestrino wasn't overfriendly. Boyce didn't expect him to be.

He didn't like the look of his henchman Raymond either.

Boyce sat back relaxed; he didn't particularly have any feelings about Philippe, save for his bar and his malt. The young man was smart alright but impetuous.

"Mr Boyce, you are here to assist us. Can you clarify the role you have in mind? The days of family feuding are long gone. The families are no longer at war. We are more into legitimate means of making our money.

My son here, Philippe, he watches lots of movies with Marlon Brando and Al Pacino.

I was all of these when he was a child. I have grown old; you can see that for yourself, no need to be kind. What is it you do, Mr Boyce? Are you the one who pulls the trigger, plants the bomb, hey?"

Boyce lit a cigar, coughing a little. Philippe pushed an ashtray over to him, glaring at his father. Raymond studied Boyce, taking no interest in Philippe or his petulance.

"I am the fixer, Don Maestrino. I try not to get my hands dirty if I can. A man of your experience will know that as much as it is desirable, it is not always possible," said Boyce.

Don Maestrino strained to see Boyce's face which unnerved him. The cigar smoke seemed dead in the air. "How many times Philippe have I asked you to let the light of God into this room?" he said, getting impatient. Philippe rose to open a window.

"Who is to be shot and who will do the shooting?" he asked bluntly.

Philippe stopped in his tracks half way across the room. The question didn't bother Boyce. He took another long drag, exhaling the smoke in spasms.

"I will kill the woman. Philippe, he will organize the explosives to kill Don Dino. We will arrange it for the parish priest of Cucuron to kill this faith healer, he will be left with no choice." Boyce was speaking from a script.

"Philippe knows nothing of explosives," Don Maestrino said, standing up. Philippe had reached the table but still had not sat down.

"Don Maestrino, you and your good servant Raymond have used explosives many times. It is well documented in our files." Boyce spoke like he was ordering dinner.

Philippe finally sat down, watching his father go to the window and take out a cigarette. He lit it making sure he blew the smoke out into the air.

"Philippe can't do explosives, how can you expect him?" Don Maestrino said.

"You and Raymond can. Don Dino will go to Volterra on Sunday to protect Toby at a baptism. We can be sure of his journey, one road in, one road out. You can assist your son. After all, I am led to believe it's a family business." Boyce stubbed his cigar out as if to punctuate the meeting.

As Monica sang the crowd gathered, most sitting out front in the cocktail bar.

Gardiner liked her voice. It held strength yet was soft and melodic.

He thought back to his meeting with Eva, the reaction of Quinn and Kellerman to his news. They were shrewd, could never be accused of giving much away.

Kellerman said, "Right, this doesn't sound too good," whilst Quinn gave his by-now customary, "Gee, ain't good, hey?"

Gardiner didn't mind, duty done.

He left out the eerie Agnolino, any personal observations he made. Right now it was none of their goddamn business.

Monica sang "Dream a little dream of me." She sang it with real conviction. Gardiner felt his chest heave as he sought to control his emotions.

He thought of Susie when they first met, how she let her head rest on his shoulder.

It was nothing and yet it was everything. It was like a daughter taking comfort from her dad. Susie, the girl who had been hurt, her mother so ill as she grew up, then dying so unexpectedly.

Those nights he cuddled her and felt her warmth seep through. He could still feel the tingle of her hot skin. She who breathed so softly in his ear.

It was she he pined for on those lonely wet nights waiting at dig sites for bones, for half-rotted corpses.

Where was she now? Maybe that's what hurt the most. He had nobody to dream of anymore.

When Monica finished the pianist called a ten-minute break. Gardiner watched as she walked elegantly to the bar, ordering a soda.

He followed her, ordering a gin and tonic.

"I really like the music," he said.

Monica, used to tourists complimenting her, replied, "thank you, it is nice to hear."

"We have a mutual friend," Gardiner said casually.

"Chi?" Monica said.

Gardiner chanced, "Eva, la tua amica." She tried to walk away.

"I spoke to her. She is concerned for Toby."

"Non posso,"

"I don't have time for games. If you want to help you better talk to me." He put on his best hard-nosed look.

"I don't have time, Monica."

"Come fai a sapere il mio nome?"

"Please, it's for Eva."

"OK, where do we meet?" she said finally. Gardiner sighed, taking a sip of his gin.

The Don touched her, his gentle hand wiping perspiration from her shining forehead. She stared up at him in awe, ashamed. Gregor and another man were there but left on the Don's command.

"I can't believe it is you. I see you only as you were when Father Burdon brought you to me."

She could see tears moisten his eyes, they held back by glue.

Don Dino refused to wipe his eyes wishing for the tears to develop.

"My Don, you have lost none of your compassion even in old age. You remain a better person than I could ever hope to be!"

"Sssh, ssh, my Eva, don't waste your energy on me. I have come with good news. I will protect all we have left, you, Toby, and my own mortal self.

I want you to go stay in the house in Bagno Vignoni. It is arranged, I will keep you safe there. The waters of St Caterina will cure you like before. They will wash away all your demons. You will once more see the spirit of your child. I will watch over him in Volterra. I will mind him like he were my own flesh and blood."

Eva closed her eyes to stem the tide of her own tears. The Don rubbed her forehead once again. "When you are well, Gregor will take you. I wish my son Benedetto was still here. Toby reminds me of him."

A tear fell down the Don's cheek, winding through his ravaged skin, falling in small drops upon her.

Monica felt out of place. Rosa served her dry white wine. Monica smiled at her. She was Italian, from the south. Monica knew by her dark skin. Gardiner watched her drink.

Monica was uncomfortable with him.

Gardiner leaned forward.

"Eva may have some information for me?" he said pitching his question softly.

"She has many enemies." Monica said as she drank her wine like somehow it might be poison.

"Who are these people?" he asked.

"Mr Gardiner, I dunno. Eva and her son don't talk about any of this. You want to interrogate me."

Gardiner knew he had to act quickly.

"No, I have no wish to interrogate you. I must speak with Eva. She has contacted me. I fear for her. She may be in trouble."

"She never mentioned you. I don't know where she is. That's the truth."

"I see," Gardiner waited for her to continue.

"Is she still in Bagni di Lucca?"

Monica stared at him. "I have told you all I know. I will say nothing more."

She left, passing Rosa who sighed, giving him a hangdog look. Gardiner was sure she thought him rude.

In bed, he couldn't sleep. It was too warm, the sheets sticking to his skin. He sat up, cursing his luck, taking his Lipitor. He had forgotten as was normal.

Monica was holding back. She couldn't hide the fear. What were Kellerman and Quinn so worried about anyhow?

He called Bateman, he had no idea exactly what he wanted to ask. It just seemed like a good idea.

19.

I have always found it easy to fall in love. I fall in love with places, with women, with their faces. Really I don't know if visualizers are capable of love, real love as humans understand it.

Is seeing a woman standing naked midst a field of sunflowers anything to do with love? Don't get me wrong, I know what love is. I believe visualizers know what love is. We just can't feel it.

I can't feel this empathy towards things or if I can it comes in fits and starts, never ever-present.

Going through phases, beautiful woman standing in a sunflower field, or maybe a lavender field. I love the aesthetic. It is not the blood, the guts, the body function, the juices, hot and cold, cramps, the pain. Never the human touch. Only the aesthetic is real.

Just wonder, do other men have more empathy for their partners, their children? I view the world as a sociopath. In the end all the attention falls back to me. I feel the dread, my mind weakened by brain flu. Fatigue enters my conscious; all things around me are distorted. The pain is real in itself, it manifests with headache and nausea, light headed, looking over my shoulder, each fear numbered one to ten. When alone some rationale returns, eventual dismissal, the same miserable pattern each time. I imagine the chemicals, black, oily turning slimy green, clear water flows strong, kills ninety nine percent of all known brain flu.

Lucia and I got a map from the guy in the Castellare. He

outlined our route for us. Lucia was navigating. We headed south from Siena.

As usual I was thinking about other shit. I wondered, is this why I do things for people? Is it why I smile, make funny comments, try to please them?

Have I always known there is part of me that's not very nice, maybe even intrinsically evil?

Often I wonder about the people who served in the Nazi death camps, or who worked for Stalin, or the guys in the movies who made people dig their own graves.

These people had brothers, sisters, kids, parents, aunts and uncles, cousins.

It's like in my own mind I sort of forget that these beauts are exactly the same as me. They were all little babies crying in the pram.

Each one may have been frightened by the dark, mothers sang lullabies for them.

Funny, isn't it, how I somehow thought they all fell to earth in a meteor shower?

Like most of us I imagine them to be alien.

Or maybe we believe they are human, twisted by dictators like Hitler, Mussolini, or Stalin.

I dunno, I think maybe people are intrinsically evil. Is this why we get so much shit in the world?

Lucia would say, "What about all the doctors and nurses and people who help the starving and the poor?" I reckon they are all in it for themselves. They just don't know it.

They're feeding some giant ego with purity drops. Hell! It can't be that bad.

Lucia spoke, now mustering great enthusiasm.

"OK," she said holding the map out flat on her knees,

"We need to go to Asciano, then Abbazia d. Monte, Oliveto Maggiore."

"Grand, just don't let me take the wrong road."

I looked at her. The sun was whitening her whole complexion. Again as she read she reminded me of my father. I enjoyed her enthusiasm, the speed of her delivery.

She surprised me with her continued map reading.

"Then we go to a place called Pienza, on to the Quírico d' Órcia, after that some place called Bagno Vignoni."

I tried to be funny. "Why did he send us to that joint?"

"Oh," Lucia said. "He said it has healing waters, like the whole centre of the village is a spa. I read up on it in the guide. It says St Caterina of Siena bathed there."

"Wow, St Caterina," I said, trying to be smart and steer the car along the most beautiful hilltop roads with some of the most wonderful scenery I have ever laid eyes on.

Lucia ignored me as she was used to my silliness.

I felt like some giant hand was going to frame the landscape, capture all living things. It was like if God wanted to adorn the walls of heaven with his creations, he would have chosen this view. I stopped the car, opening the windows, enjoying the delight on Lucia's face.

She touched my knee with a friendly pat.

"I love Italy," she said innocently.

I too looking beyond my thoughts, felt the calm of her and the landscape combine. They were an irresistible force.

Bateman gave in, he admitted defeat.

"Sure as I ain't no faggot ass Gardiner, you take the fuckin' Mickey, hey? Every time I tell you the same shit. You don't work here no more. You're on the horn to me every goddamn day lookin' for shit. If it's not weirdo Italian kids, it's this shit. What the fuck you want to get on the CIA? I mean you know as well as I do Steve, these fucks don't exactly publish their resume on the net, got me? You wanna know about this guy Robert Quinn and some fuck called Jack Kellerman? Ring the goddamn Pentagon. Fuck you, Steve, I dunno, you call a favour, that's ok, but favours, hey, every day a favour? You want the dirt on these CIA fucks.

You know sometimes these fucks take you out for knowin' their name. Get me, Gardiner, hey?"

"Joe, you get this one, I promise, no more. Just get me some background, will you? I wanna know who they report to. What areas they move in. Just get me that, will you?" Gardiner as always remained calm to counterbalance Bateman's excitement.

"Last time, Gardiner."

Toby was taken aback. "I don't understand, Matthew. This is totally out of character. He has never shown you the slightest respect. For your parish priest he is like a stranger. We both know he certainly would have dumped you if he thought he could get away with it. He is afraid you may have too much information."

"I knew James Burdon a long time, I was his friend and confident. Marie Abele is less than ten years my senior. He is like a very old man. He has changed Toby, he has mellowed. I think he looks forward to retiring."

Toby interrupted, keeping an eye on Monica who was treading water in the pool. She was cool and fresh on such a hot day. "It is strange he should be called to Rome then suddenly has a change of heart and wants to assist us at the baptism?"

"He says it is his final act, he will retire with the grace of God, having made good with his long-suffering curate," said Father Matthew, half hidden under the poolside umbrella, like his words offended his natural naivety.

Toby, his voice slightly raised above the sounds of the sprinkler, responded, "Matthew, I will have to inform Don Dino. It sounds wrong. Whatever we think of Marie Abele, I am sure he is not a soft sentimental sort. It would be more like him to go missing in retirement or send you a snotty letter based on your conflict of idealism. To assist at the baptism is to allow him spy or have some agenda." Toby, sounding worried, put his sunglasses on.

Monica splashed at the far end of the pool. She looked different out of the glare.

"It was Argüelles he blamed, Argüelles. He says the Spaniard threatened him. It gave him time to reflect. He said he felt scared. I will see out this baptism with you as penance, for I sinned against you."

Toby shook his head. "Matthew, it is too risky. You must decline his offer."

Father Cryan sighed, lying back on the poolside sun chair. He knew Toby was right, yet the thoughts of refusing Marie Abele made him uneasy.

Boyce laughed as Philippe poured the malt.

"We have so much to celebrate, my new friend," Philippe said, pouring slowly.

"Don Maestrino has already ordered all we need. I think his cooperation is vital.

I don't mind confiding in you Mr Boyce, it means so much to me to have him on board." Boyce raised his glass, smiling at his new Italian friend. "The Cardinal is a very powerful man, and also, lucky for you my friend, a very wealthy man. Let's drink to him!"

Philippe copied Boyce by downing the glass in one shot. Boyce held out his glass for a re-fill.

"You know," Philippe said, straining to pour steadily, "I never realized the respect with which my father is held in Rome. He was very active in assisting these clergymen when he was young. To think they still respect the Giordano family to this day!"

Philippe watched Boyce carefully to see if he might down his drink once more. To his relief Boyce just sipped.

Raymond came in from the shadows. He walked, hunching slightly, which made his hair trail behind him.

"Don Maestrino waits in his car," Raymond said ignoring Boyce.

"My father wants me?" Philippe said, surprised.

"He is waiting in his car." Raymond was even more deadpan than before.

"Excuse me, Mr Boyce; I must see what it is Father wants. Help yourself to malt."

Philippe followed Raymond from the shadows into the light. It left Boyce in good mood, not having to make small talk, a half bottle of malt to be consumed, free at that. There was something still alive in him from his Methodist upbringing: anything free is good.

He topped up his glass, sitting back on his high stool, enjoying the calm.

The evening Rock didn't show, Boyce wasn't unduly concerned. He looked out the window of his quarters at half past seven. The sentry on duty was pacing up and down. It was starting to rain, as it did most autumn evenings. The boy is probably delayed, something on the farm. Maybe he is gathering information. He was improving, learning to accept his lot. Boyce reflected, it is like the prisoner forced to dig a ditch, the better he digs the more he is given to eat. Still it wasn't like Rock, he was normally on time.

When they found the third body Boyce felt nervous, he wondered should he call a halt.

The priest was causing trouble. The commander was questioning.

Some politicians were asking for an investigation. The IRA were making bland statements about their operatives not being directly involved; they were launching their own investigation.

Boyce knew he was making headline news around the world. There were things he was finding out, things that would only make sense to him. One of his key operatives had gone missing in South Armagh a year earlier.

These bastards knew what happened to him. More importantly he had vital information about operations in May 1974. How could he risk that hornet's nest exploding in his face? Boyce was sure a specialist Provo unit operated in his area. He knew it wasn't from Mick Devlin's farm, yet he was smoking them out. The priest was the problem. He somehow was learning the rules. He was active against him like he understood. Rock was never late. Something happened.

When they arrived the house was deserted. The captain allowed the squaddies to go first. All the lights were off, he followed the corporal into the kitchen.

Soon they found the light switch, he could see the door ajar beyond the darkness of the small parlour.

The corporal pointed to the blood on the floor and then to the sight of Mick Devlin lying against the cold stone wall.

They found the body of Dwyer just inside the parlour door, both men were shot through the temple at close range.

The squaddies found McCabe's body in the barn; he was tortured. His head slumped forward in the chair. The only light shot to pieces.

The Provos had completed their investigation, Boyce thought. How very thorough they were!

They even shot the dog. He lay prostrate on the gravel at the barn by the side of the house. The blood oozed from underneath his belly, a dark spring.

There was no sign of the girl; he checked his watch; it was 2.15 a.m.

20.

Lucia ordered us cold spring water. My tummy was playing up badly, needing hydration. I had to visit the loo. A small room, I tried to be quiet. I heard waiters and kitchen staff pass by, their lyrical voices disturbing my concentration.

When I returned, I found her sitting at an outdoor table in what was the monastery garden. The building was old, certainly impressive.

We had walked over a moat with a drawbridge to gain entrance. The place was modern, built around old. It wasn't packed, yet a few tourists sat ordering refreshments. Inside, a kind of long bar done in an old style, the food displayed as a buffet. By the time Lucia and I figured it all out the hunger had gone off me.

Being with Lucia in this type of place was a little like leading a child by the hand round a national monument. I always got the impression she didn't quite know where she was or what she was actually doing there.

Heck, it is good for the odd photograph, to show any casual observer who may feign interest. Personally I can never remember being remotely interested in anybody's holiday snaps. I would patronize unashamedly with things like, "Oh, very nice"; "It looks a lovely place"; "Oh really? That's Niagara Falls?"

Unless you're there yourself, you tend not to give a damn.

We eventually decided to explore, like it wasn't every day you found yourself an ancient monastery deep in the heart of Italy.

Lucia followed me blindly up a series of winding stone steps till we finally ended up in a turret-like room.

I pulled the gold handle of a heavy door expecting to find a secret passage or a long corridor. Instead it was a modern bedroom, the bed adorned with what looked like a child's clothes. We hastily made our exit save that we be accused of prowling or with intent to do harm. We laughed returning to the car.

"Where now?" I said to Lucia, still chuckling at the thought of a mad monk chasing us through the car park.

"Pienza," she said, enjoying her pronunciation.

As we drove on, Lucia went quiet. The countryside became even more beautiful, if that were possible. I felt like we were in the foothills, some artist drawing aimlessly, waiting for us to rise from the valley, to find the high mountains away in the distance.

"I think that's Mt. Amiata," Lucia said. Then she surprised me, as if the heat of the day was taking its toll. "You know, when you went for your op, remember I waved goodbye to you?"

"Jesus, yeah," I said, trying to be brave.

"Did you ever think we would make it here, Steve, ever?"

She was looking at the whistling countryside, the golden lush of straw. She was gazing at the unbroken lines of perfect small trees that railroaded the hills. She watched as goats and young horses grazed.

Capturing the sky, somehow it belonged to her. Far from the clinical atmosphere where she watched her husband wheeled down a long corridor to be greeted by eyes hidden by masks.

Where did she go the day I fell asleep? For the first time I asked myself, what did she do? What did she think?

Could she concentrate? Did she pray with the children? Maybe they all just sat round the dinner table as usual making small talk? I couldn't imagine it. All I could see was the darkness of my own slumber. The kind eyes behind the masks, female eyes doing their job. You know they freeze you for twelve hours somebody told me. They thaw you back to life slowly.

In effect you're really dead for all that time; a machine does everything for you. We by-passed Pienza for absolutely no reason other than we took a wrong turn. I was prone to do

135

this if Lucia was in any way fatigued herself and missed a road sign. "I often thought about it, if things turned out different," she said, studying her map. "I don't know," she continued, "they never allow for the effect of all this on families, it's like the patient is the focus, just lying there getting better, the body does what it does getting a little better every day, so you can walk two laps of the corridor. I remember the colour coming back to your face, I could see the whites of your eyes, the dreadful pale look gone," Lucia laughed, crumpling the map to indicate she had decided our route. "I would have told the children how kind you were, how I felt so safe with you, but what else? I dunno, you would have to write something down for me." I glanced at her, she brushed her fingers against my hand. I sensed her smile at me, her heat falling on my face. "Lets go to Bagno Vignoni." She said kindly, tidying the map on her lap.

Eva heard the car pull up; it came to a halt with a loud screech, sending gravel stones flying like bullets against the side of the house. She thought nothing of it at first. Then she heard voices shouting.

"My God!" she thought, getting dressed, "it's McCabe, Dwyer." Her father promised there would be no more. She knew Dwyer and McCabe were around, she saw their van earlier over by the barn.

She tried to steal a look out the side window on the landing but saw nothing in the dark. She heard Rusty bark and her father's voice pleading.

She moved cautiously down the narrow stairs leading to the parlour. Maybe it was the captain again and the army. That was all she could think.

She tried to steal a glimpse through the parlour door, but it was only slightly ajar. She listened.

A man with a strange accent was shouting, he told her father to be silent. She heard two strange voices. The one with the loudest voice did most of the talking.

136

"That boy told us nothin'. What da fuck, Mick Devlin, you makin' a mockery of the IRA. You tie up with fuckin' MI5. Fucked up our operations for fuckin' years round here."

Her father tried to speak in his defence, but the lesser voice screamed, "Shut the fuck up dont fuckin' speak. If you speak you will be shot." Her father went quiet. "We have McCabe in the barn. You just hope he tells us what we want to know because the boy wouldn't tell. So he'd better, you give us this fucker, Boyce, da you hear?"

This time Dwyer went to speak, but he too was drowned out with, "Shut the fuck up if you want to live."

Eva tried to remember where her father stored the gun. He hid it in different places it wasn't anywhere near her more than likely in the barn.

"I want the truth, Mick Devlin. You work for Boyce, right? You're an informer for the British. All three of you are informers, right? When are you due to meet him next? That's what I need to know. Tell me when, tell me where." The man's voice was louder than before.

Eva sat involuntarily on the floor; her legs given way with fright.

"I can ee tell you what I don't know," Mick Devlin blurted like a frightened child bullied by an overzealous teacher.

Eva heard other men enter the room. She heard the shuffle of feet and the creak of the door. Rusty stopped barking, she wondered why?

She had heard his constant yelp in the background like the grinding of a machine and then it stopped suddenly.

"McCabe has told on you, all of you. Anyone else here?" the man shouted.

"No, no, just us, just us. We wanted to report in..." Mick Devlin blurted.

"Shut the fuck up," the quieter voice said. Eva cowered, partially hidden by the soft couch that made the parlour respectable.

"I hear you have a daughter, where is your daughter?" The man's voice was even louder. Eva was sobbing now. She tried desperately to keep silent.

"We will find her. So tell us where the fuck she is!"

"Away, she is away in Belfast visiting her sick mother." Her father's words held terror.

Eva longed for somebody to comfort her and take away her fear.

The shots weren't loud. She barely heard them it was like somebody said "Psst," just a bit louder. She heard one, then another.

The parlour door swung full open. Dwyer, his face all red, fell forward cracking his head on the stone floor.

All she could see were flashes of light. Only the kitchen's dim light was on; the parlour was dark.

"Let's find the girl," the quieter voice said.

"No, fuck it. We're here too long let's get the fuck out."

She waited for a few minutes till there was no more sound save the old grandfather clock in the kitchen.

It ticked slowly before it chimed for midnight and then started ticking again. Eva eventually mustered all her strength and walked past the still body of Dwyer.

She winced as she saw the blood formed three different pools around his head. Her father was slumped against the wall, like he just sat down for a quick rest. There was a large hole in the centre of his temple. The blood was thick like stew; it came from the rear of his head, flowing down the whitewashed wall like lava.

Eva wanted to touch him and see whether there was still life in him though she knew he was dead. She had seen death three times before. He had that same grey look; it was almost like peace descended but with a look of surprise.

It was the expression of final acceptance, she saw it before also. His face showed anger – anger hopelessly defeated by acceptance.

She walked out to the yard. It was cold, the frost already settled on the windscreen of Dwyer's van. She walked a few paces calling, "Rusty, Rusty." She whistled him as well, her last call pathetic. "Russteee."

She found him slumped by the side of the barn, she could

tell he was gone. He lay motionless in the dark, black rivers running from underneath him.

Inside the barn by the light of the moon McCabe, his dark body strapped to the chair.

The glass on the ground made it useless to try turn the light on.

She closed the barn door out of habit.

When she phoned the priest it wasn't so much to ask him to come and help her, more to attend to the dead. Father Burdon arrived and was shocked. She could tell by the way his head shook slightly when he spoke. He kept all his questions and replies short.

Ordering her not to touch anything but to leave everything as it was. Turning off the kitchen light he coaxed her into his car. They drove down the meandering drive to the side road. It was the last time she ever saw the place.

Boyce told the corporal to call the police and let them tidy up.

Back in his quarters he prepared for bed. The knock was slight, just audible.

"Yeah?"

"The police have called in, sir."

"Yes, Corporal, what is it now?"

"They found another body, sir."

Boyce looked at the door, getting dressed all over again.

"Spit it out, Corporal." Boyce was having difficulty with his buttons.

"Our boys are checking for booby traps, sir. We can't go in till first light."

"Fine." Boyce started to undo his tunic once again. "Let me know when we can go in then, will you?" he said to the door.

"There's something you need to know, sir." The corporal felt foolish talking to wood.

Boyce, finally relenting, opened the door, half dressed. "What the blazes is it, Corporal? Spit it out. We may get a couple of hours' kip, hey?"

"They think it may be your informant, sir. The description matches. They can't be sure, obviously, till we can get close."

Boyce stared at the corporal for what must have appeared too long. The corporal moved uneasily, worried by his stare.

"Alright," said Boyce, finally shutting the door.

21.

The road to Bagno Vignoni winds uphill. Halfway up the hill on the left are car spaces; I parked tight between two vehicles.

Lucia led the way. A small park with kiddies' slides and small trees was silent across the road.

On the brow of the hill the old pits used in mining sunk into the cliff edge. Lucia was taken with the little trenches with tiny rivers of sulphuric water.

Some were full, others completely dry. Lucia peeping over the hill could see people down the cliff face. It was like something in Arizona: the rock formations, the scrub grass, twisting animal-carved tracks.

"Wonder what they're all at?" she said.

"I think they're swimming. There must be a pool down in the rocks," I replied.

"Jesus," she said, "how the hell do we get down there?"

I found the way. The path down-hill was treacherous, the small stones moving under our feet. In places it was very steep

We went sideways at times. I held her hand in case either of us slipped. At last we arrived at a tiny bridge.

On the other side about five people, ranging from the elderly to children, bathed. Once again I was worried about the water depth. The pool was long and narrow, vagrant water from above showered through the rock, filtering to the pool like relaxing bath water.

The pool filling a space which nature welded into the cliff, hidden at one point, to reveal a dead end with a platform of solid rock in an empty grotto. The water was completely green in colour, so I had no idea how deep it was.

A young woman swam along its middle. To my shock, when she stood the water barely reached her thighs. She then leaned over placing her arms 'neath the surface.

The young woman, pretending not to notice us, raised her hands; they were soiled with muck from the ground below. She smeared it all over her face like a face cream.

She turned green in an instant. "How interesting," Lucia said. God, I thought, who needs face packs?

Lucia, taking off her shoes and socks, waded in, encouraging me to do likewise. Reluctantly and still not trusting the depth of the water, I waded in. The bottom was slippy. It was akin to trying to skate on ice for the first time.

Lucia, touching the bottom, getting clay on her hands, making sure not to get her top wet.

"Pity we didn't know," I said. "We could have brought our swimsuits."

"Yeah," she agreed, as more people arrived and were as surprised as ourselves to find the little oasis.

Lucia insisted on photos as soon as I had dried my feet.

A beautiful specimen of Italian teenagehood was hovering in and out of the pool. She was beautiful in her darkness; her skin breathed the shine of youth. She was still childless, perfect, her buttocks looking pert and strong through her one-piece swimsuit.

It was morphine to the spirit to watch as she covered herself with the sulphuric water allowing its green slime to enter the pores of her dark perfect skin.

She washed away, smiling towards the heavens, wondering at the sky she descended from.

"Try one of me here," Lucia said, she used the grotto as background.

Soon we made our ascent, slipping and sliding once again. I expected to see snakes, as if snakes belonged in such terrain.

We reached the top, by the old stone pits, exhausted.

"Let's have a drink," Lucia said.

I knew she meant water. The bar was clean with modern wooden furniture. The girl who served was friendly and very efficient. We both ordered spring water with gas and ice. I asked the bar girl whether I could look upstairs. On this level was a gallery-type structure with handrails. It had only a few tables, the walls were adorned with pictures of the jazz musicians who played there over the years.

To be honest, I didn't recognize any of them. The pictures were good, so I had a look at all of them along with any curios that came my way.

We stepped outside, refreshed after our arduous climb and strolled down towards the centre of the village. We passed a civic policewoman giving advice to a bemused tourist.

The village soon changed from the modern façade to the old world as we reached its centre. This was Bagno Vignoni. The whole square was walled, the interior a hot spring.

We could actually see the sulphuric bubbles as the gases burst from the centre of the earth. The spring was divided in two by a walkway. There was a small oratory, it gave the place an ease as if the saints held vigil to uphold its peace. On the opposite side were several small restaurants and a glamorous hotel. Further on were some small bric-a-brac souvenir shops.

Lucia took photos of me with the bubbling water in the background. She marveled at everything around her. This was where St Caterina of Siena bathed in the warm sacred waters of Bagno Vignoni. I saw her stand, the waters dark, cooled by time its ripples touched her skin. Anointing her forehead she saw me, her skin fresh and white. Smiling, pointing to her breast, pure water filtered through the fibres of her peasant clothes. Lucia disturbed me wondering did we need more spring water for the car. I left St Caterina to bathe with the spirits thinking of Lucia who walked ahead.

I liked the way Lucia asked whether we could stop for water every so often. She acquired a childish plea to her voice. It wasn't the first time I felt she was childlike. I knew in some way a childish innocence still dwelt within her.

At times it unsettled me and made me feel guilty or wrongly gifted with power. Yet in the main I found it to be her most attractive quality, that and her sense of justice.

She was, despite her maturity into womanhood and motherhood, still unaware of the dark ways of the world around her. She was a visualizer too, in some ways even more so than me. Little things like ladybirds, plants, the softness of animals, pleased her and gripped her senses. She was brave, waiting to see if her husband thawed from the cold; waiting to adjust, to amend, maybe struggle on without him if she needed to; wondering if nature was going to bite her, to take her down in the fields of golden corn.

Her spirit was part of the reason she could rise again, forage for new, fly against the hardest of breezes to protect her nest.

She was one with St Caterina, bathing in the green waters of Bagno Vignoni.

The cold inside him made him shiver. He never felt cold like it, the morning air was devouring his organs. He moved slowly like he needed a hip replacement. The troops lined up on either side, some in the ditch. Watching their young faces painted with ridiculous markings.

They were in awe of him, these ferocious fighting men.

The corporal walked back slowly, afraid of slipping and looking foolish.

"Well," Boyce asked breathing steam.

"They're nearly done, sir. Ten minutes maybe." The corporal spoke slowly, like in some computer space movie.

"Just keep the fuckin' priest away!" Boyce noticed Burdon's car, the soldiers keeping him well back. He promised himself he wouldn't look around again. The Jesus-like figure was shouting abuse up the tiny dirt road. Boyce could barely make him out.

"Murderers!"

The corporal was waiting further instruction. "We will wait till the bomb disposals are finished. Have your men secure the area, Corporal," Boyce said disinterested.

"Yes, sir," said the delighted corporal.

"Yes, Corporal. When we do move in, keep Paddy Priest back beyond the cordon."

Boyce gave his junior a cold look, as if to say, "Do you think you can manage that?"

As they moved forward Boyce stayed about third in line. He knew a sniper would always target the first, it was business after all. The body face down, naked, arms outstretched with burn marks on both wrists.

Blood clotted just below the hairline. "The cold," Boyce thought. "He probably bled like a pig."

It matted his curls straight with damp and tiny specks of ice.

There were marks on his shoulders between his shoulder blades like he was beaten with some implement.

"Will we turn him over or leave it to the police?" the corporal asked.

"Turn him over," the captain commanded.

The corporal did, using his boot. Boyce stared at Rock, his face grey with hints of blue.

Loose chips from the road surface stuck to white frost felted on his forehead. His left eye was shut his right hung from its socket like a worm dangles on a hook.

The body resting on its back, his eye slotted neatly to one side almost out of view.

The sides of his jaw were smashed. His mouth was fast shut like some prankster had used superglue. The round of his neck was cut deep like slashed with a knife. Boyce knew they were rope marks.

Down further, his nipples were stretched. Someone had pulled them with pliers.

His genitals were kicked, smashed till they resembled rotted fruit.

Boyce tried to stay calm, examining Rock's face to see what sort of sentiment death had bestowed on him. There was nothing, only death.

Walking back, a few officers from the constabulary mocked, "Another good day's work, hey, Captain?"

145

He ignored them.

In the distance all he could hear was that damned priest screaming, "Murderer." Burdon was joined by a swelling crowd from the village. The noise grew louder and louder as the patrol drove through them. They were beating the sides of the armoured cars with their fists.

Eva didn't know what to make of it at first. It should have hurt, yet it didn't. She wasn't sure if she really understood it. Was it a good thing or a bad thing?

The priest thought it was a good thing when he was doing it. Yet afterwards he sat on the corner of the bed and cried. Then he got to his knees and prayed fervently to God, asking for forgiveness.

He had taken her to his house and served her tea, piping hot with lots of sugar.

After a while the trembling stopped. He had loaned her a jumper as her whole body was shivering.

Soon he too got cold and went searching for another jumper. Eva only managed to pack a few things in an old bag. There was nothing warm, not even a coat.

Father Burdon told her not to worry; he would look after things. As soon as she finished her tea he would show her the spare room.

When he returned she could tell the jumper he wore was years old. It was too small for him and had holes under the arms. She offered to swap; he wouldn't hear of it. He made her drink her tea and patted her on the head gently.

He asked her if she was hungry, offering to make scrambled eggs. She refused, saying food would only turn her stomach. She was too tired for anything. Farther Burdon brought her up the narrow staircase to the spare room.

He turned on an electric blow heater and told her to turn it down if she felt too hot.

Soon Eva lay under the blankets, leaving her underwear on. Even with the blow heater, it was still cold.

After a while she heard him go to bed. His door shut quietly; it had a kind of click sound that pierced the darkness.

She tried to sleep, tossing and turning, switching off the blow heater because of the noise it made. Eva tried to make out shapes in her new surroundings. There were street lamps outside. She was wondering what she would do. She probably had only one change of clothes; her father was dead; her mother maybe dead too.

She felt the tears brew inside her. A sense of panic had taken hold of her whole spirit so often recently. What had she done? Three times she put those boys out of their misery, saved her father, saved herself; three times she had answered their screams for help.

Was God punishing her now? Was this God's revenge?

Had he come in the middle of the night to get her, to punish her, to put her out of her misery?

The door opened. It was a smooth door and barely made a sound.

"Are you alright, Eva? I thought I heard you stir."

"Yes, Father Burdon, I was havin' a bad dream." Eva lied.

He walked over, the floorboards creaking softly. "I can't say how sorry I am for you, child. I have known you since you were a wee girl."

"I know, Father. If it wasn't for you, we'd have nobody."

She tried to sound grown up. She felt his hand pat her forehead and liked the warm rustic feel of it.

"I was thinkin' about those boys. My Daddy couldn't do it. I tried to help him. I swear, Father, those boys, they were half killed already. They were beggin' to be killed."

"Ssh Ssh," said the priest, "we will not talk of it now, not this night."

Eva wondered whether she should tell him about her dreams, those little daydreams where she would marry him.

She thought not. She could sense a difference in him, like he wanted to say something to her but was afraid.

"I think maybe you and I can get out of here; maybe we will!" Father Burdon said cheerfully. "I have a friend in France; I will give him a call and see if he will take us in for awhile."

"France! My teacher, he goes on about France. He says it's much bigger than this wee place." She moved her head so his stroking covered the width of her forehead.

"Aye France is bigger, even bigger than England."

"Bigger then England?" Eva whispered as if she couldn't believe it.

She felt him move closer as if he was tired and wanted to lie down for awhile, she wondered whether she should move and make room for him.

His breath was upon her. It wasn't foul like most men who bent over her like the Doctor on a visit.

It was sweet, fresh. She felt the soft bristle of his stubble brush faintly against her skin; it tickled. She giggled, she wanted to ask him what he was up to, then she felt his lips against hers. At first she was frightened as if she was been sucked up by a mad Hoover.

It felt soft as he dragged her lips towards him.

She felt he was trying to fit into the small space left beside her. Sure he would fall to the floor, she moved to allow him more room.

His tongue wet her lips. Touching her flat tummy his hand with gentle strokes. Removing her underwear, she was suddenly exposed.

He lifted himself to his knees. She could just make out his face in the dark. Filling her he cried out as he went, "Haw-haw."

She lay still as if in wonder of what this fullness was. When he finished he stared at her, shadows from the street lamp changed his face till he looked young. Eva saw the eyes of a boy. Father Burdon was still, tears streaming, raindrops draining along the softness of his face.

22.

I remember the day I first told Lucia about the pain in my throat. I can still see her eyes going dead as if she didn't want to hear.

"What kind of pain?"

"Dunno. It's like it's hot all the time."

"You had better see a doctor."

"I'll be fine; it's nothing."

Sometimes it would burn me bad. I would lie down for awhile, maybe sleep and it went away.

Funny all the time in hospital it never burned at all. If anything, I just looked really tired with huge bags under my eyes. Couldn't sleep in the ward; the nurse used to flash her light into my face.

I would give her the thumbs up. The young nurse walked away exasperated at my lack of sleep.

Hospital is akin to being in prison. Early morning call, a light breakfast, a few minutes to shave and wash. Then the consultants, followed by a team of white coats.

The worse thing about public hospitals in Ireland is the complete lack of privacy.

The consultants as usual bark out their questions in earshot of everybody else in the room like pulling the curtains makes for privacy!

"So how are we today?"

Everyone answers, "Fine."

The poor old consultant is addressing one patient.

You await your turn. As if uninterested you pretend to read

the newspaper or a book. The consultants arrive with their entourage.

They were very nice, I'd have to admit not in the least stereotypical, as in condescending.

I had a laugh with them. It was like they were the friendly guards in a prison camp.

One particular man who was near retirement used to challenge me intellectually like he wanted to check that my spirit was still intact.

He held his stethoscope against my heart, asking me was it alright for his juniors to have a listen.

I don't know how he'd have taken it if I'd refused. Heck, we all have to learn.

So now he said, "What do you hear?"

One young bright spark volunteered, "The heart beat is too fast."

Another would act dumb as if they hadn't heard anything at all, which concerned me as much as the consultant.

"No, no, there is something very important here that you are missing."

His students looked at him blankly; the shadow nurse was shushing the other patients.

I felt like saying, "My heart is beating so fast it's like John Wayne riding into the sunset," quoting the consultant from the previous day.

"The third beat," the consultant said at last "You must listen for the third beat."

He thanked me for my patience, which is sort of weird when you are a patient.

Marching off he said to his senior registrar, "Think we will find heart disease there as soon as we do the..."

I interrupted, his senior almost angry that I had spoken. This guy read my notes aloud, in a manner not unlike a fellow in first class at school.

"Sorry, did you say I have heart disease?"

"Supposition," the consultant said, unconvincingly. "Supposition."

Trying to stay calm, I said, "That's ok then."

The consultant gave me a wry smile as the small party left the ward.

It was so different in the private hospital. My own room, a shower and a nice view out the window.

The registrar was very direct. "If we hadn't found you perhaps you may not have made it to the hospital."

The anaesthetist was even more comforting, going on about the contusions in my brain like I had minor strokes, yet the bypass was more urgent. Wonder how Lucia didn't pass out with the shock.

They were only short of saying I was fucked, lucky not to be more fucked, I didn't realise how lucky I was.

They sent this kid up to shave me. He was like something out of The Munster's; it was like the great undead met the very soon to be dead for some sort of shaving fetish.

I digress. My children came to see me the night before my operation. I felt like I was on death row. I expected somebody to shout, "Dead man walking," at any second. They were nervous, brave, uneasy at seeing their dad so sick.

I didn't know what to say. We watched TV. I remember laughing at Jennifer Aniston in Friends; it chilled us all out.

Amanda left first, kissing me softly on the cheek. I had seen a kiss just like it once before, I couldn't remember when.

James, trying to be manly, waited till last.

"Well, Dad, you will get through," he said bravely.

"Yeah, I know." I lay back on the hard pillow, feeling tired. "But you'll take care of things for me if anything goes wrong, wont you?"

"I won't let you down," he tried to disguise the shake in his voice.

"Is your mother coming back up?"

"Yeah, she is."

I will see you when this is all done, OK? So...," I could not say more. I hugged him somehow not getting emotional; nor did he, having composed himself.

Lucia was upbeat. "I will be in early before you go down just to be here with you, Steve."

If she was emotional she didn't show it. I guess, like all of us, she knew what had to be done. "Dead man walking."

As I drifted to sleep I remembered where I had seen a kiss so soft, so measured, with so much love.

Years before, my father laid out in his coffin, his time capsule to another world. My older brother placed his fingers round his forehead gently stroking his pale blue skin. My sister leaned across kissing my father's right cheek. I knew even though he was dead he had to feel that kiss; it allowed him pass through the universe into never-ending space, his heart at peace.

Marie Abele put the phone down looking directly at Argüelles. "This is madness," he said. "They will never agree."

"What do you suggest then, old loyal friend?" Argüelles said sarcastically.

"I dunno." Marie Abele looked pleadingly at Drozdan, who watched like a barn owl.

He picked up the phone once more and dialled, speaking only for a minute.

"Well," said Argüelles,

"Father Cryan says he will consider it but ultimately it's not his decision."

Marie Abele sat down looking at the automatic Argüelles gave him. It lay harmlessly on the table.

"I think you will have to persuade your curate, Abele. After all you are his parish priest." This time it was Drozdan who intervened,

"I have no jurisdiction in Italy, Your Grace. Perhaps you could intervene; my gut feeling is they might refuse even you,"

Marie Abele was better when he felt cornered; his bluntness was covered in sincerity.

"I doubt if Your Grace wants to import your problem Abele. If you refuse, or cannot accept our request, we will view you as a traitor. We have other sources in Viaréggio. I am sure they can help us."

"What is it, Abele? Have you not the stomach for it? Come

on, you're the man whose indiscretion led to the deaths of the three main leaders of Sodality. What do you take us for?" said Argüelles. He was on his feet pacing the room, speaking only in angry short bursts.

"Edgell left us very graphic notes in his files. It was his worry Father Abele you were indiscreet perhaps when Don Dino spent some months in Cucuron. Is that the case?" Drozdan asked quietly.

"Monsignor Argüelles's tone disturbs me, Your Grace. I have never killed a man, whether or not he was my enemy. I was compliant with Cardinal Edgell. I am as loyal a servant to Sodality as anyone. I have great difficulty accepting criticisms from some jumped up—"

"Now, now, gentlemen, please!" Drozdan said as Argüelles went to confront Abele. "Be seated," he said almost sadly to Argüelles.

The Monsignor obeyed, giving Abele a growling look.

"I don't think we can count on your loyalty—not in the light of the serious doubts Cardinal Edgell had about you, Father Abele. You know the rules Sodality has. No middle ground. Our cause is too important, too vital."

Drozdan tried to sound self righteous, yet compassionate. Argüelles smiled mockingly at Abele.

"Your Grace, surely I am not to be tried and convicted on the basis of suspicion. Of course it is a matter of historical record that Don Dino spent some months in Cucuron after the death of his son. I was present at the meeting with Don Dino six months later. At no time did Cardinal Edgell ever indicate to me he had reservations about my loyalty; the opposite is the case. I was to keep minutes and observe the others. If he was worried about anybody, it was Fucilla!"

Argüelles looked at the Cardinal, as if eagerly awaiting his reply. Drozdan, whose head was bent low over the table, now looked up slowly to square up to Abele.

"The parish priest of Cucuron doubts me, a Cardinal, the leader of Sodality?

Abele, you have been given a chance to prove your loyalty,

to show us that we have misinterpreted Edgell's notes. You put obstacles in our way. Tell us you cannot comply with our requests. What is it you want me to do? Send you back? Let you retire, go out to pasture and live out your days knowing all you know yet not willing to be complicit yourself? Talk sense, man." Drozdan banged the table for effect.

Argüelles eyed the Frenchman gleefully.

"Your Grace, I beg your forgiveness. It was not my intention not to comply with your wishes. I was merely pointing out the difficulty in implementation."

Abele went to stand; when he did his true frailty was exposed. His back was hunched and his head bald with a red rash like psoriasis.

"I will take the weapon you supplied, Monsignor Argüelles. I will comply with your request. It must be done. I wish you both a good day. I will report to you when I have carried out your bidding."

Abele gave Argüelles a dull look, like nothing else mattered anymore.

Abele stood facing the bathroom mirror. His suite was of the highest quality. He slept for an hour comfortably, his thoughts were not as laboured as earlier; gone was the disappointment, that awful feeling of time wasted. He smiled; the mirror smiled back, he made a lot of money out of Sodality. The money was still there; it gained interest for over thirty years.

He could go to America. It was the place to go; a person could disappear easily there.

Yet no matter how hard he tried he could not visualize himself walking alone along a deserted beach. Drozdan would see his reputation was ruined, a wasted career, his parishioners whispering behind closed doors, their parish priest a fraud.

Walking was difficult now. With his arthritis getting worse, he was destined to become a bent old man. The face in the mirror was sad now.

Abele reached for a Kleenex to dry his eyes; the tissue stuck in the hollow of his face.

What was it bothered him most? The thoughts of one indiscretion causing the death of his colleagues.

There was so much more to that chain of events, so much more than he was responsible for. Don Dino did the despicable act out of his lust for revenge.

It was Father Burdon who told the Mafiosi. Why did he betray the one man who allowed him to stay incognito, allowing the girl to carry her child? Marie Abele never passed on the information to Rome, he just wanted to control Burdon, he never betrayed them.

The sad face in the mirror had enough. The man who looked back at him didn't belong in the world of Argüelles, Drozdan, or even Edgell.

These fanatics were against the teaching of Jesus Christ; their views were even more perverse than Fr Cryan and his liberation theology. No, the money could serve the poor, do some good; he had willed it that way. Marie Abele took the automatic that Argüelles so mockingly handed him hours earlier.

It was ridiculous to watch it against the side of his temple.

He wondered whether he would see blood flow like in the movies. Would it splash all over the mirror glass?

Abele squeezed the trigger.

His body crumpled in an instant like a folding deck chair and slumped hard against the well-crafted tiles. The blood formed two distinct small rivers, one under the wash basin, the other to the base of the toilet bowl.

23.

I remember nothing of when I was dead. I think that bothers me.

I came back to the real world with nothing to report.

Hardly worth being dead at all.

When I woke, the night nurse said soothingly, "You made it, Stephen. You did great."

A few hours later I was sitting upright in a chair.

They transferred me back to my room propping me upright; the chair had a sort of wide feel to it.

It felt like I'd been attacked by thugs and left for dead. I had this wounded feeling.

I lay back, thinking I was reincarnated as Jesus Christ.

Earlier they removed the drains from my chest. The nurse told me not to look, a little like telling a child not to touch the ice-cream. God allowed me to peep at the core of my being.

To see your blood vessels, the living insides of you, float like dark liquid then solidify into the green tartar of a dormant volcanic crater.

They left little marks on both my right and left side—reminders of life's pitiless centurion. Each day I got a little stronger, they eventually put me back to bed.

Later the nurse took the catheter out of the head of my penis. I got daily injections in my tummy; it was like being stabbed every evening at eight o' clock.

I had to take Warfarin tablets due to the diagnosis of a tiny clot in the lung.

Two green, one blue, or one blue, a yellow, two green. Can't really remember. All that's clear was it made for an extra three days in hospital as my "INR." didn't stabilize.

I became a total expert on my medical condition at the time, Lucia even more so.

She read the 'How to Recover from Heart Bypass.' book backwards. She practiced her cooking for a dietary diabetic with the zeal of Delia Smyth.

Women in general aren't impressed with illness.

Don't get me wrong. It's not that I think they don't sympathize. In general they do.

It's just when you show them the missing artery from your arm or mention dietary diabetes, they sort of freak.

It's like a whole set of church bells ringing in their heads. They can see the undertaker arrive.

I don't think they ever think about the insurance, more the terrifying prospect of having to nurse a sick husband or partner.

This goes back to when we lived in the trees. If the monkey got sick, he was kicked out and replaced by some able-bodied monkey.

Yet, as I say all this to myself I have to be honest, when you catch the concern and indeed sometimes the visible pain on the waiting wife or girlfriend's face, it is impossible to justify such a comment.

I suppose a part of me thinks it's just down to the deep deliberation taking place, the web of female intrigue, should I look for someone else or what?

Still I am sure my musings are being affected by the daily cocktail of drugs I consume. However I only needed to take the rat poison for three months, much to the relief of Lucia and those closest to me during my recovery, as I became a real big pain in the ass.

I suppose I was always afraid of death and dying. I lost my father quite suddenly when I was just a kid.

I had only ever been in hospital to visit him. Then once, years later, I was in hospital for a hernia operation. I was twenty years old then.

Visiting my dad was a sort of ritual guilt thing: a thirteen-year-old who opts for walking up the cold steps of Mercers hospital on a bright summer's day.

My father was in a ward with about twenty men, all laid out with legs in steel braces or asleep buried under blankets. It was like something you would see in a military hospital in World War I.

My dad, forever cheerful, was popular with his fellow patients and the nurses.

I watched the man in the bed next to him. He looked too old to have the children who played cards with him. The boy was ten, maybe eleven, the girl was eight. They played snap and some other game I didn't know. This was their ritual. They rarely spoke; they just laughed or smiled when somebody got the upper hand.

The greying man sat astride on his bed, his dressing gown faded in colour from age.

Dad stayed there at least twice. I can't remember if these people were there on his first or second stay.

Anyhow one day I climbed the cold steps. The strong sun was warming the pavement outside. Dad was subdued; there was a curtain drawn round the bed beside him. He told us the man had died the night before; the nurses had been upset and crying.

My God, I thought, what about his children? Who will they play cards with now?

I had no concept of death or illness or anything else, my fixations were firmly planted in the mundane world of a young boy.

When I had my hernia I was sure I was in the same ward as the one my father eventually died in.

This was our local hospital in Dun Laoghaire. Somehow it played on my mind, this was a place of death. I lost it, even at twenty years old. Hospital where people die, I knew for the first time how fickle my life was.

Gardiner watched as the man walked from the bar looking perplexed, searching up and down the street.

How odd, Gardiner thought. It's like he has lost somebody.

Gardiner wanted to walk the cycle lane along the length of the prom. The constant ringing of bells, shouts in gruff Italian, forced him to join the throngs of people walking the prom properly.

He decided to walk as far as the harbour and see what the place was like.

The walk took him by numerous secret entrances to the beach. He passed the gelaterie and fashion stores till it opened up into a kind of square. As he made progress the stores and bars got more numerous.

This was the older part of the town. The harbour itself was surprisingly long with little marinas dotting the centre. He sat to rest his legs when Bateman rang.

Gardiner had a little difficulty hearing above the summer wind until he switched the phone to his left ear. So he started his conversation with "Who," and got, "Bateman, you prick," in reply.

"Joe?" Gardiner said laughing; he could hear him better now.

"Where the goddamn hell are you? Out floatin' in the ocean? I can feel the wind blowin' from here."

"Hold on, Joe," Gardiner said turning towards the harbourside eateries and stores.

"Yeah that's better Steve, got you now, loud and clear. I got nothin' from the CIA on these pricks, Quinn and Kellerman.

They are so deep under cover Steve they don't exist. Either that or you got them all wrong, my friend, they ain't work-in' for the goddamn agency at all,"

"You're talking shit, Joe. They came through your office looking for me," Gardiner said, trying to sound as tough as he possibly could.

"Steve, I am telling you my old pal, these fuckers aren't CIA. I checked and double-checked, you got that?"

"Well who the fuck are they, Joe? Where the fuck are they? These guys have been contacting me for a year. My bank account is full of money. Hey, so what's going on?"

Bateman was quiet for a second, as if he was trying to compose his words.

"These two fuckers are FBI, not CIA. That's as far as I get."

"FBI?" Gardiner sounded worried.

"Steve, these guys have taken you for a ride. If I was you I would make contact with them and find out what the fuck they're up to. Ok, got to go. My mistress wants to get back with me, I just had my ex-wife send me a note wanting to try all over again. Can you believe the shit, Gardiner? Of all the motherfuckin' things to happen!" Bateman was gone.

She sat in the same deck chair, under the same parasol.

Susie had Shaun with her but not Marsha. Gardiner waited for her to move. She walked upright, her firm buttocks barely hidden. She sensed his eyes trained on her. Rodent like, her nose, faded features, tanned skin all over, she used a sun bed. He didn't look away as Shaun ran the boardwalk to greet her.

She must have wondered why he was alone, the wash spraying his head, surf shampoo lingering down the bend of his back. Susie knew he was eyeing her, choosing her.

At times he saw children play with Shaun, little boys with names like Alessandro.

Susie saw them reel in small fish, put them in plastic buckets. Alessandro shouts,

"Ne abbiamo preso uno." Older boys fix the rod. A young girl watches them, she is abandoned, careless.

Gardiner saw Susie at dinner, where the fat waiter tried to be upmarket. He watched her on the roof top terrace, where she was abandoned also.

Nightlight, endless neon reflecting dreamlike ice-cream, he sat sipping gin, talking to waitresses with names like "Petra." Lost city, rivers flow, thousands of them. Turn, stare, dark dress, shoulders bare, shaped in a light of her making.

Everywhere he hears Italian. Small hoarse voices shout to parents. Another wave of surf knocks him over. Gardiner catches warm air. He spies Susie, she is avoiding him. Rat like Susie walks upright, she is lost in the brilliant light.

Boyce got tired of waiting for Philippe to come back. He drank all the malt. He was worried because he only felt tipsy when he should have been drunk.

Walking out into the warm air didn't have any effect either. He just felt the heat hover over his bald spot determined to give him an instant shine.

Boyce looked all round him. Up and down, the prom was full of tourists, locals going about their business.

'The idiot must have forgotten me,' Boyce thought, finding the idea half amusing. There was nothing for it but to return to his hotel room to report in. Then an instinctive nervousness swept over him.

What was Philippe up to? Had he set up a double cross? Maybe the henchmen followed him now, waiting to pounce.

He looked over his shoulder. His hotel was close by, less than a two minute walk. Nobody would try anything silly midst the crowds. Still, his training flooding his brain, keep walking quickly, not too fast as to attract attention; stay with the crowd; don't become isolated.

Back in his hotel room he dialled Argüelles; the phone rang for a minute before the Spaniard spoke.

"It is you, Boyce?"

Boyce related the story about Philippe.

Argüelles taking it in his stride said,

"It is of no importance. I would suggest he has got cold feet or at least Don Maestrino has taken steps to protect his son. I don't see them being any threat to our security. We still have you, our main man."

Argüelles sounded very pleased with himself. Boyce thought for a second, his experience taught him to sense danger; he sensed it now.

However it was not in his interest to impart his fear to

Argüelles. The monsignor was a pompous idiot; he would only make a mockery of him. Perhaps the whole deal would be cancelled, leading to a complete waste of Boyce's time, with of course the thought of no pay day critical.

"We proceed, that is my advice," Boyce said sternly. "I will go to Volterra in the morning early, as planned."

"Yes Mr Boyce. This is what we want you to do."

"I cannot take responsibility for any action against Don Dino as Philippe has lost contact. It makes my mission more dangerous."

Boyce chose to be matter of fact, in an effort to confuse Argüelles, who replied straight away,

"This is why we picked you, Mr Boyce. You came with the highest of recommendation. It is important you make sure our business in Volterra is completed. We cannot rely on our French priest. You were always the ace in the pack. We will deal with the woman and Don Dino later. I accept you are only one, I will consult with the Cardinal and see how best we can assist you. Contact us from there."

"Indeed, Monsignor."

Boyce ended the call. He didn't like Argüelles, or the men of the cloth in general. He reckoned it all stemmed back to that bastard priest Burdon.

He went to the mini-bar; they had only one small bottle of malt which would never be enough. He drank it anyway, before calling room service.

Gardiner dazzled at night. The flow ringing of bells, scooters drone. Happy train passes, children wave. Women of good stock go eat with well dressed young men. This was his once, his time with Susie; she is now with a portly man who is rich, smokes cigars.

Faded, the young waitress who brings him his cheque. She is flirting with him. Dark skinned youths sell him flowers even though he is alone. Back lanes are ordered with bicycles, lovers aloft ride by him.

Susie blows thick smoke over her head, she hides behind it.

Gardiner notices she is not pretty, just has a good body. Lines of people joining hands walk the prom, this is Viaréggio.

In daylight wash turns to dead water makes Heidi Heisler, careless abandoned. He reaches for Shaun, but she sees him. Gardiner reaches into the fire, feels his heart, nurse tells him not to look but he does.

Viaréggio waves recede who is alone careless. Gardiner talks to Romanian waitresses, he eats chocolate ice-cream from the gelateria, talks business with fat owners.

The crowds flock all is normal. His heart needs Lipitor, wakes with Aspirin, and EMCOR. Thousands, all centurions, bronzed gold, litter the golden sand, his eyes bought by decomposition.

24.

The day before my hernia operation they brought this American guy in. He robbed a local bank using a stolen car and a water pistol.

When the cops gave chase they shot out the tires of the car, he busted his leg in the crash. So he was under twenty-four-hour guard.

Personally I liked the guy, he attempted the whole escapade to fund his wedding to a girl he only met a couple of days earlier.

I think his parents sent him to stay with relations in Kerry. He flipped, stole the car, and drove to Dun Laoghaire.

If anything it distracted me from thinking about the ward and my dad.

I suppose, like all matters of the mind, it doesn't pay to dwell.

I still think it was cool to wake up and not be dead. To tell the truth, I think I was more scared the first time than the second, even though a hernia operation is a piece of cake compared to a heart bypass.

Strange, it's like the age you're at is relative to the level of your anxiety. There is a correlation between age and the impending sense of doom.

I suppose its one thing to die aged seventy-five having lived and done what you had to do as they say, another to die young, or even when your kids are young.

My dad died when he was fifty-two, leaving a young family the youngest only eight years old.

Lucia never really got to grips with my past. She had her own issues, though her parents were still alive and healthy.

Her mother had suffered from depression most of her life, Lucia didn't inherit the gene; sadly one of her brothers did.

Sitting up nights comforting one another, hey she would probably contend I never got to grips with her life as a child either.

Who can honestly say they are capable of wearing someone else's shoes especially when they are young shoes?

The world is different for a child. It all appears in black and white, good and bad; there is no middle ground.

Childhood is an unquenchable thirst for all things pleasurable. When we become adults, we tend to replace this with alcohol, drugs, or sex—not necessarily in that order.

I suppose maybe that's why we end up disappointed. We must stimulate the physical senses rather than the visual or the simplistic.

I am unfair to women in this regard as I always reckoned they had the upper hand being the hunted, men the hunters getting the raw deal and dying younger.

Women contend that men at least have the ability to evade the isolation and loneliness they feel. How many eligible women spend their evenings watching soppy soaps on television with a sleeping infant upstairs?

How many are propped up on sofa pillows downing copious glasses of red wine with a bitter taste in their mouths?

Of course, the answer to all ills is marriage, the great producer of children, of respectability, status, and normality.

Maybe at one time in social history it made real sense. It grounded men and I suppose it made women feel safe.

Nowadays I think it's more of a business arrangement, like two financiers meeting up every now and again to make sure the mortgage is paid. Each time a little more procreation takes place.

For what? To provide a safe haven for the off spring, a good education, and a nice piece of real estate to leave when you die.

Anyway I preferred being a kid over being an adult.

I never expected either of my parents to have any physical, personal, or psychological desires outside of me and my next meal, the way to go or what!

Lucia rubbed sun cream all over her legs and arms; I did her shoulders. They were burning red.

I told her to mind herself, thinking of sleepless nights or wasted afternoons.

"Yes, Daddy," she teased. She lay back under her brolly. The pool was attractive in a freezer-like fashion.

The birds were dive-bombing, picking minute drops of water with imaginary fingers.

Suddenly without warning I decided to leave Lucia.

I had no intention of physically removing myself from our marriage, upsetting our children, her parents, my mother, and so on.

I just decided to remove my heart from her. There wasn't and still isn't any intention of replacing her with either an older or younger model.

No, I was making a last stand against living, life in general; this is what heart bypass surgery does to your brain, makes you want to be alone.

"Philippe, you are my son I love you with all my heart you must tell Don Dino all these plans. This man Boyce, he goes to Volterra to kill what is essentially the Don's flesh and blood. Don't you see how you must help us stop this?" Don Maestrino implored Philippe, who sat like a spoiled child at the opposite end of the room.

Both Gregor and Raymond stood close watching him.

Philippe stared at Don Dino, who had taken position on the old piano stool.

Don Dino could see that youthful vigour present in Philippe's eyes. It was foolish, yet Don Dino half understood it.

The boy felt cheated, humiliated, abducted by his own, brought to the house of his father's mortal enemy.

The boy was stubborn; he would have to see sense.

"Philippe," Don Maestrino said once again.

Don Dino shook his head politely.

"My son Benedetto is dead over thirty years." Don Dino said to Philippe, who stared at the floor. "He is dead because I failed in my duty to protect him; his wife and my grandson. What does that make me, Philippe? I am an old man now, admiring the vine. Every day I cry for my son. When your father came to me, I was suspicious. We are sworn enemies since we were children in Volterra.

Don Maestrino tells me he is worried for his only son. I say to Gregor, what shall I do? My enemy is here. If only we could turn back the clock.

If I had asked your father for help? Maybe together we could have stopped those bastards from Rome."

Don Dino stood, turning his back on the ensemble to dry his eyes. He turned back to his audience slowly, saying,

"I will make an offer to you, Philippe Giordano. I will plead with your father to release you. It will be your choice. This is, I think, fair? Philippe, is this a fair choice, hey?"

Philippe, looking defiantly at the Don, said, "Yes, Don Dino."

The Don sat down again on his piano stool. "Philippe is free to leave at any time. He has a choice; let him decide."

"What are my choices, Don Dino?" Philippe said suspiciously.

"You can contact your friends in Rome, help them. Or you can assist us, the two greatest families in Toscana." Don Dino looked kindly at his old enemy.

"Your reward Philippe will be honour. Your choice, Philippe!" Gregor opened the door that led to the terrace exit. "Gregor will drive you wherever you want to go. I warn you, Philippe," Don Dino continued softly.

Philippe went to stand, looking at his father and Raymond who were passive as if they didn't quite understand what was going on, "If you go, you will no longer enjoy the protection of our families. I think Don Maestrino will agree." Don Maestrino stood staring at Philippe in a way that unnerved the younger man. "Walk through the door Philippe; you will never come back to me."

The old man showed no trace of emotion. Philippe moved silently to the door.

Boyce couldn't understand himself, another hectic day planned. He succumbed to another bottle of malt. Swallowing the dregs of the bottle, the last drop catching his throat.

He rushed to the toilet where he got physically sick, the vomit filling the basin.

It missed the drain and filled up round the edges and onto the taps, soiling his hand as he tried to clean.

Running the bath water he changed his mind and sat on the toilet, kicking away his underclothes.

His waste was mixed with dark clots, the black he knew was blood; he vomited again, this time onto the floor, over the clothes he just discarded. Boyce started to cry; his body was now his tormenter. After half an hour he suddenly felt relief. As his body relaxed he felt the fullness of fatigue.

In the fields, soldiers crawled, sometimes they rested their heads on hard cow pats. Boyce smiled at the image, fighting men living in rotten ditches. The fields belonged to the ancients' drumlins with hideous hedgerows, mock boundaries. The rain lashing against his face, always cold at first, then warm. Over the hill Mick Devlins farm, tossed mud fields half ploughed, crows darkly picking at wasted seed, the rusting tractor still by the broken fence. She was gone, she didn't belong there, she was summer. The lightening strike bringing the first of dawn made him shiver, this was his winter.

He cleaned up as best he could, stripping naked and hiding his soiled clothes in the base of the hotel laundry basket. Managing to have a shower, he wrapped himself in hotel towels and returned to his armchair shivering, not quite sure why.

Ringing room service, ordering another bottle of malt. This was his second; somehow he knew he could not sleep without it.

Sipping it slowly, he tried to make it last longer, hoping he would drift to sleep before it was empty. He felt his eyes close a few times, but the speed of his thoughts kept him awake.

He saw her once again. Midst the desolation she was the only real thing, she found bodies for him, opened cell doors. Now he wanted to destroy her, why didn't he finish it years ago when she was vulnerable? He made the choice, let her go, yet her people murdered his. Why destroy the surveillance tapes, all save for her tumbling down the hill. He remembered the house on the hill, the triangular field with three telegraph poles falling to the boreen. She falling through straw, in close up eyes made of iron.

25.

I was always so sure I'd marry my childhood sweetheart. Lucia interrupts, asks me am I going for a dip? I choose to lie back and dream; she gets in slowly. She acts like the cold water makes her sunburn hurt. She starts to rescue ladybirds again.

An Austrian couple come out for a swim making two couples at the pool. How dare they?

I lie back, hiding behind my shades, thinking of the glowing blonde from a different world and a different life. Lucia is at the edge. She deposits at least two ladybirds and brushes away at least three large ants.

Her name was Linda; she was the swinging-gate girl, funny the things you remember. When we were kids the girls who wanted to run to the loo actually grabbed their own crotches.

Linda used do it all the time. When we robbed orchards she stuffed the cooking apples down her knickers which made for a great carrier bag.

However it was all innocent stuff, nothing further was ever ventured, her actions were regarded as natural.

I often wonder is she why I worshipped woman, the texture of her skin, the shining glass of her eyes? She was a beautiful fair child. She became a very beautiful woman.

I remembered her wearing a summer frock leaning over her garden gate. We had long conversations about nothing until soon I was disappointed if she wasn't there.

I spent my summers chasing after her over Killiney Hill. This girl was really fit. Taking off by the green shed, racing after her till she'd get to the low wall which allowed a panoramic view of the Wicklow Mountains.

Having caught up with her, gasping for air, trying to pluck up the courage to ask her to go out with me.

She whizzing away again up to the Obelisk. By the time I caught up with her again I was so out of puff I couldn't say a word.

No wonder I ended up with heart disease. I wonder does she know?

Funny how people from your childhood, sweethearts or not, disappear from your life. All those faithful buddies, gone; where to?

Linda might have been my childhood sweetheart but I don't think I was ever hers.

Even though we did have those long conversations at the gate I am sure she was just teasing me and amusing herself.

Some of the hards used to tease her about her advancing breasts.

As they grew it was like she'd placed two underinflated tennis balls up her blouse. I was mortally offended on her behalf when the local hards teased her.

One time three lads, two girls, Linda and myself, had a day excursion up the Sugar Loaf. We decided to climb it from the front. We got the old red bus to Bray, walking the rest of the way. We climbed it all the way to the top, the hard way over loose stones.Scraped by briars, stung by hidden nettles in the heather.

Our descent was even more dangerous, the loose rocks shifting under our weight. We made it to the safety of the meadow grass. As usual Linda ran like a gazelle with me chasing after her.

She stopped, sitting on a bank where the grass was lush and thick. It was lined on both sides with heather and wild flowers.

"Come on over," I said feeling an urge, new and odd.

"No, you come over here," she said smiling.

I thought of my night dreams of her, the hidden passageways through our next-door neighbour's attic leading to her attic, down to her bed. Yeah, the possibilities were endless.

As I got to my feet to move over to her, she took flight.

I never did catch up with her. She gave me the odd smile as she crossed the path on her way home from school. I might catch the occasional sneaky look through my bedroom window as she dismounted from the bus.

It was like something happened to our bodies; they wanted us to grow, spread our wings, leave our seed elsewhere, never to infect the memories of childhood.

Gardiner tried to ring Quinn. His cell phone was dead, Kellerman's was the same. Something was wrong; he felt a little nervous.

It was 6.00 a.m. He hardly slept. Once again he forgot to take his Lipitor. He poured a glass of spring water into the foul-smelling plastic cup, swallowed his Aspirin, his Emcor, and lastly his Diamicron. Later, new supplies, the Pharmacy on the side street. The pharmacist suspicious, maybe just curious.

Now he tested the blood. Shit, seven point six; it should have been under seven. What the hell did he eat? It was the medicine he took for his cough. There it was, the offending bottle, on his bedside locker. Eva surprised him.

"Well Mr Gardiner, tomorrow, Sunday," she said. "We need to talk."

"Where do we meet?" he asked.

Eva gave him directions to Bagno Vignoni.

White uniform stretches over his bed. Gardiner is blinded by her. She whispers soft things, telling him not to look, a line of dispensing fluids.

She needs assistance to lift them. Gardiner looks for his soul, it is buried among blood tissue, his lungs heave.

Susie sees him again, this time she walks across the cycle path to the road. Her rear is firm, shaping the sarong she wears as a disguise.

Gardiner wants to be on the roof to spy her. She looks round to where he sits drinking gin. Petra serves him, smiling. Petra walks inside where it is dark. Gardiner is sure the small cafe is cluttered with unused tables.

Boys pass, tall, blonde, with fishing rods, little boys scamper after them. Susie wears the expensive shoes from the display window opposite. People pass by pleased with the world, Viaréggio day care centre.

Fat women are jealous of Susie, eating ice-cream, disturbing their skin with sun block.

Gardiner wanted Susie there when the drains lifted, hand cranes left wet cement. Susie is gone. He is left to view the hordes, modern centurions. Petra thanks him for the tip. He is dazzled by the sun, the sirens in his head. Agnolino lives here, passing by in various disguises.

Boyce left early. It was dull, the lowlight suited his mood. His hired car was too small for him; he felt cramped. Yet the road to Pisa was good.

He was sure it would become winding and narrow. His directions were to bypass the city itself, take the main road to Firenze, turn towards Montecastello. Boyce felt really tired. The Ruger strapped inside his jacket cut against his left breast when he turned the wheel. He charged his phone and searched the road behind him. Mostly trucks and holiday makers; nothing caught his eye.

"Well, there he goes Don Maestrino," Don Dino said sadly. "It appears youth has no affiliation to honour. Raymond will pour you a drink."

"Have no worries my friend, he will come to no harm, not from us. Gregor will leave him safely in Viaréggio."

Don Dino stood and walked to the drinks trolley to help himself. He preferred water at this time of day. Don Maestrino asked for brandy.

"I feel nothing but shame Don Dino, for Stella, Monica, and for Raymond, my faithful loyal servant for so long."

"I have no regrets," Raymond said, handing him the brandy.

"Well, to be honest Don Maestrino, you are right. Your son lives with Al Pacino in the movies yet he is smart enough. You are lucky. These clerics underestimate him; that is good.

I promise you Philippe won't cause us any harm. My men in Viaréggio are keeping a close eye. He may serve a purpose in identifying where we might locate our two religious friends. They move like rats around Rome, appearing at night, crawling from their dustbin, eating scraps. We will find them Don Maestrino, all is not lost."

Don Maestrino drank his brandy without pausing, smiling at Raymond.

Drozdan wasn't happy. Argüelles tried to make light of it.

The windows of the study were wide open. The air conditioning was down again.

"We will fry in here Monsignor," Drozdan observed. "The city is burning. I feel a little like Nero."

"Should I fetch a fan?" Argüelles asked insincerely. He was quite comfortable, preparing for a heated debate.

"No, no, there is the faintest of breezes. I can feel it against my skin," Drozdan said, much to the Monsignor's relief. "Problems, problems, more problems. We are fast slipping into the mire. Edgell taught us this lesson my friend, yet we fail to learn."

The Cardinal sat back on his chair, stretching to relieve a pain between his shoulder blades.

"Your Eminence, our man is in place. He goes to Volterra. When he completes his task we can review our strategy." The Monsignor was ecstatic.

"Monsignor, you presume so much. How do we know Don Dino hasn't persuaded Philippe to divulge our plans? Even if this were not the case, Don Dino is protecting this 'faith healer.' Mr Boyce will not walk into the church going boom boom!"

The Cardinal mimicked the sound of a gun to the deflated Argüelles who stared at him across the desk, like it took a moment to visualize the Cardinal's comments. "Your Eminence, I spoke to Philippe by phone not twenty minutes ago. They tried to persuade him to change sides. He refused. He swears his loyalty to our cause."

The Monsignor was out of breath with excitement. Drozdan, moving forward and resting his elbows before him, scowled. "Monsignor, Philippe is a fool. Don Dino will have his information, he is very powerful. I am sure his men are watching for Boyce all over Volterra. He is probably watching his every move. As soon as Boyce takes out his gun, he'll be shot to ribbons! The plan was to take Don Dino first. Cause confusion to negate them. This won't work!"

Argüelles sat back, wondering whether he should go get the fan for himself. "Philippe is trying to gain the expertise in Viaréggio. He has contacts," the Monsignor said weakly.

"Contacts with whores! Put everything on hold till I figure out what is best."

Drozdan stood, pacing across the room, clapping his hands inappropriately.

"What about Boyce?" the Monsignor said; he didn't know whether to follow the Cardinal or not. He went to stand.

The Cardinal returned to take his seat. "Monsignor, leave Mr Boyce and Philippe. Sometimes wounded sheep are best left to lie. The wolf will be fed. My speech to the seminarians this evening, we will concentrate on that. We have made errors, basic errors. We underestimated the power of Don Dino. We gave too much respect to Don Maestrino. Let us try Edgell's old friends in Rome.

Think, Monsignor, what difference does it make? If the faith healer heals today, Don Dino breathes more air tomorrow. The woman, she will be taken care of in our own good time. My friend, for now we write a speech."

Drozdan clapped his hands again. The Monsignor felt his

heart skip a beat. "Your Eminence, I will get the laptop. Do you require refreshment?"

"No Argüelles, we require inspiration." Drozdan banged his desk with his fist in anticipation. "My words will enlighten these seminarians. They need to hear the truth."

26.

Lucia's upbringing was far removed from mine. Yet there are many similarities between us.

It could be just down to the type of people we are individually, or our parents and the values they put on things. Maybe in truth it was a little of both.

When James was born I remember looking at her striving through labour. I thought to myself, my God, I will love and cherish this woman forever.

She was so brave, yet so scared. I watched him come out. It was the first and only time I ever saw a miracle. I missed Amanda as she was born in the back of the ambulance on the way to hospital.

Some nights when we are cosy Lucia and I comfort each other remembering the good times.

In a way it is the life blood of people staying together knowing they have sailed the high seas in small boats.

Yet I cannot help feel there is a natural resentment between the sexes which sort of fucks up any notions of harmony, maybe even love, in the sentimental sphere.

Reading these theatre reviews or film reviews, the reviewer might say, "What a load of sentimental rubbish."

I dunno. Would they prefer the world to be ice-cold?

All pinstriped suited and serious? Yeah, I know some who would.

My father had drawers full of medals for sentiment; he was unashamed of it. I think he regarded them as an asset in his short life. That didn't make him naive or feckless in any way, filling up our heads with magical stories from the past.

Lucia came from a wealthier background. With her mother's depression, I suppose she finds it hard to be sentimental, or even fond of her childhood.

I often get the impression she feels cheated, even a tiny bit jealous.

On the beach at Viaréggio she often talked of the good times times when her dad brought her and her brothers into the water on a beautiful sandy beach in Kerry.

Her dad of course full of rough and tumble, swimming out and retrieving beach balls.

Handstands, diving under, shark catches her leg.

Lucia's mother had her good times too. She was an excellent cook, going to extraordinary lengths to get the packed lunch just right.

She is funny too. Like Lucia she has a razor-sharp wit and can tell a great yarn.

Lucia told how her mother complained bitterly about the general hordes encroaching on her space.

The poor woman erecting the windbreak when the Huns arrived with their footballs.

The carefully prepared sandwiches were only issued when the football landed spraying sand through the air like a scene from Lawrence of Arabia.

In her mother's good times she taught Lucia to sing and play the piano. Like all of us we tend to neglect the talents so hard won in our youth.

I don't think Lucia has played the piano for years, even though her mother still plays at Christmas.

Isn't it great though, how women can remain so loyal to their offspring? In general they regard them in a completely different light from men. Woman, the maker and defender of the nest; man, the feckless wanderer through the forests of time. Man forages for food, maybe a little glory, gets a new suit, watches sports, reads serious articles in the newspaper.

Woman is the family representative, the president, the public persona of what is hers; all is hers, all is precious.

Once when we left our little outdoor restaurant in Volterra

I felt Lucia go quiet, somehow I sensed the sound was turned down.

She was subdued as we stared out over the vast valley below and over fields changing colours in the blink of an eye.

"You know, I am not sure if I really like this world," she said. I was surprised; it was un- Lucia-like. "No," she affirmed. "I don't, I don't like life at all."

"How can you say that?" I ventured, all false, trying to remain upbeat.

"Ah, I like the sun, the fields, children, other things; life itself though is not great, is it?"

"We have to live." I said earnestly. She whispered "Death will come when thou art dead, soon, too soon," Lucia rested her head on my shoulder, "something my mother used say." We watched as cloud puddles flowed, filling the craters below, making dark shadows.

Boyce felt the pain rip through the lower part of his body, his legs cramping at the thigh and his stomach burning, his outer skin touched by a branding iron.

He pressed the button for the electric window. It opened obediently.

He noticed the sign for a rest area ahead. When he pulled over he took his half bottle of malt from the glove compartment.

"Thank God," he took a swig. The malt tasted like diesel oil.

He could feel the perspiration drop from his brow; it made tiny pools on the knees of his pants.

Trying to get out of the car to remove his jacket, but the pain shot through him like explosive bullets.

He felt his underwear soiled.

The perspiration now molten, his head an active volcano, he gasped for cool air.

Feeling for the lever that allows the seat to bend backwards, it moved easily, the seat falling until he was prostrate.

His eyes closing, he needed sleep. Images flashed beneath

his eyelids— pictures of night, of day. Clouds fast against a clear blue sky; soon dull rain.

The priest eyed him warily. Boyce made no attempt to move or get past him. Father Burdon relaxed a little.

"What can I do for the murdering scum?"

The priest had a vicious accent which unnerved Boyce.

"I came to see the girl."

The priest, standing on the step, looked down at the Englishman. "Well Captain, doesn't it appear a little late, with both her parents gone?"

"I didn't ask to see you Burdon. I want to talk to the girl. If you want, I can try again later in my official capacity. Either way I get to see her. Thought you might like this way better."

Father Burdon eyed a package the Captain held in his hand. Saying nothing he stood back almost sideways to allow him enter. The girl was in the kitchen; she sat astride a stool like any girl her age. She looked lazy. Boyce noticed she was wearing a pretty white frock with black spots as if someone amended a chess board.

She went cold at the sight of him, eyeing the priest nervously. Burdon smiled at her, rubbing her hair gently as he passed.

"I brought this for you," Boyce said, in the softest voice he could muster.

"It's film from the farm. I thought you might want it!"

"You hardly expect a thank-you now, Captain?"

Father Burdon didn't want to excite the girl.

"No, no, I didn't. I wanted her to have it, that's all."

The Captain turned to leave, looking at the girl, her eyes of steel.

"What are your plans?" Boyce asked.

The priest answered for her, "dunno." "Just make sure I am updated, this could be a mess for everyone," the Captain said.

Eva said, "Why Captain? Why did you do it?"

Her voice ran through Boyce's brain, it entered the wrong compartment. He froze, turning back to look at her.

"Because there is a war on."

He eyed the priest who just shrugged.

"I mean why did you bring me this film?"

Eva glanced at the priest. Her movement revealed the whites of her eyes; her pupils almost disappearing.

The Captain didn't answer her; walking quickly he left the room.

Boyce struggled to catch his breath, his perspiration mixed with the smell of foul waste.

He tried to think. His phone, he needed an ambulance; where was his phone? It was where he left it on the passenger seat. He lost all strength, unable to move forward. What was the Italian for ambulance? "Ambulanza," yes, he remembered. Trying once more to move forward his stomach exploded in pain. He cried out, "Help me. Ah, my God, help me." His voice descending to an inaudible whisper.

The morning was frozen. The corporal kicked over Rock's naked body. Rock's eyes, once so deep, were fish-like. Boyce knew he was heading to meet those eyes—naked innocence lying cold, forgotten.

He threw himself to one side. The green vomit spewed over the driver's door. Bits mixed with blood spattered through the open window, dripping like treacle, attracting flies. His mouth locked open. Edward Boyce was dead.

Gardiner his dream: Susie the rodent bathes, he watches black women carry baskets on their heads. Susie is running up the boardwalk. She sees Heidi Heisler, the small one with the spectacles. Gardiner is unconcerned, her face was on the television, in every crime magazine, this place was thrash. Bodies float ashore unidentified. Susie screams at the ambulance, it goes too fast speeded up, it is made in a nineteen thirties gangster flick. Yet he is too hot, beads of sweat lubricate him, wiping his brow more than once.

Agnolino watches, he is with the body decomposing at the shore.

The flies meant nothing to Gardiner. He witnessed dead children, their bodies rotted. Opening the door the stench hit him, forcing him to step back.

Flies walked in and out of the man's rigid mouth. Gardiner noticed the gun strapped to his left breast. He removed it, checking for bullets. The Ruger was fully loaded. Checking the glove compartment, covering his nose, he found more ammunition. Moving away slowly, Bateman's words echoed in his head:

"Nobody gives a fuck 'bout you when you're dead, Steve. See, nobody can screw you for nothin' when you're six foot under."

Leaving Susie was easy. She was with the fat man; Shaun didn't reckon him, each day entering the beach at La Pace. Susie undressed like a stripper, her thong barely covering her rear. Sometimes he took to the sea to fool her, thousands of people watching him. Older people with funny white hats eyed him suspiciously. They got their feet wet at the water's edge. Children ran through their legs wildly cheering, shouting, the wash hid him for moments.

27.

One day back in St Maxime, I got really scared. I don't know why.

We had taken another trip to St Tropez, this time by road.

Lucia was dying from the heat even though the car had air conditioning.

The roads were very busy with holidaymakers, camper-vans, and scooters.

I stopped at a beach; it took about five minutes to find a parking spot.

Lucia fancied a swim. The beautiful people sat back; they adored the sun.

Walking to the edge it seemed to get deep very quickly, like a few feet in you were out of your depth.

Lucia enjoyed the cool of the water. She once again gave me that strange 'what the hell is going on in your head,' look.

I must admit to being slightly bored sitting there pretending to play with the sand.

Even the sight of beautiful women passing with their fashion-model bodies barely covered by their swimwear failed to excite me.

I was pissed with myself, all my life cursed with this irrational fear of things. One such fear is deep water where I can't stand; I must have drowned in a past life.

There are others, but who cares? I decided to burn on the beach.

Burn I did, watching Lucia swim up and down waving at me like it was the first time she ever saw me.

I was sulking I guess. I was thinking about Boyce and Gardiner; at that stage I hadn't a clue what was to happen to them.

How much of oneself do you put into any character? Should a character be truthful to you or themselves?

I guess I was still fragile. The operation was less than six months back, as Lucia reminded me again and again.

Maybe on the beach that day I figured it out why men don't tell the truth about what they think.

If there was a jail for thinking things, I think I would get life imprisonment.

Years ago I went to see this psychiatrist. He was counselling me for stress management or brain flu, whatever you like. I told him I thought I was crazy or about to go crazy at any second.

He probed, I answered telling him that in the middle of a normal conversation with someone I would get this dreadful surge right through my body.

I would actually visualize myself hitting this person for no reason.

I used to stare so much in the rear-view mirror of my car to make sure I hadn't knocked anyone down I became a danger to those ahead. Driving looking backwards not a great idea!

The guy did the watch thing on the desk in front of him like in the movies; he reminded me of the man who played the quack in the film Ordinary People. Can't think of his name - Judd, something. Anyhow this guy was a ringer.

After much probing questions, honest answers, he got me to try this deep-breathing technique.

It worked very well. He told me things like I could run my own business. I was very smart. He sent me upstairs to a colleague who had some new innovative way of checking actual stress levels.

I broke the machine. She hadn't seen such a case of mental self-abuse in her lifetime. Funny, after I bought her relaxation tape I did feel better. She said I would, that the stress stroke anxiety was always there; it sort of popped its head out more when there were changes in my life.

"Probably it was all triggered by the death of your father," she said.

I looked at Lucia, thought, then dismissed it as being unfair did she understand the operation had reopened so many old wounds? Things which I had come to terms with, made my peace? They came at me like they had risen from the grave all zombie-like.

Questions, regrets, sad times, happy times that went sad are all I seemed to remember.

I kicked the molten sand with my foot, the burning grains attacking the soles of my feet through my sandals. What was it I feared most? Death?

My illness returning unexpectedly, falling down half dead in a crowded street, people gathering round wondering 'what has happened to him?' Or was it living again that frightened me? This sense that I should have died, I deserved to die? Why did I deserve to die? Because of things I thought when I was thirteen years old?

Is all of life to be like this? Is fantasy in itself a crime? Is male fantasy a crime?

Are all men, I say men 'cause women don't seem to fall for this rubbish in general, all demonic in our makeup? Do we just wish to know about perversities for the sake of enlightenment, assist our understanding of it?

Is it cool, to say to some fella in a bar you want to see what she did to that horse?

I dunno. I remember listening to a song once, the chorus went, "I'm looking at the river but I'm thinking of the sea," how many men will think, "Oh yeah, I have thought that."

How many men will say, "Of course, but what we think is not an offence? Isn't what we do corruptive or abusive?"

I think men get into pornography when they're tired. I think there is a direct link between mental exhaustion and sexual perversity.

When she went to Cucuron she was frightened. She pleaded with James, as she now called him, to bring her back to Ireland. He sat rubbing her hair gently.

"We can never go back, Eva," he whispered. "It's not safe for us there. We must stay here for a while, at least till it's safe to move on." James Burdon had powerful whispers. "My friend, Father Matthew, is a student here. He can intervene with the parish priest, Father Marie Abele. He may let us stay."

Father Burdon rubbed her tummy. She was starting to show. He pressed lightly on her bump, "We have to be careful my child," he said, trying not to look directly at her. Eva searched for his eyes. Finally he gave them and she was reassured by the spread of gentleness before her. "I have wronged you Eva but we have to be careful because our dreadful secrets are connected. I fear for you, not me. Whatever they do to me won't be enough, but you have everything in front of you!" Eva felt tears come but they refused to fall.

"I will have to lie to protect us, but this will be short term I promise. We will move on soon, where I will protect you, keep you safe." His whispers comforted her, his hand against her cheek turned the tap, tears abandoned her eyes.

The parish priest accepted his explanation that the girl had been raped. Marie Abele approved, she wished to carry the child full term. Father Burdon gave his services on a part-time basis to the parish.

Marie Abele accepted on condition once the child was born they would move on. Father Burdon agreed, thanking the already balding Marie Abele.

Eva was half way through her seventh month of pregnancy when Don Dino arrived. She watched as the limousine pulled up at the front of the parochial house.

When the Don stepped out she could tell he had once been heavier but weight had fallen from him very fast. The driver carried his case to the front door. The Don glanced briefly upwards where she left the drape pulled back. She closed it with mortal embarrassment. Don Dino saw her for an instant in the evening light.

186

Weeks went by; she heared the Don shuffle about in his room as she stopped on the middle landing. Sometimes if she listened hard she heard him weep; she didn't like the sound he made. It was like he was trying very hard to stop yet couldn't help himself. The Don took his meals alone in his room. Occasionally he would allow one of the priests to visit him. This was mainly to perform a religious prayer.

Don Dino requested his confession be heard. He asked if he could receive Holy Communion. Eva couldn't figure out what sins he could have committed between confessions, he never left his room. She asked James about this.

James sat her down on the sofa, gently patting her tummy where it was sore.

"In the teachings of our church, Eva, we can sin by thought. A person does not have to be physically anywhere in particular, like you and I here, we could think something bad that may be sinful."

Eva was quiet. She liked him patting her tummy, his hand eased the pain.

"I don't like that rule, James. Do you think it a fair rule?"

James looked at her astonished, his hair flapping from the draught of the open door.

"Funny, you know, Eva, Matthew and I were having a chat only this morning. There's a thousand things we don't agree with. Aren't most of these rules only man made? Clever devices to control people! There's new thinking in our church you know. Don't know if they are gonna get away with this sort of thing much longer."

"Does he believe it, James?"

She started to rub her own tummy as James stopped to stand up. "He is very sick, Eva. The poor man has lost his only son."

"How did he die?"

Father Burdon looked at her youthful figure sitting legs crossed, her bump showing through the loose-fitting red dress.

"He was killed by car bomb," the priest said finally, going to close the draughty door.

"My God," Eva said frightened "They have bombs here too?"

"It's not the same, child, not the same over here. Doesn't happen very often if ever, not like at home with armies of occupation. Over here it's all just about money."

"Aye," she said not quite getting it.

28.

The first time I remember feeling unwell was in Siena. It was a pity because we had a great day. Lucia drove, I did the mapping bit.

To my surprise it was much harder than I had imagined, indeed I looked upon it completely differently after that. It was a skill all on its own.

For example, there was no way Lucia would miss an exit because she was looking at the floodlight pylons of some lower division Italian football club.

Lucia drove us down a one-way street.

"Jesus," I said, "keep going."

She shouted, all excited. She did, and we were fine.

Siena like much of Italy is a mixture of the old and the new.

The old walled city is brilliantly restored, it's gateways stood stately on the top of a very steep hill.

We had the video camera. I volunteered to use it. I hope I did to good effect.

The place was buzzing with people. Around the race track, which is gladiator-like, magnificent old buildings and churches, leading to a huge central square.

Lucia entertained me no end in the morning reading aloud from The Lonely Planet, her enthusiasm straight out of my dad's school, she making everything sound exciting.

Perhaps we were a long time without food. I remember Lucia going into this large church I videoed for posterity, sitting outside to wait for her, feeling tired.

Now I wonder was my body already starting to fail me.

Someone well-informed would quite rightly remark I had indeed failed my body for years; as the man says that's another story.

So there I was sitting on the warm steps of this colossal church in the heart of Siena; the day trippers, beautiful girls, the old and the decrepit, all walked by.

My dad played piano; I still hear the sound. I can't name the tunes, yet the sound is indelibly stamped in my brain.

Once when I was twelve he brought me to Cork; it was a Saturday; he was working overtime.

We stopped in this restaurant in Mitchelstown. Now, you may wonder what the hell a fella would be doing in the middle of old Siena thinking of Mitchelstown.

There you go. He played the piano in this restaurant; maybe seven or eight tunes. Evidently he and his fellow cronies (there were three Lorries in the convoy) always stopped in the same place. He always played the piano; it was a matter of duty at this stage.

I think I only thought of it because I was sitting there like a prat, still trying to get the odd artistic exterior shot of the beautiful buildings.

Maybe I always wanted to be an artist after that. The music spreads round to soften my brain, yet my Dad died unknown for his artistry.

A few people knew how talented he was, but not the general public. He was talented enough to be famous. Once we all came along, time to forgo all his dreams, put food on the table. Is it this that leads me to believe artists have to be selfish to succeed? Some people knew his worth alright.

The people in Mitchelstown sent a wreath to his funeral they knew they could never hear his music again.

A part of me hates people. I hated them when my dad died.

I hated all my friends, all his friends who came to sympathize, all my relations. Everyone in the whole world became my enemy. They all sinned against me for not dying too.

Most of all though, I hated waiting on the steps of that goddamn church in Siena. Can't explain but something funny was happening in my body. It went away for a couple of years but I knew it would come back.

Father Burdon went to see Marie Abele. He was about to knock when he heard the parish priest pleading.

"The man is distracted, Cardinal. We made a mistake, one that should never have happened. Yes, I am sure I am alone. I am only saying that killing Benedetto was an error of judgment, not in the best interests of Sodality

Yes, Your Grace; I will continue to talk to him. I know, Cardinal, I understand what you say. It may be a clever device. Yes, she might get close enough, yet she is so young. I can't, hand on my heart, advise. Yes, Your Grace, I will talk to Don Dino. Sorry, Cardinal, I do. I know we cannot change the past, I know that. I am quite sure Don Dino has no suspicion, none. OK then, but you agree we may need to modify our plans in future? I will try to talk to him, fine!"

Father Burdon heard the phone placed back on the receiver. He stood still for a moment, afraid to make a noise. If he knocked, Marie Abele might become suspicious.

He turned to retrace his steps when he heard the creak of the door behind him.

"It is you, Father Burdon. I wasn't expecting anyone!" Abele said shocked.

"Father, I came to see you to discuss where we might go when the child is born.

I heard you were on the phone or maybe you had someone with you, so I…"

"No, I was on the telephone. Come in," Marie Abele said nervously studying Burdon's face as he walked by save he betray any sign of excitement.

James Burdon was calm. "I spoke with Father Matthew.

He's returning to Paris to complete his studies. He is trying to help us get an apartment," he said quietly.

Marie Abele took a seat, offering one to his subordinate.

"Father, I have noticed a certain attachment between you and this young girl.

Since you came from Ireland it has cemented even more. Don't get me wrong," Abele said in his studied manner. "Perhaps you should consider your role as a priest. Naturally I was duty bound to inform my superiors in Rome, despite your excellent record in Ireland. Well, I am sure they will take a dim view of the situation. The church, as I keep reminding Father Cryan, is not a political party. We do not allow room for differences in interpretation of ideology. Father Cryan is naive; I expect him to mature. Father Burdon, some of your recent homilies are nothing short of Marxist propaganda."

Abele spoke without anger or any conclusive passion. Burdon looked at him, went to speak, then changed his mind reluctantly. He said, "Are you suggesting I leave the church because of my politics?"

"No, I am not," said Abele firmly. "I think you should review your politics, perhaps get it more in line with current Vatican thinking. Remember, the church is very strong on the vow of celibacy."

Marie Abele went to stand to indicate the meeting was closed. "Am I to be de-frocked? What are you saying?" Father Burdon asked without real anger.

"It is not my call, Father. I can only report it as I see it."

"So Father Cryan will be safe, his relatives own the largest vineyard in the region, even though he shares my politics?"

Father Burdon was sorry he said this. He had no wish to implicate his friend. "Father Cryan has never indicated any of the left-wing claptrap you have inflicted on the poor people of this region. I do remind you, Father Burdon, I report what I see," said Abele.

Burdon hesitated again. He could sense the fear in Abele; it made the air in his study putrid. "As you wish, Father. I want to inform you of our departure as soon as the child is born."

Burdon turned and walked out. Abele stood, his head bowed wondering what future he had left.

Father Burdon listened to the Don; he spoke at length about Benedetto when he was a child; how he tried to cultivate him as a complete man, not instill any of the old family ways into his blood.

"I only confess my undying love for my son," said Don Dino.

Father Burdon hesitated, "I too have a confession to make, Don Dino," he said.

Burdon related his story. The Don moved the muscles of his jaw involuntarily as he listened to the details about Eva, even how she became pregnant. Burdon then went on to explain his theology, how it differed so much from the main stream. The Don was impressed with his ideas, sitting up and taking notice, whereas earlier he was apathetic, almost docile. Burdon told him about the conversation he overheard Abele have with some Cardinal. Don Dino was calm, yet he asked Father Burdon at least three times to be absolute and sure he was correct. At last the Don was satisfied; a dead weight was lifted from his shoulders.

"Father, you say you have some half-baked plan to go to Paris. I, Don Dino, have always been a fighter like you, I respect your cause, the way you stand up to oppressors and to your own church. I want you to get the girl and come with me. In two days my car will be here; we will go. Don Dino owes you protection for all of your life. You bring the girl; we say nothing, not a word. See?" Don Dino put his finger to his lip to indicate silence. "Marie Abele is not to know why I bring you. He thinks I feel better, a little stronger, yeah? I take pity on my friend, Father Burdon, with the young girl carrying her sweet child. It is all he needs to know!"

Toby was born in Bagni di Lucca. Eva presented him to his father in private. Don Dino arranged they could cohabit. Such was his power, the local people never mentioned the matter in public. It was the Don's expressed wish. He also arranged for Father Burdon to assist at the local

church, setting up a fund to assist the political activities fostered by his trusted priest. Father Cryan was never aware of the Don's patronage.

Eva loved Bagni. Don Dino arranged for her and James to live in a quiet village around 10 kilometres up in the hills. The three of them would often sit on Don Dino's terrace, the men supping Chianti and Eva having a soda whilst breastfeeding Toby.

"I have had a letter from our friend requesting a meeting," said the Don.

"Who?" said Father Burdon reading a paper Matthew Cryan sent.

"The parish priest of Cucuron wants to congratulate you on the birth of your child, my dear." Don Dino smiled, which pleased Eva as she had grown to love him deeply over the past few months. "They want to set up a meeting, to offer us a deal."

"A deal?" Father Burdon asked.

"Ssh, James, let him finish," Eva said.

Don Dino smiled at James. "Yes, they know of your reputation, my dear. Evidently British Intelligence has made enquiries regarding your whereabouts," Burdon looking worried continued to listen, "They want to send a delegation here to discuss the possibility of you assisting them in completing a certain task."

"Sodality," Burdon said putting his paper down.

"Who?" Eva asked.

"These people think the Third Reich should have won the war. Cardinal Edgell is a Nazi."

"I don't understand, James." Eva said innocently.

Father Burdon explained; When James finished the Don said, "I will ask your forgiveness later, Father Burdon. I must avenge Benedetto. I must." Tears filling his eyes.

Eva handing the infant to James, went to comfort him. " These people are my enemies, my nemesis, yet I can't condone murder." The priest was trying to be soft, pulling Toby close to him.

"This is not murder; this will be revenge!" Don Dino said ruefully.

29.

Returning from Siena, Lucia stopped to get petrol. We couldn't, for the life of us, figure out how to open the petrol tank. Its security door didn't even allow for a key. We tried and pressed every lever, every button.

Lucia started to read the manual. Three older Italian men, attracted by Lucia's blonde looks and tight red dress, offered to help.

After much discussion in fast Italian, and obvious disagreement, they all agreed there must be a lever some place.

On reflection, they could have robbed the car with Lucia now sitting in the passenger seat and taken her away.

However, in reality, they kindly found the correct lever and the security door fell open.

We thanked them profusely in English; they gesticulated pleasantly, though incoherently, in Italian.

The weary drive back, the golden light illuminated her, she warming me with her beauty. Me, fatigued, falling to a past of meadows deep with slug spit, burnt patches with broken glass.

Camps made of fern where small boys huddled and yearned. Hours of labour, usually ended when someone shouted 'lets wreck it.' I always imagine Lucia there, although this was impossible. She fitted in though. How can a fantasy form around what you already have back to a time you didn't have it? Lucia is wary of my meadow, as groups of people hide there, the good me, the bad me, the pretending to be nice me.

So we all rolled naked, getting the sun. What a farce my sun burnt arse. Young girls using mats hanging on clothes lines as weather maps, ruin their game, still look at soft skin, soft white with small brown moles. Lucia sees me, strapless, wading through grass, wet, the slug spit sucking my knees, after that jealous dreams, she understands just once as we descend by golden gate, stacks of yellow hay, just once she sees the path, where girls in frocks pose stately far away, she watches athletic boys run jump skip hop dance, Lucia smiles at the red arses on them. I tell her I am tired of walking straight lines, never really getting anywhere. Something happened me to resent normality. Smug women living on the back of success. Arrogant men with camera's and deep voices. My meadow, I lost in my long grass, my sweetheart runs naked to woods.

By the pool Lucia allows me hide. I turn my back, search the hedgerows for lizards. The drift of her hand makes a cool wave in its shadow. When she stands I am her sunbed. She says bland things about food, about medication. She mentions the children and something funny about Aunt Mildred. At last she gives up, watches the dive bomb birds. They spill small amounts, lands near her handbag. After a pause she says, "where I'm from we have dark bog holes. You go in there, nobody will ever find you."

Philippe swallowed the gin using the bottle; he smashed the glass earlier. Argüelles told him to stand by and do nothing till he made contact again. It was a complete waste of time. How would he fund his move to New York? The bar was losing money. What was there now?

His father had disowned him, as his sister had already done. Also, he was now the mortal enemy of Don Dino. He drank, wondering why they allowed Boyce to continue and not him.

Raymond walked from the shadow; he entered from the harem-type extension.

"What is it, Raymond? Have you come to finish me?"

"Philippe, I have come to give you the news," Raymond said, the shadow making him look taller.

"What news could you possibly have that might interest me, Raymond? Not unless you're new-found crony, Don Dino, is prepared to bribe me."

Raymond ignoring him said, "You will find no peace in drink, Philippe. Your father sends you this message: Boyce is dead."

Philippe let the gin bottle sit on the bar and turned to face Raymond full on.

"You have killed him?"

"No," Raymond said. "The police found his body. They suspect natural causes."

"Shit, come on, Raymond. Natural causes?"

"I tell you from the mouth of Don Maestrino. You have not stooped so low as to brand your own father a liar."

Philippe was quiet for a second. "I have not, Raymond. Forgive me; I have been drinking. It seems my friends in Rome no longer need me."

"So be it. They are strange people, Philippe, not like us."

"Does my father send me any other news, like how he and Don Dino are suddenly allies after forty years of hatred?"

Philippe lifted the bottle again but hesitated as Raymond moved closer. "Don Maestrino wants nothing from you. He values your life.

He is an old man now. Old men cannot compete with the young. He knows you may set your own trail of destruction. It is your call. He is responsible for you whilst you're here in Viaréggio."

"I can mind myself, you tell Don Maestrino, I can do that," Philippe said, as if reading from a Mario Puzo novel.

"Don Maestrino was desperate, he didn't know where to turn. He is guilty because he needed to tell Don Dino some things which shamed him. He put himself at the mercy of Don Dino," Raymond said and removed a package from his jacket pocket placing it on the bar.

"Don Maestrino at the mercy of Don Dino? I am ashamed of him!"

This time Philippe took a swig. The gin hurt as it went down, making him want to spit it out.

"There is two hundred thousand dollars in the package. Don Maestrino says it's twice what this bar is worth. He wants you to take it and go to America. You will find the names of family in there. Go see them. You are no longer the responsibility of your father."

Raymond turned to face the shadow, when Philippe said, "You tell my father I am no longer his son, this money buys my bar. Tell him, one day I will head the family in New York."

Philippe tried to make Raymond out as he left through the dark room but couldn't. He walked away like he was painted black.

Don Maestrino was nervous, yet he was too old and unconcerned for himself to be visibly shaken. His arrival with Raymond had gone unheralded. Don Dino's security escorted them, led by the suspicious and surprised Gregor. Raymond surrendered his weapon. Don Maestrino didn't carry a weapon, never had. Don Dino took his usual position on the piano stool, allowing Don Maestrino sit in a cosy chair. The old man almost disappeared into it. It surprised Don Dino how frail his old enemy had become, after all he was just two years older.

The older man got straight to the point. "It has been many years, it is always like a dream to me, us two running round the streets of Volterra. Did it happen ever? Does my mind trick me, play with my memory? I cannot thank you enough for this audience, because you have great reason to mistrust me. You may even hate me, though you may not know fully why you do."

Shifting for comfort, Don Dino was impressed by the clarity and delivery of Don Maestrino's monologue. He guessed, despite his old enemy's appearance, Don Maestrino still had a keen and active brain. "I listen with great anticipation," Don Dino said cordially. His failing in the past had been his readiness to committal before he heard the fullness of facts.

"Don Dino, I have a full and dreadful confession to make. I also have a plea to make of you. It is within your remit to punish me in whatever way you feel is just.

I am hoping that when I relate my story, you will see I wronged you. Maybe you will realize that I too was used, ignorant to the fall out of my participation. On hearing this, I hope, and pray, you may help me save my only son Philippe." Don Maestrino paused, awaiting a reaction, but continued when there was none forthcoming. "When they came to see me, they played up the fact that we were enemies. They tried every trick in the book, citing the families from Roma, saying they recommended me! Cardinal Edgell with this Archbishop Damasky came to see me."

"Only them?" Don Dino interrupted. "Not a Monsignor Fucilla and a parish priest called Marie Abele?"

"No, no, I don't think so," Don Maestrino said slightly flustered "Maybe the priest I think. Yeah, the priest was there; he was a Frenchman. Yeah, he took notes."

"Marie Abele," Don Dino said.

"At first I refused. They wanted me to provide explosives, expertise. They told me it was just to frighten you. Pleading you were vital to their plans, without your assistance they were spent. They said they needed to force you to help them. They wanted to suck you in, intimidate you. Don Dino, I swear to you, I flatly refused. Raymond will testify to that. May God be my judge?" He looked around at Raymond for comfort. "This Cardinal Edgell gave me huge sums of money to assist them. Then this other man, Damasky, he was Polish, he said the families in Roma would be upset if I didn't oblige. I had a young child, he indicated he might not be safe. I said I would provide the explosives as long as they were not used against you, Don Dino, or any of your family personally; they gave me their guarantees." Don Maestrino stared at the floor. "I fixed it for a car. I thought the target was your car standing empty, idle. As you approach, boom, allow you to see the Roma families were vexed, we should support this Sodality. They did the rest. I don't know who planted the explosives. The next thing is, I hear about Benedetto. I go, 'Oh my God, what have I done?' Bloodsucker I am, Don Dino, I took their money. We were run out of Roma. Left with nothing. Stella was going to leave me.

Don Dino, I am weak, not strong like you. What should I do, hey? So I come to you for your judgment, to plead for the life of my own son, Philippe."

Don Maestrino hung his head in shame. The old man looked like a stroke victim.

30.

Can it be real? Lucia shows me around the narrow streets of San Gimignano.

The little narrow passageways lead to small restaurants, also some private addresses. Lucia thought there was a walk going right round the city walls. It consisted of cul de sacs.

I dream, is any of this real? Standing with Lucia, her taking photographs of dark alleys. Surely I died. I must have died!

When I was at school another class came to sit with us for a full day. Their teacher was sick. I suppose we were in about third class.

This boy sat beside me, fair hair, his eyes light blue. He was my friend for the day mid the smell of chalk, a room of stale air, dubious perspiration.

I tried so hard to mind him. I don't know why, he had such innocence.

The teacher was sneaking drinks of water from a plastic cup. Did I believe the story that two of the hard boys pissed in it one day? Not really. The man drank lots of water as if he suffered from permanent dry throat or was he an alcoholic in need of hydration?

I knew I was mad loving eyes that were not mine, feeling the faint heat of his body beside me.

We were like two victims, all soft this love, never sensual, born only of curiosity.

All soft, with boys' tattered satchels, wooden rulers chipped, protractors, implements of tired learning.

We were sums, views from windows with high walls,

footballs lost. Those back gardens were grandiose for those who lived there, a certain falsehood. Many were boarding houses, cheap bed-and-breakfasts. Then, as now, everything was time, incalculable as forever we exist, live, or die.

He went home. I went home. Just another day. All gone home.

A week or so later, I was having a bath.

My mother towelling me dry said, "Did you say you had a boy in your class, one day a while ago?"

"I did."

I said, "he lived over in Gresham Terrace, beside the Christian Brothers."

"I thought you said that." She eyed me sadly.

"Why?" I asked.

She patted my back gently with the towel. "Ah, the poor boy died," she said. "Meningitis."

I still hate that disease, maybe more than any other. Child stealer, secret visitor, the hooded one, dark angel.

I still see his face; sometimes he visits me.

For years our favourite pastime was to go to the swimming baths in Dun Laoghaire.

I was afraid, of course; the five feet was too deep. The big tank, far too deep.

There was a slide at the five foot. You splashed into five feet of water I suppose. I was just four foot. I was always afraid of drowning. I don't know, swimming wasn't really my brief.

We spent a lot of the time sitting drying off. Me pretending. I, the swimmer, was just too cool to swim. Lying back, I let the sun dry my skin. The real swimmers paraded the little jetty behind me. These were the people who could swim a mile or so, out into the open, choppy sea.

Brave swimmers the locals from Dun Laoghaire. Agile, they dived from the high wall opposite at Bug Rock. One guy came up with blood all over his chest, when his dive took him too deep. I was no good at this type of thing, never any good!

Sitting there, pretending to belong, splashing crossways in the pool.

Afraid of falling in, scared every time I passed it, brave and delighted every time I made it safely. Staring at the white hairs on the legs of the girl beside me, wondering why she had white hairs and I had black. It is so easy to glorify the past, what is it, the present, ten years on? People do it I think as a lament for youth.

Who wants to grow old, grow up?

I still see the walk home from Dun Laoghaire baths, keeping our bus fare for sweets.

Horses jumping in gardens, my horse clearing every obstacle till he reached the top of Sallynoggin hill.

When I think of it, I realize I went mad long before my operation or Viaréggio.

I don't know for sure if I actually went mad, my counselor said that going mad was easy compared to what I had done to myself.

What do you think?

Going mad to me meant two things: really tight haircuts and lots of saliva.

So I let my hair grow as long as I could. I didn't produce saliva for at least a year.

Going mad meant becoming a visualizer.

Now there is something important one should explain about visualizers before it's too late. Not only do we see things in graphic terms. We also, for our sins, record every single goddamn thing for posterity.

Shame, pain-in-the-ass stuff I know. Don't you ever mess with a visualizer because we will remember! We will never forgive, 'cause like every day this same thing comes on the camera replay. Press the memory button, it's there.

So I was mad the year I was leaving secondary school. I was really mad, honest.

I was in love with three girls, all visual. Went to my Debs with a fourth, who I had no real feelings for. How can a visualizer ever have feelings? You either look good, stimulate the imagination, or you don't.

One girl I visualized went to the Dominican Convent. I

had this thing: us making mad passionate love to the music, 'The Great Gig in the Sky.' from Pink Floyd's Dark Side of the Moon, vocal by Clare Torry.

Making love in the middle of Sussex Street among tiny cuts of glass debris of a bomb blast. Drawing blood, fake incisions, the music, Clare Torry screaming, orgasmic sound. My lover oblivious to the mayhem, only the music goes soft; the vocal goes, "Who said I was frightened of dying?"

Softer still till the image faded, all the debris sucked up into the atmosphere. She returned to her schoolgirl curls, I watch from across the street, the piano finishes with an intentional bum note

Gardiner tried Kellerman. His phone was dead. Quinn was on voice mail so he didn't leave a message. Why pretend to be CIA? As Bateman said, they were FBI. He went over their previous meeting, searching for clues.

Why Hilton Head, why meet on Daufuskie Island? Gardiner spent a week there looking for a kid's body. They also searched Brooklyn backwards. He kept driving the road to Firenze.

Susie watched him leave. She was relieved she saw him by the body he reached into the fire, he took the heart, she saw it beating in his hand. Gardiner smiled to show he wasn't bothered, the rodent, slipping by the Bonito cafe late at night. Elegant, upright, rich husband to mind her. What did she do for him?

The night in Viaréggio allowed him to hide, sipping wine on the roof top terrace. Rosa befriended him, topping up his glass arbitrarily. The bland musician smiled as he sang in pigeon English. Gardiner spied Susie on the street. She was sleek emerging from the alley.

The scooters droned, the ringing bells, cars cruised, people panicked on the pedestrian crossing. Young people laboured at the gelaterie, tired looking it was getting late. Soon bed, drugs, jumping pains in the morning. Mind racing, soft hurdles, dark grass. He bought his prescription, the assistant was suspicious. Agnolino watched, the heart beating better then expected, keep it alive, keep it ticking.

The car hire people asked so many questions. Gardiner put his shades on. The musician smiled. He turned to the pale couple seated next to him.

"Jesus, it's not right," Toby said.

"Well, maybe we should call a halt," Matthew said upset.

"No, I don't mean ..." Toby moved in the driver's seat to ease the heat in his groin. "What I mean is Marie Abele and me are opposites, total complete opposites. He is the moon, I am the sun. My God! What drove the poor man? It is this I am concerned with. It was so out of character, him asking to assist us."

"Yes," said Matthew. "That did cross my mind."

Toby steered the car into rest area, to give them all respite. "Perhaps he just went mad," volunteered Monica. "Has he been acting strange of late?"

"Yes," said Matthew.

"It's not like Marie Abele. He was a clever man, make no mistake. In many ways, he wasn't a bad man either," Toby said taking a bottle of water from the cool bag.

"Why did he want to help out, Toby? To me it sounds like people were pressing buttons. I don't know. I am just trying to help." Monica was almost apologetic.

"It must have been no good if he decided he couldn't do it," Toby said very seriously.

Matthew looked directly at him. "Do you think we should cancel, Toby?"

"No," was Toby's emphatic reply. "Don Dino will take care of us as always."

"OK," Monica said.

Matthew was silent.

When Gardiner reached the outskirts of Siena, his phone rang. He pulled over. It was such a relief, the whole thing was playing on his mind.

"Wow, you won't believe it, Steve, you know all that dying shit, don't fret. Be glad you're still breathin the Italian air."

"What is it, Joe?" Gardiner asked exasperated.

"Well, holy shit didn't I just track those two assholes down."

Bateman sounded really pleased. "Where the fuck are they? I have been tryin' to make contact," Gardiner said like a small boy.

"You will never guess, Steve." Bateman said cryptically.

"Joe, where the fuck are they?"

"They are only out on Daufuskie Island. Ain't playin' golf either. These assholes are right behind you, Steve. They are in some hurry, boy."

Bateman was gone. Gardiner dialled both his contact numbers again, with the same result as before.

Toby said to Monica, "Why is it sometimes you look out into the dark, you see shapes, faces of people you have never met, coming before you then leaving just as quick when you try to make sense of them!"

"Dunno, Toby. Go to sleep. Your mind is racing."

"Yeah."

"What is bothering you?" Monica said turning on the bedside light.

"When I was a kid, Don Dino brought us here to Volterra, to this place.

I don't ever remember it being this dark. I could always see the lights of the city through the drapes," Toby said blandly.

"You're just worried for tomorrow it should go well!"

"Yeah, maybe I am more worried for Matthew," Toby said sitting up.

"Why?" Monica asked innocently.

"Matthew is such a good man, Monica I hate to think I may let him down. He doesn't deserve that!"

"Let him down?" Monica stared into his pale blue eyes. "You cannot let him down, Toby. No way, no chance." She kissed him softly on the cheek. "You are here for him my love, so you cannot let him down."

Toby turned to hold her, feeling her warmth seep through him. His tired brain turned it's worry to his mother. "We must ring Mother first thing in the morning to check on her," he said.

"We will," Monica said wearily, half asleep.

Gardiner drove on. He was tired. He pulled over to a roadside café he noticed to his right. The place was a bit rough, with truckers and bikers. He didn't care, a sandwich, some coffee, and he would be right as rain. Once more he thought about calling Quinn or Kellerman but thought better of it. Surely it was up to them to make contact with him if they were really concerned about the information he was gathering. He ordered a coffee with a readymade salad sandwich. He was eating it slowly. The news came on the television mounted on the wall.

What he saw unnerved him. It was in Italian. He could tell by the pictures more or less what the news story was about.

Gardiner could see it was about Viaréggio, how a child repelled a would-be abductor. He felt a sudden pain in his tummy, needing the toilet. He ran through the drugs in his head: Coversyl, don't forget your Lipitor later on he reminded himself. Heidi Heisler, her face on the newspaper cuttings shooting through his brain.

He was on the hill again, breathless, the sweat in beads on his forehead. Agnolino sitting on the rail, the mobile pressed to his ear. All the time, the minibus ambulance siren. Returning to his car he closed his eyes, images banged, stuck to his eyelids.

The yachts alongside the deep channel advertising wealth, white sail drifts by. The marble hills tower over everything.

Dark shapes hide in the distance. A monument to Italian emigration is spoiled by sun worshippers. Gardiner admires the territories, secret entrances, miles of sand, city dunes. Agnolino close by floats beside the rotting flesh. Gardiner longs to immerse in the deep, he sees the red sea part, naked he sails forever, beyond searching for his lost heart. Agnolino kicks at the sand, the corpse burns, the remains of the sea is lost in chest drains. Gardiner drinks water, the cold is no comfort, the parting waves collapse.

31.

Lucia and I were discussing deep things like the meaning of life.

I was going on about the Garden of Eden.

Maybe because we were sitting at the garden table in the hotel Villa Belvedere.

It was exactly as you imagine the Garden of Eden to be.

"I never thought of things like that," Lucia said.

"You believed all the crap about Adam and Eve and the snake?"

"Where did we come from then?"

Lucia was just being innocent, she knew about Darwin and such like, she just wasn't in the mood for thinking deeply.

"Don't know. They say we crawled out of the sea."

"I don't like that idea," she said. "Are you trying to tell me, at one time we had fins, did this with our mouths open?"

Lucia imitating a goldfish is a sight to behold. I laughed.

"So they say. But sure, who knows? We then became monkeys or apes, then we turned into Neanderthals."

I was trying to be clever when she said, "Yeah, I used to meet a lot of them at dances when I was a kid. Just think of it, here we all are, the sons of Adam, the daughters of Eve. The products of illegal fornication. I presume the apple bit was for children." Lucia laughed.

"Makes sexuality bad, what a way to control hearts and minds, making the basic instinct to procreate the seed of sin, wonder what fuckin' genius worked that one out."

I was away on my soapbox. Lucia sat forward.

"I think I will go to the pool and cool down. You stay here, its nice in the shade," she said.

"Take Moses, there he was stuck out in the desert with his tribe. What do you think this lot were up to? Rape and pillage and more rape, adultery, men flying into jealous rages as their women were seduced by younger specimens."

"Yeah," said Lucia yawning, "I do need to cool down,"

"So what does Moses do surrounded by such mayhem? He treks up a mountain and comes back down with all these rules carved in stone."

I was really on a roll. "Really?" Lucia said. "Like, 'Thou shalt not kill', 'Thou shalt not covet thy neighbour's wife?'"

"Yeah," I said. "You can see where Moses was coming from, can't you? Surrounded by mayhem."

"But you're crazy, Steve. You don't like people, human beings. You especially dislike women."

She spoke lightly. "Now," I said, "when have I ever demeaned women? Didn't I fight for women's rights, for equal pay when I was only eighteen?"

"Don't know did you?" Lucia looked at me blankly. "Never told me, if you did."

"I did," I said insulted. "I was only working in the factory as a summer job."

"You're always giving out about women."

Lucia was standing, her towel draped over her arm. She mimicked, "Oh that's women for you, can't trust a woman, women are so compliant, it is why the education system suits them."

She started to walk away. I turned my thoughts to the men I knew, grabbing my own towel, hardly prize-fighters either. Anyway I had my own particular gripe with men and their egos.

The room was basic. He was only twenty minutes from Bagno Vignoni. Gardiner tried the television, to get an update on the news. Most channels were showing game shows. Some were reviewing World Cup soccer matches. He took his Coversyl and dialled Susie.

"You pick your moments, Steve, just bringing Father to the hospital, yeah, he's gonna have his surgery," Susie said, speaking very fast.

"Pity," Gardiner said. "Give him my best."

"I will."

"How are Shaun and Marsha?"

"Same as ever. Shaun is doing well with study, he will ring you soon."

"Great."

"Listen, I got to go, father is panicking about the time."

Susie started to speak even faster. "OK then, keep in touch," Gardiner said, clicking off his phone and cursing, "bitch."

He threw the phone on the bed in temper. It was hot, he needed to open a shutter and allow air in.

It was a different type of heat, not like South Carolina where the air was dead, his body dripping sweat, forests so dense, small creeks where alligators often destroyed vital evidence. Washington State was so cold. He sifted through deep snow looking for a child's body, buried deep, preserved, death deferred. Leaving Viaréggio was easy, he left through Marco Polo. People crossed on the pedestrian ways without fear. Twice he braked hard.

They cycled up one way streets the wrong way. Girls with golden thighs stopped beside him on scooters. Older people peered from shop fronts. Were they glad to see him leave, Heidi Heisler left to tell her tale, the beach at Viaréggio so busy.

Hide in the waves appear through the white surf, dark eyes peer, cold fish.

Birds jostled in the branches high above him, debris falling on the dry earth. The concrete bridge led to the green, the sprinkler system activated suddenly, he welcomed the wet. The creek, dark water lettuce stalking. A gator moves away as driftwood dead water washes on stone. He looks around, the lavish fairways are empty save for morning gulls.

The church was full, Don Dino placed his men in the background, strategically watching proceedings, blending with the congregation. Don Dino was a master of such events. His men were not all thin, dark-shaded foot soldiers. Some were old, but loyal and seasoned campaigners. Father Matthew nodded to Toby who sat by Monica in the front row. Marea arrived carrying Donata in her arms. She walked proudly towards the marble font. There she stopped, presenting the child, who was doll-like, to Father Matthew.

"Battesimo," Father Matthew smiled at her; the girl smiled back.

Father Cryan went through his liturgical duties steadily, without rushing. Donata cried, only momentarily, when the water was splashed on her head. Father Matthew gestured to Toby that he had finished. Don Dino's representatives were rigid, watching the congregation for any uneasy movements.

"Ne sono certo." Toby said, placing both his hands on Donata's head. Marea stood, watching him in awe. Toby leaned forward, kissing the child softly on the forehead. He then whispered into the child's right ear, "Ti voglio bene." As they left the tiny church older people raised their hands to touch Toby. He smiled at them; many blessed themselves as he passed. Blinded by sunlight Toby looked behind him at the smiling Monica. The light captured the church till it sparkled, reflecting gold.

Drozdan went over his speech one last time. Argüelles smiled at the same highlights each time the Cardinal read it aloud.

"I don't like it, Monsignor it is flat, stale, like bad bread. I need something to lift it, to make it more dynamic."

"Your Grace, I can tell you it is perfect as is. Changing it now will only upset its rhythm. There is no point in changing something just for the sake of change, it has to make sense. Believe me your words make perfect sense."

Drozdan wished to check the level of his sincerity. Once satisfied, he said, "OK, Monsignor, I will read it once more so listen carefully."

Drozdan read it aloud. The Monsignor listened intently however, on completion Drozdan was just as worried about it.

"No, no, Monsignor, it lacks something let me think." Argüelles went to speak but Drozdan put his hand up, to indicate silence. The Cardinal was pacing the room. This always made Argüelles nervous. After what seemed like an age, the pacing stopped. Drozdan looked at him. "Edgell, what would Edgell have said, eh?" The Cardinal went to his desk, sliding the drawer open, removing the file on Edgell. "The answer lies in here I'd bet. Argüelles, we may never get another chance to sell the values of Sodality to these seminarians again. We must seize this opportunity my friend." Drozdan read, then re-read the file until suddenly, to the great shock of his companion, he banged down the file on his desk. "Monsignor, I have it. I know exactly what we need to do."

Argüelles felt uneasy at the vigour in the Cardinal's voice. "Think of it my friend, the world under the Third Reich or the world under Stalin. I will show how Sodality will change the whole social order, how everything we have tried so far is unreliable. We shall speak of new beginnings. I will reach a crescendo with how we, the church, will save the world, how we must prepare for the invasion of the infidels from the East. Yes, Monsignor I assure you, we will convert many to our cause this very night."

Argüelles smiled at the self-satisfied Cardinal sitting opposite. "We will take our own car, but have the driver pull to the front of the building rather than the back, Argüelles. Make sure it's our regular man." the Cardinal said. The Monsignor went to make the call.

32.

After my operation Lucia was lost in a state of fear. Her world changed, nothing was certain anymore. She tried to deflect her angst, pretend she adapted to the perilous world she now inhabited. At times her care was overwhelming. She fussed around me, I could sense the anxiety spawning from her core. Yet sometimes she was stern, even cold, like she was fighting the dragon with her sword. I tried to rationalize her icy determination, imagining a world where women cracked up if anything went wrong.

Hardly women's fault, this urge to survive, the granite will to continue, to allow the species develop; this is the property of women. Lucia collects this will; she has it in abundance. I have the greatest failing of all: emotional dependence, instruction manual included. This in itself is not a sin; it is misplaced against one self. It's probably the most destructive force in existence.

It begins in childhood, with a complete unadulterated fascination with women.

Of course all is entirely visual, as you can imagine.

Women are objects of beauty, the figures who stand naked in golden fields, the ultimate in aesthetic art, the reason for being.

Long dark hair curling, cradling the breast. Firm-buttocked blondes, their radiant eyes burst through your skin, burning your heart, yet leaving no mark.

This is my nemesis, the one element of desire to hold, embrace, feel the nakedness press against my skin, true desire, the only reason to breathe, to feel her heat. Of course, reality isn't like this. I possess a childish selfish view. I have never grown out of it. Why, for instance, were all my amateurish early efforts at writing poetry dedicated to women?

Follows naturally, all my favourite songs are love ballads?

On what premise did I forget the world? Search only the so-called beauty, the mystery of the opposite sex? For Christ's sake, what hopes and dreams do I attach to this?

Even now I am emotionally lost. I don't really believe woman is man with different sex organs. Allowing for their diverse emotional structure

I am rudely awakened by any resemblance to humanity or likeness to maleness as in coughing, sneezing, farting, or defecation.

It was a major shock to me at one stage of my evolution, discovering women actually could die. To still hold with this emotional savagery in middle age, a worry indeed! Lucia thinks I am crazy. She says things like, "What do you expect me to do? Go red, swell like a balloon, then burst?"

I dismiss this type of reply as being rude in the extreme and feckless to the sensibility of the visualizer.

I was eighteen in 1976 I visited London for the third time in my life.

Julie was my best friend's sister. She was twenty one. It was late in the year, the start of

November. She lived in a squat with some college friends.

Dunno, I think they were on a year out. She used to write to me, telling me all about life in London.

I imagined the squat as broken down, full of rubble, sleep rough kind of joint, but she told me she had her own room in a normal house.

As I have admitted to already, this visualizer was so in love I could not eat, sleep, or relax. I daydreamed of her, night dreamed of her.

All else in the world faded to insignificance, perhaps, most cruelly, me, myself. My love for her, in all its infatuatory self, consisted of wet paint to be brushed over my ego and self-esteem.

I regarded that, and maybe still do to this day, as a truth, the artist hidden beyond what is more wonderful, but all outside of yourself. She greeted me at the bus station on Gloucester Road.

It was perfect. She ran towards me, her face beaming, her arms outstretched. I was wiry, scraggly hair high in curls, made no sense, the partings like aimless streams running downhill into a dense wood.

To put things in context, I would tape the theme song from Love Story, not the movie, but a series of weekly plays on the ITV channel.

All the way on the tube Julie kissed me, whispering things into my ear, asking me to share her bed.

My God, I had only known her six months. I loved her so much.

We had our relationship by stealth. My friend didn't know about us, or at least he didn't pretend to know.

I was a virgin. I think even at twenty one, she was too.

At night, lying face down on the bare mattress, writing ad lib verse in my copybook. She was a student of English, cleaner of the houses of orthodox Jews. She read it finding it pleasant and innocent.

I think Julie regarded me as sullen and immature, though she never said so.

Standing at night by the window, watching as the London trains went by, I was out of my depth, thinking women were impressed by intensity and romance. London itself was a nice place. I saw everything was older; home was whiter, all new.

The squat was in number nineteen, Glasterton Road, in the Borough of Stoke Newington, within the environs of Stamford Hill. At night, we walked to the pub linking hands, the full Moon, soft light making shapes playing with clouds in the night sky.

November in London was cold. Having a beer, warming myself by the calor gas fire, listening to tunes like Chicago, "If you Leave me now," and the Hollies, "The air that I breathe," written, of course, by the more talented Albert Hammond.

Julie, aware of our age difference, grew to resent my silences. I was afraid to speak save for saying something stupid. Her friends were ribbing her. One particular pain in the ass referring to me as 'the child.'

Eventually we had a row. I stormed out finding a strange bar full of black men and hippies. When I got back, Julie confronted me. I told her out straight I thought she was embarrassed by me. She didn't deny it. Also I chided her for our misguided and frustrated attempts at sexual fulfilment.

She became defensive.

"Where is your condom?" Julie wanted to know.

This was 1976, for God's sake, condoms were some sort of item to be classified under, "Very bad, very, very bad, dangerous, for grown-ups only, only pagan English grown-ups at that."

I had seen the machines in the toilets but was scared to go near them.

"Well," I replied, "who else would sleep naked beside you for fourteen nights, brings you to the point of no return, then actually turn and do a runner?"

I heard later that she had been with this English Bin man guy who wore leather, he was tall and slick. This happened about a week before I arrived.

I don't think Julie went all the way with him either. You never know with women, do you?

She got the tube back to Gloucester Road with me, tears streaming down her face, as I boarded the bus to the airport.

I think my friend probably did know about me and his sister. He never said anything about it, the sort of thing your mate understood, even if he didn't approve of it.

Through him I saw her again a few times. She wrote me a very poignant letter a little time after I got home. She asked me to wait for her:

'For God's sake, wait for me.'

I waited like a dope keeping the heart, painting over my ego, my self-esteem, for three years.

218

Once I danced with her full of hope at a night club in Greystones,

I quoted from her letter, told her I waited. She laughed, saying how she moved on, sure we could always stay friends.

I thought back, walking through Heathrow Airport three years before, playing Supertramp in my head as I went to board the Aer Lingus to Dublin.

"Na nah, Na nah, dreamer, nothin' but a dreamer, can you put your hands in your head? Oh no, oh no." Freeze frame.

Benedetto was uneasy. Anna didn't look well; his wife was too full of blood.

Her cheeks were rose red, her legs were bloated. She looked like she was swallowed then regurgitated by a wild boar. Anna insisted on coming with him. It was odd, she normally stayed behind to keep an eye on things. Today she was insecure.

The pregnancy fatigued her, made her fearful. He was too tired to be putting up arguments. She was present with these shoe manufacturers from Milano before.

He would leave Theresa in charge; she was capable. Her English was good; she could deal with the tourists. Benedetto checked his watch. Anna would keep him late. She was so slow getting ready he stepped out into the doorway, by doing so he might send a subliminal message to his wife to get a move on.

He left the car half on the sidewalk to allow him to keep an eye on it, save he get a ticket from the Carabinieri.

The meeting was in one and half hours in Siena. They planned to stop briefly in San Donato to deliver shoes to Anna's mother. She promised not to delay.

Benedetto sighed in frustration. It was a warm close day in Firenze. The air was heavy.

Suddenly there was a loud clap of thunder followed by a flash of blue lightning. The rain started to fall heavily.

It pelted off the roof of the car like a thousand hoses were trained on it. A good cleaning, he thought. Anna arrived; her pregnant body paused; she surveyed the deluge.

He saw the rain was mixed with hail, most unusual for the middle of June.

"Have you got Mother's shoes?" he asked, his hands reaching out to take them.

Anna handed them over, unsure as to whether to make a run for it, the rain was so fierce.

There was another clap of thunder with a flash of lightning. It might have forewarned the end of the world.

Benedetto wondered whether it was safe for his wife even to go the few metres. The world was dark and wet. They were sheltering from a great violence.

Across the street the other stores: Il Formaggio beside Pizza Franco, he could just see the sign for Guido Longilette, lastly La Pelle.

"We will go, my love," he said pointing to his watch.

Ten seconds later, they were in the car, soaked as if having stepped from the shower.

Leaving the city, the streets resembled small streams. The shopkeepers down near the city gate were worst affected, sweeping dirty water from their stores. One brave soul attempted to unblock the drain causing the waters to rise. Benedetto found the roads drier outside as he left the city heading south. Eventually he turned for San Donato, driving uphill.

Taking a sharp turn right, he proceeded up to the village, where he parked by a closed food market.

Anna said, "You turn the car, Benedetto. I won't be long."

Anna walked up the small hill along the narrow street where her mother lived. Benedetto turned the car, watching as the villagers moved again after the rains. Anna was true to her word.

"OK, let's go I brought a dry towel for you," she said as she got in.

He guided the car down the narrow street, turning left down the hill past the old church. He turned left again, taking the road for Siena.

"I wanted a girl," Anna said. "But the more I love you, Benedetto, the more I want a boy," she added laughing.

Benedetto was silent for a second. He checked his wing mirror before moving on to the main road properly.

"As Don Dino says, let our child be healthy."

"Yes, your father is right!" Anna said smiling.

Catching the perfect white of her teeth, thinking she will be back to her beautiful self as soon as the baby is born. They would have a happy life together.

He could see his empire of shops grow rapidly to cover the whole of Italy. Yes, life would be good.

When the car blew up, it was just as he had slowed because of another cloud burst. The lashing rain failed to dampen the roaring inferno. The flames rose 20 feet to challenge the storm clouds overhead.

33.

Watching Lucia by the pool rubbing cream on her arms and legs, thinking of lost romance.

It was like great Cupid built a wall between us. If either of us ventured over, he shot us straight through the heart with his arrow.

We spent our time trying to find some common ground.

I felt removed from her in every way: emotionally, intellectually, our views of society, the world around us.

A person finds it hard admitting he is a visualizer. By my very nature I am insane. I was always waving goodbye in my dreams, at the end of the lane soft boy waves goodbye to his girlfriend.

I only feel comfortable with people who challenge me intellectually. If they can undermine my thesis all the better, gives me a chance to invent another outrageous proposal.

These moments usually take place totally accidentally in bars, anyway with barstool philosophers.

I have a hatred of all things normal, things to conform to.

Conformity is my neurosis. I cannot defeat this dreadful emotional fear.

There must be paint, add on paint. I must block my self-esteem, my ego.

I'm ulcerated by precociousness in any of its guises. I run, scared this is the architect of bad feeling, of mistrust.

I am a visualizer. I can tell by a person's eyes whether they are benevolent or malevolent.

Lucia sees the world as most people see it; she sees it the correct way; she interprets it the correct way.

My world allows little light and little room. My ego is bashed and broken.

The first year after I left school I went to work in an industrial laundry. It was a way of making money. Friday was my favourite day. It was my turn to load the huge washing machines known as the Cascadex. The machine had different compartments, which I filled from a portable container. I think it was twenty-one towels to each compartment, then soap powder and the switches, I was good at switches. They needed to be pressed and opened in sequence. After twenty minutes you had to open your drains.

The water gushed out into trench-like gullies to disappear into the drains.

After my process was finished, things moved on to a giant pressing machine. The women removed the rubber bands from the towels, feeding them by hand.

Once they reached the other side, other women would remove them using a roller to make the towels fit the dispensers in toilets. I often had the job of packing the rolled towels into their sacks to be loaded on the van the next morning.

The whole place went at a hundred miles an hour right from the start of the process at the "Flaker," where the towels were fed through a flattening machine and then tied with rubber bands on the far side.

It was my first experience of work, its characters, the good, the bad, the frenetic pace we were expected to work at. I learned about women too! The girls at one end of the pressing machine didn't speak to the girls at the other end. This silence between them lasted the whole time I worked there. I never found out what the hell the argument was about, and who started it or why.

It just didn't seem to matter, they didn't speak, that was it.

The foreman was a tall man called Mick. He came from an upmarket estate near Johnstown Road. The lads joked that he walked out of his house each morning with a briefcase, wearing a suit.

By the time he reached the laundry, he would get rid of the suit and walk around in an old vest, which allowed the hairs on his chest show through.

The briefcase, of course, contained his egg and tomato sandwiches.

Of course it was horseshit, but I half believed it. At my age I believed most things.

Mick turned out to be one of the best human beings I ever met. He was exceptionally kind and generous to a young idiot like me.

His favourite trick was to take out his false teeth in the canteen as the night ladies clocked in, rubbing them vigorously with a nail brush and industrial soap. The women ran out to their work stations in disgust, but laughing just the same.

Years later, Mick bought a pub in the city, which I think didn't do so well. Afterwards he drove a van. I suppose life just moved on. When I came out of hospital, an old colleague from the laundry told me that Mick died of cancer.

I was with Lucia in a pub. It struck me that she knew nothing of me, nothing of my early life. If I had died during surgery she'd have mourned a man she hardly knew.

Don Dino wasn't sure why he asked Gregor to drive him. He was still undecided as to the benefits it might bring, people differed on these matters. Some thrived on revisiting the past, others tried to forget, move on. It was of no value to hold the memories of their loved ones so close in their hearts.

Personally he'd rather forget the past, pretend it didn't exist. He wanted to spread Benedetto's ashes in Volterra but Anna's people were from San Donato. They wished to scatter the ashes in the hillside village.

Anna's grieving mother was sure they wanted to view the mountains and serene valleys forever. Falling in love, watching over the trees, they planned to build a new home in sight of the church Anna loved, the ding dong of the bells and the perfume of wild flowers. Benedetto longed for the peace of his evening stroll, the tiny road where he looped his way back to the village making small talk with the people he met.

The police had taken so long to hand over the charred

remains of their children and the tiny infant inside his daughter-in-law's womb.

The Don was happy they were hearing the church bells calling to all the living things below, resting in peace listening to Gods music. Gregor allowed him to walk down the little road by the church alone. The Don swallowed the thin air of the hills, smiling as he remembered his son far more as a child than as a man. He sat for a moment to catch his breath; the heat making his brow moist.

Benedetto as a child! Going to Certaldo to see his Aunt Vittoria, the Don's sister. She had loved the boy like her own. Don Dino lifting the boy on his shoulders, walking halfway up the narrow cobbled street to where Vittoria lived. Greeting them warmly,

"Amore mio!" she said.

Benedetto, six years old, shouted, "la mia Vittoria!"

Picking him up, his tiny legs kicking the air.

The Don remembered, walking further up the hill alone. He entered the old city out of breath for the climb, turning left up the narrow street, walking into the church which was dark and forbidding. Praying silently for many things, mostly for the sins he committed.

"Mio Dio, abbi pietà di Benedetto."

The light and the silence of the church made him feel closer to God.

In Quírico d' Órcia Gardiner sat restlessly on his bed. He cleaned the gun at least ten times with a bathroom towel till the barrel glistened. The news was disturbing. The child in Viaréggio had given a description of the attacker, police were compiling photo fits. How many times had he seen it before? So many times he placed his hopes on those photo fits. They showed a picture of the little girl herself, she was probably six years old, fair, not Italian. Gardiner tried to translate her words. The girl was Austrian, on holiday by the sea. Gardiner looked at the screen in panic. She was so like her, so like Heidi Heisler. She even wore small spectacles, they rested on the bridge of her nose. Her tiny face, so small, could barely support them.

He picked up his phone dialling Kellerman. The cell phone was dead. He tried Quinn; his phone was switched to voicemail.

"Why are you guys never there?"

He threw the phone on the bed in temper feeling the heat rise in the room. He had to get out, if only for a few minutes.

Alessandro was shouting to nobody in particular. His job to fill the plastic buckets for the older boys. They went about their work with zeal. Alessandro followed them everywhere. A small blonde girl wearing spectacles took an interest in the small fish. She followed blindly, watching Alessandro's every move. Gardiner watched her from the cleansing surf. Susie stared uneasily, her eyes partially hidden by the afternoon sun.

"Take me to Certaldo," Don Dino said.

"Certaldo?" Gregor said, looking over his shoulder at the Don.

"Don't go the main roads. Go to S Casciano in Val di Pesa. Bring me across country to Fiano, go that way!"

Gregor looked at him. It was hot, his forehead dripping.

"Don Dino, why now? They're all gone, you know there's nobody in Certaldo not now Vittoria is dead. Who is it you want to see?"

The Don looked at the floor of the car. Sadly he said, "I want to see the countryside. Benedetto and I used to go this way. I want to go to the church in the old city, say a prayer. We can take our time, Gregor. You can stop for water, if you are thirsty."

Gregor nodded. Setting off in silence past the church, he turned left and continued along the quiet road. He had to stop to allow traffic through, the roads narrowed in the small villages. They drove on, winding their way uphill, rounding endless hairpin bends. The Don sat scanning the countryside trying to fuel his memory. It was a long time since he last touched Benedetto's skin, heard the gentle sound of his voice. He lived out among the vines and the olive trees, the dry earth had stolen his spirit.

The road through Fiano was just one lane. Gregor stopped to allow a blue bus through. Don Dino said nothing as they approached the city. Gregor parked in the large square to the left.

"We will get the train up to the old city," the Don said.

"I will wait here!" Gregor sat on a cold stone step.

The Don entered the dark church, as always so quiet. For a moment he felt nothing had changed, yet so many years had passed. He sat uneasily in a pew near the rear, the paintings invisible in the shadow. Fate was conspiring against him, spying, searching for signs of weakness. His thoughts turned to contrition. Perhaps it was the only way to save his soul. Was he contrite? Did he forgive them? Those who destroyed him, stole his only child, his son? He hated them even more now. They had denied him.

Before he held the anger of youth, now it was the whining sound of an old man shedding bitter, angry tears. The sense within of fragility, of powerlessness, of loss. They could have tortured him, made him bleed, torn out his tongue. Why do worse, torture his soul forever. You can only kill a man once, get your revenge. His thoughts turned dark.

'I would have killed them a million times if I thought I could. Even I can't raise the dead. I have not the power to resurrect them so I can kill them once more. I sit alone in this dark place looking for forgiveness.

The purity of my soul, will it spare another love?'

He knelt forward, the silence making his mind race. 'Who could imagine the world to be as dark, so dreadful, as this place? How vacant and lonely must God be?'

"Faccio un Atto di Contrizione." he whispered through

his hands. The pressure of his fingers against his eyes formed shapes of light against the silent dark. He saw the faces of his son and Eva. Feeling only fear, his insides hurting, his heart beating so fast.

34.

Her mother's depression was a huge thing. I often wondered how terrible it was to grow up with. Lucia doesn't talk about it very much.

A child of seven doesn't want to hear her mother say she is going to kill her.

The woman did actually mean it literally. Her father spent all his life compensating, maybe even spoiling her at times.

As Lucia aptly says, 'Sure, doesn't everyone have a cross to carry?'

When we are intimate she likes to talk, tell me about little things she did when she was a kid. When she went missing, cycling for miles into the countryside on her own. The days spent on the beach, the family picnics. She is right though, everyone does have a cross to carry. I often think it's my greatest failing as a human being, my intolerance, my total failure in offering a helping hand to those who, for one reason or other, have crosses heavier than my own.

We were driving to Asciano, winding our way through the beautiful countryside.

Lucia was taken by the name, so we went for a flip-flop stroll around it.

I was all grey-haired, sun glassed. I watched her stride ahead, wondering about her, what fast cars ran through her mind?

How much of her early life is hidden from me.

She wore a blue frock a little too heavy for the weather, we struggled up the hill passing the elevated fountain.

I was amazed to find the water was so clear. The Italians are a clean race, putting Ireland to shame.

Somebody once said, if you see one Italian village you have seen them all. Honestly, they could not be more wrong.

Each place has its own charm; the people go about their business with dignity; they keep their streets clean. The buildings are old world, people have style. I find they have a modernist disposition. I always found the people outside the main cities to be friendly and courteous. Asciano is a beautiful old place. By the time we reached the top of the hill, Lucia didn't know whether to go right or left. We went right.

We stopped at a small bar for 'Aqua frizzante.' The shops were sparse, but clean and upbeat. I could imagine the GIs walking these streets in 1944, '45.

They must have felt they were a million miles from home. Italy is like that. It really must appear very old to Americans.

Lucia took lots of photographs at the fountain, ones of me, then I took one of her, before some passer-by took one of both of us.

Whilst I worked in the laundry, I decided it was time to break out on my own.

I was turning nineteen when I got this flat in Monkstown. It was in Longford Terrace near the Purty Kitchen pub. I think, looking back, I was too young. Not that normal nineteen-year-olds are too young. Girls sharing are never too young

I freely admit! I hadn't matured enough to engage in responsibility.

At the time my friends were into smoking grass, the odd LSD tab.

So there were lots of all-night sessions with plenty of sounds and smoke and the usual supply of beer.

Three girls lived in the rooftop flat above us. They had to go through our flat to get to the clothes line, so the lines of communication were well open.

Of course, me being the visualizer, I fell in love with all three of them. My two flatmates didn't bother. Another mate, who sort of half lived with us rent-free, got my girl. Sure, wasn't he right!

I nearly got one of them one night. She got rightly stuck into me. I always said the wrong thing, or blew it, my cross, still is to this day.

I was also in love with a girl from the laundry. She was from Bray, had a motorbike, sexy or what?

Even better she decided to move in. Manna from heaven, this girl sleeping in the room next to me. As I warned, you could count on me to blow it.

I managed to find her bed one night. She was cool, we chatted. She allowed me to stroke her hair. I could feel warmth drift inside me.

Just as I was about to explore all the possibilities she said, "Hey, Ste, do me a favour, will you?"

"Sure," I said, thinking I would walk the West Pier and back.

She said, "Turn out the bathroom light, will you?"

"Sure, not a bother." ' Bathroom lights? I can do that, turn them out.'

I had my foot back in the bed, waiting to cover my body with the warm bedspread, when she said, "Hey Ste, do us another favour, will you?"

"Yeah, like what do you need?"

"Go back to your own room," she said.

Life never changes does it?

Eva looked over her files, her eyes hurting, the faces in the photographs haunting till she felt nauseated. The photo of Heidi Heisler brought tears to her eyes. She was thinking back to what the Don said earlier.

She wondered about him. He gave the appearance of pillar like strength yet maybe he wasn't strong at all! She felt he was soft underneath. Perhaps it was his rationale that made him vulnerable and sad. His words about contrition made her think, not so much of the Don or his life, but more of herself. Who was she? How contrite was she?

Excuse after excuse, James Burdon was the master of excuses. Eva Devlin was not contrite, in many ways she doubted if the Don was either. Was it just a game? The lodge was much bigger, more plush than her own small house in Bagni Di Lucca. The gin was good. It calmed her and stopped her hand from shaking.

She took another sip. Soon the effect soothed to make her more emotional, more removed from life's realities, like placing a hand on a lit candle and not feeling the burn. Eva was tired of it now. She wondered whether any of it was a good idea. Was her mission a passion born from guilt? Don Dino put it so eloquently, an act of contrition without mouthing the words. Since James died, religion was unimportant. The fact that James was a priest was irrelevant once they moved to Cucuron, he faded as a cleric. Eva could only ever see the man, butcher, baker, candlestick maker. At night he always slept naked, close, glancing his hand off her side; she would play with the fur that graced his chest like body gorse.

He might whisper things to her, his voice gentle like he was hearing the first confession of a small child. Sometimes Eva talked of those dreadful cold nights in the barn; James listened for a long time without reply. Every now and then she would pull playfully at his gorse to check if he was awake. He would let out a tiny scream, whispering, "I am listening." Eva smiled to herself realizing his softness exonerated her guilt.

"Every time I close my eyes, James, I see those boys. I see what we did to them. For what? I ask myself. For a few lousy acres, for the IRA, for what? James, you cannot imagine the terror in their eyes."

Eva stopped playing with James's gorse to place her left hand on his warm tummy.

"What good does it do, Eva Devlin, to be living it night and day, when you were only a child yourself? The world you lived in was chaos, worse than Dante's inferno."

He spoke softly, so as not to upset her.

"I know, James, no matter. I took those boys away from the world. I took them from their families, the people who loved, cared for them, their mothers, fathers, sisters, brothers... maybe they had sweethearts?"

Eva sounded shocked, as if she had just thought of it for the first time.

"The madness had gone too far, girl. One of them would have pulled the trigger. You did it for your father, to save your home, to put those poor miserable boys asleep out of their torture, their misery."

As she placed the photographs back into the file, she looked at Heidi Heisler once more. Same age, she thought, same Aryan looks.

"So what is it he likes about you?" she said aloud drinking a mouthful of gin.

It left a bitter taste in her mouth.

Gardiner kept to the shadows of the trees at the Hotel Casanova. It was warm yet cloudy overhead, the air was dead. The traffic nearby mainly tourists, worried-looking as they might be lost. He returned to his room. It was darker, the evening was closing in. He checked his watch. Smiling to himself he rang Bateman.

"Joe, it's me," he said.

"Steve, the fuck? You let a guy get some rest, huh?" Gardiner ignored him. "Your problem, Steve, is that you should have died. You didn't pity that big mouth of yours, man, you can sure say it all when you're out of it!"

"Joe, I want to know, did he ever take any kid that wasn't Aryan? This guy went missing. I'm convinced he is here, in Italy."

"Fuck, Gardiner, you guys have all the information. Those medications, they are driving you crazy, man."

"Fuck you, Bateman."

Gardiner switched off throwing the phone on to the soft carpet. He felt dejected and lay on the bed sipping water, taking his Coversyl.

Soon the room went dark and he drifted to sleep. In his dreams they appeared again, Quinn and Kellerman, the ambulance, its siren sounding; Agnolino sitting on the rail;

running up the hill, the perspiration saturating his brow; Susie with the children by the pool; the beach; the hawkers selling their wares. Suddenly all was deserted: the pool, the beach, the hill. Gardiner woke sweat forming on his chin like a drip from a tap. He clutched his chest. The pain wasn't like before; it was just numb. Sitting up in the bed for what seemed like an age, his damp skin turning cold, making him shiver. He wanted to call Susie, but it was too late. She might be asleep. How he longed to hear her voice!

Susie follows her portly husband up the boardwalk. Agnolino stands by the fire, salt water bathes his feet, he cools down. Eyes search from the sea fixed hard on the reflection from tiny glass. Agnolino allows the water cool the heart, it beats alone. The blonde boys search the bucket, little fish gasps for air, sand clouds his water, his fins destroyed by sandpaper. Alessandro gets more water, he pours from one bucket to another.

"Ne abbiamo preso uno." Alessandro shouts to his Mother who is busy reading a book, "Grazie Allessandro," she mutters.

35.

Lucia never understands when I speak of emotional attachment. I think it's because she spent most of her childhood trying to detach.

Or, in fairness, it is more likely detachment was forced upon her due to her mother's illness.

When my father died, emotional attachment became like the swill that feeds the pig. I take life very seriously for a man. I am easily moved to tears, at least I used to be till I had my operation. It is like you're walking on black ice all the time, slipping and sliding, waiting for someone to catch you. The dread and awful realization is when you realize there isn't anybody to save you.

Everyone deals with bereavement differently. Some lock it up, store it away. Others face it full-on, fight it every day.

Me, I blamed myself for it, everything was my fault. I often wonder. I read these psychological profiles of people who do dreadful things.

There is always some point in their lives when they go off the rails, maybe when they were really young, or over a relationship that ends, or money.

You hear of women driving their cars off piers into the sea with two kids strapped in the rear, or the man that shoots his entire family, then himself. Weird, isn't it?

The Saturday my dad died, I was having a bath. Don't ask me, we were all on tenterhooks. My older sister already warned my younger brother and me.

She told us that Daddy wasn't going to get better.

My younger brother, he didn't really understand, he didn't know. Maybe his dad would get better.

Me, I couldn't stand it; not knowing is the worst thing.

I kept thinking: give me a result, a final score, tell me is my dad going to die or not, the not knowing nearly drove me insane.

I went for my normal Saturday bath. Funny, when things go so wrong, you still occupy the same space, do the same little things you always do.

All week had been a nightmare, ever since I got home from school the previous Monday.

My mother told me my father wasn't well. An ambulance was called.

When I went into his room, it was on the pretext of combing my long hair using the dressing-table mirror.

Dad lay, grey looking, propped up in the bed. I thought his breathing was unusual.

"The ambulance is coming for me," he said.

I tried to make light of it, continuing to comb my hair.

"You will be alright, Dad," was all I could muster, looking at him through the mirror; he was struggling to catch his breath.

My Dad had rheumatic fever twice, once as a child, once as a young adult. His problem wasn't to do with his coronaries. There was vegetative growth around the valves of his heart.

This type of thing was lethal in 1972. Now they could cure him in a few days, or at least fix his problem, and re-fix as necessary.

When the ambulance arrived, he laughed and joked with the crew who carried him down the short stairs of our house.

I ran out the back to the shed frantically filling the coal bucket.

Out of guilt, I ran back just in time to see him go out the front gate to be lifted by strangers into the back of the ambulance.

Strangers in a strange vehicle took him away from the house he lived in for close on twenty years.

I tried reading the newspaper to distract myself, the night

was endless. The phone rang. People called to see my mother, to check on my Dad's health.

My mother made way through her visitors in the sitting room to answer the phone. The hospital, we were to go quickly, my father was very ill.

I remember being sent to summon my older brother from a neighbour's, about a street away. One of our visitors, a man from down the street, came with me.

My older brother was eighteen. He was practicing guitar with a few of his mates. They had a dog who looked fierce. It sat guarding the front door, sitting on the mat, growling. The neighbour hesitated, but I kept going, my adrenalin up; nothing was going to stop me.

My older brother, to this day, is one of the bravest people I know.

I said, "Come on, Dad's very sick."

He just said, "OK," simply, and accompanied me home.

All week he sat outside my Dad's ward. He was hardly a man, yet he had to play a man's role. He dealt with things his way.

He is quiet, never speaks about it, he carries the weight.

The world stole from him that terrible day.

"I will pay no attention to it Toby," Monica said.

As they walked from the car, she felt the clouds heavy, the sun stolen. The valley below was misty, like little bonfires were lit at irrational intervals.

"It's Don Dino who worries me," Toby said looking back at her.

He has an odd look of resignation on his face.

"She is just resting, Toby, she cannot be in trouble. It is so stupid for her to want to be alone. She was worried for you, the baptism. Now all is fine, she is gone missing."

Monica gave a sort of mock laugh.

"The Don assures me, he knows where she is. I just know he is holding things back."

Toby turned the key to the side door. Soon they were

inside. The light was dim as the shutters were closed. The villa held an odd smell as if it needed to be aired.

"I will open a window," Monica said.

"Leave the shutter open. Don Dino has gone without a word, even security doesn't know where he is." Toby said.

"Try Gregor on his mobile. He always has it on."

"Good idea," Toby said, sitting down. "OK, Gregor? Yeah, will talk later. Yeah, OK."

"Well?" Monica said sitting opposite.

"You won't believe where our Don is," Toby said.

"Try me," Monica replied standing up to go pour a drink.

"Certaldo."

"Certaldo? What is he doing there?" Monica asked pouring a drink for Toby.

"Gregor thinks he is losing it. The Don is in repentance mode, has poor Gregor exhausted driving the roads."

Toby's mobile rang. Before Monica could answer it, he picked it up.

"Yeah, Matthew? Sssh," Toby indicated to Monica, who was rattling glasses.

"Mi dispiace." Toby said and then sighed. Monica saw his eyes swell with tears. "Grazie infinite Matthew, ho provato a fare tutto il possibile." Toby looked tearfully at Monica; she had already stepped towards him. "Donata è morta."

"Marea, povera ragazza." was all that Monica could say.

Don Dino allowed Gregor to help him into the car. When he was seated comfortably, he opened the window. The air was soft and moist, not Toscana weather. As Gregor drove he reflected on the old city, its church, how it had allowed him the peace to think.

She made her position clear; the money was for Toby and his children. 'I served the earth badly,' he remembered her words. Don Dino smiled for rarely had he met a person so true, no matter how unusual a life she led. It was time to go home, cut his losses, leave the world to providence. What a pity the evening was so dull, he would see little.

Drozdan tried in vain to make himself look taller than he was. The podium was old style. It felt more comfortable to lean on it. He hunched his shoulders. Argüelles gave him encouraging looks from the front row. The room was full with the fresh-faced, eager-looking students, even if, to his distaste, some were of mixed race. Drozdan took his pen and circled two paragraphs he might need to pass over. In all, maybe sixty students and ten of their mentors were in attendance. The room was quiet barring some vagrant coughing, the sound of latecomers scrambling for seats. At last he could start. He chose not to smile, but to shock.

"Each and every one of you is guilty," he began, watching the young faces move from light expectancy to serious frowns. "You sit here, each and every one of you, smug, compliant. You belong to a church that means nothing." Drozdan stopped abruptly. Argüelles beamed his support. It was the other faces he studied, the mentors in particular. Some of them seemed astonished, but interested in his style, his approach. Others he knew were enemies.

He could see the hostility in their demeanour already. The students ranged from amused to skeptical.

"Nothing." Again he paused as if to allow his audience to digest his words. "Where I come from, in Croatia, the church means nothing.

Where the good Monsignor comes from, in Spain, you're right, our church means nothing there either." He pointed at Argüelles, who beamed broadly. "Why is this? I can hear you say. Why is this? The Holy Roman Church meaningless all over the world. Worse, my good friends, is it used to mean something before it handed itself over to the liberal left, who, in all truth, have more in common with Jewry, than the message of Jesus Christ," Drozdan paused again. Some of the mentors, he could see them, recognizing the enemy, they moved even more uneasily in their seats. The students were discussing his statement when Drozdan raising his voice. shouted, "To move forward, we must go back, back in time to when the church stood for the protection of the decent. Philosophers, men like Cardinal Edgell, could see the truth. We need to be militant in our quest to realize it." The students were bickering among themselves as Drozdan allowed the dust to settle. One mentor, Drozdan recognized him as a liberal American, walked out followed by three of his students. "We allowed Stalin to live, think about it, Stalin, godless, merciless, we allowed him to own half of Europe till finally the demon seed he laid came to an end.

Think of today, we undermine the efforts of the righteous governments. They lead the fight against the infidel in non-Christian countries. While our enemies are quoting the gospel according to Josef Stalin. Think, my friends, think back, imagine the world had Adolph Hitler being feted rather than rebuffed. Would we have this dispassionate Catholicism we have today? We could rule the world with the truth. Whatever goodness man has is born with him. A man's race is the mould from which he spawns, it must be a good mould ..." Several students and mentors got up to leave. All the coloured students marched to the exits. Argüelles, fearing impending disaster, stood, waving people back to their seats. He stood, pathetically eyeing the Cardinal, who looked exhausted, his spit dribbling down his chin. A handful of students cheered; Drozdan waved at them to be seated. "I cannot water down the truth. It is this thinning of our basic belief which has sown the seed for the meltdown of our church. We in Sodality are committed to change, to return to the basic values of our Fathers, leave a legacy to the children of the world saying God's love is earned by right, one which is inherited at birth."

36.

How can I say it without falling down? I sat in the bath listening.

I hoped it was true. There was noise downstairs, sounds of people crying.

My aunt was on the phone, imparting the news to relatives. She was in tears and could hardly get her words out.

I was glad, I almost smiled to myself, thinking it's over, it's all over. I won't have to worry anymore. The pain in my tummy receded.

I dried myself going into the same room my younger brother was in the same bed my father lay in a week earlier.

"What is wrong? he asked."

"Nothing," I chided, bullying him into not asking anymore questions.

He didn't, he was eight years old.

Ten minutes later I sat on the stairs, my head in my hands, crying.

My older brother comforted me, telling me not to cry. We could look after everyone, the two of us.

Relatives and neighbours arrived. I watched my older brother wipe the tears from his eyes. They were single and unwanted, still they came.

I didn't cry again, not for a long time. I didn't cry in the church. I choked my tears at the graveyard.

I winced. They started to shovel the cold earth into the grave as we left.

The man who played music, the piano, the strong tenor

voice, who was talented enough to be a professional, was gone.

Him lying there, in that dark coffin. A million times I went to visit his grave.

I think it was around this time, when I was aged thirteen, I first hated the world and myself.

I still hate people. Most people are obnoxious, not genuine or true.

I still hate myself. I suppose that just about evens things out with the world.

We don't discuss my father as a family. Sometimes we say things like 'It's Dad's anniversary today.' Or my mother might say, 'your father used to say that, or sing that.'

In general we all sort of pretend it didn't happen.

In some ways it's like he didn't exist. Instead of bringing us closer as a unit, I feel somehow his death wedged between us. As if each one of us entered into our own world of confusion and regret . We all marched up the hill to our own private crucifixion. Lucia doesn't understand death, the way it affects people.

All her family are still alive, she has never been to Calvary. She has never had to smell the plastic container; it's foul perfume. The stench of flowers, withered before your eyes. Lucia says it was around this time I first went completely mad.

Drozdan was pleased a group of about ten students remained to give him a standing ovation. Their cheerleader was a plump little fellow with a tight, bowl-like haircut. He smiled as he clapped and cheered. Drozdan waved back from the podium. Some of the students at the rear gave Nazi-type salutes. The Cardinal wasn't sure which way to react, so he placed his arms in the air, imitating the type of pose adopted by artists when they depict saints. Argüelles, standing, turned to smile at the students. He knew the process of recruitment was difficult, recruiting would be slow. Their numbers need not be great to start, they already had their generals; the foot soldiers could be handpicked. He was surprised by the amount of noise the students made. They were clapping and cheering. Some were stamping their feet, shouting, "Drozdan, Drozdan." like they were at a boxing match.

Finally, the Cardinal dropped his arms to indicate to the Monsignor the meeting was over. Perhaps he might sign a few pamphlets the Monsignor had given out. As he walked from the podium, the students rushed forward to greet him, many with their pamphlets open, ready for his signature. Argüelles tried to offer security by standing in front of the Cardinal. The first group of students came to an abrupt halt, forming a sudden queue. Drozdan smiled as each one held his pamphlet out for signature. The students were complimenting him, bowing, and kissing his ring. The last in line was the plump little fellow with the bowl-shaped head. He held his pamphlet sideways over his arm. Passing Argüelles, he smiled broadly,

"Grazie," he said.

He handed the pamphlet to Drozdan. The Cardinal noticed the shine of the gun straight away. Argüelles thought it was a toy of some sort. The robust young seminarian shot Drozdan straight through the temple, his silencer making a sound like a small metal object being dropped. Argüelles, looking on in disbelief, tried to take cover. The seminarian, still smiling, turned and shot the Monsignor straight through the chin. He fell to the stone floor, hard, like he was made of lead. The young man walked by the shocked students out to the foyer. He discarded his gun into the waste bin before walking outside where he boarded a waiting scooter, taking the time to put on his helmet.

The scooter left slowly before turning right down a narrow lane to disappear.

Gregor did as Don Dino requested. He stopped at the village outside Bagni di Lucca. He didn't mind so much as they were almost home. He just couldn't grasp why the Don insisted on walking up the hill alone. Don Dino took his time, walking slowly, feeling a faint chill, disappointed by the unseasonable weather, wondering when things might improve. Comforting himself he thought of her. This was her place, the place where she spent her happy years with James. When James died, she reverted to her youth. Somehow James managed to protect her from herself, her dark past. It was his great skill, one inherited by his son.

He reached the brow of the hill. Looking back Gregor was parked safely, just by the road. Behind him the hillside full of trees, forests thrived as far as the eye could see. She had chosen this place, dark and hidden. She lived here, like in a fairy tale. Don Dino checked his pocket for the package she left.

Gregor watched from the car. The Don was walking by the rail protecting the meadow. Gregor's phone beeped; he read the text. Ah! The Don will be pleased, his enemies have been dealt with, his repentance already made. Gregor watched as Don Dino retraced his steps down the hill. There was lightness in his movement.

Eva was tired, looking over her files for the umpteenth time. She sipped her gin slowly. She needed her wits about her; a special effort was required. She was looking at the photographs, almost like she expected the faces to change. They always remained the same.

Eva saw the same look of innocence. The ones she hated, the gruesome pictures taken for the pathologists, the innocence became resignation, shocked, crushed, anger. What would James Burdon have made of all of this? She could still see him in the flush of his youth, his earnest face, fighting all alone vicious wolves, animals so fierce, they could devour him. All that time, he withheld his natural male desires. A man out of place, out of time, in conflict with himself, his own conscience, his own frailty.

Never did she think badly of him. Life is, in essence, revisionist. We revise our opinions, our thoughts, our sureties, on a daily even hourly basis. Of course, he was wrong to do it, he took advantage. She was at her weakest, most vulnerable. Yet, was it she that wanted him to do it? Even though she had no idea of the mechanics of love, was it her desire? James cried too, wetting the pillow, his tears so intense; his regret so large. No matter what she might say, he could never forgive himself. Before he died, he confessed to Matthew. Matthew gave him absolution, yet James held the view, some sins were unforgivable. He confided in her at the height of his illness. "My violation of you was preceded by a year of thought and torment," Eva thought of her own sins, gin finding the gateway to her soul.

Sometimes she watched him, as he sat drinking coffee, or in the chair on the small terrace. She imagined what was running through his mind long into the night, lamenting on his ravaging of her, restless cries of torment. Despite it being sinful, it was also illegal. So he ran away with her. Was it under a false pretence? Was he running from the law, from spite? The disgust within the community he served might have destroyed him. Yet they led such a good life together, loved their child, befriended and consoled Don Dino. Could life have served them better if they stayed in the dark rains of South Armagh? Did James Burdon deserve to be jailed for what he did? Was it not him who fought against the injustice so violently executed on his flock? Should she herself not have gone to jail?

Eva took more gin. It crept into her, half afraid to be swallowed. Was this her potion, allowing her to forget her own crimes? Allowed James to forgive her in exchange? They were two sinners exchanging forgiveness in order to continue normal lives, the rock on which they built their lives dried dust. How convenient!

James and Matthew sitting in the scullery drinking coffee, talking about liberation theology, speaking grandiosely about the poor, the association between Jesus Christ and the individual, the co-relation with the politics of communism, even anarchy. Highbrow nonsense! Or is it just part of the human condition? We take chances, we do dangerous things, not only to ourselves but to our loved ones. They are at risk, by default, if we abandon responsibility. Was James not just as morally reprehensible as Boyce? What was the difference between Boyce and James? Is not all moral and political ideology bankrupt?

Her father was too weak to stand up and face the bullying of Captain Boyce. Mother, straw chewer, child, baby, Mummy. The terror in the eyes of the boys, congealed blood seeping from their souls, blood replacing tears.

Their pleading and screaming, begging for their lives, loud at first, then softer, quieter, their breathing falling, irregular.

The gin was forming patches to plug holes. She felt drilling in her heart till the pictures became deformed. She could not see any before or after, staring to the past to find her body shiver with cold. Was it enough to feel guilty? Did it add a certain glow? James was no longer around to ease her conscience.

37.

The night in Viaréggio was special I was sitting on the rooftop terrace with Lucia. We were flirting with the Italian air. The sea silenced the crude sounds from the street below, drowning all, allowing only a faint breeze.

Gardiner was only an afterthought, happens sometimes when I drink too much wine.

To me he was too compact. Lucia thought him to be ordinary and nice.

I probably found him too middleclass. It's a secret hate of mine. I hate the middle classes, their values, their morals. More importantly, the way they reproduce themselves with arrogant authority.

Don't get me wrong, I hate the upper classes even more. As for the working classes, where I come from, don't get me going!

Right now, I just want to pick on the middle classes, mainly because it's easy.

As I say, Gardiner was too neat, he had middle-class written all over him.

I can tell by the clothes they wear, the way they sit, the way they address waitresses and each other.

Middle classes now are the new horse manure, all diligent, hardarsed business types married to their desks.

They have little or no time for their families, barring to put the bread on the table, relaxing, playing low handicap golf, driving new expensive cars, bragging to their cronies, who they meet once a week in the bar. Buying a new car, passing their old one on to the wife.

They're nothing unless the kids have been to Florida, Sea World, in New York for shopping.

If they're really on their game, they organize for the wife to go with the daughter or a friend. Staying at home to play more golf, clear their desk. Good old ordinary normal middle classes do this, like Gardiner who writes copy, "Welcome to Marlboro country." and shit like that.

What is wrong with me? Why don't I want to be happy? Is there a part of me all jealous? Maybe me as middleclass is all I ever wanted!

Just to be normal, three-bed semi, mortgage, happy kids, happy wife, live, die, like the rest of the goddamn world.

Why do I watch people happy, dancing, think sad things once the alcohol hits the system? I remember the painted ego, the self-esteem, covered with black bin liner.

Viaréggio at night, where I dreamed so much looking out over the city from the roof of the Grand Palace Hotel. I watched as the world moved politely, without fuss, with such order, such beauty, yet I felt I didn't belong.

The summer after Julie, I went back to London again. This time by ferry with my friend Tim, a thin guy with delicate looks yet women found him very attractive. He came from a very traditional Catholic family, yet he seemed to reject all of this.

I remembered when I was young watching his family troupe down to Communion in age order, announcing their family's respectability to the world.

His people were decent. Tim was intelligent and very good academically. When he left school he got a really good job in the laboratory of a multinational manufacturing company.

However Tim liked to rebel so he threw the job in and started to take copious amounts of soft drugs.

We became friends because we both liked live music and long hair.

He came to stay in my flat in Longford Terrace. Then we decided to go see the world and head to London.

We arrived in London early morning, with just about the price of breakfast. Tim had the address of another crony of ours called Tony. He lived in a place called Hackney in North East London.

The first time I saw Beck Road it reminded me a little of two streets in Sallynoggin, save for it was longer.

The streets I refer to are Sarsfield Street and Parnell Street. Both were made of artisan-type dwellings. Families of ten and more were brought up in these two-bedroomed houses.

There were lots of Irish still heading to London, even in the mid-seventies. The economy wasn't good at home. The educational opportunities which are available now, were unheard of back then.

Funny though, a great deal of the people I met there were roughing it, yet many of them came from what I regarded as a better social status. I mean from places like Blackrock, Booterstown, and Foxrock, like this guy Tony was from Foxrock.

I think his father drank and was rough with them. I could never understand it, how a fella could downgrade his old man who was living. As far as I was concerned it didn't matter what your father was like as long as he was above ground. These guys were lucky.

Looking back, I suppose, I was just naive.

Don Maestrino sat staring at the empty bar, the place abandoned, the musty smell of closed windows, people gone, leaving only dust. He thought of Philippe, though not in an emotive way. His boy jumped ship, he was mixed up. America was the only place for him now. He received bits of news. It wasn't good, reports of fights, excessive drinking. His cousins keeping an eye but there was only so much they could do. Don Maestrino knew Philippe's life was finely balanced. If he threatened the wrong people, got involved with drugs, maybe just rubbed up some people the wrong way, God only knows. Helping himself to a whiskey, not realizing how much he poured. Where had he gone wrong? What words of wisdom had he failed to impart? Maybe he allowed him grow too quickly? Philippe had the mind of a twenty-year-old when he was only ten. Was it because Stella died when he was young he became precocious? Fate conspired and visited his own flesh and blood. Was it by example? Did the boy see in the dark figures of Raymond and his henchmen heroes to follow, worship? Boy, he thought a chip off the old block. He tried to remember back in time to when he was young. Don Maestrino, the man, when he first met the beautiful Stella.

He drank more whiskey, soothing his nerves. His memories became more vivid. He could see himself with Stella, dancing to violin music in the kitchen of her house. Her brothers sitting round the table, clapping, break dancing like Russians do when full of vodka. Yes, and these fellows would think nothing of grabbing a shotgun. They could blow a hole in an enemy's chest midst a row over land or a dispute over the honour of a sister. Volterra, the golden fields often hid rivers of blood, trenches dug deep into the night. Who knew where people ended up? Their families came looking, silence can belong to a community. Recently he noticed, animals stay within the confines of their own, their likeness, their sameness. Humans do also.

So Philippe watched his father, tried to emulate him. In the end he was left with one choice, to try and be better, more ruthless, successful. But for whom, Philippe? To please his father, so his father should be proud of him! He drank more whiskey, finding that his mind was even clearer now. The reasons made more sense; the memories were more real, true to life. Don Dino believed him about the explosives. In truth he didn't know they were to kill Benedetto. 'How did I not suspect? Can Don Dino forgive me? I was aware it was for an attack on his family. I didn't know it was for Benedetto. Does that soften the blow?

No. The Don was too forgiving, too nice. Maybe he hatched a plot in his head. Perhaps he was saved through Monica. Don Dino liked Monica. He may care for my daughter, like she is part of his family.'

He took more whiskey. The drink was cold till it was swallowed, its heat internal only. Knowing the power of Don Dino, it was the greatest he had ever seen. He remembered when they were young, imprisoned in the city prison in Volterra, Don Dino arranged things. It was here they resumed their rivalry from childhood.

It was over small things at first, like who was in control of smuggled goods like tobacco or alcohol. Don Maestrino controlled his section, Don Dino, the other. One day, he sent his runner on a delivery. The young runner was gone for a long time. Don Maestrino waited patiently, wondering where on earth his charge had gone, till at last it was night and lock up time. He was almost asleep when a tray was pushed through the flap of his cell door. On it, covered with a napkin, was the severed finger of his courier. Don Maestrino recognized his ring, it read, 'Alberto.' So this is why Philippe hated his father. He had turned his back on the very core of the activities which made his family rich and strong. The final insult to go seek protection from Don Dino himself. Don Maestrino was getting tired, his vision was blurred and his head shaking.

He had consumed most of the bottle of whiskey, only a half glass left. Raymond stepped in from the shadows. Don Maestrino eyed him contemptuously.

"I am not ready to leave here, not yet," he said harshly. "I will lock the place up, it will have new owners soon, 'New York Bar Viaréggio.' Raymond didn't answer. He stood still, looking sadly on his long-time employer. "What is it, Raymond? Is there bad news from New York?" Don Maestrino asked, his eyes squinting at his tried and trusted.

"No, My Don, there is no news. I just have not seen you so drunk for many years."

"Yes, and you know why I am so drunk?" He turned to stare into Raymond's eyes. "It is because I have failed, my whole life has failed. Philippe is right, I lost my bottle. I am not like Don Dino going in search of God, do penance every time I have to do a hard thing, kill or maim an enemy! A snake does not apologize for its poison."

"True, My Don. I will bring you home."

Raymond moved to assist Don Maestrino from his stool. In the limousine, Don Maestrino fell forward with the effects of drink. He hit his head against the dash. Raymond was concerned.

"Are you ok?" Raymond turned on the interior light. A blue and purple bruise had already blotched the old man's skin.

"Bring me home."

Don Maestrino slurred his words. Raymond turned the ignition. The doors of the limousine blew, the driver's side smashed into the side window of the bar, the passenger side went skywards. Then the roof blew off, the two occupants burned till it looked like they were dummies in a test environment. The front wheels rolled across the promenade, on fire. Late-night stragglers thought some street theatre group were performing.

Almost immediately the front of the New York Bar blew onto the promenade, its glass flying everywhere, causing cars to swerve and inflicting superficial wounds to people on the cycle path.

38.

At the end of Beck Road, St Joseph's Hospice. I often stopped, when leaving the house, to gaze up at the people in their dressing gowns, sitting in a sort of lobby area watching television.

One of the English guys staying with us, a speed head, told us the truth. He said simply, "They go there to die."

I have to admit, this unsettled me. From what I could see, most of the inmates were young, like in their twenties or thirties. From where I stood, they were just chatting amongst themselves.

Sitting normal-like, staying in a hotel or something. I wrote Julie a poem about death. It went childishly, "If I needed to be rescued, would she come?"

It was a sort of play on words. I was trying to explain to her the experience I had of watching the walking dead every day. This was set against my own silly infatuation with her. It was meant to parody me, in context what had I to worry me? I don't think she got it.

Tony, myself, and Tim played football in the local park. I thought maybe some scout would notice me. I might end up playing for some first division outfit.

They didn't, and we needed to get money.

One of our other mates, who visited us in Monkstown, we nicknamed Scissors. This was in the days before joyriding became an epidemic.

This guy could start a car, using scissors, which was some feat. I met Scissors through Tim, he was due to follow us over.

The DHSS were kind to Irish boys who were too lazy and weird to work, so the in thing to do was sign on.

I, in my mad way, could justify it using reverse logic. I was drawing from the British State, thus hurting their economy, helping redress the balance of eight hundred years of colonization.

I am sure the eight pounds a week I got broke the country. Our English counterparts kept calling me Paddy. This made my effort at destabilising worthwhile, yet silly, rather shameful when I look back.

So we became the great unwashed, the great underused. Ambition was replaced by alcohol and soft drugs with a complete loss of self-esteem.

Tim and I decided on account of Tony (who actually did work on a building site, as a labourer), who was heading home, to move house.

There were various reasons for this. One was the speed head who ran us ragged in Beck Road. Also the state of the place, with guys pissing in the kitchen sink. The toilet was outdoor as well, with no toilet paper, it was littered with piles of pornographic magazines.

Next-door was worse; this place was more rundown than ours.

A Dublin guy called Peter lived there with an English girl. She was much older than us. Brian, this English guy we befriended, said they had intercourse one night when they were all smoking. Didn't care who was looking.

Intercourse was a strange thing to me. I was a virgin. I don't think Tim was a virgin, because he had a girlfriend called Louise back home. There was alcoholism in her family, I dunno. From what I have seen alcoholism is a dreadful disease; there is nothing that robs children of their childhood like it.

Anyhow, it was then we decided to move to Casterton Street, a little cull de sac made up of two squats.

We moved in expecting Scissors, also a visit from Marie, one of our female flat neighbours from Monkstown.

I didn't know, me silly idiot, sending flowery poetry about

dancers to her, that she only had eyes for Scissors. So there
you go, that's life.

"I fuckin' hate you," Monica said hysterically.

She beat Don Dino's chest so hard, Toby had to pull her
away.

"No Monica, calm down," Toby chided.

"Look what you have done, big fuckin' man, Don Dino. You
have killed my father, sent the only person left in my family
who could have stood up to you, into exile. Jesus! Did you see
the newspaper, Toby? He killed the Cardinal, the Monsignor
as well. You're an evil, evil man."

Monica went to beat at Don Dino's chest again, but Toby
restrained her. Gregor stood by at the sliding terrace doors.

"Is it true, Don Dino? Are you responsible for this?" Toby
asked, almost ashamed, airing his own naivety.

The Don had taken a seat, his lips curled beneath his harsh
white head.

"You expect too much from Don Dino. I am an old man.
I am retired. These religious bigots were responsible. Toby, it
is clear they targeted Don Maestrino because of this Cardinal
Drozdan, Monsignor Argüelles. It was an act of revenge,
totally outside of the Bernado family's control."

Toby stared at the Don to try see through him, find some
version of the truth.

"Liar!" Monica screamed. "Wait till my brother returns
some day, he will return to avenge his father."

"Monica," Toby implored, as if to remind her of respect.

"Philippe will return. I know my brother. I am so exhausted
by guilt, I got it wrong, not him,"

Toby went to comfort her, but she withdrew from him,
sobbing.

"It is with great regret I heard of the demise of Don
Maestrino. We know each other since childhood," said the
Don. "I cannot be responsible for the evil works of rogue
Cardinals and Monsignors. I hear this Drozdan and Argüelles

were patrons of the Roma Mafiosi." The Don still held his lip curled. "It is her right to be angry, Toby, she believes I have killed her father, she is without blame."

Monica had slumped into a garden seat. She was shivering and shaking. Toby offered her his hand, but she refused. He looked at the Don ruefully.

"She thinks you are responsible?" Toby said standing and watching the Don's eyes.

Don Dino also stood, staring back at Toby, their eyes held as if in a trance.

"E' importante che sappia che sono innocente."

He waved his hands excitedly.

"Assassino." Monica said under her breath, looking at the Don's curled lip. "I will leave here now. Are you coming, Toby? I cannot share a house with such a person."

She stood. Toby looked at her then at the Don, who stood impassively. His lip twisted, like he had something stuck in his mouth. "You come now, Toby, or forever you are doomed to live with this evil."   Don Dino sat down again as if exasperated, sighing still twisting his lip. Toby noticed his eyes made of glass. "Make your decision, Toby," Monica semi-mocked him. "Come on, miracle man, save whatever's good."

She went to leave.

"Monica," Toby shouted. "No, wait," he pleaded.

"If I leave without you, I will always be without you, Toby,"

she smiled, stopping at the sliding door. Don Dino sat, his head bowed.

"Ti amo," Toby said passionately.

Monica turned her back on him, walking away. Gregor watched as she walked through the dark interior, slamming the door. Don Dino looked at him quickly, shaking his head. Gregor watched Toby slump into his seat in silence.

When Monica reached Viaréggio she had no choice but to book into the Grand Palace Hotel. Her father's apartment was sealed off by the Carabinieri. She went to the rooftop terrace to have a drink, to think. The drive through Lucca was long and weary, especially at night. She asked the waitress for vodka. Soon her head was relaxed, things started to clear. Things she had been so unsure about for so long started to make sense. Philippe heard his father's stories, it became part of his brain, part of the folklore.

When she met Toby, she thought he was the best, most faithful and attractive man she had ever laid eyes on. He was so kind to her. When she felt unloved, unwanted, a woman struggling in a man's world, Toby took her by the hand. Toby the lover, the faith healer, stray son. He had an alcoholic mother, his father older, deceased before they even met. Who was this man? Why did Toby live under the protectorate of Don Dino? Toby thought there was no God like Don Dino. Eva, felt there was no God like him either.

Monica hesitated, taking a sip of her vodka. She knew her habit, she was speaking aloud, people would look at her. It was clear in her head. Don Dino had organized the murder of her father. There were things to attend to. Philippe must return from America. He would find her different now, she had changed. She was not like before trusting them, Eva and Toby, they were non-people. They only existed because Don Dino wielded such power. Her father had trusted him to save his only son. Don Dino abused her father's trust. Philippe knew, he knew all along, knew the rules of the game. Don Maestrino was old and mellow.

Monica moved uneasily in her seat. If they should come after her she was alone. Toby was no longer her lover. Don Dino wouldn't think twice. She calmed herself. Toby was a simple boy who believed all his mother told him, or was it the other way round? Did Toby hold the power and Eva believe everything he said? She sometimes thought if Toby said black was white, Eva would consider the possibility.

She suddenly became nervous, checking the tables around her, watching for sudden movements, knowing she had no way of defending herself. Out of habit, she thought of dialling Toby.

Silly, earlier he made his choice; he would not protect her now. She must get a gun. She didn't know how to use a gun. She tried Philippe once more, no connection. She tried again using a different area code and it rang a strange ring tone.

"Hello?"

"Philippe? Thank God! Where are you?" Monica cried.

"Drinking beer in Manhattan. Why, Monica? Why do you call me? You don't like me."

His tone was matter of fact, without malice.

"Philippe, you must come home straight away. They have killed father and Raymond. I am so scared," There was a silence at the other end of the phone. "Philippe, Philippe," she said.

"Yeah, I'm still here, when did this happen?" he asked sadly.

"Last night a car bomb..." I tried to get you earlier but I was dialing the wrong number,

Monica spoke too fast. Again Philippe was quiet.

"Where are you?" he asked finally.

"In the Grand Palace Hotel," Monica said nervously.

"OK. Stay there till I get back in a couple of days. I have to make some calls. Stay there, Monica. Don't leave the hotel."

"Alright." she said, shaking.

Philippe was gone.

She looked around, feeling isolated. Rosa was coming to give the bill. It was time to leave. As she got up, two men and two women at the next table got up to leave also. She was half way to the sliding door leading to the small bar when she realized she left her bag on the table. Monica turned to retrieve her bag. The man from the next table followed.

"I have it for you," he said.

His companion, about a year younger, stood close by with a blonde lady.

He said jokingly, "We are all rich."

Laughing pointing to the bag.

"Grazie," Monica said, turning to leave once more.

She felt the weight of both men as they lifted her. Monica felt herself carried, her feet flailing. She was held over the parapet.

In all it took about ten seconds. The women, uninterested, chatted idly,

"There is an envelope on your table. You are no longer under the protection of Don Dino," the taller of the two men said harshly.

Monica returned to a standing position. They left, the women laughing. Monica went to her seat, her body numb from the neck down. Rosa returned with her change.

"Are you ok, madam?" she asked.

Monica nodded, holding up her hands and gesturing for Rosa to keep the change. Picking up the envelope, she walked out blindly.

39.

When Scissors arrived, things got better. He had a calming, almost ridiculous charm.

Tim respected him, doing whatever Scissors told him to do. We shared the house with Brian and two other English guys.

Scissors came from a big family. He was from a nice house out in Blackrock.

He didn't need to sign on and always had enough cash for a meat pie in the shop opposite, which was run by an Irishman and his wife.

The owner spent his time advising us to go home; we didn't take a blind bit of notice. Eating his meat pies, listening to "Captain Beefheart." drinking snakebite, smoking Lebanese draw.

One evening, we drank a lot of snakebite, smoking our Leb and listening to sounds.

Tim had a funny way of toking. He inhaled very deeply, his face pale, contorting into rubbery shapes, eventually turning purple before exhaling dark clouds into the air. Scissors sat winking at me, laughing.

The English guys didn't get us at all, a crowd of paddies in their midst.

Brian was the most decent of the English lads. He didn't get on with the only other resident on the street, a Bryan Ferry look-alike named Bill.

The other two English guys, Reg and Mike, used to wind him up about it saying things like – ' that ponce next door is out to get you, mate.'

Anyhow one day we were all pissed and smoked out of it. All of a sudden two police cars pulled up.

I have never seen fellas leg it so fast. The Dublin term is 'scatter', pronounced 'scattterrrr.'

Out the back, half way up to the railway track, so doped out of it all were laughing.

The cops, of course, went next door to arrest our good friend Bill. We trailed back, one by one, to our little room to see them escort Bill into a police car, a heavy hand on his head.

Much to Brian's delight his arch enemy was escorted away by the police.

When Marie arrived, I had no idea she had the hots for Scissors.

I thought I loved her. Once again, it was just one of my silly infatuations.

Befriending her and her flatmates in Longford Terrace, their flat a large spacious place with huge bedrooms with a beautiful view over Dublin bay.

We became friends, a certain ease descended like we were friends and always would remain so. Marie thought us funny, if not a little mad.

One night, when we gathered in our flat, I plucked up the courage to ask her to go for a walk. To my surprise, she agreed. We walked down Salthill towards Seapoint.

After a while we sat on the cold stone wall protecting the railway line.

It was a beautiful night the full moon lit her face. She was small, with lovely reddish hair her cheekbones were full, allowing her eyes to dance. Marie was soft, with a beautiful laugh coming from her heart. Her giggle was infectious. Often people laughed with her not knowing why. She was quiet watching the moonlight cast dark shadows across the water, save for the shoreline which retained its blue. Lights danced as electric fish jumped and were swallowed. She watched as the dark shadow pushed towards us, leaving the spirit dancers drift further away.

We chatted. I told her about my past. She was cool, her reaction wasn't over played.

Like, no matter what I might say, she reacted the same way.

She told me about herself, her family, about a brother she lost when she was young.

I fell back a little somehow I couldn't quite understand somebody's loss could outdo mine.

She was cool about it. In her own measured way there was no give towards drama, never an inkling. She never required understanding or pity, like she was saying, 'This happened to us. I guess it's the way life is'. I, silly put my hand up to stroke her cheek.

Her skin was firm, female, pure. Marie never flinched or acted different, like she expected me to kiss her, get closer.

She stayed cool and controlled her beating the world, her anger at the elements before her, the sea, the moon, and the stars in heaven.

Monica looked at the envelope, its contents spread over the bed, one hundred thousand Euros in used bank notes. There was Don Maestrino's estate to consider, his lawyers said it could take years to complete. The police were investigating his death and also his assets. His lawyers could not be sure what might eventually pass on to Philippe and herself, his wealth or debt. She felt the tears swell in her eyes, how she needed him to come home! How she prayed he wasn't too afraid! Frightened, scared of Don Dino, would he want to care for and protect his sister?

Maybe she should contact Toby? See where he stands now, whether he has had time to think? The tears started to fall as she suddenly realized she was powerless to do anything. Where on earth had she gone, her whole identity stolen?

She the daughter of Don Maestrino Giordano the sister of Philippe, the lover of Toby. Who was Monica, what had the world left to offer her? In an instant, she sat on the bed, the bank notes crumpling under her weight. She held her head in her hands, her eyes wetting the tips of her fingers.

Maybe go to London, she heard there were good opportunities there for singers. She might even invest some of this cash in singing lessons, one day she might get to sing in Convent Garden. "I will go soon, in the next few days," she said aloud. Should she wait for Philippe? She might entice him away from Italy, maybe he would go with her.

Don Dino watched Toby as he lifted his glass, his right hand shook. Maybe he was getting a debilitating disease. Holding the newspaper, it also trembled.

The Don was about to say something when Toby, feeling his gaze, lifted his head and said, "Tell me we are innocent?" Don Dino smiled at him softly.

"I swear to you, Toby, we had nothing to do with it. This has all the hallmarks of our friends from Rome, I tell you."

"These reports from Rome, Don Dino, what do they mean? Drozdan and Argüelles, dead, shot by an assassin. People will suspect us first and foremost."

Don Dino sighed, exasperated, "Don't you trust me, Toby?"

"I do, I do."

"I swear on Benedetto's grave, I had no hand in these events. Is that not enough for you?"

Toby nodded, putting the paper down. He picked up the glass once again; his hand shook slightly.

"It is Monica, isn't it? You miss the girl?" the Don said.

"She thinks we are bad people. I doubt if we should ever change her mind now her head is set against us. She is so sure."

"She is wrong!" Don Dino said, considering Toby's comments. "What hurts me is she wants me to make a choice. She wants me to come out and say, 'Yes, Monica, Don Dino is a murderer, a common criminal,' huh?"

"I can't say that," Toby continued.

"It is more likely she is upset. After all, she was very close to Don Maestrino, he doted on her. Her brother, he runs to hide in New York. He is of no help to her. She wants you to make choices, so she can get a hold on you, have you forever at her beck and call." Toby studied the Don's expression; he was angry.

"I love you, Don Dino," Toby said, half embarrassed.

Don Dino went to rise from the table. He looked away, as if embarrassed himself.

The fields looked dead they needed a little rain, then three solid days of sun just to bring them to life.

"I will tell you about love, Toby," he said sitting down again, the light wind brushing his face.

"Love is non-existent between man and woman. There is no love, only arrangement. You may be fooled Toby, but you are not a fool." The old man rested back in his chair, watching Toby. The younger man's eyes falling to stare at the steel table, to reflect. "Love is what a parent holds for a child, or a child for its parent, brother has for sister. There can only be true love through blood. All other love is transient; it is with condition, on condition. It is subject to status, to rule. You are no more in love with Monica than I. You are a man, Toby. She has a delicious body for you. You are lean, perfect for her. Where do your minds meet? As soon as she gets bad news, it is your fault. Her anger is vented on you. Has she tried to contact you since?"

Don Dino was angry.

"No," Toby said finally, as he shakingly lifted his glass once more, "she has not."

"Well," said Don Dino, "I felt so sorry for her, in spite of her warped opinion of me. I offered her money to go away, to allow her think, reflect. I left her a considerable amount. Has she returned it, told you she is sorry? She is wrong. Disappears with the cash, just like the rest of them. Toby, don't be fooled."

Toby finished his drink, standing abruptly.

"She accepted your money, yet still discards me like I

was shit. I see," he said and turned to go, but the Don wasn't finished.

"Your heart is like a hole. You must fill it with concrete, or else people will pollute it and it will wither and die. It is your fate I fear."

Toby eyed his elder, his light blue eyes uncomfortable in their glass cases.

"I have learned, learned so many things," he said as he left, to re-enter the house.

The Don felt a sharp pain down the side of his face, a trapped nerve. Feeling it tighten he rubbed it, massaging with his fingers deep below the ear.

The sun made a sudden appearance beyond the distant hills. The heat helped him relax his muscles, till soon the pain receded. Benedetto would understand. No point in upsetting Toby, not after all that had happened, or what might still happen. It was alright to lie alright to do things, and justify them, even bad things, if they were for the best.

Don Dino stood and walked to the grass watching a small lizard break for the heat of a stone. He thought it was the essence of living to seek comfort and protection. Right now, his sole mission was to protect Toby at all costs. Soon he may have nobody else. The boy sought refuge, comfort, with Don Dino, anything else useless. He sighed as he turned back to the darkness of the house. Toby might never understand his actions, or his motives. Forever he would deny his participation in the death of Don Maestrino, the tracks would become overgrown.

Monica let Toby's number display. She wanted to ring him now in all her panic. She knew him he would come to her comfort her. Toby was never angry or vindictive. The news of Don Maestrino shocked her, upset her. He'd understand the things she said were in the heat of the moment. Of course she loved him, loved him dearly, always. It was the right thing to do. All this thinking of London, was she losing her mind? An Italian girl, alone in a strange city like London. Yet as she went to dial, she stopped. What could Toby do? She asked him to make a choice. He chose Don Dino. It was clear. He didn't follow her, find her like a lover should. No Toby's intentions were clear, he let her go. What if the money was his idea? Maybe he persuaded Don Dino to give her the money so she could go away. What if the Don was grooming Toby, as he might his son? After all those wild rumours about Eva, perhaps it was Toby who killed her father?

40.

I knew Marie wanted Scissors, when she stayed overnight in Casterton Street.

Something tells me it wasn't that I wanted her so much really I didn't want anyone else to have her.

This I listed under the heading, 'More bad luck for me.' Frustration, really.

I could hear them, Scissors laughing as they horsed about on the couch.

I adopted this heavy brick-on-my-shoulder syndrome, which I carry to this day.

When Marie headed back to Dublin, I could see Scissors get all emotional in Euston Station.

The way he watched the train as it left, like his whole life was on it. I knew then my feelings were no match for his.

The realization hurt even more, for, as sure as anything, I knew this wasn't a fling, one day they would get married, and they did.

Tim was getting restless. We needed to find work the DHSS were hardly feeding us.

I applied for a job in a supermarket chain in Hendon. Did the whole lot, references, letters, got called for an interview.

My social money was laid out for a haircut, then, the English boys told me Hendon was miles away, like too far.

I was gutted. I got the tube to Baker Street. There was an agency there. You could get work washing dishes, cleaning the underground. Going back on the tube I kept catching the eye of this pretty girl opposite. Looking down, then up. She was doing the same, somehow our eyes met accidentally. The more we tried to avoid it, the more contact we made.

She smiled at me. I was falling in love. Eventually, of course, she got up to leave.

I was almost tempted to follow her. She walked away without looking. She enjoyed a bit of fun that was it.

Back at the squat things were getting worse. We weren't eating properly, losing weight, smoking dope, drinking lots of snakebite.

I sat in the kitchen, drinking coffee. Somehow it all got too much. I had such hope when I rented the flat in Monkstown, I just wanted to grow up, be independent, mature.

I only wanted to live a self-sufficient life, have a regular girlfriend, live a normal life. Here I was, with a crowd of English lads calling me Paddy, sitting drinking cold coffee from a filthy mug, without a red cent in my pocket.

I don't know what came over me. I just fired the mug through the window in frustration. It smashed the glass and shattered into the yard.

The English boys never called me Paddy again. Tim and Scissors gave me anxious looks whenever I walked into the room. I knew it was time to admit defeat, to go home.

I sometimes wondered what was wrong with me. London has lots of little parks, adorning every urban area.

Walking through, mid-November, the leaves lay in heaps by wet tree trunks. In my mind's eye, I saw naked girls, girls I wanted, could never have. They danced naked, beyond.

I could imagine them anywhere, parks were a special place.

Was my life just a whole series of dreams? Why were women shy of me? I held my head down in their company. I felt my nose was too long, it made me ugly; my skin was tarnished with teenage spots, so ugly.

Still kept my culture though. One night, Tim and I went to see James Joyce's, A Portrait of the Artist as a Young Man. We even had a drink first.

The film was preceded by a wildlife documentary by Patrick Carey, then a short about Joyce's life itself. This included pictures of Killiney and Dalkey, home from home. The small audience was made up of young English students.

They were touched by the sincerity, the intellectualization of it all.

Little did they know, Tim and I had walked the same streets as Joyce, had shared the same beach at Sandycove!

I promised myself, if I ever wrote a novel, I'd try out-do Joyce, stealing from his characters, Stephen, I would call one of my female characters Lucia, after his daughter.

The film was pretty good. I loved Maureen Potter as the aunt arguing about Parnell at the dinner table.

With Joyce's work, it is impossible to make a film without bending to the surreal and the offensive. I don't think Joyce wrote for film as such, maybe he wrote for the mind's eye. The only good movie of Joyce was John Huston's, 'The Dead.'

Gardiner woke with a start. It reminded him of his operation, hearing a voice calling his name. It was soft at first, distant, then, got louder, like a beating drum. The nurse's voice coaxing him, "It's all over now; you did great!" Slowly, slowly, he came to his senses. He realized the room was empty, the shutters were closed fast. The faint light broke through cracks in the wood. The sun was making a comeback, still weak, like it just found Earth. Gardiner was cold through. Pulling the duvet around his shoulders, it gave instant heat, surprising him.

Instinctively he reached for his bag. He noticed the automatic and was taken by the silver glitter. He moved it, taking his medicines in three separate packs: Aspirin, Diamicron, Emcor. He washed them down with small sips of water from his nightcap glass. Checking the time, he dragged his upper body up. The pillows supported his neck and back properly. It was early, 5.50 a.m. He could rest a little. Closing his eyes he heard once more her voice, so sweet, so true, "You did great; it's all over." The intensive care ward, so neat, so compact. His mind jumped from one thing to the next. The nurse was watching the monitor behind him. The junior doctor was writing copious notes. Opposite him an old man lay unconscious.

"Boy, you sure talked a lot. You're coming around, you're sayin' all sorts," the nurse said innocently.

The other nurse came to help; they discussed removing drains from his chest.

"Don't you look," said the nurse who woke him.

Gardiner studied her deep brown eyes she looked younger than she actually was. He searched them for intelligence. Her eyes were innocent, he concluded. She cared only for him. Gardiner stared at her hair all tied up under a wiry hat. Yet she was still pretty. Her mouth was strong, with thick lips. She gave her name, Pam. Good it was an easy name to remember. The other nurse was small, fat, dark. She was foreign.

She assisted and in unison they said, "Now."

Pam said, "Don't look."

Gardiner looked. They pulled a bar full of tubes, cold steam rose from his chest. He felt lighter, swish. His insides were exposed the body started to seal, all dark in there, dark internal sea. Swish, it washed his internal organs. When he slept, he met Agnolino in his dream. For the first time, he saw the steep hill; the white rail guarding the soft meadow; the ambulance with the siren bellowing; Agnolino with his mobile phone stuck to his ear; the perspiration draining down his cheeks; running up the hill; on the beach at Viaréggio; the hawkers passing him were trying to sell; the emptiness; Susie waving from the shore; Shaun and Marsha were waving in unison. His mind switched to the pool, Susie on the sun lounger, feeling a sharp pain, his chest about to burst. Gardiner drank the last of his water, time to get up. As he moved, he could see the marks, the red scars, manholes, drains, cuts in his chest, the hollow eyes of the porter shaving him the night before surgery.

"Joe, what've you got?"

Bateman hesitated on the other side. "Steve, I know I shouldn't be doin' this. I got you all wrong, friend. Way off target this time, buddy! No sooner do I pass, you shit, you, go change everythin.'"

"Joe what the fuck, you on? Hey, just tell me where the fuck Quinn and Kellerman are."

"They're in South Carolina, buddy. They are headin' out to Daufuskie Island."

"Right," Gardiner said. "What the fuck do they expect to find there?"

Bateman hesitated again.

"They are looking for some kid's body Steve. The same as being dead, when you're knocked out like that."

"Yeah, I'm with you, Joe."

Gardiner sat on the bed facing the mirror. It was three quarter length, allowing him see down just below his navel. The drain marks in this light became no more than tiny scrapes of self abuse with a knife.

"Joe, you find out who they're lookin' for 'cause I need to know. These guys are freaking me. No contact, see? So I dunno what the fuck they're at. One minute CIA next FBI. I can't deal with shit like that."

"Got you, Steve I'm sure gettin' tired of this. Yeah, I'm tired. My mistress is tired, even my old mom she says, 'Who the fuck is this Gardiner? What's he got on you, Joe?' I say, he gave me extra days' vacation. You're fuckin' with me, Gardiner."

"Good luck, Joe."

Gardiner clicked off opening the shutters slowly so as not to allow the light to blind him. Slowly light filled the room, rising, making shadows on the walls opposite. What was dark and dreary disappeared. His torso looked pale in the mirror. He covered himself with a towel.

Shower, some light breakfast, and he would hit the road. Maybe he would skip breakfast. Gardiner was about to ring Susie. Susie was asleep, he went to shower. Sadness descended now. If only he could talk to Susie, listen to her advice; let her tell him mundane things like how Shaun and Marsha were getting on. No, Susie was gone from him now, he was alone. He didn't like the mirror over the wash basin. It was steaming up as the water level neared the top. He faced a blind shave.

"Just some hot water and you can't see your goddamn face," he said. He didn't like the look of himself through the mist it made his bristle more conspicuous.

The crease in his chin sank deeper, his lips and cheeks were red. His blood pressure was up, shit. He ran the disposable razor down the side of his chin. It wasn't new and caused tiny trickles of blood to flow. The minuscule dots pieces of his skin gone. Yet as the mist cleared, his image became more benign. He could see the clarity of his eyes. They stared back, they found a stranger.

Running the cold water, he splashed it on his face, cooling him, waking him up. At once he felt fresh. The water was dark with the mix of foam and beard; he could feel its darkness. Just like he saw it before he remembered the East River, as a boy. The stench of sewage at low tide, funny it is cleaner now. No he saw it somewhere else. He stared at dark water. Looking for a child! That was it, waters so cold, tangled weed, lost forest. At one time he felt so bad he called the child's name. Two months later, he got his heart attack. The shower wiped away stray shapes of foam from his cheeks and brow. Gardiner kept his eyes shut, save it might sting.

Franziska felt cold even though the sun was burning the boys. Eyeing her, fierce, she stood rigid filling the bucket at the water's edge. The surf dissolves, tiny waves breaking against her feet.

She managed to adjust her spectacles, brush away the condensation, the surf spray blinding her, eyes upon her, hurting her. She wanted to run to Mama, she was shocked. Alessandro called out, "Ne ha preso uno." She didn't understand. Eyes approached, a liquid ran through her. As the man came close he spoke softly.

Placing his hand on her shoulder still speaking slowly, softly. Franziska walked a yard with him her tiny feet sinking in the sand. Alessandro watched her run loose, fast up the boardwalk. The man shuffled away. Agnolino smiling kicking sand over the ashes. Time to allow the fire die, the heart was gone.

41.

I watch Lucia swim in the pool. Her long body glides through the water, white horses swim alongside her.

Lucia smiles, with froth around her lips. She waves and I wave back.

Small birds hide, glide, awaiting their turn to wash. Large birds are more aloof, flying higher, out of reach. The plants, the bushes are the parameters where she exists. This world has imprisoned her in a small space, to her liking.

Her outstretched arms caress the water; they have massaged my shoulders. There is strength in Lucia. Her energy seeps through the tips of her fingers, haunts my shoulder blades. I feel their weight against the small of my back, just above my buttocks.

All life left in me belongs, is owned, by this woman.

Sometimes she goes red with embarrassment when we meet new people, a strange world for blonde girl to survive.

Her strong arms do not reside in her soul. She drowns, yet is afraid to let go, just to feel the experience. She sleeps, her face soft, falling on the white of the pillow. She wakes, her words muffled; the sound is infected by feathers and dust.

I hear comments about the world, her friends. She tells me stories from childhood, happy ones, sad ones, stories tinged with suspicion, regret, fear. Lucia drinks, she drinks to calm the part of her already calmed by alcohol.

She writes postcards almost as an exercise. Her victims are teased into entering the tiny prison created by her.

From thousands of miles away, they are invited to spend

just a few minutes, see what it is she sees, feel what it is she feels.

At the Bar Priori, in Volterra, she discusses our children. I allow her time and space. She is rampant, her opinions of them, of me, her own personal tragedy, one that is lobbied by her sex, are glued by imperfections, imperfection is not tolerated.

I see myself as a mass of rubble, skin and bone, a body that once functioned. Her world is populated by the worth of things that matter, of future possibility. This world is better than mine, for, at least, she has hope.

I am dubious. I confuse passion with lust, love with need, emotion, with anger.

When Lucia is soft, she is different. Every so often she drops her guard and wonders about James. Was she too hard, too pushy?

Did she turn him off, make him compliant, angry? Was Amanda too smart for her, playing the eternal female game?

Lucia swallows her Rose, she would love another. It is barely lunchtime I want to find this church.

I confuse it with a baptistery, it is indeed a church.

Lucia mentions my illness, how awful it was, how it frightened her, took away so much, gave back only temporary things.

I wonder why nothing has really changed since my illness, maybe save for me. I get fatigued so easily. I spend my life walking the tightrope in the neurotic circus.

Lucia touches me, she rubs the back of my hand, she disturbs the paint. My ego, my self-esteem crawls from the damned. I don't want her to rub my hand and not change things. Even the thought disturbs me, burns my belly.

How can she change what she fails to see or admit?

I am lost to her, my insides cringe. I scan the world for possibilities; that's all they are. Lucia is real, at least this almighty fear, living alone.

The crowds are listening to the mellow guitar as the man plays Italian style. All is fit for romance.

I left love somewhere. The drains were extracted, I looked for comfort, saw none.

This is my guilt, how can I show her my heart has left her?

Quinn said, "No, this isn't the place."

Kellerman looked at him, like he lost it. How can you be so sure? Quinn caught hold of his left arm, his grip relaxed and friendly.

"She said, walk by the house with the Gator, on a 100 yards into the wood."

"I knew we should have brought her down here, Bob. Don't see how it could have hurt."

Kellerman started to walk, making Quinn let go.

"You know, Jack, I don't get it. Each time, each place, we went by the book, right? We find nothing. I dunno, like the guy wasn't fully with it. Could be just dickin' with us."

"Nah, he's just got lucky, that's all. We have only some pieces we ain't got the jigsaw."

Kellerman kept walking with intent, Quinn quickening to keep up.

"How many diggers?" Kellerman asked, passing the house with the Gator replica.

"Ten."

"Are they good?" Kellerman asked, looking at the tape in front of him, his white forensic suit lying across his waterproofs, spread neatly across the hood of the jeep.

"Jack," Quinn said, grabbing his own forensic attire.

"Alright, Bob just checkin'."

Kellerman started to change. The digging had started. The site was 80 yards to his left.

"You know this heat here in Daufuskie won't leave much, not above ground anyhow. Sure, who knows, maybe he never found him, gators got fed."

Kellerman spoke with such an air of resignation, it unnerved Quinn. He watched the disappointment in Quinn's eyes, his face now masked.

There were bones, most likely animal remains. Still the lab will examine them, in case there was a mix.

Quinn watched as the tired diggers continued. They were not deflated by their lack of success. Around him, large tree trunks led to the darkness of the interior.

The cries and screams of animals gave an almost tropical feel. He could hear the swish of water, tiny creeks were explored disturbing gators, play suspended on the golf course.

Quinn could smell the sea. The same sound he first heard as a kid when holding a seashell tight to his ear.

As darkness closed in, the diggers wanted to try a new site about 20 yards on. They were willing to work on, using the generator.

Kellerman shook his head, "We come back in the morning, folks. You guys go get some food hey, have a beer or whatever?" The diggers gave him a mournful look, walking away slowly back to the vehicles, their feet plodding, breaking stray branches, almost falling over small roots.

Quinn drank his beer. Kellerman was lost somewhere in the remit of his brain.

A few diggers chatted away. They were tired, sitting with their backs propped against the couch. One of the more energetic, youthful ones invited a Buddy to a game of snooker. They had an early start; youth will have its fling. Kellerman said, "Hey, Bob, order a beer, will you?" His tone was light. "I don't get it, Bob, this guy has us chasing here, there, everywhere. He spills the beans, maybe he did, maybe he didn't, right? Then he disappears, just when we got him. You know, he's like a bear wanting to walk into a trap. You know what I'm sayin'

He is sayin', come catch me, I can gnaw off my own leg, no problem?"

"You sayin', Jack, this son of a bitch got our asses!"

"Dunno, maybe." Jack said taking his beer.

"We cant find this kid. We looked in Washington State, we searched Brooklyn backwards, we dredged the East River. Now, Daufuskie. What have we found? Fuckin' piss all. I tell you Bob maybe this son of a bitch got us running. He is laughin' at us for sure."

"Wouldn't mind," Quinn said. "We don't have a clue where the son of a bitch is."

"No," Kellerman said, drinking half of his beer. "We ain't got a handle on him. You know, if we were to follow every attempted abduction."

"Yeah, I guess this guy has no pattern. Jack it is killing us, most of the kids are blonde and blue eyed, but then he breaks his pattern with the black kid." Quinn decided to drink some of his beer, it tasted bitter but he drank most of it down.

"I know. This black kid's daddy was in the diamond business. He is a multimillionaire."

"No pattern," Quinn commented. "I suppose that's a pattern?"

"What you mean?" Kellerman asked earnestly.

"The pattern was there, save for the last one. Blonde, blue eyed, under, eight years old, mostly female, one male, then this last one was twelve years old, Negro. I don't get it, unless the same guy didn't do the last one or maybe he did to give us his pattern, not ours?" Quinn looked Kellerman in the eye. "I think, yeah, you're right. This guy is fuckin' with us. What about his admission? There ain't... no way... you could make it up, is there?" Kellerman said. "Bob, give me your phone." Kellerman grabbed the cell phone, half watching the young digger break, the balls spreading randomly across the snooker table.

Robert Quinn stood motionless with his back leaning against the Jeep.

The divers were down a long time. The creek ran between the putting green and the wood. The trees towered over as in parental duty

Kellerman was on the landline all morning talking to this expert then another. The answer was always the same. You cannot lie, it is impossible.

Kellerman reluctantly accepted this, as one accepts a sinister diagnosis of cancerous tumours. Every now and then a diver would surface, swimming to the side, tugging on his safety line.

"We need more light, these torches ain't worth a damn," Quinn said, eyeing the tech supervisor and keeping an eye on the armed backup in case some giddy gator wanted an early morning bath.

Three divers down below. Quinn watched as they faded slowly midst the swampy foam, slimy algae, mutant, vegetation.

The synchronized swimmers, all three divers surfaced at once. First Quinn thought that they were coming up for food or to replace their oxygen.

He noticed the leader carrying something.

Quinn recognized it as a child's tennis shoe attached the remains of an ankle, just the bone… yellow.

The dive-team leader placed it on the ground in front of him like a dog leaves a game bird.

Quinn felt his stomach heave as he saw the tennis shoe full of holes. It was like a beach stone, ravaged by the sea.

Kellerman rushed to him. In his fright he went to pick it up.

"No, Jack." Kellerman withdrew his hand, like he nearly got tangled in a machine.

"What is it?" Kellerman asked the vomiting Quinn. The divers were climbing from the creek.

"It looks like our girl got it right." Quinn said, wiping his mouth.

"Gators?" Quinn nodded, "Let's hope he was dead when he hit the water."

Kellerman looked at his partner, his face pale as if he had lost litres of blood.

He got the medic to check Quinn out, even though he knew it was just shock. Sugar-filled coffee forced down soon settled the issue.

Jack Kellerman stood looking into the creek. It was innocent in its calm depth.

He felt no elation or excitement. The breakthrough was unimportant, just like the others, and they still hadn't found the little girl. In a sense they lost him,

God knows, they had lost him. As Quinn said, all they could do now was offer hope to the family, give them some closure. Allow them to grieve. It was their right, at least they knew for sure now. How many others were gone they didn't even know about, where did he leave Heidi Heisler?

Kellerman saw Quinn drinking his coffee from a plastic cup. He was shivering in his forensic garb, yet the evening was so hot even the mosquitoes left the scene, abandoning them to go eat living things hidden in the forest.

42.

Where did I the soft boy go hey, piano player, to whom do I owe the music? Is it bitterness against life, a God anger thing, jealousy, louder, just sheer good banter? Western cruel twist of fate, to meet the devil at the gate, my rooms now are speckled in small villages with old Protestant churches asleep on tiny hills. All trees are evergreen, middle-aged women on the edge of frumpiness with a taste for fine wines, a race to grumpiness, heck what common ground!

Why is it she stayed a laughin and a smilin a courtin whilst I agonised over it all every second as if this wasn't just another chance, my last chance, my last crippled crucified chance. There are times when the plane lands from the woods across the damp grass, sometimes her warmth overwhelms me, I have touched my true love. Do I risk it? Spoiled gob-shite, I see through the armour of plane landing. Postponement because she smells the man in me is all dark meat. Who was crucified? Stand up, look, do you see the birds are all flying, circling, stacking, is it me up there staring down at this wet earth, maggot hands, through maggot clay.

Is it not my brief to have a permanent companion, an everlasting place so my incredulous children can visit? I know it must land to the rear of trees. I want to scream shout the madness that is me every second of every day.

The first time I went to London was way back in 1968. We

all went the whole family. I was about ten years old and the memories are cloudy.

Sitting on this leather chair – it was half on deck – the mail boat sailing out of Dun Laoghaire. It was dark and cold.

Feeling sick, my father watched over me. Eventually, I vomited over the side.

On the train, I remember standing between the carriages, looking out at England, noting the names of the stations we passed through. Names called after football teams, famous names like Crewe, Wolverhampton.

Back then, things were the same as now, save for time has moved on, fashions changed the look of things, the way people perceive the world.

People who were alive then are dead now; people who were not born then are born now.

In 1968, we went to my father's nephew's flat to watch the European Cup final.

It was in black-and-white. As we walked the dark streets back to my uncle's house, I fell in love with the city. This dark place where some of my family were exiled.

I fell in love with English playgrounds and parks, gobstoppers transforming into chewing gum. I never realized how much this dark city with school villages, such order, would change my life forever.

    didn't see it comin' didn't see it at all
    where is all the sense of it where does this bright snow fall
    I've been feelin' kinda wicked fresh in the crisp breeze
    didn't see you comin' didn't see you at all
    the cold wind blows across the playing fields
    I smell the grass from long ago
    I guess that's where I could go
    didn't you hear the trains steal by in the dark
    couldn't you have led me to waterlogged fields at dawn with
you in a nightdress me on a white horse you know this kind of
wickedness does not suit bleeds my gums back to the day when

I did search for you by the playing fields you moved frosted face with a carry case your school villages infected by a lack of real invective what I lost was one embrace I learned to hide my face save for my nose which was straight from a woolly hat didn't see it comin' didn't see it at all where the wind blows shallow along the tarred path it sneaks into your room beside the disused railway track where once as a mere child I stood beyond laced curtains to scream my childhood back was met by the rustle of youth crawling through surface water bled the tiny pools never found your safe eyes again after that mind wanders inside the dawn soldier winter coat.

Don Dino listened to Gregor, who was wiping his brow, feeling the heat. He helped himself to iced tea. "He said he doesn't care, he wants his revenge. He is willing to up the ante, whatever it takes." "I see," Don Dino said, taking an olive to chew. "He has no doubts?" "None, the latest information, Don Dino, they are certain now." "Of course, Eva is in position we must rely on her..."

Don Dino didn't finish his sentence, removing the olive from his mouth, throwing it into the waste basket. "Gregor," he continued. "Perhaps, we should make sure, what do you think?" Don Dino stood facing the garden, as he liked to do. Gregor, still feeling the heat, hesitated, then, wiping his brow, said,

"We promised her, Don Dino to go against her wishes she has never let us down. I am inclined to leave what isn't broken, so to speak."

The Don turned to him, a considered expression on his face; his cheeks puffing slightly, he allowed the flow of air to ease his brain.

"Yes, I agree," he said, taking a step forward. "Yet this may be the end, Gregor, there may be nothing more. The money will stop. Perhaps, as you say, we should honour her wishes. I am old, my money will last me, what you think? Only if this one pays out. I dunno, Gregor, I wonder, should we take out insurance?" Don Dino sighed; he turned to look over his garden again, looking perplexed. He hated turmoil.

"Think of this insurance, Don Dino. I can see your motive so clearly. I think your insurance might be your undoing. Maybe she sees what we have done, she will think betrayal. She may not carry out instructions; she may change her mind about everything. It will leave no payday for you. Eva left you her note she may think you are trying to stop her, what then?"

Gregor's voice was about as excited as the Don ever heard. The old man turned once more to face his faithful servant.

"Can we not just lie in waiting, out of the way, just in case, hey? How will she know that?"

The venom in Don Dino's voice surprised Gregor, his rationale broken.

Gregor drank the last of his iced tea, "You have your say, Don Dino. She has never failed us, I doubt if she will now. It is her final task, as they say, she is committed to it."

"Insurance, Gregor, we should take out a policy. I may be losing my reason, as you say she has never failed us, why now?

I am so nervous, like this is my swan song. I am afraid to be left without my final payday!"

"It is natural to worry. You should chew it over. He said he will wire the money as soon as he gets confirmation."

"Yes confirmation, Gregor, is what is needed here." Don Dino was watching the birds glide into his ornamental pool. They wet only the smallest part of them, save for the water may weigh them down.

Monica was surprised to hear the phone. It didnt ring all day, the last call came from her father's lawyer.

Maybe it was Toby. She thought of him when booking her tickets to London.

"Monica." Philippe said, in a hushed voice.

"Philippe?"

"Where are you?"

"Ssh... Ssh... you must listen. I have returned, I am back, do you hear, in Viaréggio. Are you still at the Grand Palace?"

"Yes." She wanted to tell him about London, but he interrupted.

"What room?" Philippe sounded different, it unnerved her.

"26," she replied, nervously.

"Sit tight."

He was gone.

Monica glanced sadly at her tickets, the money in bundles on the bed. Then she felt the tears as the emotion took hold. Philippe came back for her.

As Matthew Cryan walked slowly through the cemetery he felt uneasy.

In life they never agreed, they were enemies. So why, after death, should he afford Marie Abele respect.

The heat of the sun withered the existing flowers placed by some faithful parishioners. The roses Matthew brought wouldn't last too long, at least they were fresh.

Matthew placed the flowers in a pot. Noticing the pot was dry, he looked around for a water source.

A tap was dripping by the narrow path about 10 metres away. He was careful not to stand on old graves as he brought the container over to fill.

He watched the cold water splash into the dirty container. He felt the heaviness as it filled, till at last there was enough. The journey back to the grave of Marie Abele was uncomfortable with the added weight.

Perhaps he was a hypocrite, maybe Toby was right. He surely was in strange humour when they last spoke.

He had never heard Toby lapse into such a depression, his will to live seemed diluted. Toby was devastated by the sad news of Marea and her baby Donata.

It was almost like he was admitting he was a fraud, yet Matthew still believed in him and his curative powers. Toby told him about Monica, and Matthew understood the poor boy, his heart was now broken. What was so strong has now proven to be so brittle. He wondered about Don Dino, something James said, all those years ago.

James confided not long before his death, that trouble followed him all his life, from his earliest memories. He moved from a war zone to the criminal life of Don Dino. 'You can wipe the dirt from a man's face, can you cleanse his soul?' Matthew had no doubt Don Dino was capable of anything. Toby now, as his father before him, belonged to this world.

Funny how life turns out. He read the inscription on the headstone of Marie Abele. It was innocent and kind. How much we sanitize the dead, Matthew thought, how often we excuse the living. He turned to walk away, back across the narrow paths to the exit. He wondered should he call Toby, invite him to Cucuron, and allow him find the truth about himself? Toby would refuse. He awaited his mother, who had gone away again, the poor stricken woman. James tried to explain her to him, so many times. Matthew felt the soreness in his throat once more. He tried to swallow but it hurt more.

It comes and goes, he thought. I should go and have it looked at. If not I will be here soon in this place, pushing up the daisies. Maybe Toby would come to visit if Matthew said he needed him once more. Not in his present mood, he may see Matthews's symptoms as another failure. He looked back as the sun-lit webs appeared over the half-broken wall glistening against the granite in the headstones furthest away.

Why did he come to this place to put flowers on the grave of a man he mistrusted, didn't respect? Was it out of Christian values of love and respect, or was it that very soon somebody will be putting flowers on his own grave. He shuddered at the thought, retracing his footsteps to his car.

43.

Sometimes I see him he walks abreast of me
slides by with the rain pelting on his hat
don't worry
he has given me the contemptuous look
one that failed him in life.
He can crawl inside my head pick the bones of memories
cold dark vacant the vagrant ones slip uninvited
into the soft chair.
Small furry rodents crawl up under my sleeves patter
down my back
little rodent bear didn't know whom he feared me or
the rodent.
Is that why I am so serious cause every laugh since
was useless
each smile each bead of sweat all moments in love-
making useless
all pain chest pain all gain guilt.
Sometimes I see him drive by in old cars with old hats
when I fall from derelict bar stools
my mind tricks me into believing the A40 could
do a hundred.
Fat chance daft power me up the noggin hill
where years past I rode by on my bike fit as a fiddle
in gardens there are trees which lasted longer
what was it that got me
he was gone never coming back or we were all humans
none of us strong enough to save him.

At the mercy of St Paul St Jude, St Michael the
fiery archangel.
Where was God to hold us and comfort us
    what strange red roaring fire filled universe did we
inhabit.
    I have guilt it being in the thoughts you know
beads of blood sweat pour little tiny ice-filled droplets into
my eyes fill tired blood piping vessels with cringe powdered
slime so much so I feel the power of devils burn brands of
shame forehead urns burns.
    Till I remember am thankful for the soft.

Once when I met her our eyes held for a second, just a
tiny second too long.
So now each time I see her I search for that.
Somehow she knows, her eyes cold upon intruders.
    I am lost, endless flicker of light as it escapes.

It came upon me before I was ready.
Crawled up the open road, cut a path beyond my control.
In there my two old dancers,
return to those days if only.
Saw the tears she took her chances,
counting how many children we have raised.
Came round so unexpected,
wanted my intellect yet.
I need a hug a cuddle,
wanted me to burst her bubble.
It always seemed so hard,
the vanity mirror where she was lost.
Making children run away
so all time could stand still.
She broke up with a minor artist,
befriending clear blue men.
Teach him golf ever after,

thought I heard her laughter bend.
It came upon me before I woke up,
crawled my way from the bed.
Fell into dried sea dazed.
All of us sent to find a mountain,
one sends its seekers west.
Saw her starring in a creep show,
there were no more mountains left.
It came upon me before I was ready,
crawled up the open road.
She stood alone without her suitcase,
plans to spend her time alone.
Broke up with her only boyfriend,
to keep small rats fungus toads.
Tried to fire three burnt out muskets,
we just could not afford the clothes.

Eva allowed the light to hurt her eyes. The pain in her tummy was central, as usual.

The bottle lay flat, as she had left it. A drain in the end soaked the flex of the lamp. She tried to lift her head from the pillow, but gave up on the third go.

Nothing for it but to allow it sink in further, watch the black patches of light going swish big, then small, beyond her eyelids.

Loud music played uncontrollably, her soundtrack unsuitable to the mood.

She attempted to sit up to make it stop but she hadn't the strength. Giving in to the music, it tortured her. Her clothes were strewn across the floor, like there was a robbery.

Her underwear between the bathroom and the bed laid as a pathway. So many years since she had a man, a real man.

It goes with the drinking, who wants to cuddle up to an old hag smelling of gin?

Not even Don Dino. Why should he when he could have the best prostitutes from Firenze? Once he brought girls in from the South of France. Men, what is it about their loins? Their ego's need to be washed daily, their needs never satisfied.

No wonder women resorted to stealth, no wonder!

She could see the hills awash with light, yet clouds gathered to the west. Soon she forced the issue, getting up as her appointment was in two hours.

The files, she left them comfortably on the dressing table. Her gun, Super Redhawk, was in its case.

It was a forty-four, Magnum, ideal for the task in hand. My God, this was the most crucial job in thirty years. Retirement ahead, permanent retirement.

James hated the idea. He was practical, he knew they must live. He knew her enemies were ever present; the protection of Don Dino was the only option to survive.

James in his a way could justify things. Honestly, Eva could never fully buy in to his logic.

What started out as a little girl taking on the world, led to appalling things!

There was no hope she had already crossed the line entering the realms where most people fear to thread. No refusal, no going back.

Don Dino gave her instructions. She didn't hesitate in crossing the line again.

Eva mustered her energy, aware time was ticking away. She made herself listen to the pounding music, it hurt her brain.

Repeating to herself, 'I don't care about shit anymore.' she somehow found her way to the bathroom. Eva managed to run the shower, which she took cold.

The cold water was soft against her skin. James, how quickly he gave in.

Going back to Cucuron was an admission of defeat on two fronts. Firstly, his feeble attempts at atonement, secondly, his complete failure in realising his doctrine.

His failure to communicate with his son was another reason, probably the starkest.

Priests are not meant to have children, not by commandment of the church. Really, like top businessmen, they don't have the commitment or the time.

James always paid lip service to Toby, for some reason he wanted the world to guide him.

It was a case of I created him, isn't that enough, in my saintly image too? James was no saint as, deep down, he knew. Perhaps he hoped for a St Toby.

James spent so much time in England and Rome he hardly ever saw his son. Some people thought Don Dino was Toby's father. Don Dino, bank roller, provided everything all of these years: Toby's education, the investments Toby lived from the dividends. Eva allowed the fantasy to develop if her son was to work for a living? She wondered. The water was getting warm; the clock was ticking. She put on her bathrobe, at last drowning the internal music. Eva started her hair dryer looking out her terrace doors.

The sky cleared a little. She could now see over the sandcastle, all the way across the valley to Bagno Vignoni. Soon she will meet him there. The Red Hawk Magnum primed. He would be armed also!

Why do this, why dry my hair? Do I want to look my best? She caught a glimpse of herself in the small mirror set into the wall.

She had aged so much. Her eyes, once the fanfare of her face, receded. Made of glass, her countenance was sweet. It was painted with flesh paint. Her artist painted her with a large brush, soaking the wrinkles.

Eva looked for the files again. The real wonder, old evil hag finds solace as she makes her final exit.

Can evil be traded? Who is most evil, the one who knowingly kills for profit or the deranged mad person corrupted by life?

How would James view her plans? Would he approve or not? 'People do irrational things when they are at war!' In her life, she was always at war.

From the moment she took her first breath, war screamed. Eva heard its sound, way across the barren landscape.

Right inside her war raged. As one day led to another her mind was stretched to endurance, beyond comprehension.

Soon she shall leave the lodge. Bagno Vignoni in eighteen minutes, a bottle of gin, the Red Hawk Magnum. She will need them all.

Eva couldn't help herself, pouring a gin, opening the file. Her head calming as the taste folded round her throat.

The pictures, innocence at play. Alcohol mended her sense of horror.

Pathology pictures in files, honourable job to finish with! A little like a sports star, bowing out with a lap of honour.

Toby was coming at her in an instant, he was almost a stranger. Should she call him, say goodbye? Was it best to allow Don Dino give him the note, the DVD? Words, useless. Could she say anything to him, would it make sense?

Toby, he'd try to stop her, come after her. She left her phone dead, must be countless messages from him. Time to allow him to go. He has his own special place now. With Eva gone perhaps he could grow like other young men. Was it the violation of her as a child, ending under the protection of Don Dino, all that goes with it, a loss of identity, loss of normality? Eva, her head so cold. Why did God spare her? People killed in bomb blasts, those killed in aircraft disasters. Her own people murdered by an Army of occupation. All so fucking arbitrary, she concluded. Give me a name, date, a place, a reason. Fuck the reason. This is the only time I ever had a reason. Eva gathered her things. Checking her watch she locked the Don's lodge. The morning was crisp at the altitude even though the sun fought valiantly to break the frosty spell.

44.

Listen to the leaves falling, a bird moves in the undergrowth startling starling a rat in a maze. Couldn't tell if it was him, just the rustle of the wind, hound comes running down, he is old and cold with a zombie frown most unhappy hound around. An old man died about five houses up, the mafia did the funeral, stood by their fancy cars. Dark shades shadow beards, thought they were out of tuner.

I think comin' for me now own a white coat, latest news I will run out of fizz. Their money is safe, they know it, you may see this horror for what it is.

Share with the hound a sense of hopeless profound. Every passer-by is dead, people walk in the park with me, see them fat, small, some very tall. Large ladies, small boys, pretty girls in children's frocks, they're all dead, no one says hello back when I nod my head.

I know for sure that like me they are no longer living, the storm is a farce as is walking so fast. Left my last will and testicle, in my heart diseased heart.

Look at the photograph
at what it says,
five figures at dawn
early days on the lawn.
crows circle winter coats collars up, where is this path.
Three girls long flowing hair, two boys need love.

crows scream, know who we are, can't say a word,
the mockin' grey clouds overhead.
 yellow light, wants to capture the moment.
Faces fade, caught you,
Still look at the photograph.
 look at what it says, never trust a moment
or girls with long flowing hair.

Do you see the same things as me, all the bare trees
dark crows.
Yes you semi nude I spy you in dreams I see you.
 Through a dark glass your figure is hurting my eyes.
 Fighter hands up, horseshoe gloves, still can't get it,
tougher now than before.
Want to spill my own blood.

When I look at Lucia, I see her at all respective ages,
right back to when we first met. The big things in our lives
appear before me. The day we met I was taken with her quirky
sense of humour, the way she blinked her eyes as if to signify
intelligence.

When we got married it was almost forgetful, save for the
fact she was radiant and so full of hope. Women derive pleasure
from such things. I wonder how many men would marry if it
were down to choice?

I suppose a fellow likes to put his feet up at some stage. It's
a respectability issue, a status symbol.

For women, the rites of passage mean finally they are at
one with their peers. Women carry a satisfaction beyond
comprehension, little self pleased smiles, lost in consumable
eyes.

The beads of sweat making love, the soft touch of a hand
around your neck as it gently massages, the daily banter over
cups of hot tea.

Are husbands and wives like football teams 'We'll support
you, ever more?'

Like me, Lucia has grown dark with age. Her body is caving in with multiples of minor aches and complaints.

Is love retrospective or do I mix love with passion? Are men not just loin creatures, potential rapists, pillagers?

Just think we are all set to face life, with all its dangers and all its expiry dates. Be content learn to live only in the present.

I think women have learned to adapt to this much better than men. They have no sense of their own mortality yet can accept a man's, with just a little too much grace.

Monica said the obvious, "Philippe it is you?" She thought he looked a little older. "How's New York?" She was ashamed her words sounded false, contrived.

"I came to see you Monica, I was concerned." He sat over by the window, looking out onto the street. Things were quiet in the late afternoon.

A couple followed by some older people walked by lazily.

"I found out my friends in Viaréggio are few, there is nobody to protect you. Is it true, what the lawyers say about fathers' estate! We may never see a cent?" Philippe moved to the bed and sat on the corner, as if exhausted. Monica sighed, throwing her eyes to heaven.

"I arrived this morning. What happened between you, and Toby?"

Monica related the story slowly, in a sad voice, trying to hide the tears.

"You won't believe me, my sister. I am sorry that you are sad. Maybe you are wrong about Toby.

His blood is not family blood. I cannot see him hurting anyone, least of all father.

No, it was Don Dino, he is capable of it. His reputation in New York is legendary. Mainly for the ruthlessness he shows when dealing with his enemies!"

"Father went to him for help, his only concern for you his son. He opened his heart to Don Dino, telling him truths of

294

the past. Father was foolish he probably signed his own death warrant. He did it to protect you, Philippe. I know you had your differences but he loved his son." Monica's voice was shaking as she turned to face her brother. Philippe was eyeing the bundles of banknotes and travel documents lying on the bed beside him. Monica noticed the tears in his eyes,

"What are these?" he asked.

"I am going away; I didn't know what to do so I booked tickets for London."

"London, what is in London?"

"Dunno, a new life, a fresh start. Supposed to be good for singing, I dunno." Monica pretended to tidy the writing desk. Philippe interjected, "no my sister I will bring you to New York.

London is no good, not for you. We have cousins and family in New York. We can take some kind of refuge there, at least till the lawyers are finished."

"Cousins? What do they intend to do about Don Dino? Allow him go free ?"

She sat on the spare bed, her head down. She was subliminally examining the patterns on the carpet; they were triangles, then rectangles.

Philippe last saw her so sad when he was ten years old. Monica stared at him tears streaming down her cheeks. "Don Dino is too strong, Monica, even the Roma families fear him. The New York families will not touch him. He is old school; he does not interfere with their operations. They don't want him involved so they keep a distance. He is so dangerous he is not to be messed with. For us there is only escape." Monica could see the sadness and the swallowing of pride as her brother went to the window to check the street once more.

"We cannot stay here in Viaréggio, we must go. Throw those London tickets in the bin we fly from Pisa, in the morning." Monica nodded, bemused. She was thinking of Toby and how this could have happened.

Toby walked a pace behind him. Don Dino found the hill steep. Toby didn't want the old man to rush.

"I own all of this, a thousand acres, going south!" The Don pointed to the meadow beyond the rail, then to the bend in the road, on to the small village where Eva lived.

"I let the people live here for free Toby, they farm this land. It's not much. I try to help them as much as I can. They are content. That is my way of giving back to the town of Bagni."

Toby caught up with him, now it was he that found the walk hard.

"It is a good thing you do!" Toby said genuinely.

"Ah yes, there you go Toby. You may feel I am good and selfless. I assure you many favours are owed and were received by me over the years. Let's call it a two way street, boy, hey. You don't think this old man is a registered charity do you?" The Don clapped him on the back and started to walk slowly back down the hill.

"I want you to have all of this Toby. My people are drawing the papers as we speak. Someday you can decide to sell it. This was always the deal as long as these people get first option to buy. They know its coming. They just wait for the day."

"But how can they afford it?" Toby asked.

Don Dino smiled. "They have lived here rent free all their lives farming selling their produce. They have no overheads they must be the wealthiest people in Toscana. Let the moaners or those who begrudge move on, we have no time for them."

"I don't know what to say?" Toby said, deeply moved by the Don's gesture.

"Does my Mother know of this? I have not heard from her since she went on retreat."

"No," said Don Dino. "I have not told her yet. I will as soon as she returns hey?"

Toby could see Gregor standing patiently beside the car, wisps of his hair blowing backwards, covering his balding head.

"Why does she choose not to speak to me Don Dino, it is

like she disowns her own son. I cannot tell her about Monica or anything going on in my life. You must know the answer Don Dino?"

The old man stopped, he too looked at the waiting Gregor, his loyal servant, waiting for him patient as ever.

"Toby you know how ill your mother is. She needs complete rest. Her doctors have ordered complete rest and recuperation. I am responsible for her disappearance, her lack of contact, because she is so ill. Toby I fear that without complete rest she may not come back to us at all. It is for her sake and for yours that she stays away. Her drinking is out of control and at dangerous levels."

Toby shrugged. As usual Don Dino spoke sense.

Don Dino waited whilst Toby did some business in the post office.

"Well Gregor, I have made my mind up. We need insurance for sure. We cannot leave things to fate. I have thought long and hard. I have made my mind up, you must be there early. I want to make sure he cannot slip through, you understand?"

"Yes I understand." Gregor said, peering back at his master, removing his sunglasses. Don Dino slumped back in his seat; his lips curled as they always did when he was thinking.

"Double the security whilst you're gone. I hear this Giordano is back in Viaréggio. I don't expect trouble from him, but we are having him watched just the same."

"I won't intervene in Bagno unless it becomes necessary, Alright?" Gregor rested his hands on the wheel.

"You will need a rifle, make sure it's telescopic."

"Sure." said Gregor, spotting Toby walk across the car park.

"This time our employer wants results, we cannot leave it to chance.

As I said Gregor, we need to buy an Insurance policy."

"You are wise Don Dino." Toby re-entered the car. Seeing both men were silent he thought the Don must have fallen asleep.

"I sent Matthew a letter. Maybe when Mother comes home I will go visit him in Cucuron."

Neither Gregor nor Don Dino acknowledged his statement; the car slipped away, the sun sparkling on its bonnet before it turned left.

45.

I don't believe in God. I think people can use God for good or for evil, most times in history God has been used for evil.

It really doesn't matter, which God you're into, the story remains the same.

People are basic. Our basic is evil. Most of us are afraid to follow our instinct, which is good. Otherwise, we would all end up in a complete state of chaos.

Most people in the world think they're good. Why are they good? Have our instincts changed so much?

Ask yourself the question, why the Holocaust? Why the atomic bomb? Why do we forget each outrage, each tragedy, as it passes? Normal life resumes. The great surviving human.

Don't you think the boys in the trenches of World War 1 thought they had died and were in hell? Why serial killers? Why not?

If you were to examine religions all over the world, how many people have died because of them, for them, against them?

Are people intrinsically evil? Is it what we do that matters, or is it what we think?

Gardiner left Quírico d'Órcia, the road was clear. All round him the sun kissed fields, cut straight from cereal advertisements. Seek her out at last; it was so tiresome. He longed for home, for Brooklyn. Maybe Susie would allow the kids to spend the night. In his excitement he thought of calling Bateman, but changed his mind. A single Carabinieri behind made him slow down and concentrate.

It was a cool, fresh morning and the hills beyond held mist. It indicated dew. He imagined the cold and damp.

The Carabinieri sped past as a truck ahead pulled over into a self service gas station. Gardiner saw the sign for Bagno Vignoni, it was big and bright. Climbing the hill slowly he knew from his research to turn left down a dirt track. It started with tight bends. His car bumped over the uneven ground.

Bateman called, "Jesus, Steve, they're pulling up some heap of shit here I can tell you. Jesus Christ, they found the body of this kid, see, in South Carolina, this joint ... hey, Daufuskie, yeah you got it. Now they're digging every goddamn place. Up in Washington State, here in New York, they're drainin' the East River buddy, drainin' it. You know where you went fishin' with your old man, as a kid? Jesus, Steve, you're some man. Havin' a heart attack, you got to keep the mouth shut when you're asleep. Nurses are kind of smart."

Gardiner turned off his phone. Her four-wheel drive was parked a hundred yards ahead.

He checked the Ruger .357 Magnum. Placing it neatly in its holster, he fastened the last two buttons of his khaki jacket. He left on foot over the uneven ground till he found the steps up to the rock pool, where he knew she was waiting.

Eva wanted to get there first. This was home ground, where she first bathed Toby. In this place she first noticed the look in his eyes.

James brought them here; it was his homage to St Caterina of Siena. Driving the loop to Asciano, on to the Monastery at Abbazia di Monte Oliveto Maggiore eventually arriving in Bagno Vignoni via Buonconvento, James loved the drive. She remembered the weather was beautiful. Their rock pool was deserted, since it was too early for tourists. Locals were still turning in their sleep.

Eva moved deftly across the narrow causeway leading to a

semi Grotto, listening for the sound of an engine and watching for the rising dust. She placed her bag between small rocks. How should she handle this? First a drink. She drank the gin straight from the bottle. It relieved her anxiety, spilling to her insides hot, burning. She eyed the sulphuric waters and longed to bathe. Eva's thoughts were disturbed by the sound of a car to her left, she could see the dust rising. At last he was here.

The remains of the half built sandcastle sat on the hills. It always looked so childish against the landscape. Away to her left was the valley of trees, more water unevenly spread, discarded by nature. Gardiner walked up the path. Eva wasn't surprised by him. He was true to his photograph, though he tried hard to disguise himself. Perhaps it was his walk, the slight bent look. He stood at the far side of the pool, afraid to get closer and standing upright, in a bold bid to correct his error. "Buongiorno." Eva said standing as upright as she could. She could sense her hands shake, doing her best to hide it.

"I have come. So, what is it you have for us?"

Eva was silent for a moment, unsure as to what to do or say. Should she show him the file? It was ridiculous, he was too far away.

Gardiner spoke, "My people want to know what you want?"

"Infanticida." Eva said. Gardiner stood impassively.

"Having lived here so long, Mr Gardiner, I was sure you'd have a wee bit of understanding of the language."

Eva reached into her bag to get her file. She saw him flinch. Through the corner of her eye she saw him reach inside his khaki jacket.

Gardiner stopped as he saw her produce the Manila envelope. "What have you there? Your file on Auldridge, Edgell?"

"You have lost me." Eva said. "It's a file on the children they reckon you have killed." Eva stepped back a little unsteadily. Gardiner smiled, "God you really are crazy, hey? I'm ex –NYPD, the best tracker in the business. I even found you!" Eva gave a wry laugh.

"They said you were nuts, my man. I thought I was nuts till I met you."

"We met before?" Gardiner said, holding his forehead with his right hand. "We met in Bagni di Lucca, we did!" He said holding his head, like he was struck with a blinding migraine.

"See this file I got here." Eva said. "Got photos of all the kids you killed both in the USA and in Europe. Yeah, you're the tracker, alright. Like to give the kids an odd, hey? Before you hunt them down?" Gardiner was recovering his composure; she was playing with his head. "Thirty years in the NYPD, I got commendations, lots of them."

"I will show you these photographs; they will jog your memory. Melissa Kaufmann, Sara Berger, Jonathan Pressman, Heidi Heisler. I should have said, Mark Harper. The biggest mistake you ever made. This wee boy's Daddy has lots of money." Eva threw the file half at him, into the green rock pool. Gardiner watched it sink, half tempted to go retrieve it. He didn't.

He clapped his hands in mock admiration, "Well darn it, Bateman. I went and opened my big mouth when I should have been sleeping. If it weren't for the goddamn nurse, I'd be in the clear, hiding out in Europe. Those guys in Interpol, they liaise with the FBI and the CIA. We all should be shitless, Bateman. Who gives a shit about you when you're dead? Nobody Steve, nobody gives a rat's shit." Gardiner stared at her across the pool.

"You fucked me, that's for sure. I had that kid on the beach in Viaréggio. Fucked me with all the shit about disguises and warning parents. You shouldn't fuck with things you don't understand." Gardiner roared at her. Eva winced taking a step back.

"I'm gonna call Susie. You don't know Susie; she will know what to do!"

Eva saw him reach into the pocket of his khaki jacket; she felt the screams from him filter through the sacred water. She could feel her hands shake as she reached for the Red Hawk.

Gardiner, his voice wailing across the valley, "I can see you. You're hiding from me in the dark. I can smell you, you piece of shit!" Then, "come to Papa, you little bitch."

He pulled out the Ruger.

It was straight and firm in his hand. His shot went through Eva's throat, burning a hole and exiting to strike the rock behind her. Eva fell head first into the water. The splash made the water white for an instant, loud, then it was calm, going soft.

Gardiner watched as she floated face down, her blood made silly colours yellow and light blue. He returned the gun to its holster out of sight. He was thinking of Quinn and Kellerman, how pleasing, he terminated her as requested. Final payoff, all go home. The bullet from the M21 went through the bridge of his nose. Blood spouted forwards in a great gush like a garden hose let loose. Gardiner dropped forward, his body falling slowly.

Gregor climbed down the cliff face. He watched Gardiner's body sinking, his legs the first to go under.

It was time to go. Walking, he saw Gardiner's head submerged, bobbling at the surface, barely visible. Gregor saw green froth attached like worms to his hair.

Eva was gone, the pool swallowed her. He waited for a second, calling Don Dino on his mobile. Don Dino listened in silence.

Toby was reading on the veranda. He was digesting his breakfast when Don Dino pulled up a hard chair opposite.

He made a lot of noise; Toby automatically lifted his head from his book.

The Don poured orange juice in silence, and coffee, still he did not speak. Toby watched him, bemused.

"Don Dino, are you out of sorts this morning?" Toby asked lightheartedly.

"My heart aches," Don Dino said gruffly.

"What is it?" Toby said, putting his book down and pulling away his chair at the same time.

"Your mother's dead, Toby. There has been an accident with a firearm,"

303

"Jesus." Toby was on his feet. "Where is she?"

"Sit down, Toby. There is nothing to gain going crazy. Sit down, I will help you, sei arrabbiato, listen to me."

Toby tried to calm himself, but he was a jack-in-the-box with a faulty spring.

"Your mother, as I told you, was very ill. See, the drink, eh?" Don Dino pointed towards the orange juice, then his mouth, "got a hold of her head, her brain, see that?"

He pointed to the side of his head, tapping it gently,

"She has killed herself." Don Dino banged his fist on the table, the glasses and cups shook. "Here, look," Don Dino said fiddling in his pocket. "She says give this to Toby if I do not come back." He handed Toby a scribbled note and a package.

Toby immediately read the note. It was in his mother's handwriting; it simply said, "Ti voglio bene."

46.

I was in love with Viaréggio at night. I loved the little outdoor restaurants; the children who came by to play tuneless accordions then take the hump when you didn't subscribe to their musical education.

The African guys who could come to your table five times in a sitting trying to sell you flowers.

They were amazing; as you nodded your head to say no, they stood for twenty seconds in disbelief. A slob like you failed to treat his woman to such a beautiful red rose.

He would only leave when he realized his sales technique had failed. Within ten minutes he tried again.

Honestly, some of the high powered world corporations should study these fellas for lessons in persistence. Lucia and I said goodbye to the night up on our terrace. We looked over the parapet, watching the people disperse, the cycle lanes thinning, as the night wore on the pedestrian ways deserted, even the road traffic was sparse.

When Viaréggio goes to sleep, it sleeps.

We woke up to our last day, our last breakfast. Don Maestrino was there, bursting out of his ill fitting uniform, directing his charges with ease, much as a conductor might soft music.

The food was as usual top drawer, with beautiful fresh rolls, ham and salami. Lucia ate scrambled eggs.

The Italian woman her beautiful daughter and fat hubby were deep in conversation.

He was doing most of the yapping, so I guess he was in charge. I saw Gardiner again he walked right up to our table.

305

"I'm really sorry about this, you guys. But you know, I tried on this goddamn jacket this morning, I find a wallet that ain't mine. It sure as hell looks like mine so I have a look. Got all this Irish stuff, so I figure, I must've picked it up by mistake when we were up top that night, eh? One hundred bucks in there too."

He was right, the hundred euros was still there, my notes folded incorrectly in the zip pocket, my credit cards, my identity card, all still there. Of course, I'd cancelled my credit and debit cards. "Sorry, buddy," he said, marching away.

"Well," said Lucia, "credit that for a bit of luck."

As we left, Viaréggio was lost in bright daylight, innocent, without darkness.

We headed towards Marco Polo. Lucia was quiet. I was thinking back to when I woke up in hospital, the nurse said, "You have made it. Well done, Stephen you did great."

I wondered, did I say anything when I was dead? Do dead people talk?

"I'm glad we're not going home yet," Lucia said. "We have another week to look forward to. Did you check your sugars, love?"

"Yes," I replied. "I took my Aspirin, my Diamicron, my Emcor."

They freeze you, so you won't bleed whilst they fix you,

'hey, I took your heart out, it was beating ok,' the surgeon said, like he was telling somebody about a missed putt.

The heart is tied to your being. I don't know if cancer is the same. To put it bluntly, it is like somebody taking out your emotional self, and beating ten different colours of crap out of you.

Bypasses are two a penny, no big deal you hear people say.

Lucia laughs when I play on the Walt Disney character, 'Steamboat Willie.' by calling myself 'Bypass Willie.' I was forty-six when I needed my bypass and was diagnosed with type 2 diabetes. Yeah, it could have been worse. I spent the rest of the journey composing lyric poetry.

Sun starer in blonde-filled eyes listens to the wind deserted skies she feels its desolation grow into a storm only she could know she runs naked midst cows jumps hedges to the south she disappears into the woods.

A long time ago, I had to stay in for school lunch. I think I was given money for the Lido, chip shop. I may have eaten a packed lunch, I can't remember.

It was before Daddy died. I was still in primary school.

Harsh winter, I remember it was windy, the rain stopped yet the roads were full of surface water. Deciding to go for a walk, I headed down the Dun Laoghaire seafront,

smelling the sea as I left Sussex Street, striding down Eblana Avenue, to Marine Road, passing the Elphin Hotel.

As I came closer to the Mail Boat terminal at the Carlisle pier, I could see the harbour was in storm, small craft battered about, their moorings unstable.

The sea was washing up on the lower level of the East pier; the wind picking up, blowing hard across Scotsman's Bay.

I was wearing a dark navy overcoat, buttoned right up to the neck, pulling the collar of my overcoat tight. I saw the world for what it was the yachts tied fast caught in the rage of water, the sky dull yet full of reds and purples, yellow stripe behind cotton wool. My world was plastic, unreal.

The East pier, which was normally thronged with people, was empty save for me hugging the wall, dark swell lashing the lower walls. Wooden floors where small boys ripped the knees of their pants and were afraid. I marveled at the seabirds, how they controlled their flight, hovering always just out of danger, diligent birds, workers in the wind.

The waves grew stronger as I passed by the bandstand, some even reaching the upper level. Waves splashing and threatening, coming stealthily from outside the walls. The world of sea, come soon; splash on my boyish face, lash me with the floggings of time, of lost smiles, human faces own the sky, I first saw the fire.

I moved on, terrified a giant wave might come up to wash

me away and it did allowing the cold air attack sore muscles in my chest. I walked lobsided, my head is pushed back out of its socket, the heart is beating, alive within the crematorium. I made it back to the promenade, running back to school excitedly.

I told my Mother later of my adventures, expecting her to scold me for walking the pier during a storm. She glared at me saying, "Don't be walking down there on your own, you wouldn't know what dirty oul lads are hanging around there."

At last Lucia and I arrived at the Hotel Villa Belvedere. Before long, we were walking by the pool, taking in the magnificent view. I stopped, staring into the water, feeling it cool without even getting wet.

If only, I wished! I stopped the clock, somebody could have said, do this, do that and you won't get ill.

Walking each morning, the first day I power walked all the way up the hill into San Gimignano, to the park outside the city walls.

Lucia said it was too much, I might push myself too hard. I obliged walking twenty minutes down hill, then up the slight incline back to the hotel.

Lucia awaited me, stretched out by the pool.

I am morose since my surgery, not the same person at all, tired and irritable all the time. Every day I live, I think I am about to die. I am obsessed with death and all that goes with it. I like to include it in conversations whenever I can.

When I am drunk, I get all brave and become all blasé. I think of everyone I have ever known who is dead.

I imagine them decomposed in their graves, so cold. My waking hours are captured by these morbid images. I think I will fall down off my perch, I too will decompose.

I tell my family I want to be cremated, tell them where I want my ashes spread. Lucia thinks I am crazy. She reckons I need help.

Don't know, maybe if I could pay somebody to lie to me, tell me all is going to be good, it would make me feel better.

Over two years after my operation my chest is still sore my scar is still to heal. Inside, my pins crash and tip, like the inner crust of the earth, fault, sliding, slipping.

Sometimes I am so fatigued I think I will fall down. All I want is cosiness and comfort.

I don't want the real world of politics and bad news. I don't want to hear the truth.

There is but fate. I am no better, or worse, than the next.

Some of us live, some do not, it is the way of things. Some get sick, others don't.

Lucia has lost my heart. Why has this happened, when I should have found her after my illness.

What harsh dweller lives within me that makes me not want to love?

Is it her guided independence that infuriates me, or is there other things at work?

What more could she have said or done for her husband? Did I expect her to have the operation and recovery for me? Is it a matter of pride? What is it?

This woman I have slept with for over twenty years, this woman has gifted me two healthy children.

I don't love her anymore because she doesn't care enough for me.

It's what we do, not what we think. She will not unveil the rest of her life for me, she does not implicitly love or trust me, this is her respectability.

I am haunting myself. I live on the edge of the cliff, constantly falling over, only to cling on for dear life. Lucia come and catch me, is that too much to ask of another? I wonder what it is I will leave life, this is the measure my parents have left me.

Is it fortitude on my mother's side? My Dad, it all happened so long ago, I barely remember him. Diligence comes from my mother's side as well, let's not forget that.

Yet, he haunts my waking hours during fatigue it is frightening to say the least.

What did he leave me, I don't know! Maybe a sense of good, maybe that good is there and really exists, I like to think that.

Sometime I hope people will see the world for what it is, that is my real wish. The powerful can't always win at the expense of the innocent. Some will disagree, say they can, they have, well hopefully not.

People will sigh and say isn't it the way it has always been, always will be.

Someday I will sit back, hear him play again, it is what he left me, the sound of piano music always in my head.

Sweet music creates, silence, distant bells calling to church, high on the hill we went, dark nights, in the early morning, sweet voice, the words carry over sad houses where lives lived and people bled, come soon the night to where a small boy sleeps.

Gregor wasn't sure whether to knock they were in the lounge for ages.

He put the tray of soda down on the sideboard in the hall, placing his ear against the door to listen. No sound! He thought of going away.

In fact, he picked up the tray to walk back to the veranda but changed his mind again and went back.

Resting the tray as gently as he could, knocking quietly on the door he strained listening for a reply. Slowly he turned the handle, it made a creaking sound as he pushed against its weight with his shoulder. At first he was frightened, the room was in darkness. Gregor noticed a flicker of light from the television screen built into the wall. Walking forward, he saw the outline of Don Dino, beside him the thinner frame of Toby. "Don Dino, is everything OK?" Gregor asked, glancing at the screen. The light wasn't constant, the movie old cine film. Every now and then it would wash the face of its audience. Gregor could see both men had tears running down their cheeks. Glancing at the screen once more, there she was, not more than thirteen years old, tumbling downhill, through meadow grass. She was doing hand stands, half revealing her underwear then sitting, thinking, the sun dazzling her hair, the white of her skin, biting straw pale pink tender lips. She is tumbling once more. Don Dino and Toby cry loudly, each one trying to outdo the other. Gregor turned on the lamp. "Can I offer you a soda?" he asked.

The End

About the Author

Paul Kestell born 1958, Dublin Ireland.
His previous work includes a Radio play "For a few Weeks in June." broadcast on Irish Radio. Also his short story "Ballinglanna" was published by the "Willow Lake Press." on the internet, Viaréggio is his first Novel. A second Novel, "Wood Point." is due for publication in 2010.

Lightning Source UK Ltd.
Milton Keynes UK
03 March 2010

150867UK00002B/2/P

9 781438 901909